Praise for Steve Cavanagh

'This guy is the real deal. Trust me'   Lee Child

'Plotting that takes the breath away'   Ian Rankin

'If you read a thriller as good this year, it's only because you've read this one twice'   Mark Billingham

'Steve Cavanagh must have sold his soul to the devil at the crossroads outside of Rosedale, Mississippi in exchange for becoming one of the world's best crime writers. Steve is 5/5'

Adrian McKinty

'A dead bang beast of a book expertly combining his authority on the law with an absolutely great thrill ride. Books this ingenious don't come along very often'   Michael Connelly

'A brilliant, twisty, ingeniously constructed puzzle'   Ruth Ware

'Eddie Flynn is fast becoming one of my favourite fictional heroes and Cavanagh one of my favourite thriller writers'

S.J.I. Holliday

'Smart and original. A belter of a book'   Clare Mackintosh

Steve Cavanagh was born and raised in Belfast before leaving for Dublin at the age of eighteen to study Law. He practiced civil rights law and was involved in several high-profile cases; in 2010 he represented a factory worker who suffered racial abuse in the workplace and won the largest award of damages for race discrimination in Northern Ireland legal history. He holds a certificate in Advanced Advocacy and lectures on various legal subjects (but really he just likes to tell jokes). His novel *The Liar* won the 2018 CWA Gold Dagger award while his follow-up novel *Thirteen* won the Theakston Old Peculier Crime Novel of the Year Award in 2019. *Twisted* was a *Sunday Times* Top 10 bestseller. He is married with two young children.

To find out more, visit Steve's website or
follow him on Facebook and Twitter.

www.stevecavanaghauthor.com

 /SSCav1

 @SSCav

FIFTY FIFTY

An Eddie Flynn Novel

STEVE CAVANAGH

ORION

An Orion paperback

First published in Great Britain in 2020
by Orion Fiction,
This paperback edition published in 2020
by Orion Fiction,
an imprint of The Orion Publishing Group Ltd.,
Carmelite House, 50 Victoria Embankment
London EC4Y 0DZ

An Hachette UK company

1 3 5 7 9 10 8 6 4 2

Copyright © Steve Cavanagh 2020

The moral right of Steve Cavanagh to be identified as the author
of this work has been asserted in accordance with
the Copyright, Designs and Patents Act 1988.

A CIP catalogue record for this book
is available from the British Library.

ISBN (Paperback) 978 1 4091 8586 4

Typeset by Born Group
Printed and bound in Great Britain by Clays Ltd, Elcograf S.p.A.

MIX
Paper from
responsible sources
FSC
www.fsc.org
FSC® C104740

www.orionbooks.co.uk

To Luca Veste.

In thanks and admiration, for being my Podbro,
for inspiring me, for writing great books that entertain me,
and for making me sore with laughter.

Thanks for all the goats.

JANUARY

EDDIE

For a trial lawyer, there are two words in the English language that terrify us more than any other. These two words stared back at me from my phone. They'd come through by text message seconds ago.

THEY'RE BACK.

The jury had been out for all of forty-eight minutes.

There's a lot you can do in forty-eight minutes. You can have lunch. You can change the oil in your car. You can probably even watch an episode of a TV show.

But one thing you can't do in forty-eight minutes is come to a fair and balanced verdict in the most complex murder trial in the history of New York City. That's not possible. It was probably a question from the jury, I thought. This isn't the verdict.

It can't be.

Across the street, on the corner of Lafayette, is the Corte Café. From the outside it looks inviting. Inside, it's coffee and breakfast sandwiches on plastic tables and chairs. Usually three or more lawyers cool their asses on those chairs. You can always tell the ones who are waiting on a jury. They can't eat. They can't sit still. They unnerve the place like a guy sitting there with a machete on his lap. I used to go there when I was waiting on a verdict, but the sight of another lawyer in jury limbo is enough to put anyone off the coffee in the Corte Café. And the coffee is good.

So instead of chewing on the furniture, I grabbed a coffee to go and headed out to walk the square. I don't know how many times I've walked Foley Square. My record is three days. That's how long a jury took to acquit one of my clients, and I damn near burrowed a trench into the sidewalk with my heels. This time, I had only just stepped out of the Corte Café, coffee in hand, when I got the text.

I dumped the go cup, crossed the street, and made my way around the corner to the Manhattan Criminal Court building. The stars and stripes flew from a flagpole thirty feet above the entrance doors. It was an old flag. High winds, rain and time had not been kind. Its colors had faded, and the flag was torn almost in two. Some sections of stars had unraveled and were lost in the winds. Huge threads billowed outwards from the red and white stripes, almost reaching to the paving below. There was money to replace it. Times were hard, and only getting harder, but the flag was usually kept pristine even if the roof was leaking. I thought they should keep this old flag – the sun-bleached colors, rips and tears somehow seemed appropriate in these times. I could only guess the justices felt the same way. With children in cages at the border, the stars and stripes had lost their luster for some. I'd never known my country so divided.

A raven perched on the end of the flagpole. A large black bird with a long beak and sharp claws. The first ravens to return to New York City were spotted back in 2016. Normally found upstate; no one knew why they had come back. They made their nests in the high corners of bridges and overpasses, sometimes even telephone or electrical towers. They fed on garbage and the dead things that curled up in the corners of alleyways all over the city.

As I passed beneath the raven it let out a sound – *croaaaak* – *croaaaak*. I didn't know if it was a greeting or a warning.

Whatever it was, it unsettled me.

Before I took this case I didn't believe in evil. Up to that point in my life I'd met and fought with men and women who did evil things, but I put it down to purely human weaknesses – greed, lust, rage, or desire. Some people were sick, too. In the head. You could say they weren't responsible for their terrible crimes.

As I was waved past security in the court building lobby, I couldn't stop these thoughts. They invaded my mind – poisoning it. Each thought was another drop of blood in a cool glass of water. It doesn't take long before all you can see is red.

Most killers I'd come across I could make a stab at some kind of explanation for their behavior. Something in their past or their psychology that held the key to their reasoning and criminal behavior. I was always able to rationalize it.

This time, there was no easy explanation. No key.

This one I couldn't rationalize. Not really. There was something dark at the heart of this case.

Something evil.

And I had felt its touch. It had hung over this case like the ravens hanging over the city.

Watching.

Waiting.

Then swooping down to kill with a sharp claw and razor bill. Dark and black, fast and deadly.

There was no other way to describe it. No better word for it. People can be good. There is such a thing as a good person. Someone who does good things because they enjoy it. Why, then, can't the opposite be true? Why can't a person just be evil because they enjoy it? I hadn't thought of it that way before, but now I could see the sense. Evil is real. It lives in dark places, and it can consume a human being like a cancer.

So many had died. And perhaps more would die before the end. When I was a kid growing up in a small, cold house in Brooklyn, my mom told me there was no such thing as monsters. The stories I'd read as a kid about monsters and witches and taking children away from their parents, into the forest, well, she said they were just fairytales. *There are no monsters*, she said.

She was wrong.

The Criminal Court building elevators were old and painfully slow. They took me to my floor, I got out and walked the corridor to the court room, following everyone else inside. I took my seat at the defense table next to my client. After the huge audience was seated, the doors were closed. The judge was already ensconced on the bench.

A hush fell as the jury filed in.

They had already given the paperwork to the clerk. Paperwork they'd completed in the jury room. My client tried to say

3

something, but I didn't hear her clearly. I couldn't. Blood roared in my ears.

I was a pretty good judge of which way a jury would fall. I could call it. And I was right, every single damn time. I knew before I took a case on whether my client was guilty.

I'd spent many years as a con artist before I turned those skills into a law practice, with little adjustment. Conning a drug dealer out of two hundred grand isn't a kick in the ass away from conning a jury into bringing home the right verdict. Innocent people went to jail all the time – but not on my watch. Not anymore. I'd learned – in bars, in diners, on the streets – how to read people. I was good at it. So when it came to plying my trade in the courtroom, I knew whether my client was guilty from the first meeting. And if they were guilty but wanted to maintain their innocence in court, I wished them good luck and waved them goodbye. I'd been down that path years ago, and the cost was too great to bear. I'd ignored my gut, let my client walk. He was guilty and I'd turned him loose. He hurt someone. So I hurt him. In some ways, I was still paying for that mistake. No one is infallible. Everyone can be conned.

Even me.

Reading clients and reading juries was my bag. This case wasn't normal. There was nothing remotely normal about it.

This was the first verdict that I couldn't call. I was too close to it. In my mind, it was an even split. The verdict may as well come down to a coin toss. A fifty-fifty. I knew what I wanted to happen. I now knew who the killer was. I just didn't know if the jury would see it. I was jury blind.

And I was tired. I hadn't slept in weeks. Not since that dark red night.

The clerk stood and addressed the jury foreman.

'In these matters, have you reached verdicts upon which you are all agreed?' asked the clerk.

'We have,' said the jury foreman.

PART ONE

SISTERS

Three Months Earlier

911 Call Transcript

Incident Number: 19 – 269851
October 5, 2018, 23:35:24
Time: 23:35:24

Dispatcher: New York City 911, do you need police, fire or medical?
Caller: I need police and ambulance. Right now!
Dispatcher: What's the address?
Caller: 152 Franklin Street. Please hurry, she stabbed him and she's coming upstairs.
Dispatcher: Someone has been stabbed in the house?
Caller: Yes, my father. Oh my god, I can hear her on the stairs.
Dispatcher: I've got NYPD and EMS on the way. Where are you in the house? Where is your father?
Caller: He's on the second floor. Master bedroom. There's blood everywhere. I'm . . . I'm in the bathroom. It's my sister. She's still here. I think she has a knife. Oh God [inaudible].
Dispatcher: Stay calm. Have you locked the door?
Caller: Yes.
Dispatcher: Are you injured?
Caller: No, I'm not hurt. But she's going to kill me. Please get them here fast. I need help. Please hurry . . .
Dispatcher: They're coming. Stay down. If you can, brace your feet against the door. Okay, you should be safe. Take a breath, the police are on their way. Stay calm and stay quiet. What's your name?
Caller: Alexandra Avellino.
Dispatcher: What is your father's name?
Caller: Frank Avellino. It's my sister, Sofia, she's finally gone full fucking crazy. She ripped him to pieces . . . she [inaudible]
Dispatcher: Is there more than one bathroom? Which one are you in?
Caller: The en suite in the master bedroom. I think I hear her. She's in the bedroom. Oh Jesus . . .

7

Dispatcher: Stay quiet. You're going to be fine. NYPD are only a few blocks away. Stay on the line.

Caller: [inaudible]

Dispatcher: Alexandra . . . Alexandra? Are you still there?

Call ended 23:37:58

911 Call Transcript

Incident Number: 19 – 269851
October 5, 2018; 23:36:14
Time: 23:36:14

Dispatcher: New York City 911, do you need police, fire or medical?

Caller: Police and paramedic. My dad's dying! I'm at 152 Franklin Street. Daddy! Daddy, please stay with me . . . he's been attacked. He needs a paramedic.

Dispatcher: What is your name?

Caller: Sofia. Sofia Avellino, fuck, I don't know what to do. There's so much blood.

Dispatcher: Your father's been attacked? Is he in the house?

Caller: He's in the bedroom. She did this. It was her . . . [inaudible]

Dispatcher: Is there someone else in the house? Are you in a safe place?

Caller: I think she's gone. Please get someone here, I'm so scared. I don't know what to do.

Dispatcher: Is your father bleeding? If he is, try and press on the wound with a cloth or towel. Keep pressure on it. The police should be outside any second. I see there's another call from the property.

Caller: What? Someone else called you?

Dispatcher: Is there someone else in the house?

Caller: Oh my god! It's Alexandra. She's in the bathroom. I can see her shadow beneath the door. Shit! She's right there! I have to get out. She'll kill me. Please help me, please . . . [screaming]

Call ended 23:38:09

ONE

EDDIE

I hate lawyers.

Most of them. In fact, nearly all of them with only a few notable exceptions. My mentor, Judge Harry Ford, and a few old-timers who hung around the Manhattan Criminal Court buildings like ghosts at their own funerals. When I was operating long cons in my late teens, I knew a lot more lawyers than I do now. Most lawyers were easy to con because they were dishonest.

Never thought I would be one of them. The business card in my hip pocket read 'Eddie Flynn, Attorney'.

If my father, a gifted conman in his own right, had lived to see this day, he would've been ashamed. I could've been a boxer, or a con artist, or a pick-pocket, or even a bookie. He would look at his son, the lawyer, and shake his head and wonder where he'd gone wrong as a parent.

The main problem is that lawyers tend to think of themselves more than their clients. They start off full of good intentions: they saw *To Kill A Mockingbird*, maybe even read Harper Lee's book too, and they want to grow up to be Atticus Finch. They want to represent the little guy. David and Goliath stuff. Then they realize they won't make a decent living in that line of work, that their clients are all guilty, and even if they do write a speech worthy of Atticus, the judge isn't gonna listen to a goddamn word they say.

Those that are wise enough to know it was a pipe dream to begin with figure out they need to join a big firm, work their asses off and try to make partner before their first heart attack. In other words, they figure out that the law is a business. And business is booming for some.

Standing outside 16 Ericcson Place, I was reminded of how much money big-time criminal lawyers made. This was the address for NYPD's First Precinct. The parking bays outside, usually reserved for patrol vehicles, had been taken by a fleet of expensive German engineering. I counted five Mercedes, nine BMWs and a Lexus.

There was something going down inside.

The entrance to the precinct was by way of blue and white painted mahogany doors with iron studs punctuating each ornate panel. This led to the TSO's desk, and beyond, the duty sergeant's booking desk. That's where I saw the argument in full flow. A plain-clothes detective in a yellow shirt was sticking his finger in Sergeant Bukowski's face while maybe a dozen lawyers on the other side of the desk argued among themselves in the waiting area. The waiting area wasn't more than twenty feet long by ten feet wide, with yellow tile on the wall. The tile could've been white at one stage, but cops smoked a lot in the seventies and eighties.

Bukowski called me twenty minutes ago. Said I needed to get down here fast. There was a case. A big one. That meant I owed Bukowski Knicks tickets. We had an arrangement. If something juicy came across his desk, he called me. Only problem was Bukowski wasn't the only cop in the precinct on the take, and judging by the crowd of lawyers, word must've gotten around.

'Bukowski,' I said.

He was a butter-ball of muscle, body hair and fat in NYPD navy blues. Ceiling lights caught the sweat on top of his bald head as he turned, winked at me and then blithely told the detective to take his finger out of his face or he would insert it somewhere in the detective's mother. I didn't listen to the details.

'I've had enough, Bukowski. They get one minute each with the suspect. That's it. After that she picks her lawyer and we go straight to interview. You got it?' said the detective in the yellow shirt.

'That's fine with me. Seems fair. I can handle that. Go get some coffee for half an hour. Or call your mother, tell her I'll be by when my shift's over.'

The detective stepped back, nodding continually at Bukowski before swiveling on his heel and making his way through the steel door at the back of the waiting room.

Bukowski addressed the crowd of lawyers in front of him like he was a bingo caller explaining the rules. 'Now, here's what's going to happen. Each one of you pricks takes a number, when I call it out you got a minute with the suspect. She don't sign your retainer, you're out of here. Got it? That's the best I can do.'

Some of the lawyers threw their hands in the air, then began pounding their cell phones with their fingers while others just continued to complain while they jostled toward the ticket machine to get a number. The tickets were for members of the public who waited in line to make a complaint – not for lawyers waiting to see a client.

'What the hell, Bukowski?' I said. 'What's the point in me buying Knicks tickets for you if you're going to call every damn lawyer in Manhattan?'

'Sorry, Eddie. Look, this is a hell of a case. You'll want it. This ain't nothin' to what this place is gonna look like in the morning when there's an army of paparazzi outside waiting to get a picture while we take these girls for arraignment.'

'What girls? What's the case?'

'The ESU brought in two girls at midnight. Sisters. Both in their twenties. Their pops was lying upstairs in the bedroom, torn to pieces. The sisters called the cops on each other. They're both saying the other one killed him. This case – it's gonna go big.'

I looked around the waiting room. The cream of Manhattan's criminal defense attorneys were gathered, all the big players in their thousand-dollar suits with their assistants tagging along behind them.

I looked down. I wore a pair of black and white Air Jordan Low's, blue jeans and an AC/DC tee under a black blazer. Most of my clients weren't concerned with my sartorial appearance after midnight. I clocked some of the suits nudging each other and nodding in my direction. Clearly, I didn't look like any kind of competition for these guys. But what I didn't understand was why this case was such a big deal.

'The sisters claim the other one did it. So what? They got money or something? What's brought all the lions to the riverbank tonight?'

'Shit, you haven't seen the news, have you?' said Bukowski.

'No, I've been asleep.'

'The girls are Sofia and Alexandra Avellino. Frank's daughters.'

'Frank's dead?'

Bukowski nodded, said, 'I talked to one of the ESU responders. Frank was gutted like a fish. Torn up with a blade. The responder told me this was a bad one. And you know the ESU – they see a lot.'

The Emergency Service Unit of the NYPD operated like a smart SWAT team. There wasn't much they hadn't seen – from terrorist atrocities to bank robberies, hostage situations to live shooters. If someone in the ESU said it was bad, that meant it was straight out of a nightmare. But it wasn't the extraordinary level of violence involved in the crime that had brought out Manhattan's finest criminal sharks – it was the victim and the alleged perps.

Until November last year, Frank Avellino had been mayor of New York City.

'What are the chances of me getting in on this case when I'm at the back of the line?'

'You're at the front of the line now. Carol couldn't get the client signed up. The guy in there now hasn't got a prayer. I'll take you through in a second,' said Bukowski.

'Hang on, I was third in line?'

'Carol Cipriani bumped me a grand to be first, but she couldn't get the client signed up. Sorry, Eddie. I gotta eat.'

'Hey, what are we? Chopped liver? What gives here?' said one of the suits.

'Don't worry, take it easy. He's not bumping the line. You'll get your chance,' said Bukowski. 'It's okay, Eddie. Most of these pricks are here to see Alexandra. You're seeing Sofia.'

'Hang on, we're not here to see both sisters?' asked one of the suits, and they all raised their voices to complain.

Bukowski was my guy, along with half a dozen other duty sergeants who would tip me off if they caught a big arrest, and I always looked after them in return. This time, the NYPD smelled a big case and every cop who had a lawyer feeding their pockets got on their phones. I'd seen it before. The detectives in charge of the case would complain to the sergeants, but as long as they didn't cut into the arrest time too much there was nothing they could do. The detectives wouldn't complain to their superiors because then they would be ratting out a fellow officer.

In the NYPD, rats die in holes. Some of the lawyers here would get their shot and those who didn't wouldn't complain. If they did complain then they wouldn't get any more calls. The clients wouldn't complain because they got the pick of the best lawyers. High-profile homicide was Christmas time for uniformed PD. Like most things in this town, a little corruption and a little money on the side helped to grease everyone's wheels.

Welcome to New York City.

'Let me grab my keys and I'll introduce you to Sofia.'

'Why am I seeing Sofia?' I asked.

Bukowski leaned in close, said, 'I know you. You won't take the case if the client is trying to get off on a crime they committed. Alexandra, I got my doubts about her. This chick – Sofia – well, you'll see. I get twenty to thirty people come through my cells every day. I can spot the real perps same as you. She ain't a perp. But I gotta warn you, don't make any sudden movements with this chick. Don't hand her nothin', don't leave any pens or paper with her.'

'Why?'

'Well, the custody doc thinks she's crazy . . . But she won't attack you. You're gonna be her lawyer.'

TWO

KATE

Kate Brooks slept soundly, wrapped in layers of woolen blankets, wearing her Taylor Swift PJs over her gym gear, and two pairs of thick, white tube socks. No matter how much she tinkered with the old radiators in her apartment, she couldn't get them to heat up. The studio apartment had been advertised to let as *'A bijoux living space with central heating throughout'*. Two radiators at either end of the room technically counted as heating throughout. As a consequence, Kate got dressed before bed every night. When the winter really kicked in, she didn't know what she was going to do.

An alert signal began to chirp on her phone – an electronic bell that got louder every second. Kate's arm swung out of bed to the nightstand and she swiped at the screen twice to silence it. She quickly tucked her arm back under the duvet, and turned over without really waking up.

The phone began chirping again.

This time she forced open her eyes. The noise coming from her phone didn't sound like her wake-up alarm. She realized it was a call from her boss – Theodore Levy. Not only that, but she'd hung up his first call.

'Hello, Mr. Levy,' she said, with a croaky voice.

'Get dressed. I need you to swing by the office and pick up a document, then meet me at the First Precinct in Tribeca,' said Levy.

'Oh, sure thing. What do you need me to bring?'

'Scott is in the office right now running down some leads, but I need him here. I need you to get a retainer agreement for Alexandra Avellino. Bring it down here. I'll need it in the next forty-five minutes. Do *not* be late.'

With that, he hung up.

Kate flung the covers back and got out of bed. This was the life of a newly qualified lawyer. She was close to six months in the job, the ink still drying on her law license. Scott, another baby attorney in the practice, was in the office already, and why the hell he couldn't pick up whatever Levy needed didn't affect Kate. Levy barked orders and people jumped. Didn't matter that there might be an easier or quicker way to do something; so long as everyone was in a frenzy, Levy was happy.

She checked her watch. She would need a cab. Twenty minutes to the office from her apartment. She tried to guess how long it would take to get from her law firm to the First Precinct, and decided it would probably take another twenty minutes.

No time for a shower.

She hauled off her pajamas and gym-wear, put on a blouse and business suit. Her skirt had gotten creased, but it didn't matter. A ladder appeared at her right calf as she put her tights on. Her last pair. She swore and went hunting for her shoes. Her head thumped off the archway dividing the bed from the small area where she had managed to fit a couch and a bookcase – the area that masqueraded as her living room. There was a small cut to her forehead, which stung, causing her to take a sharp intake of breath.

'Shitbird,' she said.

A pair of Adidas cross trainers lay by the front door of her apartment. She put them on, grabbed her overcoat and purse and left.

Twenty minutes later she stepped out of a cab on Wall Street, asked the driver to wait and ran toward the entrance to her building. Using her pass to open the front door, she rushed into the glass-fronted reception area where a security guard sat behind the desk. The elevator pinged. The doors began to open and Kate took a step forward, ready to leap inside. Scott came bounding from the elevator, a file underneath his arm. He bumped into Kate, shoulder to shoulder, turning her around.

'Sorry, Kate, I have to dash. Levy's secretary is still printing the retainer. I didn't have time to grab it and Levy wants me at the precinct right now.'

'Wait, I'll be two minutes. I've got a cab outside,' she said.

Scott, nodded, turned and ran for the front door.

Kate pushed the button for the twenty-fifth floor, twenty-five times, counting out each one as the elevator rose. Levy's secretary, Maureen, was grabbing pages from the printer. She put them in a folder and handed them to Kate.

'Is that the retainer?'

Maureen nodded. The pages were still warm from the printer.

Why couldn't Scott have waited and taken this with him?

She had long since given up trying to answer such questions. In the world of the big law firm, no one worried about deploying twenty lawyers and fifty paralegals if it gave you a moment's advantage over your opponent. She had been dispatched to get the retainer because she *could* be dispatched to get the retainer. Kate went back into the elevator, selected the ground floor and then hammered the close-door button with her middle finger. She mouthed *'come on, come on, come on,'* under her breath as the doors slid closed.

When the elevator doors opened on the ground floor, Kate rushed out. The security guard stood as she approached and used his pass to unlock the door. He grabbed the handle and pulled it open for her.

Kate said, 'Thank you,' breathlessly as she ran into the cold air.

And stopped dead.

Her cab was gone.

Scott.

What a shitbird.

Frantically, she looked up and down the street. No cabs. She opened the Uber app on her phone. Her father hated her using Uber, and had warned her against it many times. The app said there was a driver two blocks away.

The car arrived within seconds and Kate got in the back. It was a metallic blue Ford. The car was old and smelled like dog. It was too dark to get a good look at the driver, but she could tell he was fair-haired, skinny and had tattoos covering both arms.

Scott was a TOTAL shitbird.

Scott had gotten a job as an associate four months after Kate. The firm of Levy, Bernard, and Groff was a complete-service law practice. That meant they could hide your millions so you wouldn't pay squat to the IRS, screw your spouse out of their divorce settlement, sue whoever pissed you off for whatever reason they liked, and if the shit truly hit the fan they had Theodore Levy – a master litigator and criminal attorney. Kate had been floated around a few of the departments and finally settled in Criminal. She had a knack for the work. And it showed. Levy had a dozen lawyers in his team, but he liked to work more closely with the new associates on his own cases so the more experienced lawyers could concentrate on billing their hours.

Kate noticed that Levy especially liked to be close to the young female associates.

Scott had arrived in Criminal a month ago and hit it off with the boss big time. He was Levy's blue-eyed boy. Kate could tell. She had only been to one lunch with Levy and she had been in the department for two months before Scott arrived. In the four months since his arrival, Scott had already had four lunches with Levy. While Levy was small and toad-like in his appearance, Scott was tall and rail-thin with cheekbones you could use to tenderize steak. The associate's angular appearance was crowned with two dark blue eyes, which somehow appeared to be back-lit, as if a small bulb burned brightly behind each orb.

He had taken Kate's cab, and she promised herself to have it out with him as soon as they had a moment alone.

The driver stayed quiet, and it wasn't long before she got out of the car and headed into the precinct.

Inside was a circus.

A crowd of lawyers from the top firms in Manhattan, all waiting.

She spied Levy and Scott, sitting on an aluminum bench at the back of the room, and deep in conversation. In order to get there, she had to squeeze past a dozen other lawyers in the cramped waiting space. Some she recognized from TV. Some she knew from their commercials or pictures in the *ABA* journal. These were the lawyers who were always photographed at the New York Bar events. They were all over forty years old. All white. All rich. All male.

All ignoring her.

'Excuse me,' said Kate as she tried to make her way through the crowd. Some of them were engaged in group conversation. Golf. Rich white lawyers all loved golf. Others were arguing and some were on their phones. None made eye contact with her. She kept her head low, moved forward politely muttering 'excuse me,' in soft tones. In the center of the crowd, shoulders brushing shoulders, there were hands on the small of her back gently easing through, and as she moved those hands fell away and she felt another hand brush against her backside then she felt fingers squeeze first the top of her thigh, then her butt cheek.

Kate coughed, pushed a white-haired lawyer ahead of her a lot harder than he was expecting as she powered through to the other side. A ripple of laughter came from behind her. Two or three men sharing a private joke. Probably laughing at pinching her butt. Neither Levy nor Scott looked up. Kate turned, her face flushing red, and she looked at the crowd. The white-haired lawyer had moved back into place, closing the space from which she had come through the crowd. No way to tell who had touched her. The skin on her face and neck burned red with embarrassment. If she complained, she would make a scene.

From behind, she heard Levy's whiny voice. 'Katie, where the hell have you been? Scott got here ten minutes ago.'

Kate closed her eyes. Opened them. She was resetting. This had been a bad night. She didn't want to explode in front of Levy. He would only tell her to toughen up, and complain that she had embarrassed him. She let it go. She would need all her composure to deal with Levy. Only two men called her Katie. One was her father, the other was Levy. As much as she loved her father calling her that name, she hated in equal measure the way Levy used it.

She took a step back and pivoted to face her boss. He took the document folder from her, and said gruffly, 'This is a huge case for us. For the firm. We *must* secure this client. I need you on top form, okay?'

Kate nodded, said, 'I'm good. What's the case?'

Levy's mouth fell half open, and he stayed that way for a few seconds. It looked like he was waiting for a passing bug, at which point he would shoot out a reptilian tongue and grab the thing in mid-air before retracting it into his pink mouth.

'The former mayor, Frank Avellino, is dead. He's been murdered in his bedroom, stabbed . . . what was it, Scott?'

'Fifty-three times,' said Scott.

'Stabbed fifty-three times, my dear. And we are going to represent his eldest daughter. Both of his daughters were arrested at the scene, and each of them is blaming the other for the murder. One of them is lying, and our job is to prove that it's not our client. Understand?'

There was a patronizing sting to Levy's words, and Kate ignored it. The *my dear* phrase was not meant to be gentlemanly. She'd gotten used to most of the shit she had to put up with, but *my dear*, or *little lady*, still made her grind her jaw. She fought down the anger as this was the moment she had been waiting for since she joined the firm. Creepy guys in bars, and general everyday sexism on the street she could handle without a problem. When it came to the men who held her career in their hands, it was different. She knew it shouldn't be, that this wasn't right, but she thought it best to keep her lips sealed and her head down. For now. They had all the power. If she complained about this shit, her best guess was she'd be out of the job in a heartbeat – her career over before it even really began.

For months she had been writing briefs, glad-handing clients and passing out canapés at the firm's parties. Now she was on a case. A real-life, high-profile murder case. A flutter of excitement began in her stomach, and she smoothed down the front of her jacket, licked her dry lips and cleared her throat. She wanted to be ready for this. She felt ready.

'I got it,' said Kate.

Levy looked her up and down, and said, 'What are you wearing? Are those running shoes?'

Kate's mouth opened to respond, but she didn't get the chance.

'Levy! You're up!' said a voice. It was a cop, shouting from an open steel door.

'We're on,' said Levy. He stood and pulled up his pants. They were often falling down below his small gut. It didn't matter if he wore a belt or suspenders – Levy seemed to be constantly pulling his pants up.

Kate saw a small bunch of lawyers leave via the steel door. They had obviously been inside talking to the potential client. Their heads were down, and they looked tired. Levy would get the case. Whoever the client was. It didn't matter. This was Levy's forte. He was good with clients. Got them on side fast. He was a PR machine with a law license. They were going to land this case, and Kate was going to be front and center in the defense from the very beginning. She had to stifle a smile that threatened to break out on her lips – it was excitement and nerves.

'Okay, let's go,' said Levy.

Scott nodded to Kate. Kate returned the gesture. Together, the three of them took a step toward the door. Then a file came right at Kate's face. She held out her hands as the file was lowered and thumped into her chest, stopping her dead. Kate took it in both hands.

'There are some things in this file of Scott's that the client and the NYPD shouldn't see,' said Levy. 'Put it in the file storage safe in the trunk of my car. It's parked outside. The gold BMW.'

A set of keys dangled in front of her face. Kate took them, swallowed and felt a raw sensation in her throat. Like she was swallowing sharp stones.

'We won't be too long. You can use the time to think about why were you were so late getting here. When we're done I can give you a ride home,' said Levy.

And with that, Scott and Levy strode toward the open steel door.

Kate froze.

'Never mind, honey. You got the most important job. You get to watch Levy's car,' said a voice from behind her. One of the rival lawyers.

That was enough to send the entire group into thick, uproarious laughter that rolled around the room.

Kate's face flushed red. She pushed around the outside of the group, not daring to go through the middle again, and made her way to the exit. The burning sensation spread across her neck, and she recalled Levy's final words.

When he was done he would offer her a ride home. That meant he might make another awkward pass at her.

Kate thumped through the front door and onto the street.

THREE

SHE

When they brought her into the First Precinct, the booking sergeant looked her up and down, explained her rights, then told her what was going to happen.

'You'll have your personal property taken as evidence. Including your clothes and underwear. Two female officers will accompany you to a private room where this will take place. An outfit will be provided. The detectives investigating this case want to take a DNA swab, a dental impression, and clip your fingernails too. Just comply. Don't fight us. It'll only turn out bad for you. The female officers will also take your picture and your fingerprints. You'll then be moved to an interview room and the detectives will come by and ask some questions. Is there anything you don't understand?'

She shook her head.

'Do you have an attorney?'

She shook her head. Said nothing.

'Well, you will have by the time you leave,' he said.

The cop had been right. It happened exactly as he'd said it would. She had stripped, silently, in front of two female officers, and given them her bloodstained clothes, which they put into large, clear plastic bags. They gave her some underwear, and an orange jumpsuit. When she was dressed they clipped the tips of her fingernails into a bag, and ran a cotton bud around the inside of her mouth. It left a bad taste.

Then she was taken to an interview room, and left alone. There was a mirror on one side of the room, and she guessed they were watching her from behind it.

She put her elbows on her knees and leaned forward, hanging her head. Her eyes were focused on the white rubber shoes they had given to her. She was quiet for a time. Motionless and silent.

She had not spoken since the police had arrested her in Franklin Street. She'd heard one of the cops mention *shock*, and she let that play out.

She was not in shock.

She was thinking.

And listening.

The steel table in front of her was pitted with dents, and scratches. She wanted to reach out and run her fingers along those lines, to smell the table, touch it and feel it.

It was a compulsion that had started young. Another little annoyance for mother, who slapped her when she caught her touching and smelling her surroundings. She could pass an hour with a leaf, a stone, a peach. The smells and sensations were almost overwhelming and then Mother – *smack – don't touch that. Stop touching everything, you dirty little girl.*

Enjoying the sensation of touch became something else she had to keep secret. Music helped shield the compulsion. When she fell in love with a particular song, she saw colors and shapes and the music became something all the more real and physical to her, which helped keep her hands still.

The song was still playing in her head. The one that she had heard when she entered her father's home at 152 Franklin Street that evening. It had been her mother's favorite – 'She', the Charles Aznavour version. Whereas she had always preferred the Elvis Costello cover. The song floated around in her mind, playing loud and red, blanking out all other thoughts. Sitting in the small, foul-smelling interview room, she mouthed some of the lyrics as the song played only for her.

She may be the face I can't forget . . .

Her thoughts flashed images as the music played. Her father's tie. The knot still tight around his neck. The glint of white bone in her father's chest. And all those pretty sparkles of light on the blade as she tore it free from his chest, raised it and plunged it into his stomach, his neck, his face, his eyes, again and again and again . . .

She . . .

It had been planned. Of course, she had fantasized about it for many years. How good it would feel not just killing him, but ripping him to pieces. Destroying his body. Decimating it. And the thought occurred to her that all those other kills had merely been a rehearsal for the main event.

Practice.

At first, watching the light die in a victim's eyes was exhilarating. Like watching a kind of transformation. Life to death. All of it at her hand. There was no remorse. No feeling of guilt.

Her mother had beaten that out of her, and her sister, at a young age. Mother had been a brilliant chess player and wanted her daughters to be better. In her younger years, Mother had watched the Folgar sisters take the game by storm, and wanted the same for her own daughters and began their chess education early. From the age of four, she had been made to sit in a room with the board in front of her, moving pieces while Mother looked on and taught her the classic techniques. How to watch the line formations, middle game strategies that quickly moved to mates. They would practice for hours. Every day. Separate from her sister. Mother never allowed them to play against one another, not even to practice. Practice was with Mother. And Mother never let her eat before afternoon practice. No lunch; the bowl of cereal or fruit for breakfast a far-off memory. She spent many hours in a little room, with Mother – confused, frightened, and hungry.

If Mother saw a mistake in strategy, or she took too long holding a piece, feeling the grooves in the polished wood, or trying to catch its scent, Mother would snatch the chubby, offending hand that had played the move, hold it aloft, and bite one of the fingers. She could still see it now. Her mother grabbing her by the wrist. It felt like her arm had been trapped in some terrible piece of machinery that would then slowly draw her hand into a buzz saw. Only this wasn't a blade, but instead she saw her mother draw back her bright red lips to reveal two rows of perfect white teeth. Her fingers would tremble, and then – snap.

The bite hurt. It was punishment, not intended to draw blood. But to shock. To make sure that mistake never happened again. She wondered if all mothers were like this. Cold, unfeeling women with sharp teeth.

She always felt hungry playing chess. Mother said hunger helped the brain stay creative, alive. Every time she saw those teeth coming for her little finger, she felt sick, and hungry, and anticipated the pain, which was always worse than the bite itself.

She had learned from her mistakes.

She recalled the look on her dear sister's face that day when Mother fell down the stairs. Her sister cried and cried until, finally, Father came home. Sister never got over it. It made her think that even with Mother biting and hitting both of them, and forcing them to play and read about chess for hours every day, there was still some part of Mother that her sister would miss. Some connection that had been forever broken.

Even now, years later, she could still hear her sister's cries when she saw Mother's body. Sister stood at the bottom of the stairs, that stupid toy rabbit in her hand, her knees locked together and a dark stain growing on her burgundy tights, spreading from her crotch, down both legs. Sister's sobbing became so bad that it robbed her of her breath, that panicked, gasping, staccato crying.

Now, the bites and the beatings and the tears were all a memory. A part of her, something that had helped to shape her into the perfect creature she was today.

Tonight had been perfect. It looked messy, frenzied, and the body of dear Daddy had been left where it fell. A maniac kill.

That's what it looked like. That's what she had wanted it to look like. In truth, she had enjoyed it. Her kills were always controlled, and there was satisfaction in the execution, though nothing had compared to that first time. Not until tonight. She had really let go. Those impulses, which she held in check with willpower and meds – all of it had been unleashed on Daddy dearest. It felt like loosening a pressurized valve in her head – the relief was wonderful.

She had never before been connected to any of her crimes by law enforcement. Now she sat in a police precinct, facing a charge for a murder she had committed.

She was exactly where she wanted to be.

Where she had *planned* to be.

FOUR

EDDIE

Bukowski led me down a corridor with more of the same nicotine-covered tile. Behind us I heard a cop calling for the next legal team to go audition for their client. I slowed down because I wanted to see who was coming.

Theodore Levy and a young fair-haired kid followed a tall cop along the corridor. I'd come across Levy in the hallways of Center Street, but we'd never tried a case together. We were both defense lawyers, and Levy was at the high end. He worked for white-collar criminals who would pay a fortune for his services. Levy knew this case would catch the headlines, and he needed cases like this every once in a while to raise his profile. Getting your face on the front page for six months usually meant more work and you could add twenty percent to your hourly rate for the following year.

I kept walking, but let Levy catch up. At the end of the corridor Bukowski took a right and we went up two flights of stairs. Until a few years ago, there used to be four holding cells on this floor. The NYPD had dug out the old individual cells to make way for offices. The six-hundred-and-forty-pound iron doors that secured each cell had been ripped out. And they had gone missing. Cops or contractors. Who knew? But somebody made money in scrap metal and it sure as hell wasn't the city. Now, as well as additional office space for the detective squad, there was a bank of five new interview rooms.

Only two were occupied. You could tell by the whiteboard in the middle of the doors, just below the single viewing panes. I resisted the urge to glance in at my client and waited for Levy.

'Eddie Flynn, isn't it? I'm Theodore Levy,' he said, extending a hand.

27

We shook hands. Levy tucked his thumbs into his waistband and pulled his pants over his stomach. He had close-cut black hair, wore thick black-framed glasses behind which two large eager eyes moved over my body, head to toe, like he was an undertaker sizing me up for a coffin.

'Good to meet you,' I said.

'Is it dress-down Friday?' he said.

'I'll change before the arraignment. My clients don't hire me for my wardrobe.'

'Just as well. Say, you got the sister?' he said. 'Good luck with that.'

'Do I need luck? You sound like you know something I don't. I was wondering why half of Manhattan's criminal bar was auditioning for your lady. Want to enlighten me why most of them want one sister over the other?'

'Look, Sofia has had her problems. Anyone who knows Frank Avellino will tell you that. It's common knowledge. Alexandra was his golden girl. She's a face in Manhattan, and she's a sure bet in this. Sofia is the *crazy* black sheep. This is only going to go one way. I think it would be a good idea for you to talk to Sofia about a plea bargain. Save us all a lot of time.'

'I haven't spoken to Sofia yet. We'll see what happens.'

'Alrighty, good luck,' he said, and with that he gestured to the tall cop who opened the interview room door and stood aside. Levy led his associate inside – a good-looking young man who was carrying a set of papers. I stepped closer so I could take a look at Alexandra Avellino.

Even as she sat behind the desk in the interview room, I could tell she was a tall young woman. Dyed blonde hair, but a good dye job in this case. There was a reddening around her eyes, and her lipstick had faded. Otherwise Alexandra looked fit and healthy, with a milky, almond skin tone. Given the circumstances, she looked well. A certain confidence in her expression. A woman who could handle herself, and others. I could smell some residue of perfume as the door opened.

The tall cop closed the door, stood with his back against it.

'Okay, Eddie, this is Sofia,' said Bukowski as he slid the key into the lock and opened the door.

I went inside.

Sofia Avellino looked smaller than her sister, but not by much. She had dark hair contrasting with a pale complexion. The eyes were the same. Both women had their father's eyes – which were narrow, but bright and keen. She didn't smile. Her lips were thinner than her sister's, her nose too. They both looked the same age, and I seemed to recall that Frank's daughters were born within a year of each other. I wasn't sure how I knew that, but it was likely I'd seen them, or one of them, in a magazine or news article.

She looked at me suspiciously, but said nothing. Sitting opposite her was a lawyer I didn't know, but he looked as rich and as successful as the others. He gathered up his papers, said, 'You're making a mistake not hiring me,' and stormed out.

I ignored him, focused on the young woman in front of me.

'Hi Sofia, my name is Eddie Flynn. I'm a defense attorney. Officer Bukowski told me you don't have a lawyer. I'd like to talk to you a little and see if I can help. Would that be alright?'

She hesitated, nodded, and her fingers began drawing imaginary lines and circles on the table. I stepped closer and saw she was tracing the dents and scratches with her fingers, exploring the textures. A nervous response, somewhat childlike. She seemed to catch herself in the act, and put her hands beneath the table.

I sat down opposite her, kept my hands open and raised slightly. Body language cues to encourage her to talk.

'Do you know why you're here?' I said.

She swallowed, nodded, and said, 'My dad's dead. My sister killed him. She says I did it, but I swear to you I didn't. I couldn't. She's a lying, murdering bitch!'

Her hands flew up in the air and came down with slap on the table to punctuate the word 'bitch.'

'Okay, I know this sounds stupid, but I need you to stay calm. I'm here to help you if I can.'

'Sergeant Bukowski said I should talk to the lawyers, but I shouldn't make up my mind until I talked to you. I don't know what I should do . . .'

She shook her head as tears formed in those eyes, which were much greener than I'd first thought. Looking away, she swallowed down a cry, her neck muscles standing out from her throat, and instead she took a big breath into her lungs. Closing her eyes, and letting the tears fall to the floor, she said, 'I'm sorry. I can't believe he's gone. I can't believe what she did to him.'

I nodded and said nothing while she drew her knees to her chest and hugged her legs. She cried and rocked back and forth gently.

'I'm sorry about your father. Truly, I am. The truth of it is you are in the worst possible situation. The cops are coming after you, and probably your sister too. One or both of you could face a murder charge. Maybe I can help you? Maybe not. I only need one thing. I need to know that you didn't kill your father,' I said.

Sofia had been listening through the tears. She dried her face with a napkin, sniffed and began to bring herself down to a level where she could talk. If she was faking it, she was very good. I didn't see an actress across the table. I saw a young woman in pain. That was real. That was true. But whether that pain was due to the death of her father, or the fear that she might have been found out as a killer, or some other reason, was not yet entirely clear.

'Why are you asking me? The other lawyers didn't ask me if I was guilty. Don't you believe me?'

'I ask all my clients the same question. The ones I believe are innocent, I fight for as hard as I can. If they tell me they didn't do it, I can usually tell when they're lying and then we part ways. If they hold up their hands and say they're guilty, then I help them tell their story to the court, so the judge can understand why they did it, and what mercy or mitigation is appropriate. I don't fight for murderers who want to get off. That's not my beat.'

She appraised me anew, like I'd taken off some kind of camouflage and she was now looking at a real person.

'I like that you asked me,' she said. 'I want you to be my lawyer. I didn't kill my father. It was Alexandra. She did it.'

I took my time, watched her closely as she spoke. Truth was in her eyes, her voice, her face. No warning signs, no tells which could be indicative of a lie. I believed her.

Now it was time to go to work.

'Tell me what happened,' I said.

'I was in Dad's house in Franklin Street. I have my own place not far away, and I usually visit. More and more recently, since he became more forgetful. I went to the house and at first I didn't think he was home—'

'Stop, just a second, tell me how you got inside.'

'I have keys. So does Alexandra.'

'Okay, I'm sorry for interrupting. You said you didn't think he was home . . .'

'I got inside, and he wasn't in the den. That's where he normally hangs out, watching TV or working. He wasn't there. I called upstairs and he didn't answer. I thought maybe he'd gone out, so I fixed a drink from the bar in the den, finished it, and then I went upstairs.'

'Why did you go upstairs?'

'I heard a noise, so I thought he must be home and maybe he hadn't heard me come in. I went up the first flight of stairs and he wasn't on the first floor.'

'What is on the first floor of the house?'

'Three bedrooms and a gym. He wasn't in the gym, and I didn't check the bedrooms. No reason for him to be there. Then I heard the noise again, coming from the floor above.'

'What was the noise?' I asked.

'I don't know. It's hard to describe. It sounded like a groan, or a moan, or something. Maybe someone talking. I don't know, I can't really remember. I remember I went upstairs to check on him. He'd been having memory lapses. They made him disorientated. Old age or, God forbid, the start of dementia or something. I thought maybe he'd fallen. I saw him lying on the bed in the master bedroom. The lights were off in the room, but I remember thinking it was weird. There was something not right about it.'

'What do you mean?'

'I couldn't really see him in the dark, but I saw one of his feet lying on the bed. He still wore his shoes. That was unusual. My dad was always giving me sass about lying on the couch with my boots on.'

'Did you turn on the light?' said Eddie.

'No, I didn't. I just went over to him, asked him if he was feeling okay. I thought he was maybe taking a nap. He didn't answer. That's when I saw what had been done to him. I held his head and saw that the rest of his face had been so . . .' She trailed off, and then said, 'That's when I panicked and dialed 911.'

'Did you see your sister, or anyone else, attack your father last night?'

'No, I didn't see it. But I know it was her. She was hiding in the bathroom. I saw the light from the bathroom spill underneath the door. Saw the shadows as she moved in there. Ready to spring out and maybe kill me too. I knew it was her. I screamed and I ran out the house.'

'How did you know it was your sister who killed your father?' I said.

'Because my sister is the worst bitch I've ever known. I knew it was her. She's got this front she puts on for the world. Rich, successful. It's all lies. She's sick in the head. Our mom, she made things hard growing up. Alexandra is even more fucked up than me. She just hides it better. The cops arrested her too, when I told them I'd seen her in the bathroom. I saw the cops handcuff her when I was in the back of the squad car.'

A knock on the door. Sofia's eyes flashed fear as she looked over my shoulder. I got up and saw there were two detectives on the other side of the door.

'It's okay, Sofia. You're doing great. Let me go talk to these guys for a second.'

Sofia was struggling with her breathing, her eyes were wide and I could tell she was reliving that moment when she found her father. I tried to calm her again, and she nodded, closed her eyes. Her fingertips found the grooves in the table again, and started moving. I got up, opened the door, stepped into the hallway and closed the door behind me.

The first detective was the one I'd seen earlier, in the yellow shirt, arguing with the sergeant. He was my height, about my build, but ten years older and with a shock of grey hair. His partner wore a three-piece suit, dark, with a navy shirt and pale blue tie. He was younger than me, and had his hair shaved close on both sides, with a flop of hair on top of his head slicked back. They looked an odd pairing.

'Detective Soames,' said the man in the yellow shirt, thumbing his chest. He then pointed to the younger man and said, 'This is Detective Tyler,' and that was about all the pleasantries that were on offer.

Tyler filled the moment with dead air, not even nodding or smiling. Just staring. This was old-school NYPD – *the lawyers are your enemy*. Neither of them extended a hand, and they both looked decidedly pissed off at my presence.

'And you are?' said Soames.

'I'm pleased to meet you both,' I said.

'Yeah, yeah, what's your name, *pal*? We're ready to interview this suspect,' said Tyler. His slicked-back hair didn't move as he spoke. Whatever was holding it in place was industrial strength. He said the word *pal* like it meant exactly the opposite.

'I'm Eddie Flynn. I only just met my client. I need a little more time, if you guys don't mind?' I said it as politely as I could. They didn't deserve it, but I was feeling generous.

'We have to move on this. Clock's tickin'. You got five minutes then we'll be coming in,' said Soames.

'I might need longer than that. My client just lost her father. She's not in a fit state at the moment.'

'Doc says she's fine and ready to be interviewed,' said Tyler.

This was a tag-team. Tyler waved a standard custody report from an on-call doc who saw suspects from time to time for the police, just so he could collect four hundred dollars and tick a box to say that the suspect was, in their medical opinion, fit to be interviewed. It gave the NYPD some back-up in case the lawyer tried to jettison their client's version of events at a later date by claiming the poor client was out of their mind with shock, or disturbed somehow and didn't know what they were saying. It was insurance, not medical practice.

I turned away from Tyler, the barking dog, and went straight to the guy holding the leash. 'Did the doc take a look at your ass,

Soames? It must hurt with hipster-boy here sticking his head up there every chance he gets.'

'Five minutes,' said Tyler. He walked past me, bumping shoulders deliberately as he did so, then knocked on the door to Alexandra's interview room.

Instead of going back inside to see Sofia, I put my hands in my pockets and leaned against the wall.

Levy came out. Same introductions from Soames. No handshake. Levy saw me standing behind Soames.

'Look, why don't you interview Sofia first? My client isn't ready,' said Levy.

'You mean she hasn't signed your retainer agreement yet?' said Soames.

'No, matter of fact she has. She knows quality representation when she sees it. I need twenty minutes to take instructions.'

The door to Alexandra's room was still ajar. Levy's associate remained inside, and I could hear Alexandra talking to him. She was crying, and repeating to the associate, 'I didn't do it. It was my sister! She's totally crazy! Why am I here? I'm just as much a victim as my father!'

'Mr. Levy, if it helps, we just want a first account. What did your client see tonight? What were her movements? We're not talking about the whole issue with her father's will,' said Soames.

'What issue?' said Levy.

Soames took a step back, folded his arms and said, 'We got a call from Mike Modine, Frank's lawyer. That's all I'm saying for now.'

I pushed off the wall, opened the door to go back into my interview room. I needed to ask Sofia if she knew anything about her father's will, but I was also aware the cops knew I was listening. They might just be messing with us – pulling the strings on the defense lawyers – making them chase their tails down blind alleys. Nevertheless, I needed to know for sure. I didn't know Mike Modine. Never heard of him, which meant he probably wasn't a litigator. If he represented Frank then maybe he wrote Frank's will. I couldn't be sure, but if the cops were tipped off by Modine, that meant there was something in the will of interest. My best guess

– the will was motive.

I needed to talk to Sofia.

I got the door halfway open.

Stopped dead.

'Sorry,' said Sofia.

'Oh my god! Medic!' I called.

Sofia's mouth, neck and chest were covered in blood. She had bitten through her wrist. Her eyes slipped into the back of her head, she slumped off the seat and fell unconscious to the floor.

FIVE

KATE

For thirty seconds or more, Kate had stood in the cold beside Levy's Mercedes with the keys in her hand. There were house keys on the ring, as well as the car fob. She had thought about running the house key the full length of the paintwork on the Mercedes and watching a ribbon of ten-thousand-dollar metallic paint curl itself into a spiral.

She could always claim it was like that when she found it.

In the end, she put the fantasy aside, enjoyable as it had been, used the fob to open the car and got into the passenger seat. It didn't feel right, somehow, to sit in the driver's seat. Leaning over, she fumbled for a few seconds when she tried to put the key fob in the ignition. Then she realized there was no ignition. This was one of those cars that only needed the key to be near the car. Kate was a long way from owning a vehicle like this, or being able to afford to run any kind of automobile. She knew Levy's Jaguar from carrying boxes of files to and from the small document vault he kept in the trunk.

That was a memory she didn't want to dwell upon. Once a week, on Friday nights, she would ride the elevator to the basement lot with Levy. He would lean against the opposite side of the elevator car, pretend to look at his phone, while Kate stood with a box of files at her feet. She could feel him watching her, staring at her ass and her legs. She could almost feel his gaze intensifying when she bent to pick up the boxes from the floor.

Levy never carried anything heavier than his cell phone.

The memory made her shiver. She touched the control panel on the dash, locked the doors on the car and selected the heating options. Within seconds, warm air was flowing through her seat. She needed it tonight.

Looking down at her training shoes, she saw the file of papers she had taken from Levy in the station. She was supposed to put those in the trunk safe. What was it he'd said about them? They might upset Alexandra?

The precinct entrance was visible from where Levy had parked. Kate took a long look, making sure her boss didn't suddenly come charging out. He could be in there for most of the night. Kate picked up the file, opened it and began to flick through.

Scott had put together a dossier on Frank Avellino, and his daughters. Most of it came straight from the internet. Photographs of Avellino when he'd been elected for the first time. He stood at a podium, flanked by his second wife, Heather, and a much younger Alexandra. There were no pictures or mentions of Sofia in this article. Avellino ran on an anti-corruption ticket. He was going to clean up the unions, the lobbyists and City Hall.

A familiar story. And Kate knew how that had turned out.

Six months into his first term and Avellino was facing an investigation into receiving off-the-books payments from two construction unions and an investment fund that bankrolled casinos. It didn't take long for Avellino to steamroll the story.

For someone who was anti-corruption, dirt seemed to follow Frank Avellino like that kid from the Peanuts cartoon. There were pictures of Frank in restaurants and at social events with movie stars, writers, directors, real-estate moguls and well-known mobsters like Jimmy 'the Hat' Fellini. His revitalization programs always seemed to have accounting difficulties, like the two-million-dollar clean-up scheme he ran in the Bronx, which somehow had three hundred grand unaccounted for. It was a construction firm with affiliations to Jimmy 'the Hat', which carried out renovations to the First Precinct, and it had been no surprise the valuable iron doors that had been part of the old cells were inexplicably lost during the works.

There were another two dozen articles and Kate skipped through them, looking for something on the family.

Then she found a puff-piece profile lifted from an online edition of a popular magazine. It detailed Avellino's modest roots in Brooklyn, and his rise through a business empire based on flipping real estate, right up to his re-election as mayor. There were pictures taken in the family home in Franklin Street. The article was three years old. No sign of the second wife, Heather. It was just a series of photographs of Frank at home, with the exception of one picture.

He sat in what looked like a study. There was a bar beside a long desk, and TVs on the opposite wall. Frank sat behind the desk, flanked by two young women. One was tall and blonde, the other shorter and dark-haired. Light and dark. The caption said *'At home with Frank: L – R Alexandra Avellino, Frank Avellino, Sofia Avellino'*. Kate noticed that the two girls stood with their backs to Frank, and each other.

There was little mention of the family in the article. Frank merely said that Alexandra showed great promise as a businesswoman, and was already making a name for herself in the Manhattan real-estate community. And he had high hopes for Sofia as an artist. He knew his girls would make it on their own – they were smart and both had been chess prodigies even though neither of them played anymore.

Kate read some more about the family but couldn't find anything that talked about Frank's first wife – the mother of Sofia and Alexandra. Heather had been his second wife, but she had died. No information on how or when. One thing was clear, Heather was far too young to be a mother to two grown-up daughters.

She closed the file, yawned, then put the folder back on the floor. The heat was making her sleepy. She pulled out her phone, checked Twitter. So much noise, and anger. It made her feel sick sometimes. She closed the app and laid her head against the back of the warm seat and wondered when the world had become so crazy.

TAP! TAP! TAP!

Kate jolted awake, momentarily unsure of where she was, or what was going on. With the heater on she must've dozed off, but for how long? She looked to her right and saw Scott rapping the passenger window with a knuckle. She shook herself awake, then opened the door and got out.

'Working hard?' said Scott.

Kate opened her mouth to say something clever, but he cut her off.

'You're up. Theodore wants you in there to take notes. There's been a development and I have to go check it out right away. Something to do with Frank's lawyer, Mike Modine, and a will. Look, I shouldn't be longer than a few hours. I'll come back and take over later.'

'No, no. No need. I can handle taking some notes. You go run your errands,' said Kate.

She could tell he was seething at being jettisoned from the interview to go on donkey work. He stepped into the street, hailed a cab and went off in pursuit of another one of Levy's whims.

Kate locked the car with the fob, the files safely in the trunk, and was about to walk into the station when she heard an ambulance roar around the corner. It stopped outside the precinct with a jolt. A man in a black jacket and jeans came out of the station. He carried a young woman in his arms. She wore a jailhouse jumpsuit, she was dark-haired and her chest and neck were covered in blood. It was Sofia Avellino. She recognized her from the photos in the file. Behind him came two plain-clothes detectives, a desk sergeant and another uniformed officer.

The rear doors on the ambulance were flung open. Two paramedics bounced a gurney onto the blacktop and ran over to the man carrying Sofia. Kate saw a huge bandage on Sofia's wrist and noticed she was only semi-conscious. The man in the black jacket laid Sofia gently on the gurney. He leaned over, put his hand on top of her head and with his thumb he gently stroked her forehead, dislodging the hair that had stuck to her skin with sweat and blood. All the while he spoke softly. His voice was gentle, comforting.

'It's going to be okay, Sofia. I'm going to help you. I promise I'll do my best,' he said.

The woman seemed to smile, weakly, and closed her eyes.

One of the detectives stepped forward, brandishing a pair of handcuffs. He snapped one cuff onto the bar of the gurney.

'If those cuffs touch her I'll make you swallow them,' said the man in the black jacket.

'Tyler, leave her alone. She's in a bad way. One of my officers will ride along,' said the man in the sergeant's uniform.

'Back off, Bukowski, I'll go with her,' said the detective with the cuffs, Tyler.

'No, you won't,' said the man in the black jacket. 'Bukowski's man will take her. He's not on the case. He won't be tempted to question her while she's in the back of the ambulance.'

Tyler pursed his lips flat, took his handcuffs off the gurney and stepped away. The uniformed officer took one end of the gurney, helped the paramedics load her into the ambulance. Sergeant Bukowski continued to argue with the detectives as they marched back into the precinct.

Kate stared at the scene, her eyes wide.

One of the paramedics said to the man in the black jacket, 'Are you coming with us?'

'I'll meet you at the hospital,' he said.

'You can follow us,' said the paramedic.

'Nah, it's okay. I got a friend coming to pick me up. The way she drives, I'll be there before you guys.'

The paramedic snorted, said, 'Yeah, right.'

The ambulance doors closed, the sirens sounded and it pulled away. Kate heard another car coming around the corner fast. It was a black Dodge Charger. For a second Kate didn't think the car would be able to stop, but it turned and slid into a space outside the precinct, its tires squealing. A woman with short brown hair got out of the car. She wore dark jeans and a tight-fitting, brown leather coat. She skipped to the man in the black jacket, and they hugged each other.

'What took you so long?' said the man in the black jacket.

'Blow me,' said the woman.

They smiled at each other, then both of them froze and turned toward Kate, suddenly aware of her presence.

Kate closed her mouth, said, 'Was that Sofia Avellino in that ambulance?'

'You a reporter?' said the man.

'No, I'm K-Kate. Kate Brooks from Levy, Bernard and Groff.'

She was nervous, and a little stunned by the scene she'd just witnessed.

The man held out a hand to Kate and said, 'Hi, I'm Eddie Flynn. This is Harper.'

Kate stared at Eddie's hand, saw the blood on it and hesitated.

Eddie followed her eyes, noticed the blood covering his palm and wiped his hands.

'Is this kind of thing normal for you two?' said Kate.

Eddie and Harper exchanged a knowing look. One filled with shared memories of blood and killers.

Both of them nodded, and began walking toward her car.

'Nice to meet you, Kate,' said Eddie over his shoulder.

The two of them got into the car, Harper driving. She spun the tires, enveloping Kate in a cloud of smoke, then took off at an impossible speed.

Five minutes later Kate was in the interview room, taking a seat beside Levy. On Levy's other side sat the client – Alexandra Avellino. Kate had a whispered conversation with Levy before entering the interview room. Just the two of them. Levy didn't seem surprised at the events outside the precinct house, but told her to put it out of her mind – he needed her sharp. The client had signed the retainer agreement and that was what seemed to matter most to Levy right then. He told her she had to take copious notes during the interview – accuracy was everything. The cops had let something slip about a will, and he'd sent Scott to run it down.

The detectives Kate had seen outside arguing with Eddie came into the interview room. While they readied themselves with paperwork and set up a camera to record the interview, Kate took the opportunity get a good look at the client.

She looked like a skincare model. A beautiful, wealthy young woman in a terrible situation. Kate could tell she had been crying, judging by the swelling and redness around the eyes, and every now and then as Alexandra raised a hand to put it on the table, or run it through her hair, she detected a tremor at the edge of those fingers. The cops must have clipped her fingernails – they were jagged and sharp. No one who put that much effort into their appearance would go out with nails like that. Alexandra was the sort of woman who would have had a manicure that cost more than Kate's entire outfit.

'For the record, my name is Detective Brett Soames, this is my partner, Isiah Tyler, and we are interviewing Alexandra Avellino at First Precinct, New York City. Also present is counsel Theodore Levy and . . .'

Kate was writing furiously in her pad, the pen skimming across the page. She wrote, 'Levy and' and then stopped, waiting for the next word.

No one spoke. She raised her head and found the detectives, and Levy, looking at her. Waiting for her.

'State your name for the recording, please, ma'am,' said Soames.

'Oh, sorry, Kate Brooks.'

Soames nodded, bunched his lips together in a way that looked like he'd just tasted something sour, and then continued.

'Miss Avellino, at this stage we just want a first account from you concerning the recent events surrounding your father's murder. You want to tell us what happened?'

'Sofia butchered my father. There, is that what you want me to say?' she said, her jaw wobbling, her voice tremulous.

Levy jumped in with both feet.

'My client will issue a full statement, detective, once we've had disclosure. You heard her tell you who killed her father. That's it for now. For the record I know you have information regarding the deceased's will, which you have not shared. If Mike Modine made a statement to police I want to see it. Until there is full disclosure my client won't be answering questions.'

'Mr. Levy, if your client is alleging that her sister killed Frank Avellino, then doesn't she want her sister prosecuted? You're telling me she's a witness,' said Tyler.

'I found him on the bed,' said Alexandra. Levy put a fat fist on her arm. He didn't want to be so blatant as to tell her to keep her mouth shut, but he needed to give her a gentle reminder. Kate felt something else. Just seeing him put his fingers on a female made her skin crawl. Alexandra removed her arm from the table, courteously ridding herself of Levy's touch.

'Go on,' said Tyler.

'I came upstairs, and his bedroom door was open. He was laying there in the dark. I called his name but . . .' She shook her head, the tears falling freely, her throat flushing red. Now Kate wanted to comfort her, to hold her hand and tell her that she was sorry for her loss.

'He didn't move. I called out, "Daddy, Daddy . . ." and he didn't answer. I thought he might have been asleep at first. I went over to him and saw something black all over him. I touched him, and it was wet. When my eyes adjusted to the darkness I saw it was blood. I didn't know what happened, I just held him and I couldn't breathe, and then I screamed. I must have screamed because I heard myself. And then . . . then I heard her coming up the stairs. She killed him. She's bad. There's always been something wrong with her. I ran into the bathroom – closed the door and called 911.'

'You say your sister is bad. There's always been something wrong with her – what do you mean exactly?' said Tyler.

'Alexandra, that's enough. Remember what we talked about,' said Levy.

Kate glanced down at the page and saw that she hadn't written down the last question. She did it now, in shorthand. She had been so enraptured by Alexandra. This was a woman in terrible pain. And anger. She saw it when Alexandra mentioned Sofia. There was a hardness in her – something made of iron and steel – and it flashed when she spoke her sister's name. It flashed again at Levy when he tried to shut her up.

'Maybe just answer this last question and leave it at that,' said Kate.

Alexandra's eyes softened when they flitted to Kate. Alexandra was a powerful young woman – not used to taking orders from men. She needed a different approach. Levy wasn't happy that Kate had opened her mouth, she could tell by the withering look on his face.

'I'll just say this,' said Alexandra. 'Sofia thinks she's smart. Smarter than me. She's wrong. We don't talk – we haven't in years. Not since Mom died. She hates me. She didn't hate him, but she would do anything to hurt me. She's sick. Do you understand? She wants to win. She thinks it's a competition between us. You have to believe that I didn't do this.'

'Last question. Where were you before you got to your father's house? And what time did you arrive?'

'Oh God, I can't remember the time. I was jogging in the park, and then I ran to Dad's. I had to pick up some fruit smoothies for him from a place on 2nd Avenue. I don't know what time I got back.'

Kate just got everything down on paper, and then looked up to see Soames and Tyler in hushed conversation.

'Mr. Levy, we are going to charge your client with first-degree murder. She'll be charged alongside her sister. Frank Avellino has forty-nine million dollars in property, cash and assets in his estate, according to his attorney. He made a will five years ago, dividing it equally between his two daughters. Before we charge your client, we have one final question. Miss Avellino, when did you discover your father had talked to his attorney about changing his will?'

PART TWO

THE GAME BEGINS

SIX

EDDIE

For a lawyer, every case is a game.

In criminal law, it begins with an arrest and it ends with a verdict. At the start of the game you have no control over what happens, then you develop a strategy and you make some moves. At the end you get to stand in front of the jury, alone. The prosecutor doesn't matter – you have to ignore them. It's just you and twelve people. Once the final word is spoken it's all over. The verdict shouldn't matter. You did your job as counsel.

Except it does matter.

The verdict is everything. It doesn't mean *shit* how well you played, it's all down to that decision. The lawyers who make the big bucks, who drive a Mercedes home to their families in their nine-bedroom houses don't care what the verdict will mean for the accused, for the victim's family, for society and everyone in it. They can't care.

My biggest problem as a lawyer is I want the guilty to get punished and the innocent to go free. And the law doesn't work that way. Never has. Never will.

Sometimes I can tip the balance, one way or the other. Sometimes not. It matters that I try. The day I stop giving a shit is the day I quit. Sofia Avellino needed my help. It was too early to say if I believed her sister carried out the murder. Neither of the Avellino sisters looked like they could harm anyone, much less tear their own father to pieces. For now, I was involved in the case but I needed to be sure Sofia was telling the truth. In that cell, I had felt for her. I thought I had a connection. That she was open and honest with me. That was my instinct. I needed to know that I could trust that first impression.

After biting through her wrist in the precinct, Sofia had spent a night in the hospital under NYPD guard. While her wrist didn't look pretty, she hadn't lost that much blood – it always looks worse than it is. She didn't need a transfusion, but the docs made sure there was no chance of hypovolemic shock. They pumped her full of isotonic fluids and antibiotics. Her wound stitched, stats level, she was deemed fit for discharge. I couldn't speak to Sofia at the hospital, but I did get talking to the doc – a short, blonde woman called Dietrich. She had spoken to Sofia, and as far as she could tell this wasn't a suicide attempt – this was an extreme reaction to the loss of her father and her arrest.

She was charged with murder and brought to court for arraignment at noon. Bail wasn't going to be a problem. Levy had done the work for me by getting Alexandra bail an hour before. The prosecutor, Wesley Dreyer, objected to bail on the same grounds, but knew the judge would give them the same bail terms – a five-hundred-thousand-dollar bond. Why make a new decision when you could follow another? When the judge set bail for the same bond, Dreyer looked despondent. The prosecutor was a young man with an earnest look on his face. He was slim, small, and neat. He chose his words carefully, took time to annunciate and project his voice. A diligent prosecutor is always to be feared.

Sofia posted bail.

She was out, but she wasn't talking. She hadn't said a word to me in the consultation before the bail hearing, just nodding her head. She had pleaded not guilty. When the hearing was over she disappeared back into the cells so she could be taken to the court office to wait until the bond was deposited and then she could sign bail for release.

I had waited for Sofia in the winter sun on Center Street, in the shadow of the Central Criminal Court building, and ate lunch at Mori's hotdog stand, which bore a faded sign with my name and number on it. Behind me, the ragged stars and stripes flapped in a light breeze.

I thought I heard a raven's call, and then turned to see Sofia.

Sofia left the court building via the loading dock at the rear, avoiding the bank of photographers outside. She wore a black sweater, black jeans and cheap shoes, which I'd bought for her and left with the corrections department. The cops had taken her blood-soaked clothes from last night for forensics. I asked if she was alright. She nodded and we walked in silence to my car. I'd driven her to her apartment without her saying a word. I pulled up outside, killed the engine and leaned back in the driver's seat.

'Let's make a deal, Sofia. I'll defend you, but I need you to try and keep things together. I don't know how the trial is going to pan out. Not yet. We have to wait until we get all the prosecution's evidence. I don't want you to think about that yet. Just go home and rest for now. You'll have a million questions for me in a day or two. Let's meet then. For now, I have a friend who's going to get you settled in, make sure you're okay. Her name is Harper. Don't worry, she's not a lawyer. She helps me with cases, looks after witnesses, that kind of thing.'

Sitting on the steps outside the building with a brown paper sack beside her, Harper took her eyes away from her cell phone and nodded in my direction.

Sofia turned her head toward me and I saw the tears on her face. She wiped them away, drawing a pale hand over her shocking white skin. I thought of her sister, Alexandra: tall, tanned, and healthy. It was as if Alexandra had caught every drop of sun, and Sofia had lived all her life pale and hungry in the long, cold shadow of her sister.

'I wasn't trying to kill myself last night,' she said.

I said nothing. It was the most I'd gotten out of her in hours. If she was going to talk, I wanted to listen.

'I told that to the doctor at Saint Vincent's last night. Sometimes pressure builds up – in my head. I have to let it out some way. I'm not suicidal.'

By way of explanation she yanked up her sleeves and let me see her arms.

The inside of her forearms were covered in thin scars. Some remained pink and slightly raised – still in their keloid state – while others were older and an even starker shade of white. The marks were lateral, across the arm, from just below the elbow to the wrist. Both arms. Hundreds of cuts. A few looked as though they had been deeper than others. The bandage on her wrist obscured some of the scarring.

'I didn't mean to scare you. I'm sorry. Thank you for helping me,' she said.

Then she leaned forward, looking past me toward Harper.

'Is she your girlfriend?' asked Sofia.

At first, I didn't know what to say. Sofia had a child's directness – no bullshit – she told you exactly what she was thinking.

'Ah, no, we're just friends,' I said, suddenly feeling my cheeks flood red.

We were friends, but every now and again I caught myself staring into Harper's eyes or taking a moment to let her scent linger in my nose. When we hugged, as friends, I had a strange feeling as she put her arms around me. My ex-wife, Christine, was in a new relationship and, judging by what little I could pick up from my daughter, Amy, it was going well. Christine was happy with Kevin. She was in a state of contentment that I could never give her.

I was lost in thought, and the sound of the car door opening brought me straight back. Sofia closed the door, walked around the car and Harper stood to greet her. I got out and tried to make introductions, but I was too late.

'This is—'

'We already did that part, Eddie,' said Harper before turning her attention back to Sofia. 'We're going to get along just fine. I've got Cheetos, candy, frozen pizza and sodas for lunch.'

'Good thing I'm not exactly on a health kick,' said Sofia.

'Oh, that stuff's just for me. I got you celery and fat-free hummus,' said Harper, holding back a smile. Initially, Sofia didn't know how to take that answer. Then she smiled, nervously at first and then more warmly.

At once, Sofia seemed to relax somewhat. Her shoulders fell from a tense, hunched position. Her expression softened, her eyes opening that much wider and brighter.

'You grab the groceries. We'll see you upstairs. Just got to do a little business with this guy first,' said Harper.

Sofia did as she was asked, and together Harper and I watched her go inside.

'She's hurting,' said Harper.

'She just lost her father.'

'I'm just going to get her settled for a few hours. Make sure she's okay. She must be in some kind of emotional pain if she's self-harming.'

'A psychiatrist gave her a full evaluation before discharge. They don't think she's a danger to herself. I want you to make sure of that too. Don't go too deep, but try and get a sense of her. We need to know if she'll be able to hold up during a trial.'

'I'll get her to open up as much as I can. Might as well get a head start on this while we're waiting for the DA to get his shit together.'

'Agreed, but there's no rush. NYPD won't release the crime scene for at least another week. See what you make of her. She says she's innocent, and right now I believe her.'

Harper cocked an eyebrow. 'I'm not there yet. I'll let you know what I think.'

'Just go easy on her. Have dinner, talk. Settle her for the night then you can leave.'

Harper was one of the brightest agents in the FBI. Too clever, in fact. She left with her partner, Joe Washington, moved into the private sector and now she was my go-to investigator. We'd been through a lot, and I trusted her judgment. Together we made our way inside, and took the elevator to Sofia's floor. The door to her apartment lay open. Harper knocked as she pushed the door wide.

Inside was a beige and cream themed apartment. A lot bigger than anything I could afford. The grocery bags lay on the kitchen counter. Sofia stood over a coffee table, staring down at a chessboard.

'I don't play,' said Harper.

'Neither do I, really. Not anymore. Look, I'm not going to do anything stupid.'

'Good, Harper will want to talk a little. Just some background. If we're going to defend you, we need to know who you are, so we can show that person to the jury,' I said.

Sofia nodded, said, 'I'm a sucker for candy and old black-and-white movies.'

'That makes two of us,' said Harper, gently ushering me towards the door.

My phone buzzed in my suit jacket pocket. I checked the number. It was the DA's office.

'I've got to take this call, sorry. I'll see you at Harry's party tomorrow night, but call me later and give me an update.'

Harper said yes, she would call later.

I then turned to Sofia and said, 'Just try and stay level. This is all going to be okay. The press may come around, or try to call you. Don't talk to them.'

'I won't. I might go out later. I'll wear a cap and hoodie. Keep my head down. Thanks, Mr. Flynn.'

'Call me Eddie,' I said as I left the apartment. I answered the phone.

'Mr. Flynn?' said a female voice.

'Yes, if it's about those parking tickets—'

'Excuse me? Um, no, it's not.'

I knew it wasn't about parking tickets, but it's impossible for me not to play with prosecutors. I couldn't help myself. As a defense attorney I spend a lot of my time chasing prosecutors to discuss my cases. They only called me when there was a serious issue, in a serious case.

The voice on the other end of the line cleared their throat and said, 'I'm Mr. Dreyer's secretary, he'd like to see you tomorrow about the Avellino case.'

'What about the Avellino case, specifically?'

'He has an offer he wants to discuss with you.'

SEVEN

SHE

After her arraignment, she had posted bail. So had Sister dear.

The rest of that day proved busy.

Very busy.

Every effort had to be made to cover her tracks, and frame her sister. When she eventually flopped into bed at one a.m., exhausted, she realized she had eaten very little the previous day.

She had slept fitfully. Waking at five a.m., she made a peanut butter sandwich, ate it with a glass of milk and then went back to bed. She dozed and woke a few times. Her broken sleep was not due to any worry, or concern. The thought of returning to a cell for the rest of her life didn't hold any fear.

It wasn't going to happen.

Not a chance.

The interruption to her sleep was largely due to excitement. She was finally going to be free. Freedom meant money. All of her father's money. If her sister was convicted, she couldn't inherit her share of father's estate because of the Son of Sam laws. She would get everything. Money meant freedom and power. She had thought about killing her sister, and then Father – but two deaths leaving a sole beneficiary to a large fortune looked too suspicious. It would forever tarnish her with the uncertainty of facing a trial for their deaths at some point in her life. This way was better. This was clean. Father dead. Sister in jail for the murder. No loose ends. No suspicion falling on her.

She would be free.

She got out of bed around ten in the morning. In the shower, she scrubbed her skin with a rough, cosmetic stone. The ridges of that stone were a wonder to her. If she did not pay attention, she could spend half an hour touching it, exploring every line on its surface.

She dried herself and tied up her hair. Before completing her task last night, she had done some shopping. Food and essential items – some tools for the job in hand. There were still three shopping bags from a medical supply store and a hardware store by the front door. She was too tired to unpack just yet.

She dressed, blow-dried her hair and the rest of that day she spent on the couch, eating potato chips and watching a string of old movies – *Casablanca*, *The 39 Steps*, and finally *Rear Window*. An outfit lay on the bed, waiting for her. Black Lycra leggings, and an Underarmor top. She dressed, put on her running shoes and tucked her hair into the black Nike ballcap. Before leaving her apartment, she stretched her legs, back, arms, and shoulders.

On the street, she broke into a light jog to warm her muscles, find a rhythm, adjust her breathing. After Mother died, she and her sister had been placed into separate boarding schools. Both in Virginia, a hundred miles apart. It had been in boarding school when she had found her love of running. A year after Mother died, she turned thirteen. Neither sister went home for weekends. Her gym teacher had been a cross-country champion in her youth, and had given the bug to her. She loved being in the open country on Saturday mornings, watching the sun come up over the endless wheat fields, her lungs fit to burst. No one around her. Just her thoughts, and plans. The running helped keep the dark thoughts at bay for some years. Now, as a young woman, she no longer felt the need to keep those demons in check. At fourteen she had given serious thought to strangling another girl in her class. Melanie Bloomington. Even the name made her want to be sick. Melanie wore her hair long, in impossibly complex pigtail knots, her skin pink and perfect, just like her class test scores – nothing about Melanie Bloomington was less than perfect.

She thought it would be fun to strangle Melanie in the toilet block. Get her into a stall, grab her school tie and pull and twist and yank until Melanie's perfect pink face was red, then purple and then blue and quite dead. And then, she could touch Melanie's face, her eyes, her lips. But this could not be done in school. It would cause a panic. Too much attention. Still, it was hard to resist.

One Sunday morning, she found herself in a small wood on the edge of the vast school grounds. She stopped to examine a flower, its bright yellow petals looked like velvet and as she reached for it she heard a noise. A rustling and bleating. She stepped carefully over a large fallen tree trunk, and in a clearing up ahead she saw a fawn. It had become trapped in the remnants of an old post and wire fence, which must have demarcated some old boundary before the wood grew unchecked and swallowed it up. The fawn was near death. A large, murderous raven sat on a large stone some distance away. It could smell the blood as surely as she could. It was waiting for the fawn to die – which, from the look of the animal, would not take very long. Three legs had become entangled in the rusting barbed wire, and during the course of struggling to get free, it had managed to almost sever its foreleg.

The smell of blood was strong now. She approached the creature, who did not panic when it saw her coming toward it, slow and low, whispering softly. Either it hoped for rescue, or it no longer had the strength to resist. From her backpack she produced a penknife – one she had bought in a local store with her allowance. It had a pearl handle, and a sharp little blade. The fawn struggled when it saw the sunlight catch the blade, but she calmed it.

It would be a mercy to kill the fawn. She knew that.

Instead, with excited fingers, and trembling breath, she stroked the animal. The feel of its fur beneath her hand, its smell, its heart-beat – ragged and fast.

The fawn died slowly.

Afterward, she washed in a stream and ran back to the school dorm, knowing that the fawn's sacrifice was what had saved Melanie Bloomington. For now, her appetite had been satisfied. Her desire, sated.

Running kept those desires in check, and that made her feel almost normal. She used to think she had been cursed. That these thoughts and feelings were a sickness. It wasn't until she graduated from school that she realized her willingness and joy in inflicting pain on others wasn't a handicap, or a curse or a sickness – it was a gift. Six weeks after graduation she met Melanie Bloomington for coffee and shopping in Manhattan. The fawn a distant memory, her appetites raging. Melanie was excited about her summer. She was one week into her summer vacation – travelling the United States for a month with a backpack, trying to *find* herself before she started college that September. The day after she met Melanie, she went for her first long run in Manhattan, and smiled as she ran past the diner where she and Melanie had met for coffee the previous day.

Now, years later, she still liked to run in the city. It was simply another one of her many pleasures. Running in New York was almost as much fun as running in the country. It was a series of steel, glass and concrete valleys. All of them her playground.

She increased her pace and it wasn't long before she found herself on 2nd Avenue. She passed the juice bar where she used to pick up special fruit smoothies for her father. She crossed the street just before Trump Tower, and took in the reinforcements and armed guards outside the building.

She didn't care for politics on that scale. Her father had met Trump on numerous occasions and didn't much like him but knew how to use him. Life was just a game for the powerful, and those who were prepared to do what no one else would. This, she had learned from her father.

A little further and she was at Central Park. She took the sidewalk that ran along the east side of the park and checked her watch.

22:28.

She increased her pace again, finding new gears. Her legs began to move faster and faster until she was in full sprint. This was of necessity, so she could be sure not to miss her target. This run was not cathartic – purely business and pleasure. She thought again of her first run in Manhattan. The day after she met Melanie before she was heading out on her summer of self-discovery. Poor Melanie didn't find herself that summer.

Melanie's body was never found.

At ten-forty she slowed down as she came to the entrance to the Metropolitan Museum of Art. There were people leaving via the main entrance, dressed in cocktail dresses and tuxedos. She took a seat on the steps and caught her breath.

A few minutes passed before she saw him.

Medium height. Grey hair in a side parting. A tuxedo beneath a cashmere overcoat and scarf. He was talking to two elderly women, and held out an arm for each of them as he escorted them down the steps. His name was Hal Cohen. For fifteen years he had been her father's political strategist, mayoral campaign manager, chief fundraiser, and accomplice.

As they reached the bottom of the steps, the ladies thanked Hal.

She stood up, quite suddenly. Fast enough to catch his eye.

When Hal saw her, his smile faded. He quickly returned it to his face as he waved goodbye to the ladies who made their way to the crosswalk. He stood there for a moment, his hands in his coat pockets. His breath misting in the night air as he contemplated what to do next.

He bowed his head, and casually made his way over.

'Did you have an enjoyable evening?' she said.

'It was a fundraiser for a friend. Enjoyment wasn't on the menu,' said Hal. He placed a hand on her shoulder, in a paternal fashion, and said, 'I'm real sorry about your dad, kiddo.'

That's what he always called her: kiddo. When Hal began to help her father into political office, he came to the house to talk to him, meet her mother, meet the family; make sure there were no skeletons in the closet. He said if there were skeletons, he would need to know so he could bury the whole closet at the bottom of the East River.

'Thanks. He always liked you. Said you could fix anything. I need to talk to you, Hal,' she said.

'Look, I'm very sorry about what happened to your father. Frank didn't deserve that, but—'

'That is what I need to talk about. I don't have time to wait. It has to be now. Hal, you need to know I didn't kill my father.'

He sighed, nodded, and gestured to a sleek BMW parked on the opposite side of the street. They made their way to the car in silence. She got into the passenger seat, he drove.

'I'll take you home. Talk all you want,' he said.

She said nothing.

'You wanted to talk, let's talk,' he said.

Leaning over toward the driver's seat, she placed her hand on his thigh. He tensed, and she whispered, 'I know you record everything in this car. My father told me. We can talk in my apartment.'

She withdrew to her side of the car and placed her hands in her lap. Hal simply nodded, and said, 'Okay.'

She liked the feeling when Hal tensed. It made her feel powerful. Her hand had been close to the top of his thigh as she had leaned in to bring her lips to his ear. It was overly familiar, and yet she knew Hal would've gotten a kick out of a young woman putting her hands on him.

They drove in silence until he arrived outside her building and parked across the street. The building was like many on this side of Manhattan, elegant, grand, but time was beginning to take its toll. A security camera in the lobby hadn't worked in weeks. There was little crime in this part of town, so it wasn't a priority. As long as the old elevator ran that was all that mattered.

The elevator doors opened and she led him to her apartment, the largest on this floor. Last door on the left at the end of the corridor. Inside, a small hallway led them to a dining table and open-plan kitchen beyond.

'Careful you don't trip on the shopping,' she said, pointing to a pile of unopened packages sitting beside the door. Hal stepped past them, following her. She dropped her keys on the table, took off her ballcap and threw it on the couch across the room as she made her way into the kitchen. Filling a glass of water from the fridge, she said, 'Do you want something to drink?'

Shaking his head, Hal leaned on the back of a dining chair.

'So, let's talk,' he said.

'Okay, do you want to sit down?' she said.

'No offence, but I have somewhere I've got to be. And, I'll be honest, I'm a little uncomfortable. I know you're on bail, I know you could face a trial along with your sister and I could be called as a witness.'

'The cops think Dad was going to change his will. Is that true?'

He took a breath, held it in and leaned over the back of the chair. He shook his head. Then pushed himself upright and let the answer into the air as if he'd been holding it inside, like a long breath held tight under water. It burst out of him, breaking the surface of the conversation.

'I was told the same thing,' he said.

'Who told you?'

'The cops told me. They wanted to know if your father had spoken to me about changing his will. I said no, he hadn't. At the end, you know, your dad wasn't the man he used to be. He was forgetful. I don't know if it was old age or something else. We still had breakfast together at Jimmy's restaurant most days. Apart from that, we didn't talk much. He didn't mention the will. When I heard about Frank's death, and the will, I called Mike Modine.'

She drained the last of the water, put the empty glass on the counter, and gave Hal Cohen her full attention. His knuckles sat like lumps of white fat on the back of his hands, such was the pressure he applied to the seat back. He appeared guarded, wary of saying something that could come back to bite him in the ass.

'What did Modine say?'

'He said your father had made an appointment to discuss his will on Monday. He didn't make it through that weekend. Look, that's all I know—'

'Did Modine say why my dad wanted to change his will? He was paranoid toward the end, you'll remember.'

'You don't need to tell me that, sweetheart. Your father thought everyone was out to get him. He could remember who won every World Series since 1953, but he couldn't remember what he ordered for his breakfast at Jimmy's. Modine didn't tell me what your father wanted to change about the will. It may not have been anything to do with you or your sister.'

'Has Modine been in contact with you?'

'Not since I called him, the night your father was murdered. I'm one of the executors of the will, so I need to know what's in it, and if it will still hold up. Even if your sister is named in the will, if she's convicted of killing your father then legally she can't benefit from her crime. Same goes for you. I tried calling Modine today, but his secretary said he's out of the country on vacation. I'm supposed to be helping oversee your father's estate, but I don't know what I'm doing. Modine is no help.'

'When does he get back from vacation?' she asked.

'The secretary didn't know. Said she wasn't exactly able to keep tabs on the senior partner. Modine doesn't give a shit – all those corporate lawyers are the same. He's probably drinking cocktails on a beach somewhere while your father is lying on a slab with his . . .'

He cut himself off. Remembered who he was talking to.

'It's alright, Hal. Do you think my father was working with anyone new at the time he died? He seemed very distant at the end. When he wasn't raving about the IRS or whoever else was out to get him, he seemed – troubled.'

'Well, a few months ago he did ask me if I knew any good private investigators. I don't know what that was about, and again he wouldn't tell me.'

'I know you made some money working with my father. You were loyal to him.'

Hal nodded.

'I want you to be loyal to me. When this is over I'll be inheriting my father's entire estate.'

'You seem pretty sure of that,' said Hal.

'I'm innocent. I want you to help me. I will reward that loyalty.'

The promise of money put an electric charge in the air. Hal did a lot of dirty work for her father. He bribed city councilors, union bosses, journalists, and she suspected those who couldn't be bought had been put through a different form of persuasion. Politics was a dirty game, and her father played it well and stayed clean. Hal was the one who got his hands dirty.

'I can be loyal, kiddo, but that kind of loyalty doesn't come cheap.'

'You probably didn't make more than a million a year working for Dad. I can do better. Three million dollars – for your expenses as an executor of the estate, payable when I'm exonerated and my sister is convicted of murder.'

'And what would I have to do exactly?'

'Stay loyal to my father's memory. If he was going to change his will, then something must've spurred that decision. I want you to find it.'

He considered this for all of three seconds, said, 'I'll do my best. The police won't let me into the house just yet. It's still a crime scene, but I'll ask around – see who your father talked to. And I'll track down Modine.'

'Thank you.'

'No problem. Look, I really have to get moving. Mind if I use your bathroom before I go?'

She came around the kitchen island, threaded her arm through the crook of Frank's elbow and gently led him to the front door.

'I'm so embarrassed. This building is old; like really old. The toilet is backed up and I've been waiting for a plumber forever. The super is an asshole.'

'Do you need me to call you a plumber?'

'Don't worry, I've got someone coming first thing in the morning. I'll be fine.'

At the front door, she hugged him.

'If you manage to contact Mike Modine, you'll let me know what he says, won't you?' she said, gazing up into Hal's eyes.

He nodded, said, 'I'll try to get hold of Modine tomorrow.'

She thanked him and closed the door as he stepped into the hallway and made for the elevator. Her door had five separate locks. Taking her time, she made sure to lock each one. When she was done, she put her back to the wall and listened to the elevator doors rumbling closed, and then the faint thrum and bang of the counterweight moving as the lift descended to the ground floor.

Her eyes fell on the packages by the side of the front door. She sorted through them, feeling their weight. When she found the heaviest one, which was about the same size as a large pizza box but twice as thick, she picked it up and moved into the kitchen. She placed the box on the counter, found a pair of scissors in a drawer and began to cut away the packing tape. The lid opened to reveal a smaller, plain box inside. This box she opened with her nails. She peeked inside, then put the box down on the counter.

Glancing over her shoulder she made sure her blinds were closed before stripping naked in the kitchen. After folding her clothes neatly and placing her running shoes on top of the pile, she picked up the box.

She opened the bathroom door then sat on the toilet. The soles of her feet quickly grew cold on the white tile floor. She relieved her bladder while taking the item out of the box and studying it. It was silver, shiny, and had an oily smell. She wiped herself, stood, flushed the toilet and found the end of the cable that hung from the device. She plugged it into the socket above the washbasin and kicked the bathroom door shut.

She turned to the tub, pulled back the shower curtain that hung around it.

The tub was filled to the rim with bags of ice.

There, surrounded by the bags, Mike Modine's dead face looked up at the ceiling. He still wore that look of surprise. It had taken a lot to get him to her apartment. She didn't have time to wait, so she'd lured him there last night. She'd told him that her father had made another will, the night before he died. It was handwritten, witnessed and would invalidate the will her father had made some years before in Mike's office. She said she feared her sister would try to kill her if she knew that the will existed – that her sister had killed Frank thinking he had not yet made a will excluding her as a beneficiary. She trusted no one but Mike. He had to meet her now, she was waiting outside his office for him. He met her on the street and together they went to her apartment where she had supposedly hidden the will.

Once Mike got through the door of her apartment, he hadn't stood a chance. She used a Taser to subdue him, then got him into the bathroom and bound his hands and feet. An hour later, Mike was dead, her filleting knife was almost blunt from use, and she was satisfied that her father had not told him about his intention of cutting her out of his will. Her father had only scheduled an appointment. Nothing more. She had been playing a psychological chess game against her father and sister for years. Frank had found out. She was pretty sure of this, or at least he had some heavy-duty suspicions. And so, Daddy had to die. She had to make sure he hadn't told anyone before she had a chance to take him out. So far, she was reasonably sure his suspicions had died with him. Considering the work she'd put into Modine with the knife – she was sure he was telling her the truth.

Mike had not mentioned the private investigators. She already knew about them, but they had not given anything worthwhile to Frank – she had seen to that.

Now, she leaned over the tub and began removing the melting bags of ice she had used to keep Mike's body cool. These she dumped in the washbasin. Mike's skin felt freezing, but she still ran her fingers over it, enjoying the sensation. She touched his tongue, and his eyes. Aware she was becoming distracted, she bent down to pick up the device, fresh out of the box. She stopped. Hesitated, tutted. She'd forgotten something.

'Alexa! Play Elvis Costello, "She",' she said.

'Playing "She" by Elvis Costello,' said the sibilant voice from her device. Then the apartment instantly flooded with her song. She wanted the Costello version tonight.

The music would drown out the noise. She hit the power button on her new surgical bone saw, and hummed along to the melody as she worked.

EIGHT

EDDIE

Harper called me just after she left Sofia's place around five in the afternoon. She didn't get much out of her, and she was tired. We arranged to meet for breakfast the next day after my meeting with the DA.

In all my time as an attorney I'd never had a good experience with plea bargains. Even if the prosecution are offering your client a great deal on a guilty plea, with reduced jail time for saving the city the cost of a trial, it always carries a tinge of regret for me. In a plea deal, the prosecutor is the one sentencing the client, not the judge. Sure, you can bargain a little, but normally you don't have a lot of power in that situation. Harry Ford, before he became a judge, once told me that it was the plea bargains that get you into trouble with the client. Sure, they like the deal to begin with – one year of jail time on a plea, or run the risk of a trial and conviction that carried a fifteen-year sentence. That's a no brainer even for those clients whose brains don't work so good. But after six months of the Department of Correction's hospitality in a double cell at Sing Sing, with another six to go, it's surprising how many clients begin to complain about their lawyer forcing them to take a plea – that they're really innocent after all. Unfortunately, a lot of them are telling the truth. Innocent people plead guilty every day in every city in America because the prosecutor dangles a deal that means they can serve a little time and then get out and get on with their lives. Take a deal and serve one year or risk twenty-five-to-life? It ain't hard to see why people take a plea.

And while I'd never enjoyed plea bargains, I enjoyed visiting Hogan Place even less. The DA's office felt like enemy territory. Always had. Always will.

The elevator door opened at the District Attorney's office reception, and there, behind the desk, was Herb Goldman. Sometimes I think he's part of the furniture, and not just because of his longevity in the job. His skin could have been stretched across a couch and passed for fine Italian leather. Still, even at his age, not much gets past Herb. He knows all the gossip in the office, and he's older than God. Probably wiser too. I approached Herb's garish purple tie and broad smile. He leaned back in his chair and folded his arms.

'How come you still haven't been struck off, Eddie?' said Herb.

'They haven't caught me yet. I thought you were dead.'

'Me? Nah, only the good die young.'

'In that case, that tie will live longer than you. What are those things on it, turtles?' I said, leaning in for a closer look at Herb's tie. I quickly decided I didn't want to get that close to it, and retreated a step.

'My wife bought me this tie.'

'You should get a divorce.'

'Do you know any good lawyers?' he said, shading his eyes and looking all around the office like a cowboy surveying a barren prairie.

'You should be in one of those Florida retirement homes, making people your own age miserable.'

'Don't tempt me. I'd love to retire, but I can't. The DA's office keeps threatening to give me a gold clock every now and again, and I tell them the same thing – I can't retire. It's a death sentence – my wife would kill me if I was in the house all day. The DA that canned my ass would be an accessory to murder.'

'If your wife murdered you the DA would send her flowers and a thank-you card.'

Herb had a laugh that started somewhere in his belly and rumbled up through hissing pipes before escaping his lips in a high-pitched cacophonous wheeze. Like Mutley from the cartoons.

'I got you down to see Dreyer, with *this* crew,' he said, pointing with his pen to the other side of the room.

I hadn't noticed when I came in but seated to my left, on the couch, sat Levy, accompanied by the young lawyer I'd met outside the precinct – Kate. On the other chair was another young face, a guy with keen eyes who couldn't be more than twenty-five – the lawyer I'd seen with Levy visiting Alexandra's holding cell some days ago.

The presence of Levy and his team meant there was about to be a whole lot of trouble.

They got to their feet as I approached.

'Eddie, good to see you again,' said Levy, in a tone that didn't even get close to sincerity, and didn't care either. 'This is my associate, Scott Helmsley.'

He pointed to the fair-haired kid in the tight suit to his left. I'd seen him in the precinct on the night of the arrest but didn't get much of a chance to appraise him. He didn't look old enough to shave and yet he busted out a movie-star smile and extended a hand from a silk, double-cuff shirt.

'It's a pleasure to make your acquaintance,' said Scott, and he took my hand in the firm grip that some men use. I always thought the hard-handshake guys were compensating for something. The guys who can really crush your knuckles without thinking about it don't need to prove their strength in the way they say *hi*.

The woman on his right, Kate, bowed her head and angled the toe of her shoe to the ceiling and moved it around using the heel to pivot. She was dressed in a gray business skirt, white blouse and black jacket. Her hands were clasped in front of her and I could only see the top of her head. She looked up at me.

There was an awkward pause. Not long. Maybe four or five seconds, but long enough for Levy to pretend he'd forgotten about her. He had caught sight of Kate swinging the toe of her shoe, he was simply making sure she and I knew Levy's pecking order when it came to his staff.

'Oh, I'm sorry, and this is—' he said, without turning toward her, just extending a palm in her direction, highlighting the afterthought.

'Kate Brooks,' I said, loudly, stepping past Levy and Scott. 'We met at the precinct. How are you?'

'I'm fine, thanks, Mr. Flynn.'

'Call me Eddie,' I said.

Levy bit his lip. I could smell bullshit office power plays from fifty yards.

'How's your client?' she said.

'Better. She's out of the hospital, and out of jail. Yours too, I understand.'

'Yea—'

'That's right,' said Levy stepping between us, cutting off Kate mid-sentence. He hitched up his pants, maneuvering them side to side as he hauled them over his stomach like he was screwing them into place.

'So how do you want to play it with Dreyer? I say we let him do the talking, take everything out of the room and mull it over. No decisions in the room. Only thing we're set on is splitting the trial. We must have separate trials – our clients are blaming each other so we don't have a choice,' said Levy.

I nodded, said nothing. Over his shoulder Kate stepped back a pace, lowered her head again as Scott sidled up to Levy and nodded along with every word Levy said, like his boss was spilling the gospel. Two seconds ago I was talking to Kate, now the boys had basically trampled over her, taking control of the space and the conversation.

I wondered how small Levy's dick had to be for him to get this kind of enjoyment from degrading a female employee.

Pretty damn small, I concluded.

Then Herb hollered over from behind the desk, 'Mr. Dreyer will see you all in the conference room. Go on through, he's waiting. Nice to see you, Eddie.'

'You too, Herb,' I said.

Levy turned toward the double doors just beyond the couches in the reception area, waved a hand over his shoulder as if he was calling his troops to him. Scott trotted alongside him, and Kate followed last, clutching a legal pad. She reached up and took a pen from the knot in her hair. Holding open the conference room doors, Levy ushered Scott in first, without even looking at him. As Kate passed him, I saw Levy's eyes fall low to her calves. He watched Kate from behind, his fat lips puckered in a distasteful way that said he liked what he saw.

He let the door go and was about to move inside when I skipped ahead, grabbing the closing door and bumping into him. He rocked back on his feet a few steps, waving his little arms to regain his balance. Managing to grab a chair, he shot me an angry look. The heat in his gaze fed from his embarrassment. I saw Kate covering her mouth, trying not to laugh.

'Sorry, Theo, I thought you had the door. My bad,' I said.

He turned away from me in a huff, dragged out a chair and sat down.

The oval conference table seated ten. Four on one side, four on the opposite side. One at either end. A door at the rear of the room opened and in came Wesley Dreyer. He had a slow, confident stride, thin lips and receding hair. Genetic male-pattern baldness must have kicked in for Wesley in his early twenties. What remained up top had been carefully combed even though it looked thin almost to the point of transparency. He wore a different suit to the one he had on this morning at Sofia's arraignment. This one was pale blue, with a similarly colored shirt and a navy tie.

'Sit down, please, gentlemen, and lady,' said Dreyer, careful to acknowledge Kate with a polite nod.

Dreyer pulled out the chair at the head of the table. I walked around the table and took a position opposite Levy and his team. Before he sat down Dreyer unbuttoned his jacket, smoothed down his tie and gracefully put his ass in the chair. He could've been a ballet dancer. From his jacket pocket he took a fountain pen, unscrewed the top and began making careful notes in a flowing script on a legal pad. He wrote down who was in the meeting, swept his arm up in front of his face and noted down the time from his Citizen watch. He then put down his pen, adjusted his cuffs just so, and carefully laced his fingers together. Some of his movements, although graceful, had a reptilian feel. Like a snake coiling itself, ready to strike.

'I'll be brief, and I won't repeat myself so you may want to take notes,' said Dreyer.

Kate, Scott and Levy had pens at the ready, hovering over their legal pads which had the name of the firm embossed at the top of their pages in gold lettering.

I folded my arms, sniffed and waited. Without moving his head, Dreyer's eyes slotted to the left, locking onto me. While the others had their heads down, ready to write, I kept eye contact with Dreyer. Anything I could do to unnerve a prosecutor was mandatory in my playbook. It didn't seem to work. Dreyer looked right back at me like he was holding aces and he knew I had a pair of eights.

'Trial will be in January. We have most of the evidence and we have motive. You already have basic discovery, which I hope to complete soon. All I'm waiting for are full reports from forensics and a witness statement from the deceased's lawyer, Mr. Modine. I'm already in possession of the preliminary forensic results. You'll get the full reports in time, but the short version is I have forensic evidence linking both of your clients to the murder. And only your clients.'

'What do you mean by *only* our clients?' said Kate.

Soon as she'd said it, Levy tutted, and Kate looked down at her legal pad, swallowed. Levy didn't appreciate his staff speaking up in a meeting with a prosecutor. I thought it was a fair question. One that instantly came to my mind. Kate had good instincts. I liked her. With Levy, it didn't matter that she had asked a good question, it was the mere fact that she had the audacity to open her mouth at all.

'Well, Miss Brooks, I would ask that any questions you have you keep to the end of the meeting, but I'll take this one now since you've asked,' said Dreyer, not looking at Kate. Instead he looked at Levy as if to acknowledge Levy's seniority. 'Your clients were both arrested in the property. No one else inside. The medical examiner puts the time of death around the same time as the 911 calls. We're not looking for any other suspects – forensics link your clients not only to the scene, but the murder.'

Kate wrote down the answer, and lowered her shoulders to the desk, as if to appear as small as possible. She mouthed a 'sorry' to Levy who rolled his eyes and put his index finger to his lips. It didn't matter that it wasn't worth the time and energy; if I worked for Levy I would have put my fist through those fat lips a long time ago.

I thought about this new information and how it fit with Sofia's story. Frank's house was practically a mansion. Lots of rooms over three tall floors. It's entirely possible Sofia and Alexandra could both be in the house at the same time and be unaware of each other's presence.

'One, or both, of your clients murdered the victim. In that case, considering the forensics and the prosecution witnesses, this will be a joint trial. There's an overlap in all of the evidence,' said Dreyer.

A joint trial in a case like this is a prosecutor's wet dream. With two defendants blaming each other, it's likely the jury believes neither of them and both will get convicted. If one of them pulls off a miracle and manages to persuade a jury they're innocent, the other defendant takes the hit. It guarantees the prosecutor a win – no matter what.

Levy shot first.

'There's no chance in hell you're getting a joint trial. When one defendant is implicating the other, the criminal code and case law dictates we split the trials. Mr. Flynn doesn't have to call his client to testify, and if he chooses not to then it's a violation of my client's constitutional right to face her accuser. It's unfair. It's a *no* to a split trial – right off the bat. Is that clear?' asked Levy.

If he was rattled by this, Dreyer didn't show it.

He pulled at the cuffs of his shirt again, making sure they protruded from the bottom of his jacket sleeves, before picking up his pen and noting down Levy's objection.

'The fact is we would need to run almost two identical prosecution cases against your clients, and that puts unnecessary financial strain on the city. It will be a joint trial. I am pushing very hard for this.'

'Pushing who?' I said.

Levy didn't mind me asking a question, in fact he nodded along. We waited for the answer. It never came.

'Mr. Flynn, Mr. Levy, if either of you want to split the trial you'll need to apply to the court with the proper motion. We will resist that motion. That's all I'll say on that matter. I want to get to the substance of this meeting if you don't mind.'

He looked at both sides of the table. Levy and his team were quiet, I leaned forward ready to listen.

'Thank you. The District Attorney's office recognizes that your clients are both blaming each other for the murder. We feel that a joint trial will result in *at least* one conviction. It will be open to the jury to convict both defendants and you don't need me to tell you that a joint conviction is the most likely verdict. I'm offering a one-time deal. Twelve years in exchange for a full confession and a statement implicating the co-defendant. If one of the sisters confesses, they walk out of jail in six years, maybe four, with good behavior, while the other will be there for life. This is a one-time deal, available to only one of the defendants. This offer is on the table for forty-eight hours, starting now.'

And people wonder why ordinary citizens plead guilty to crimes they didn't commit. Dreyer had called it pretty well. It was likely both women would be convicted in a joint trial. The odds of one of them winning was very small when both would call each other liars and murderers. Most juries in joint trials don't believe either defendant, and convict both. In that situation, it made sense to take a plea – do four years instead of a life sentence.

Neither Levy nor I spoke. I watched Dreyer pinch the sides of his watch, and it took me a second to realize he was actually setting a timer. For real. Both Levy and I had a professional obligation to take this offer to our clients. Let them make the decision. I didn't want Sofia under that kind of pressure, not this early, but it looked like I didn't have a choice.

'If neither defendant pleads guilty, confesses and assists in the prosecution of the co-defendant, then we go to trial. There will be no more offers and no extensions. Forty-eight hours. If there's no confession, and we're going to a joint trial, then I expect both of your clients to take a polygraph test.'

'What?' said Levy.

'You heard me.'

'Polygraph results are not admissible evidence in this state,' I said.

'The old methods of polygraph testing were not admissible. Technology has moved on. Polygraphs are admissible evidence in eighteen states now. We're pretty sure we can prove our examiner's expertise in New York. As it stands, they are recognized as an important investigative tool for law enforcement. So much in this case comes down to the credibility of your clients. Who will the jury believe? One or neither of them? We will inform the court that a polygraph was offered and if it is refused we'll exploit that refusal. The judge can refer to it in his summing up to the jury.'

I'd underestimated Dreyer. That was damn smart. A real chess move. If one sister refused the polygraph, it made her look guilty. If both refused it, then it would appear as if both were in on the murder together. If one passed the polygraph, and one failed, then Dreyer could use it to convict the sister who failed it.

I put my hand in my inside jacket pocket while I watched Levy's face turn purple. He looked how I felt. Except I didn't show it. I kept my cards tight and close. A murder trial required the ultimate poker face. Levy was talking so loud and so fast at Dreyer that spittle catapulted from his lips and landed in small white clouds on the desk. I put my elbows on my knees, and beneath the table, out of sight of Dreyer and Alexandra's defense team, I opened Levy's wallet and began going through it. I'd lifted it when I bumped into him. I genuinely didn't mean to collide with him that hard. My pocket dip was executed clumsily and if I hadn't tipped him off balance he would've felt the move. As it was, he hadn't noticed a thing. I'd meant to grab his phone, but I felt it vibrate just as I put my fingers close. No way to lift a vibrating phone without him feeling it. His wallet would have to do.

Inside the brown leather wallet I found four one-hundred-dollar bills, two twenties and a five-spot. The usual array of credit and debit cards. There were membership cards for a gym, loyalty cards for different stores and a business card that read 'Discretion Supplies.' As business cards went, it looked expensive and well designed. The 'D' and the 'S' were large and in an ornate spidery font. The card itself was textured and plastic. There was no phone number and no website on the card. On the back there was a barcode for a smart phone. I put the card in my pocket, then closed the wallet and tossed it a few feet to the floor, beneath the table.

I raised my head, Levy was still in full flow, pointing a finger at Dreyer who looked on with composed distance.

'Mr. Levy—' said Dreyer.

'I'm not finished, not by a long way, the Mayor will hear about this abuse of—'

'Mr. Levy, you are finished. This meeting is over . . .' said Dreyer, inching back his chair.

'Wait, Levy, shut the hell up for a second,' I said.

The look on Levy's face amused Dreyer enough to keep him in his seat. I saw Levy's lackey, Scott, furrow his brows in a scowl vaguely aimed at me. Kate bit her lip, suppressing a satisfied smile.

With Levy still catching flies in his open mouth, I got down to the main reason I came here.

'Whatever offer you've made won't have any weight in court if you don't share some more of the prosecution evidence. The accused have a right to know the case against them. Let us see what you've got – that way our clients can make an informed choice.'

'Agreed,' said Dreyer, simply, and got up. He left the room, but only for a few seconds. When he opened the door he revealed half a dozen Assistant District Attorneys gathered in the corridor outside. They must have heard Levy's rant and come to listen. They quickly dispersed when Dreyer came out, except one of them who handed Dreyer two thick brown envelopes. He thanked the assistant, then stepped back through the open door and gave an envelope to me and one to Levy. Without another word, he left.

I left the table and said, 'Someone's wallet is under the conference table. Better pick it up. There isn't an honest man in this building who would hand it in. I'll see you folks later. I'll give you a call, Theo. One word of advice – if you want something, ask for it. It's a lot easier than pounding your little fists on a desk.'

He began to say something, but I was already out of the room. I wanted Theo in fighting mode. As long as a lawyer's blood was up, they weren't thinking, they were raging. I needed time to think. Theo didn't look like a trial lawyer. He looked to me like a pleader. He would put the deal in front of his client and tell her it was good.

I wanted to see Sofia's reaction to the deal. I needed to know for sure Sofia was not involved in her father's death. On a deep level I felt she was innocent, but there was always a small flame of doubt in some cases. I wanted her to blow out that candle.

This trial had nightmare written all over it. Dreyer was having some problems though – he had a missing witness. He hadn't tracked down Mike Modine, Frank's lawyer. When he said he didn't have that statement I had detected something in his voice, a wrinkle of frustration. Modine, whoever he was, wouldn't want to get involved as a witness in a murder trial and he was probably giving the DA's office the runaround. And there was no doubt this was a bad case to be involved in.

The worst cases all come down to who is telling the truth.

A polygraph test was a hand grenade in a case like this. It was going to blow up in someone's face. Either Sofia, or Alexandra. No matter which way you cut it – one of them was a killer. I just hoped it wasn't Sofia.

I had an idea I was about to find out.

NINE

KATE

On the sidewalk outside Hogan Place, Levy hitched up his pants and said, 'What the hell were you thinking in there, Kate?'

Kate felt the blood rush to her cheeks.

'I do the talking in the DA's office. You're a junior associate. You should know better. You embarrassed me in there, you know that? You undermined me. If you ever do that again, you'll be out on your ass. Do you understand me, little lady? Or do you want me to talk slower?'

The shock of Levy's statement hitting her caused all kinds of emotions to erupt. For a long time Kate had wondered if she simply wasn't good enough for the job. Levy's little digs at her work automatically made her feel inferior. Recently, she was coming around to the view that this wasn't about her performance – at least not all of it. This mouthful though, this had a lot of venom. She looked at Scott, who hung his head and began stepping away. She felt like a child being chastised by a parent, not knowing exactly what they had done wrong. Her mouth opened but no words followed. She blinked rapidly, stuttered and then closed her lips tight when the next feeling flooded her system – anger. She wanted to talk. She wanted to tell Levy exactly what he could do with this job. That he was a condescending, misogynistic a-hole. Her teeth ground together, her mouth went dry. Passers-by on the street could see what was happening, and they rubbernecked as they strode past the three of them, standing silently, with Levy waiting for a reaction.

Kate shook her head.

'If you're going to stay on this case then be more like Scott. We're going back to the office, but I suggest you take the rest of the morning to think things over. Get with the program, Kate. Come in after lunch, prepared, with your head in the game. If you're not up for this then maybe you should transfer departments. Wallace is always looking for junior associates in probate. Come on, Scott, we'll take my car.'

And with that, they walked away. Kate was getting used to this, and the hollow feeling in her chest grew. She wanted to be popular with Levy. He was a good lawyer. He was her boss. He could give her a great career. He also wanted to sleep with her. Of that, Kate was certain. And the more she had rebuffed his advances the more aggressive he became in his dealings with her. In the first month, Levy had offered her a ride back to her apartment and she felt then that she had no choice but to accept. He's the boss. In the car, outside her building, he began an awkward conversation.

'Nice building,' said Levy.

'It was almost condemned last year,' said Kate.

'Really, you could never tell. It looks so . . . historic,' he said, struggling to say something complimentary. 'I used to live in a place like this when I first moved to the city. All these apartments are the same around here. It would be great to take a look, relive my youth,' he said, smiling with his little black eyes.

'It's a mess, Theo, sorry. I can't have visitors to an untidy apartment,' said Kate, gripping the door handle.

'No need to be embarrassed. We know each other. We're colleagues. We should probably get to know one another a lot better.'

Kate pulled the door handle, got out swiftly, turned and said, 'Thanks for the ride,' and shut the car door. She threw her bag on her shoulder and walked into the building as fast as she could, listening for the sound of the engine in Levy's car – willing it to rev and for him to drive away – far away from her. The only sound in her ears was the beating of her heart and the idle chug of Levy's car as it sat there, motionless.

She could feel his eyes on her.

Since that day, Kate had started bringing running shoes to work. At the end of the day, when Levy was going home, she waited at her desk, her shoulders tight and frozen in dread.

'You're working too hard. Come on, I'll give you a ride home. We might even grab a bite on the way. Do you like sushi? Wait, who am I kidding? Everyone likes sushi. I know a great place on—'

'No, it's okay, Theo. Thanks, but I've got my gear. I'm jogging home. Got to find the time to keep in shape these days,' she said, reaching down to pick her running shoes out of her gym bag and then holding them aloft above her head as proof of her intentions.

'You don't need to do that. You look in pretty good shape to me,' he said.

That one almost made her puke.

Some nights Levy would persist, asking two or three times. Would she like a drink, or dinner? Levy said he'd been comped tickets for a Broadway show, or a suite at the Four Seasons for a night – would she like to tag along?

Kate said no. Every time. It didn't seem to matter. He would touch her shoulder, his fingers grazing the side of her neck, then sigh and leave. When he got into the elevator every night, Kate shuddered in pure relief, rolled her shoulders and felt the tension drain away.

In meetings he would often sit beside her, his hand slapping itself down on her knee or her thigh when he introduced her to clients or lawyers on the other side of a case. It felt wrong. It felt like he was staking a claim to her – making her his property.

Kate showered every night when she got home – not because she was sweating from a run – she never ran home. The gym stuff was simply an excuse. She washed to get the smell of him off her, the corruption that she felt when he touched her. It was beginning to affect her health.

Lately she'd been having a lot of headaches. She knew it was tension – stress. Not from the job, but from her boss. Fridays were the worst, when she carried files to his car for him, his eyes peeling away her clothes as he stood behind her in the elevator, her heart hammering, waiting for him to make some kind of move, or to touch her.

The more she avoided one-on-one meetings with Levy and made excuses not to go to dinners, the more frustrated he became. He criticized her work, under the guise of 'feedback and mentorship,' and Kate couldn't help but notice the criticism was getting worse the more she turned down his advances.

She had thought about making a complaint, but she had never felt like he'd crossed the line into harassment, no matter how many times she read the harassment policy on the firm's intranet. Sometimes he came close to stepping over it, and Kate knew it wasn't about just one incident – that a course of conduct had to be proven, but how the hell could she prove that when most of the incidents happened when it was just the two of them alone? It would be Kate's word against Levy's. Besides, junior associates who complained about equity partners often ended up on the street, with no reference, which practically made them unemployable. Kate didn't want that. She had worked too hard to get here.

As she watched Levy and Scott walk away on Hogan Place, Levy's rebuke ringing in her ears, Kate took the opposite direction – even though it was the wrong way – back to her apartment. First alleyway she saw, she ducked into the shadow. There were no tears, but she felt like crying. The fluttering in her chest that became a cramp, tightening her breath, would not clear without Kate pushing that release valve and letting it all out. Crying is good for you. She knew this. She'd read enough self-help books, but it just wasn't how Kate was made. She couldn't cry. Not anymore, not since that day. The valve was closed and locked, keeping all that emotion inside where it churned and churned. But a thought calmed her. Her heart rate fell, her breath slowed and deepened.

She wanted to go home. Not back to her apartment. Home.

Forty-five minutes later she stepped off the Edgewater Ferry, which she'd taken from midtown. When she was nine years old in Edgewater, New Jersey, she had played in the abandoned Kellogg factory with her childhood friend, Melissa Bloch. The factory was gone now, and in its place was a modern marina. Times had moved on, the factories made way for expensive waterfront condos, and with the exception of one or two companies that remained, Edgewater was now a kind of hip Gold Coast. At least half of it was, anyway. The town was divided by River Road, with the waterfront properties attracting the high prices. On the other side of River Road, in the hills, property went for half the price. Kate crossed this road into West Edgewater as soon as she left the ferry terminal. She walked past the realtors at the end of the block and turned right on Hudson Avenue – a steep climb to Adelaide Place, her father's house.

Louis Brooks had moved to Edgewater in the seventies. At that time he was a cop in the city, and his partner was Gerry Bloch, Melissa's father. It was Gerry who persuaded her father to move out here. Property was cheap because the land had been poisoned for a century or more by corn oil and chemical manufacturers. They lived side by side on Adelaide Place. It had been a magical period. A small-town childhood with a friend who was more like a sister. Life was great. Until Gerry Bloch got arrested, that is.

By the time she saw the colonial house she had grown up in, her calves were burning and her feet were sore from the climb. She had walked up the hill in her heels – her running shoes safely locked away in a drawer at work. She walked up the brick steps, painted wooden rails framing them, when the front door opened.

Kate expected to see her father. A white-haired seventy-year-old who still thought he was forty-five. Louis Brooks – always pronounced *Lou-is*, never *Lou-ee*. He would be wearing a cotton shirt, work pants, and there would be flecks of paint or oil, or both, on his lined but welcoming face.

But it wasn't her father who opened the door. Instead, she found herself looking up at a tall, striking young woman. Her black hair buzzed at the sides, long on top and swept back in a quiff. She wore a black denim jacket, navy-blue jeans with a green shirt. No make-up. Just a broad smile on the face of Kate's best friend, Melissa Bloch.

Bloch had moved away for some years, become a police officer and transferred around the country. She retired, early, from the force six months ago and moved home to her old house next door to Kate's father. This had been a solace to Kate, who had missed Bloch terribly since she'd left. Now, Bloch made a living as a freelance training instructor for the NYPD, doling out refresher courses on advanced driving, control and restraint, and investigative practice.

In her spare time Louis kept her busy helping him with various DIY projects, which he said required a second pair of hands. Both Kate and Bloch knew Louis didn't really need any help – he just needed the company.

'Shouldn't you be in work?' Bloch asked.

'I took the morning off,' said Kate.

Tilting her head, Bloch held Kate in her gaze for a few seconds before standing aside to let her in. She knew Bloch didn't buy that. Although Kate's problems at work consumed her thoughts twenty-four-seven she had yet to tell anyone about it – even Bloch. It was Kate's problem, and she was determined to keep her head down, mouth shut, and just get through it. In the kitchen, Louis was already pouring coffee. He had splotches of some dark substance on his cheek and the collar of his shirt. If he was suspicious at the working-hours visit, he didn't show it. Kate thought he was probably just glad to see her. He handed steaming mugs to Kate and Bloch and they took a seat at his kitchen table.

Kate took a drink, felt it warm her insides. It wasn't just the coffee – there was something safe and rejuvenating about being home with her dad and her best friend. Apart from being neighbors, and their fathers being friends, Kate had always felt a real connection with Bloch. They were both book nerds, and they were both highly intelligent but in subtly different ways. Kate would be the one who could breeze through class tests and exams without any effort, while Bloch would be the only one in the whole school who could tell if one of the teachers was having an affair, and who with, and for how long.

'How come you're not at work?' asked Louis.

'I took the morning off,' said Kate.

Bloch and Louis exchanged looks, but said nothing.

'Bloch and I were just talking about wood. She's gonna buy some today so we can make a cabinet. It's about time she put some furniture in that house.'

'I don't need much,' said Bloch.

Kate smiled. Bloch would have bought furniture, but Louis was running out of projects. Building a cabinet would keep him busy for weeks.

'Your dad told me you were representing Alexandra Avellino,' said Bloch.

'Ah, no, well, my firm is representing her. I'm just on the team. One of the back-room brief writers. Research, note-taking, that kind of thing . . .'

Before she could finish, Kate's bottom lip began to tremble. Her father reached out, instinctively, touched her arm and then the events of the past few days came flooding out. She didn't dare tell her father she was being sexually harassed by her boss. Louis kept several guns in the house. One of the guns even had a license. And, he was old-school NYPD. He was liable to show up at Levy's front door, stick a .38 in his face and remind him of his manners.

Kate told them what had happened that morning, and the threat Levy had made. Her father looked away, the heel of his right foot bouncing on the floor. She saw Bloch lean forward with a look of anticipation.

'He called you *little lady*? Oh, this is going to be good – what did you say back to him?' asked Bloch, moving her elbows onto the table, leaning in to catch the great come back she was sure Kate had unleashed.

Kate shook her head. 'I didn't say anything. I couldn't.'

Having clearly misread the point of the story, Bloch look confused momentarily, then stared hard at Kate. As if wondering what had happened to her friend who could wither boys with a single look and take down anyone in an argument. Back in those days, Kate had been the tough one. The one who looked after Bloch. The one who took no shit from anyone. At an early age, Kate had a way of wounding with words – they were her weapons.

Her father finished the last of his coffee, and, always looking to avoid a deep or even halfway meaningful conversation, he said, 'Let's go feed the birds.'

Kate followed her friend and her father out back to the paved yard and the two large bird feeders he kept at the rear. A single green parrot sat on a perch on one of the feeders. This was not unusual in Edgewater. It was one of the Quaker Parrots. Nobody knew for sure how or why these birds had come to nest and make a home for themselves in Edgewater. They certainly weren't native to New Jersey. Some said they escaped from a busted packing crate in JFK airport in the sixties. No one knew for sure.

Kate helped her father refill the feeder with seeds and nuts that he kept in an old barrel while her friend looked on. After a few minutes Bloch said, 'I have to take off, Louis, could I get the—'

'Yeah sure,' said Louis. He plunged his arm deep into the barrel, and he rummaged through the contents until he found what he was looking for. When he drew his hand out he held a yellow padded envelope, which he gave to Bloch.

'This is the last of your father's money. It's only a couple of grand. I hope it's lucky,' he said. Kate looked away. Gerry Bloch wasn't a dirty cop. He'd refused to rat on his fellow officers who were on the take, and with no one else to punish, NYPD brass threw the book at Gerry. The rest of the department put money away for Gerry's family. The money was probably dirty, but once he was in the firing line, Gerry didn't care. Kate had always known this, but she was a lawyer now. An officer of the court. She had a duty to report it. But she wouldn't. Not in a million years.

This was family.

'I'll order the wood from the depot today,' said Bloch. 'Thanks for this.'

Louis nodded.

Kate walked Bloch to the front door.

'This is none of my business,' said Bloch as she reached the bottom of the porch steps, and turned toward Kate. 'But you deserve to be in that firm. Take no shit. You're Kate Brooks from Edgewater, New Jersey.' Bloch sighed, shook her head and said, 'Your mom wouldn't stand for this.'

Kate watched Bloch get on a motorcycle, heard the engine scream into life and watched her roll away. Bloch didn't say much, but when she did it was worth listening. And Bloch's words fell around her now like snow, each one a cold and yet gentle reminder that she was still alive and real and feeling every moment of this life. A crushing wave of memory doubled her over and she reached out and put her palms on the floor. It wasn't pain that had brought her down – it was shame. She felt ashamed for hiding everything – for pretending things were okay, for not saying anything. Her tears made dark circular splotches on the faded gray doorstep.

Kate hadn't cried since her mother died. A year before Kate got out of law school, her mother was diagnosed with cancer. She was given a year. Kate hit the internet, found a specialist who agreed to give a second opinion. The afternoon after the appointment with the oncologist, her mom told her she had decided not to go to the appointment – that these things happened, she had lived her life and it was her time. She'd had enough of doctors. Suzanna Brooks died a week before Kate's graduation. Her mom made her promise not to cry at the ceremony, and Kate kept her promise – she had cried all through the wake, and had no tears left at the funeral. She went on to pass the bar exam, gaining the second-highest score that year and landed the job at Levy, Bernard and Groff.

A month into the job, she had to contact a couple of oncologists to arrange appointments for medicolegal opinions in an ongoing clinical negligence case. One of them was the specialist she had arranged for her mother to see. They got talking on the phone and Kate mentioned they had spoken before.

'Yes, I do remember. I don't pretend to remember all of my patients, Kate, but I remember your mom and dad. It's a familiar story. Insurance companies are the worst scum of the earth.'

'I'm sorry? I don't understand. Mom said she didn't keep the appointment.'

'Oh, well, no, they did come and see me. I told your mom we could probably give her another three to five years with this new drug. Her insurance wouldn't cover it, and it was very expensive. I'm really sorry for your loss.'

'That doesn't make sense, my dad had savings. Dad had the money for treatment. I know because he paid for my school fees—'

The realization hit her and Kate had politely ended the call, and thanked the doctor for his time. She went home and her father admitted the truth. Suzanna didn't want her daughter lumbered with student debt she could never pay. Her father had used the family savings to put her through law school. The money they could have spent on life-prolonging medication for her mom went on Kate's schooling. They couldn't afford both. Kate was the most important thing to her parents. Her mother had insisted on this.

Kate's law degree and her job at the firm were hard-earned. That's why Kate was always the first in the office in the morning, and the last to leave. Her mother gave up years of her life for her daughter. Kate could not throw that away. That sacrifice drove her. Made her stay quiet. She didn't want to rock the boat.

She thought about what her mother would say now. She wouldn't want Kate to suffer in silence. She would want Kate to stand up for herself. All those times she kept her mouth shut in front of Levy – the shame ate through her like fire, quickly cooled and turned to something much harder.

She swore to herself right then – the next time something happened in that office she would call it out. Time's up. No more running. No more hiding. No more biting her lip. Next time she would use her voice.

Because she was Suzanne Brooks' daughter.

She was Kate fucking Brooks, from Edgewater, New Jersey.

Frank Avellino
Journal Entry, Friday August 31, 2018.
7:55 a.m.

I hate writing this shit. Never done it before. I'm not a man who wants to have his memoirs published. There are enough skeletons in my closet to fill a goddamn graveyard – twice. This is on doctor's orders. This is for me only. And Doc Goodman. What the hell he expects me to write, I don't know.

I've been having – lapses. It's now eight-thirty in the a.m. I've been awake since four. Had to take a leak and couldn't get back to sleep. The usual. If it's not my prostate it's my brain. Hal Cohen finally persuaded me to go see the doc about both. I'm on pills for the prostate, and I have to write this shit for my brain. Doc asked me some questions, which I answered, and he said I was fine. But to please him, he wanted me to write down my thoughts and any symptoms I notice. He'll see me in a couple of months. He'll read this shit and it'll put him to sleep, I know it.

Maybe he's right. Maybe it is nothing. Or just old age. I've been forgetting things lately. Pills I'm supposed to take in the evening. Sometimes I'll be watching TV and I can't remember if I ate dinner. Or I leave the faucet on, running hot. Missing appointments is a bugbear of mine. If I say I'm going to show up at a place, I show up at that place. No exceptions. I can't believe I missed four meetings last week. Just forgot about them. Maybe I should hire a PA. But a PA can't call me to remind me to put on socks. I forgot those too, last week.

Little things.

Nothing to worry about. The doc said so.

I feel fine today. No problems. I remember what I'm supposed to do, where I'm supposed to be. It's all fine.

Now for breakfast with Hal Cohen.

11 p.m.

Alexandra came over tonight. Sweet kid. Smart. She'd been out running in the park again. I told her she shouldn't run in the park at night. It isn't safe for her on her own. She told me she could handle herself and I believed her. She brought me one of those smoothies I like, from the place on 2nd Avenue.

She said she'd tried calling me today. I think maybe my cell is busted. I had missed calls on that thing, but I could swear it didn't ring. I missed the meeting with the accountant today.

Again.

Alexandra gave me my pills and told me about a deal she closed for an apartment on 13th Street and 3rd Avenue. Sweet deal. Sweet kid. Sofia called. She won't come over when Alexandra is in the house. Those two still won't speak to each other. I've given up trying. But I do wish Sofia would be more like Alexandra.

Sofia will be the death of me, someday.

I'm in bed and I don't know if I brushed my teeth.

I saw someone today on the street. All in black. I think they were following me. I was on Park Avenue, and I saw them across the street. I suddenly couldn't remember where I was going so I took a cab home. I talked to the cab driver about it. He said maybe I was paranoid. I said I would ask Jane about it.

When I got home I called out for Jane. Couldn't understand why she wasn't home.

Then I remembered.

Jane's dead. I saw her dead on the stairs. Her neck stuck in the stair rail. Twisted and broken.

And the other thing . . .

Jesus.

Maybe this is a blessing? There are some things I don't want to remember.

This is awful. I hate writing this.

TEN

SHE

The timer on the Sous-vide machine began to sound a steady beat. She'd risen early to prepare a treat for breakfast and then returned to bed. There was a busy day ahead. She threw back the covers, padded to the kitchen, turned off the machine and lifted the lid. Inside was a gallon of water, which the machine had kept at exactly one hundred and thirty degrees for forty-five minutes. Reaching inside, the water felt very warm, but it didn't burn her skin. The pouch came out of the water bath and she placed it on a clean plate. Prior to taking its bath, the meat had been vacuum sealed in the pouch along with salt and thirty grams of smoked butter.

She slid a knife along the edge of the pouch releasing a warm cloud of vapor. From the cupboard by her knees she lifted a frying pan with an iron base, put it on the hob and lit it. A generous knob of butter hissed as it hit the pan. She reached into the bag and felt the liver. It was warm, but not too warm to touch. It would not burn her. The sensation of warm liver and butter in her hands was almost too good.

Delicately, she seared the liver on both sides while she licked the plasma from her fingers. She tipped the contents of the pan on top of a plate already laden with crushed avocado on sourdough toast. A few splashes of balsamic vinegar and a slice of blood orange completed the dish. The aromas increased her hunger. She took the plate to the dining table, sat down and tucked in.

She put down her knife and fork, picked up a cell phone from the table that sat beside a digital Dictaphone. The cell was a burner. Completely disposable. She accessed the reroute call app, dialed the number and put the phone on speaker. The call connected and rang out. No one picked up. She wasn't expecting the call to be answered. No one in the office at seven a.m. She was waiting for the message service.

'*This is Assistant District Attorney Wesley Dreyer, I'm not available right now, please leave a message after the tone . . .*'

She waited for the beep then hit play on the Dictaphone.

'*This is Mike Modine. I hear you've been looking for me. I'm sorry, this is all bad timing. I've been putting money away for years, and now it's time to use it. You could call it a midlife crisis or whatever you want, but I'm not coming back. Frank Avellino is dead, and I could be next. He called me and wanted to change his will, but he didn't say how or why. I suspect he was being paranoid and was in the early stages of dementia when he made the call. That's all I know. Stop looking for me. I'm not going to talk to you, Mr. Dreyer. Just leave me alone.*'

She ended the call, but let the Dictaphone play. The next voice was hers.

'*Good boy.*'

'*Is that it? Can you let me go now? Come on, please. Please just let me go. No, no don't do that. No, don't . . .*'

The sound of Mike's screams turned to static on the recording. They were much too loud to pick up clearly on the mic.

The venison liver was good. It reminded her of the fawn. Its flesh had been warm and gamey. But quickly grew cold. Soon she would know more about the prosecution case – the witnesses and forensic evidence that they would use against her. She also needed to know what the evidence would be against her sister. Lawyers could only do so much. It was up to her to tip the balance in her favor. Like that message on Dreyer's voicemail. It would lead him in a certain direction.

There were any number of ways to make sure she walked away free from the trial. Some participants in the trial would never change their minds. These unfortunates would need her special attention.

As she took the last bite of liver in her mouth, she thought the meal lacked something. Armagnac, perhaps. A little heavy for breakfast, but ideal for supper. Mike Modine had now been divided into manageable sections, each wrapped tightly in black plastic along with an appropriately weighted disc from the dumbbell set she had ordered. There any many ways to discard a body in New York. The rivers are by far the easiest. And the ferries are usually quiet after ten a.m. She would buy a ticket to DUMBO on the East River, and then, in the shadow of the Brooklyn Bridge, with her back to a security camera on the rear deck, she could toss a limb discretely from her gym bag without anyone noticing so much as a splash. She showered, put on her running gear.

She made a note on a file pad beside her. After she dumped Mike's arms in the river, she would call in to the liquor store and get some Armagnac.

ELEVEN

EDDIE

I left the DA's office with the additional prosecution discovery, and went straight to Bloom's Deli on Lexington to meet Harper for a late breakfast. I got there early, and went through the discovery before she arrived. Along with forensics were Frank Avellino's medical files. He was in good shape when he died. Only thing of interest was a note from the neurologist, that Frank had been noticing memory problems. I couldn't read most of the doctor's handwriting. After recording the history the note read: *RV 3/12 DY. Reassured and any changes to call.*

Doctors have their own shorthand, and not all are common or even noted in a dictionary of medical abbreviations. I took out my phone, checked the abbreviations in an online medical dictionary and found *RV* could stand for a number of things, but one was *Review*. The *3/12* I already knew to be three months. So it read: *review in three months*, but I couldn't decipher DY. It probably wasn't important. I was more interested in the prosecution's experts and forensic reports on the case. They made for grim reading. The DA's office could tie Sofia to the murder in all kinds of ways.

A partial fingerprint, matching Sofia's, found on the murder weapon.

Hair fiber, said to match Sofia's, found on the victim's mutilated body.

Heavy bloodstaining on Sofia's clothes. The blood matches the victim.

I've had cases in the past where a forensic expert has given me problems. I've never had a trial where there is so much forensic evidence against my client. The only potential saving grace was that I knew there was forensic evidence pointing toward Alexandra

Avellino too. If Dreyer succeeded in getting a joint trial where the defendants faced a jury together he would get the easiest murder conviction in the state's history. The evidence was all on his side.

There was something else that made me uneasy. I'd read the medical examiner's autopsy report on Frank Avellino twice. I didn't need to read it a second time, but as soon as I finished the first reading I'd felt the need to read it again, as if I'd missed something, or the report was missing something. Frank had been stabbed multiple times, even bitten. A single bite mark on his upper chest. Apart from the injuries inflicted in the attack, Frank was as healthy as a horse. His skeleton, organs, joints, all were in great condition. I'd read it more slowly the second time, but again I felt reluctant to put the report down. There was something in it that wasn't right. Maybe I was too tired, or maybe it was the horrific details of a man torn apart that was masking my thoughts.

I didn't know. I would ask Harper, see what she thought.

Harper arrived and we both ordered coffee and pancakes, and then I sat quietly while Harper told me all about her time with Sofia yesterday. So far as Sofia was concerned, Harper was just checking out her apartment for security, and then making sure she was stable and settled, that she had everything she needed. Harper's real purpose was to get Sofia talking, to find out everything she could about our new client. I worked with Harper on my last two cases, and she was incredible. Not just smart – she'd saved my life. And every time she smiled she lit something inside of me that I'd thought would never burn again.

'We talked a lot,' said Harper. 'For a young woman who never managed to finish college, Sofia is impressive. Well read, smart as you or me. She was a chess prodigy like her sister. They're very close in age – less than a year between them, but they're not alike at all. As far as I can tell the only things they shared were parents and chess. Their mother taught them.'

'I don't know anything about Frank's first wife. Who was she?'

'Name was Jane Marsden. She grew up on the Upper East Side, in a nice townhouse with a rich family. Met Frank when he was on the up-and-up. Jane was quite the socialite, and didn't have a career outside of being rich, going to parties and playing chess. Seems she wanted to pass on the knowledge to her daughters. Looks like that was all she wanted to give them. I don't think there was a lot of love in that house. Sofia told me her mother used to bite her if she made a mistake in the game.'

'Bite her?'

'Yeah, on the fingers or the outside of the hand. Jane obviously had a lot of problems.'

I nodded.

'They were both young when their mother fell down the stairs in Franklin Street and died. After that, Frank sent both sisters away to separate boarding schools. Sofia and Alexandra didn't get on at all – they hated each other, and I don't think their mother's passing exactly helped. That's all Sofia told me about her mother, but I did a little digging with the local precinct. Frank was out at a fundraiser, and it was just the girls at home with Jane. Alexandra and Sofia both called 911 when they found their mother on the stairs.'

'Really?'

'Spooky, right? Whatever way Jane had fallen, her head had become wedged in between the bannisters. Her neck was broken, and her ankle. A real bad fall. Complete accident, of course. The kids found her like that. I can't be certain but it looks like Sofia went into counseling not long afterward and her mental health began to decline as well as her grades. She never got over the death of her mother. Grades, attendance, all went down the shitter and it only got worse. She had periods where she would get her shit together for a year or so, just long enough to enroll in college or start an internship, and then bam – she would hit the wall and have another breakdown. Poor kid.'

'You felt for her?'

'I really did. You know me, hard as they come. That kid had every advantage in life and it didn't matter. Makes you think. I liked her, Eddie.'

'So she's not a killer,' I said.

Harper took a bite out of a crispy slice of bacon, crunched it between her teeth while she considered her answer and then said, 'No motive apart from the will. If Frank was going to cut one of them out of his will then I suppose that's motive for some people, but not Sofia. For some folk, money is all that drives them. I didn't get that from her. And she loved Frank. Her father supported her through her illness, she told me that. After Jane's passing, Frank turned away from both kids. Sofia took it a lot harder, I'd say. Frank supported her through the rehab clinics – it's sad that they were in such a good place and then Frank was killed. She also said her father was never the same after Jane died. I got the impression it was more than just grief. Frank had a second wife, Heather, who died of an overdose four years ago.'

'I remember reading about that. OxyContin, wasn't it? That's hard. Was it an accidental overdose?'

'Medical examiner said it could've been. No suicide note. Heather had some kind of pain problem, and she got hooked on Oxy. It happens every day. Sad, but Sofia and Heather weren't close, even though Heather was only eight years older.'

I finished my plate, the waitress refilled our coffee. Sofia's family story was tragic. Two clear accidental deaths and now her father's murder. I wondered how I would hold up if I had to go through that kind of nightmare. The hum and buzz of life continued in New York City just outside the window. A traffic cop was arguing with a dumpster truck driver while a homeless man danced around them, making faces at both men. A young girl holding her mother's hand joined in by sticking her tongue out at the cop as they passed the scene on the sidewalk. A female jogger, her hair covered in a cap, dressed all in black, ran by the window.

'Motive isn't everything, you know? Do you think Sofia could murder someone like that? Frank was ripped up pretty bad.'

'I think we're all capable of unspeakable things,' said Harper. 'I've put men down because I had no choice. I've no regrets about any of it. There are bodies in the ground right now because *you* put them there. Here we are – two educated, rational people having a civilized breakfast. No one would think we were capable of taking a life.'

'But the way Frank was killed. Neither of us could do that. At least I hope not. Do you think Sofia could have done it?'

'I don't think she did it. Why would she? This was a frenzied, rage kill. She's got anger inside her, but I can't see Sofia doing that to her daddy. Any violence in Sofia is targeted at Sofia. Did you see her arms?'

I nodded. Something Harper said made me think. I was missing a big piece in this case. There was an element of this crime that just didn't fit. Two sisters. A father murdered and mutilated and each one blames the other. Both had the opportunity to do it. Neither of them seemed to have a reason. There was a forty-nine-million-dollar inheritance and the cops seemed to think Frank was going to cut one of them out of the will. They don't know which one and hadn't been able to track down Frank's attorney. The cops thought the motive was financial. One of the sisters felt betrayed – they were going to be cut out of the will so they killed Frank before he could destroy their inheritance. That was the prosecution case. It made sense, and yet, it didn't. Both sisters had money. I was missing something.

The jogger I saw earlier ran by the window, again. At least I thought she did. It might have been the same one, but maybe not. New York is full of joggers. I shook my head, drained my coffee to ward off the déjà vu. I needed a good night's sleep – I was seeing glitches in the matrix.

'I want you to look at the forensic evidence. Dreyer gave us preliminary reports this morning. Take a close look at the ME's report. There's something in that which isn't fitting right – in my head. This trial is going to move fast so we need to be ready. Also, Dreyer is pushing for a joint trial.'

'He can't do that, not when they're blaming each other?' said Harper.

'He thinks he can avoid a motion for a split trial. He might be right. I need help with that. Someone who knows the law. Legal argument has never been my strong point.'

Harper snorted, 'You can say that again. If there was an argument for *breaking* the law you'd be all over it.'

I had needed someone to help me manage my practice for a long time. An attorney I could trust. Someone who wouldn't rob me, or steal my clients, or – worse still – clean up the office. For a while I'd been keeping an eye out at court looking for a young attorney who might have the skills. I hadn't seen anyone I liked. Now I had no choice. I needed help with this case. Harper was a great investigator, but I needed another legal mind.

'I think I know a lawyer who could join your firm,' said Harper.

'Who?' I asked.

'I'll ask if he's interested first. We'll talk at Harry's party, later. I've got to go. There's a shitload of work to do.'

'Who's the lawyer? Come on, give me a clue.'

'Well, he can't practice law anymore,' she said.

I knew, instantly, who she was talking about. I didn't think he would go for it, but I had to try. Harper was right. This person was perfect, even though he couldn't say a word in court.

I thanked her, told her she was right, and said, 'I'm going to see Sofia. Catch you later.'

Harper left the table with the papers I'd handed over. I took my time watching her leave. There was a playful side to Harper that I was only just getting to know. Through the large windows at Blooms, I watched her cross the street. The crosswalk was crowded, and I saw a woman in black jogging Lycra and a baseball hat walking behind her. The woman wore a skull cap, or something like that, beneath the cap, because I couldn't tell the color of her hair. As Harper got to the other side of the street, the jogger turned and ran in the other direction.

Probably a different jogger, or maybe someone doing laps of the same block, at worst. I pushed the jogger out of my mind again – I really was beginning to sound paranoid.

My mind wandered and I thought again about the autopsy report. I thought for a second I had realized what was bothering me about it. Then, as quickly as it came, the thought vanished. I tried calling Sofia but she didn't pick up. I left a message asking her to call me. Just as I was taking the steps down to the subway my phone rang.

'Mr. Flynn, sorry I missed your call. What's happened?'

It was Sofia. She sounded rattled – out of breath.

'It's okay. Nothing too major but we need to talk. You sound breathless, are you alright?'

'Yes, I'm fine.'

'Oh, good. Can we meet?'

'Sure. Around five o'clock? I have a few errands to run.'

TWELVE

KATE

In the ladies' bathroom on the fourteenth floor of the building that housed Levy, Bernard and Groff, Kate tucked the collar of her blouse beneath the lapels of her jacket. It was coming up on two o'clock in the afternoon and she hadn't eaten since breakfast. She was hungry, but too focused to stop for food.

Checked her reflection.

She hit the faucet, washed and dried her hands.

Checked her reflection again. She touched up her lipstick. Breathed out, nodded and left.

Kate made her way to the conference room, which had been commandeered for the attorneys working on the Avellino case. Levy had described this as the 'war room' and sure enough a battle was raging when Kate opened the door.

A long table filled with open law books, case reports, laptops, coffee cups, legal pads and pencils took up the center of the room. The group had been working all morning, discussing the discovery and potential strategies. They had to be ready to present their ideas to Levy the next morning. Levy let it be known, none too subtly, that whoever had the best work would likely be awarded second chair at the trial. Kate wanted that seat more than anything. This was her moment, and she wasn't going to let it pass. All the shit that came with the job would be worth it if she was sitting beside Levy in that trial. It was all that she could think about. The group in the room already had a head start as Kate had missed the morning session. She had now read the discovery and was up to speed. It didn't pass her by that Levy had deliberately kept her out of the office by giving her the morning off to collect her thoughts. While this put her behind in terms of work, seeing Bloch and her dad that morning had been exactly what she'd needed.

Around the table sat Scott, an empty chair beside him to which Kate returned, and on the other side of the room were three attorneys from litigation who had previously worked in the criminal department. All of them were male, all wore expensive suits that looked too tight and ties that were way too thin. They had given their names to Kate as Chad, Brad and Anderson. They didn't offer to shake hands, but one of them, Brad, hit Scott with a fist bump. She didn't know if Anderson was a first name or last name. It didn't matter. Brad, Chad and Anderson looked as though they shared the same bleached-blond personality. Jocks with rich parents and trust funds.

Kate returned to the stack of papers in front of her – a potted history of the Avellino family with more details on Alexandra and Sofia. The more Kate read, the more she was convinced that Alexandra was the functioning, organized sibling who had her shit together and her life on track from a young age. While Sofia was a disaster with bouts of drug addition, rehab stints, counseling and more than one intervention regarding her destructive behavior. It made Kate feel good to know that she was obviously representing the innocent sister, but with that knowledge came weight.

The burden of proving guilt beyond a reasonable doubt lay with the prosecution, but the burden of having an innocent client on trial for murder was a much heavier one.

Innocence weighs a ton.

'Let's blue-sky this case. Enough reading, already. We've got forty-one days and counting to lodge our motions with the court. We need discovery, motions for dismissal, and a severance motion. What've you got, dogs?' said one of the blond suits. With her focus on the case, Kate had forgotten which of them was which. She thought that might have been Anderson.

Scott said, 'Anderson, don't use that language here. We're not all dogs, there's a lady present.'

She was right, it was Anderson who had taken charge of the group and was asking for ideas. Anderson fixed Scott with an expression that said – *really?*

'Alright, alright,' said Anderson, 'dogs and *bitch*. Is that better?'

One of the suits high-fived Anderson, the other was laughing so hard he was doubled-over on his chair. Kate glanced to her side, saw Scott trying to hold in a laugh, and failing.

Kate felt the blood flooding the skin around the base of her neck like a heat rash. Her skin was prickly, and alive.

Anderson must've seen her reaction because he put both hands out in front of him, palms up, like he was trying to stop a speeding car coming toward him, 'Woah, I'm really sorry. I don't mean any kind of offence. It's just our sense of humor – absolutely nothing to do with you, personally.'

Chad, Brad and Scott calmed down and all of them apologized, with smiles on their faces – none with a single drop of sincerity. They apologized because they had to.

'He's really sorry,' said Scott.

'I am, too. So is Brad,' said the one who must've been Chad.

'Me too,' said Anderson fighting down another bout of laughter. Brad, who looked to be a little quicker on the uptake than Chad, bit his finger in an effort to quell his mirth.

'Sorry, I didn't mean it that way. I meant I'm sorry *too*. Not *hashtag Me Too*,' said Anderson, rolling his eyes and making air quotes when he said *me too*.

'Can we move on?' said Kate.

The men straightened up, now a little worried that they had offended Kate. She'd had enough of this shit. She just wanted out of the room so she could go somewhere and calm down before she said something she would come to regret. Brad, Chad and Anderson had seniority at this table, and she had kept that firmly in mind while she bit down hard in case a flurry of expletives should escape.

'By all means, you're right. Let's move on. Sorry, what's your name again?' said Anderson.

'Kate.'

'Sorry, Kate. Please, let's have your thoughts,' said Anderson.

There was a five-hundred-pound pause in the room. Thick and deep enough to drown a man.

'I've been reading a lot about the family. It's a little messed up, maybe no more than other families, but whatever went on in that house hit Sofia the worst. She's a wreck. Serious mental health problems, a history of suicide attempts, drug and alcohol addiction and an ongoing problem with self-harming. The prosecution will have an easier time convincing a jury that Sofia could flip out and murder her father.'

Taking a second, Kate looked around the table.

The sniggers and snide half-smiles had gone. Scott and the blond suits were listening – seriously listening. What Kate was about to say sounded crazy, but she believed it could work. She just needed to believe in *herself* enough to say it.

Scott said, 'After we sever the trials, we can't dictate which trial the DA will take first. Maybe they'll take Sofia's case first and if she's convicted, well that might be enough for Dreyer to have one scalp – maybe he won't risk going after Alexandra. But there's no way to make that happen. We can't dictate which trial goes first after our motion to sever the trials is granted.'

Brad, Chad and Anderson nodded approvingly at Scott, then began looking at their own notes.

'You don't understand. I'm proposing we don't sever the trials,' said Kate.

Scott looked as though he'd been struck. His head rocked back on his shoulders, he frowned and wrinkles appeared on his forehead.

'What do you mean, we don't separate the trials? If the defendants are accusing one another we have to try – they'll just destroy their own credibility by pointing the finger at each other. And what if Alexandra decides not to testify and Sofia testifies against Alexandra – we'd be screwed,' said Scott.

'It could only work if Alexandra testified,' said Kate. 'Look at it this way. In a separate trial, we have to beat the evidence from the DA. In a joint trial we only have to beat Sofia – a mentally unstable drug addict with a history of violence. Alexandra is a professional young woman, with a clear record, who is totally convincing when she says she had nothing to do with the murder. She's a dream witness. Articulate, credible, sincere.'

'It's risky as all hell,' said Anderson.

'You know the old joke about the wildlife photographers who startle a lion on the African plain? The photographer closest to the lion changes out of his boots into a pair of Adidas running shoes. The other photographer says, *You won't outrun a lion in those shoes.* And the first photographer says, *Fuck the lion. I just have to outrun YOU.*'

The meeting lasted another hour. Legal theories and strategies fired back and forth across the table. Now they would each go away and prepare notes. Not only would they present their strategies to Levy, but they were expected to critique each other's strategies for any possible weaknesses. It was all riding on the paper that Kate would now write. The meeting with Levy tomorrow morning was her shot at second chair in the trial.

Kate ate dinner alone at her desk and typed furiously on her laptop, building her theory of proceeding with a joint trial. Every now and again she flipped between the memo she was writing for Levy, and the dossier their investigators had prepared on Alexandra.

If Kate could have Alexandra's lifestyle, she would take it in a heartbeat. Until the arrest, Alexandra had been a tall, blonde, rich socialite on the Manhattan scene. Parties, limos, dinners, and dresses that Kate could only dream of buying. Her real-estate business ran itself – she listed properties for the uber-rich. And the uber-rich bought them, sometimes without even so much as a viewing. A long list of celebrity boyfriends had been photographed in the gossip and social life pages of magazines – basketball players, actors, the sons of actors, TV hosts, and even shock-jock podcasters. And she was smart, too. Alexandra had it all. A great life and great clothes. *Oh my god, the clothes,* thought Kate.

A Park Avenue lifestyle. With money. Security and total luxury. Alexandra Avellino had absolutely no motive to kill her father. He had given her a dream life. Set her on that path. She was the last person on earth who would harm her father.

Six o'clock came and went. Nobody left the office. This law firm existed on billable hours. If you weren't billing your share, your ass hit the street fast. Kate started punching in at six a.m., and usually punched out at nine. Four hours on a Saturday morning too. On Sunday she crashed.

It was past seven o'clock when the first associate left for the evening. Kate watched him go, and leaned back in her chair, thrusting her arms to the ceiling and stretching her back. That's when she heard Levy's office door open and hurried footsteps on the floor behind her. Scott came out of Levy's office. A spring in his step and a wide smile on his photogenic face. He got into the elevator and was gone.

Kate returned to the screen in front of her and read through her last sentence, careful to check for any typos. That's when she heard Levy's door again. He rarely left his office, usually only to go to meetings, or to go home. He had a private bathroom in there and a small army of secretarial staff to bring him lunch, dinner and endless glasses of chilled almond milk. She turned her head to see Levy coming toward her, hauling his pants up as he walked. He stopped behind her chair, and she resisted the urge to shudder as she felt his hand on her shoulder.

'Any response from the DA's office on my counter-offer?' asked Levy.

'No, not yet,' said Kate.

'Okay. Look, Katie, why don't you finish this up in the morning?' he said.

She felt his index finger slid across her collar bone, and not wanting to scream or turn and punch him in the balls, Kate simply swiveled her chair around to face him – forcing him to take his hand away.

'I can't, I need to write up my notes for tomorrow's strategy presentation. I should be finished soon,' said Kate.

'But you've got to eat. You should take a break. I know a great little Italian restaurant right around the corner from my apartment. And the best thing is it delivers. We could go back to my place, order in, open a bottle of wine and you can tell me all about your case theory.'

For a second – a full second – the thought of going back to Levy's apartment with him flashed through Kate's mind. She wanted second chair. She wanted it bad. But the moment passed, somehow leaving an unpleasant taste in her mouth which sure wasn't there before.

'I'm a little behind on my notes. Some more legal research to do before I can finish. Sorry, I just really want to finish this and make a good impression tomorrow. I have a strategy that's kind of unusual, but it could really pay off for Alexandra. I really think I deserve a shot at second chair in the trial.'

Levy stepped back, set his lips into an 'O' then cringed as he said, 'I just gave second chair to Scott. Sorry, I can't go back on that. I'm sure your strategy is bold, but it couldn't beat Scott's theory. It's kind of genius in a way. Ruthless, which I like, but really thinking out of the box. At first I couldn't believe what he was saying, but he convinced me. We're not going to apply to the court to sever the trials. It's going to be a joint trial. We'll put Alexandra against Sofia, and Alexandra will beat her weird sister hands down. How did Scott put it? Putting on our Nike's when we see a tiger in the jungle. We won't beat the tiger in those shoes, but as long as we outrun the other guy we're home free. Funny, don't you think?'

Kate's heartbeat quickened – she could feel the pulse beating its way through a large vein that stretched across her chest.

'When did Scott tell you this?'

'Just now. It's brilliant. I didn't see any point in delaying the decision. Scott's got second chair. If we play along with the prosecution and get a joint trial I can pressure Dreyer into a deal for Alexandra. She'll accept a felony misdemeanor, no time. So look, you don't need to have this work done for the morning. Come and have some dinner with me. My apartment is really something, you know? It's spacious but at the same time it's . . . intimate.'

Bile filled Kate's mouth. She felt dizzy, and turned away from Levy so she could hold onto the desk. She needed to hold onto something right then or she knew she would be sick all over the floor.

If she told Levy this was her idea all along the chances were he wouldn't believe her. Even with the notes she had made – Scott could say that *he* brought it up in the meeting and his bimbo buddies would back him up one hundred percent. From somewhere that felt far away, Kate was aware of Levy saying, 'Well, if you change your mind later you're welcome to drop by. I just got a jacuzzi tub installed. It's big enough for two. We could chill out with some champagne, discuss your case theory. You never know, I might need a third chair in this trial.'

She put her head in her hands.

A montage of possible actions flickered through her mind. None of them involved going back to Levy's apartment.

'No, thank you,' said Kate.

Levy backed away, perhaps conscious that he was pushing the envelope now.

Kate wanted to push her laptop up Levy's ass.

Instead, she flicked her finger across the face of the mouse, brought her screen back to life and checked her emails. She had received Brad, Chad and Anderson's notes for commentary. She printed them, and another two documents. These she collected from the copier, grabbed her coat and pushed the button for the elevators. While she stood there, she had second thoughts. What she was thinking of doing was dangerous, outrageous. It could kill her career stone dead.

The elevator doors opened and Kate got in on her own. The floor below was where Human Resources was based. She thought about hitting that button, going to the personnel supervisor and making a complaint of sexual harassment, and discrimination. The doors began to close.

She reminded herself she was Kate Brooks.

Kate hit the button for the ground floor. She'd had enough. It was time to take the nuclear option. No complaints against Levy would ever stand scrutiny. It's nigh on impossible to prove a person has done something wrong when you work in an office with that same person's name on the letterhead.

There would be no sexual harassment claims.

What she had in mind was far more damaging.

THIRTEEN

EDDIE

I waited at my office until five-thirty, then called Sofia. She was a half-hour late for our meeting, and I wanted to make sure she was coming.

She picked up my call this time.

'Oh God, I'm so sorry. I must've fallen asleep. Can I come over now?'

I checked my watch. I needed to leave in half an hour for Harry's party, and there was no way out of that.

'Is tomorrow morning okay?' I asked.

'Sure, thank you. And again, I'm so sorry.'

'No problem. Look, I could come over to your place tomo—'

'No,' she said, cutting me off straight away, 'I'll come to you. I'd prefer that.'

I hung up, and cursed the thought of the evening ahead. College parties had bored me. When I graduated law school I made a promise to avoid any and all parties, especially ones that required you to dress up for the evening. Any invitation I got that said 'black tie' went straight into the trash.

But there was no avoiding this one.

I didn't own a tuxedo and I damn sure wasn't going to hire one. I showed up to Fong's Chinese Restaurant in a black suit, white shirt and black tie. An outfit that passed for cocktail parties and funerals. In my pocket was an order of service for the last funeral I'd attended. An old con artist called Billy Bangs who cleaned out half of the golden mile in Las Vegas in the seventies. That funeral was depressing as all hell. There's no one as a lowly as an old conman. That profession does not age well. I paid my respects and got out of there.

Now I was being handed a glass of champagne from a silver platter at the entrance to Fong's and a hostess showed me through to the back room. The room was long and well lit, with Chinese lanterns and two chandeliers in the shape of dragon heads hanging from the ceiling. The party started at six, it was almost seven when I arrived. I couldn't get out of this invitation but I didn't need to be on time. Harry Ford knew I was there under protest.

I saw Harry at the other end of the room, which was filled with stiffs in tuxedos and their wives in sparkling dresses. They were senior lawyers, judges and court staff. All of them were here for Harry. Probably ninety-nine percent of them came because it was expected of them. The other one percent were there to make sure Harry went through with it. I was in the one percent category.

I was there for my friend, Harry Ford.

I saw Judge Stone behind a lectern at the other end of the room. Harry just to the left of him. Stone was coming to the end of a speech.

'Judge Ford's service to this city is immeasurable. He is one of our most respected brother judges. A fine lawyer in his day, and an even finer judge. Ladies and gentlemen of the Southern District of New York, please raise your glasses. A toast. To Harry Ford. May you live long, and enjoy the peaceful retirement you so richly deserve. To Harry . . .'

The crowd echoed, 'To Harry,' and champagne was politely sipped. I drained my glass, looked around for somewhere to place it and that's when I saw her.

A woman with a long, open-backed dress that came down to the bottom of her spine. Her hair was tied up in intricate curls and studded with bright stones. She turned, as if she felt my eyes on her.

'Harper?' I said.

She smiled and excused herself from the four or five guys around her, making her way to me.

'I knew you'd be late. I only just got here,' she said.

'You look . . . great,' I said, unable or maybe unwilling to say anything more. Harper slipped her hand around the crook of my arm and brought her red lips close to my ear. I could feel her breath on my neck, like a brush fire.

'I've never been in a room with so many assholes. Let's go rescue Harry,' she said.

Together we made our way through the crowd. I had never seen Harper dressed like this. She was a revelation. And I couldn't tell her how I felt. I couldn't say anything. It was like there was a plug in my throat. A stopper. Maybe it was for the best. Harper deserved someone better than me.

'I give you, Harry Ford,' said Judge Stone, stepping away from the mic at the lectern to make way for Harry. It was the first time I'd seen Harry in two weeks, and he looked as though he'd lost weight in that time. Harry had always carried a few extra pounds, and it suited him. Standing up there, he looked old and thin. His cheeks had collapsed.

Harper and I stopped with just a few people ahead of us in the crowd.

'I've been a dishwasher, short-order cook, paperboy, the youngest African American Captain in the United States Military, a law clerk, a lawyer and a judge. If anything, my career has been going backwards for fifty years. The best job I ever had was washing those dishes in Rocko's All American Diner. I was thirteen when I got that job. I learned everything I needed to know about it in under thirty seconds. Plates would come into the kitchen dirty, and it was my job to make sure there were enough clean plates to go back out. There was no room for ambiguity. The plates were clean, or they were not. As a lawyer my job got more complicated, and when I took a seat on the bench it got worse still.'

I looked around the room. What had begun as polite laughter, believing Harry was making a joke, petered out. There were now a lot of stern faces among the audience of lawyers and judges, staring back at Harry. Some in disgust. Some in disbelief.

And one, in anger.

Judge Stone had stepped off the small stage, and he now stood beside Wesley Dreyer, Assistant DA. Dreyer watched Judge Stone closely, as if he was reading his every gesture, sensing his emotion. Like a card player in a poker game. With lawyers like Dreyer, every conversation is a game – and the only thing at stake was what he could get out of it. And you didn't need to be a cold reader to spot the disdain and the rising aggression in Stone's expression.

'As Judge Stone takes my place on the bench I have some advice for him,' said Harry, turning now and looking at Stone directly.

'I have tried to be fair, to uphold the law and the constitution and discharge my duty to the people of this city. I've done my time. And now it feels like getting out of jail. I want you, Judge Stone, to be better than me, and I mean that. We all need to do better. The people of New York deserve no less. Thank you all for being here. I'll see you in the bar.'

Harry stepped away from the podium to staggered applause. It was a strange speech. I'd been to one retirement party before, for Harry's old buddy Judge Folcher. It had been filled with congratulatory talk, war stories and much back-slapping. Harry wasn't like that. He carried the weight of his responsibility like he'd carried injured GIs to safety in the last year of the Vietnam conflict. Harry had one quality that didn't sit well with judicial office – he cared. He cared about the victims of crime, and the defendant. Very few people in this world are truly, irredeemably bad. They've been messed up, by drugs or alcohol or life. Harry saw almost everyone in his court as a victim. That shit sticks to parts of your soul. It adheres and lingers no matter how hard you try to chip it away with rules, professional ethics or better still – bourbon.

Harry spotted me and Harper, shook hands briefly with well wishers as he passed through the crowd headed for us. Before he made it across the room, we were joined by unwelcome company.

'Unusual speech,' said a voice beside me. I turned and saw Judge Stone. Dreyer stood next to him, both men wearing game faces. If Harry carried compassion and humanity with him in every decision he made on the bench, Stone provided the justice system with the balance some say it needed. He was not a merciful man. He'd been a judge for ten plus years, but his first case was still talked about. He'd refused to accept the plea agreement the DA had arranged, and sent a homeless mother of five to jail for six months. Her crime was snatching a hotdog from a street vendor. Her kids were all in the social services system, and she had been trying desperately to get an apartment and a job so she could get them back. When she stole the hotdog she hadn't eaten for three days. It was her first offense. Under the plea deal she would've been sentenced to time served (twenty-one hours in custody from time of arrest) plus probation.

She hung herself in her cell, on the second night of the six-month sentence Stone handed down.

Stone came into court the next day, and while in his chambers he told his clerk he'd read the news reports on the woman's suicide. He said, 'That's one less cockroach in the world.' Clerks talk. Every judge knows this. Stone was a cold, racist prick and God help you if you had to appear in his court, and he wanted everyone to know it. The clerk told the story and word got around.

He had a long, pale face with dry skin that always looked as if it was coated in a fine powder. His pink lips, by contrast, appeared constantly wet and shiny, and they hid his small rat-like teeth. He had eyes that could've been black pearls, and he gave off an odor that I couldn't put my finger on. It was chemical, but not clean. Like a stink that he'd tried to mask with dead flowers.

He looked at me expecting a response. I turned away.

'I said it was an *unusual* speech,' said Stone, again.

'I heard you the first time,' I said. 'I was being polite by not arguing with you. It was honest. Harry's devoted a lot of time to this job. He doesn't want his work to be unraveled when you take over.'

Dreyer took a step closer, a look of anticipation on his face – like he was about to watch a car crash and he couldn't wait to see the blood and carnage.

'Do you think I'm not a worthy successor?' said Stone.

He took some pleasure in his question – a smug look hung around his little black eyes.

I said nothing.

'Judge Stone asked you a question, Mr. Flynn,' said Dreyer, eager to join in with the judge.

'I heard him. I thought it was a rhetorical question. But if you really want me to answer him, I will.'

Harper tugged at my arm, said, 'Hi, I'm Harper.'

She was smarter than me, and the judge and Dreyer both took a moment to look her up and down appreciatively.

'I'm going to steal Eddie away, if you gentlemen don't mind,' she said. I could tell she was pissed, and didn't like the way Dreyer and Stone let their eyes wander over her.

I didn't like it either.

She pulled on my arm, trying to get me away from the situation.

'So, Miss Harper, do you think I'd be a worthy successor to Judge Ford?' said Stone, unwilling to let any perceived criticism slide.

'Stone, what's going on?' said Harry, cutting me off before I said something I could regret.

'Mr. Flynn was just going to tell us that he believes Judge Stone will be a worthy successor to you, Judge,' said Dreyer.

Harry said, 'Eddie's not that drunk. Not yet. Stone, you wouldn't be a worthy successor to a shithouse attendant. I know your politics. I know your *kind*.'

Harry reached out, pointed to the lapel of Stone's tux. There was a metal pin there. It was small, and I hadn't taken any notice of it until Harry pointed it out. A circle with a '1' in the center.

'Your time's up, Ford. You had your run. Don't make me come after you,' said Stone.

'Let's get a drink,' said Harry, ushering Harper and me away. 'There's a bad smell around here.'

As we walked away, I glanced over my shoulder and only then did I notice that Dreyer wore the same pin on his jacket.

We made our way to the back of the room, Harry said his good-byes to some other judges and lawyers, and we split to an upscale bar on the next block. Harry felt the same way as I did about parties, even his own. The bar was part of a hotel, and we didn't look or feel too out of place in our penguin suits, while Harper would have looked like a million dollars in any room in that dress.

I got us some beers and Scotch and we took a booth in the corner.

'What was that pin Stone was wearing?' asked Harper.

'It belongs to an organization that changes its name every year or so. It used to be a white-boy gangbanger outfit out of Tennessee. They got political, changed their names from Nation First, to

American Lives First, Men of America, then something else – they split and reformed and split that many times I don't even know what exactly they call themselves these days. It doesn't matter. They don't admit women, Jews, blacks, Hispanics, or anyone for that matter who isn't white, wealthy and ignorant.'

'I thought judges couldn't be that political once in office,' I said.

'There are rules. Stone keeps to the letter of the law, that's for sure. He has his first amendment right to free expression when he's not on the bench. I just can't abide the thought of that asshole taking my place. I never thought he would get the appointment – if I'd known, I wouldn't have left, but by then I'd already put in my papers.'

'The new hotshot at the DA's office, Wesley Dreyer, he was wearing one of those pins too,' I said.

'I saw that. Dreyer and Stone are tight. Racists are weak, Eddie. They only have strength in numbers. I'm not sure Dreyer believes all the crap that goes with that pin. He's aligning himself with a powerful judge in whatever way he can. In some ways, that's worse. Stone is too stupid to recognize his prejudices. Dreyer doesn't care, as long as he's climbing a ladder. Be careful though, they're a dangerous pair. There's nothing in the rulebook to prevent Dreyer appearing in Stone's court. You challenge Dreyer for judicial bias and he'll hand you your ass,' said Harry.

We took some time to sip our drinks in silence, and I ordered another round from the waiter.

'Harper and I have been talking. You don't have any immediate plans for your retirement, do you?' I asked.

'What do you mean, plans? I don't like the sound of that, Eddie.'

'Well you can't sail a boat, you don't have any hobbies, and you're not going into any consultancy work with the big firms. You're kind of a free agent now, right?'

'I thought we could leave it at least a week before we go to Vegas and get arrested,' said Harry.

'I don't think that's what Eddie has in mind,' said Harper.

Harry pushed himself away from the table, looked at me over the rim of his glasses.

'*Eddieeee* . . .' he said, in a tone that implied I'd already done something wrong.

'I want you to work with me. I know you're not allowed to practice, but there's nothing to stop you being a consultant. I need help. I need someone who knows the law inside out. If it's any consolation, Dreyer is my opponent. I'm representing Sofia Avellino. Harper is handling the investigation. I'll handle the evidence and witnesses, but I need someone with a great legal mind. I don't have ten associates writing briefs twenty-four hours a day.'

Raising his glass to his lips, Harry took a thoughtful sip, and by the time he put the glass down he had a wicked smile on his face.

'Eddie, your cases have a habit of becoming . . . messy. Have you been beaten up, threatened or arrested yet?' asked Harry.

'Give me a chance, we haven't really got started.'

Harry raised his glass, Harper and I did likewise. We clinked glasses, and Harry said, 'Well, at least we won't have to go all the way to Vegas to get in trouble.'

FOURTEEN

KATE

It started to rain heavily when Kate pulled out one of the pages she'd printed in the office and checked the address listed at the top. She looked at the sign over the building. A panel of intercom buttons lay in the recessed doorway. Raindrops spattered the page, and she folded it and put it inside her coat pocket. Her finger paused just before she hit the intercom. Once she pressed it, there was no going back.

Her finger pressed the button, almost unconsciously. A buzzer sounded to let her know an alert had been sent to the inhabitant of the apartment above. Kate straightened her jacket, cleared her throat and swept strands of wet hair away from her face.

'Yes,' said the voice from the intercom.

'Ms. Avellino, it's Kate Brooks from Levy, Bernard and Groff. I'm one of the attorneys assigned to your case. We met in the First Precinct. I'm sorry to disturb you, but it's urgent. Do you mind if we talk?'

'Come on up,' was the response.

Kate heard a click. She pulled the front door open, found the elevators and traveled up to Alexandra Avellino's floor. The elevator was maybe half the size of Kate's apartment. The doors opened to a classic Manhattan apartment hallway. Art deco coving and lamps along the length of the hall. The place smelled like pinecones and cinnamon. She traveled up in the elevator, reached Alexandra's apartment, knocked on the door. Alexandra must've been waiting because the door opened up straight away.

As Alexandra stood in the doorway, Kate was again struck by her appearance. Tall, blonde, no make-up and wearing a white cotton bathrobe. Her hair wet from a shower. She was still the beauty Kate had seen arm-in-arm with Hollywood actors and celebrities.

'Come in,' said Alexandra.

Kate went inside and Alexandra offered to take her coat. Before she handed it over, she withdrew the damp pages from her pocket and apologized for the coat being so wet. She had left the office in a hurry – no umbrella and no document folder.

Kate didn't want anyone to know she had taken documents with her from the office. She wasn't supposed to bring anything about the case home, and she sure as hell wasn't supposed to be here.

'Can I get you a drink?' said Alexandra. 'Water, herbal tea?'

'Some tea would be great,' said Kate.

She followed Alexandra as she padded, barefoot, into the kitchen and began to make the tea.

'I guess it's really raining out there now. Would you like a towel?' Alexandra asked.

'No, it's fine,' said Kate as a drop of rainwater spattered the collar of her blouse.

'I'll get you a towel,' Alexandra said. She left the kitchen and went into the bathroom. Kate looked around the kitchen and what she could see of the living space. It was a beautiful place, with a great view of the city. Alexandra's taste was gorgeous – with carefully chosen color schemes throughout the apartment matching the couch and the chairs. The place was immaculate apart from a pair of black Lycra running bottoms draped over the back of one of the kitchen chairs. A black ballcap sat on the seat beneath the bottoms, a black top folded beneath the cap. There were some packages to the side of the front door. Some had been opened and the cardboard boxes left there, packing material nosing out of the box.

A chessboard sat on a coffee table. From the arrangement of the pieces on the board, it looked like Alexandra was playing a game.

'Sorry, I'm not disturbing your chess game, am I? I didn't know you had company,' said Kate.

Alexandra returned to the kitchen with a soft white towel, which she handed to Kate.

'No, it's okay. I'm the only person here. I wasn't playing right now. That's an old game,' she said, nodding toward the chessboard. 'You said something about this being urgent?'

'Yes, I think it would be better if we sat down.'

Alexandra poured the water into two mugs and handed one to Kate who was dabbing at her hair with the towel. The smell of chamomile warmed her through before she'd even taken a sip. Alexandra sat at the dining table, and Kate took a seat opposite her.

'What's wrong? Has the DA made another offer? I still don't know about taking the lie detector test. Mr. Levy said it was my the decision.'

'That's why I'm here,' said Kate. 'Is it okay if I call you Alexandra?'

She nodded in agreement.

'I haven't worked for Levy, Bernard and Groff for very long. Even in that short amount of time, I've had to turn a blind eye to a lot of stuff, but I can't do that anymore. Mr. Levy will leave the decision on the lie detector to you. He doesn't care about the polygraph. What he really wants is for you to take the deal.'

'What?'

'He wants you to tell the DA you and your sister murdered Frank Avellino – that you played a lesser role and it was really all down to Sofia. That way you will still be able to have a life after you get out of jail.'

'But he knows I didn't kill my father. I told him face to face – you were there.'

'I know. He'll stretch the pre-trial process as much as possible – hammer the prosecution with paperwork as a negotiating strategy and then get you the best deal he can. The only thing wrong with that is you have to admit to playing a part in the murder.'

'No, I can't do that.'

'What if he could get you to walk? No jail time. That was his last offer to the DA.'

Kate took out a piece of correspondence and handed it to Alexandra.

Kate followed her eyes as she scanned the page. Levy was a good lawyer, and he would go to trial if he had to, but if there was a deal to be made, he would break the client's arm to get her to take it.

'This letter says I would plead guilty to manslaughter, but I didn't do it. He was murdered. Sofia murdered him,' said Alexandra. 'Who gave him the right to make this offer?'

'You did,' said Kate.

'What? When?'

'When you signed the retainer agreement, you authorized Levy to negotiate on your behalf. It's in the fine print.'

'I didn't know it was there, I didn't read it. I was in the police precinct – my father had just been murdered, I didn't have time to . . .'

'I know,' said Kate, reaching out, lightly touching Alexandra's hand.

'He had no right to do this, I told him I'm innocent, for Christ sake!' said Alexandra, her voice rising, her chest heaving, on the verge of a panic attack. 'What if this got out? I'd be ruined. My reputation, my business, oh my god, I can't even . . .'

'That's why I'm here,' said Kate. 'I believe you. I know you didn't kill your father. I don't want my firm to negotiate. I think there is a sure-fire way to get you an acquittal.'

'You think you can guarantee me an acquittal?'

'I'd bet my life savings on it,' said Kate. Little did Alexandra know that Kate's life savings were four hundred and twelve dollars, which she kept in a cookie jar in her apartment for emergencies. Kate handed her the notes prepared by Chad, Brad and Anderson. They all detailed motions to sever the trial as a first step.

'When I met you that night in the police station you were scared. I don't pretend to know what it feels like to lose your father like that. And for your sister to have done it? I just can't process how that would make you feel. I don't just want to get you an acquittal, I want to make sure your sister pays for what she did to your father.'

The pages began to tremble in Alexandra's hand.

'How would you do that?' she said.

'The prosecutor wants to put you and your sister on trial together in front of the same jury. I've read everything there is on your family. I know you're innocent. I know your sister is a very sick person – she's violent and self-destructive. I think a jury looking at both of you will see that too. Basically, Levy wants to deal, I want to *win*.'

Kate outlined her plan – how she would prove Alexandra couldn't have done this while bolstering the prosecution case against her sister.

'I think that could work,' said Alexandra, finally.

'Tell that to the rest of the firm. You've seen their strategies. I think mine is the winner. They have a lot of cases – this is just another job. For me, this is personal.'

Alexandra leaned forward, she was taking care to listen to every word Kate said. Kate meant it when she said she could win, but the lie about the firm not using her strategy felt hard on her tongue. Levy and Scott would steal her ideas, and run with them. Kate wanted the best for Alexandra, and she believed she could win.

'My mom died not long ago – cancer. We didn't have a lot of money growing up. She and my father had a choice – they could send me to law school, or they could buy medication that would've prolonged her life. They sent me to law school. I didn't know about this until after she passed and I'd graduated. Look, I know what it's like to lose a parent and to carry that pain, on top of the way he was taken from you . . . Jesus, I don't know how anyone could cope with that. I want to help you. I would give anything to have my mom back. And I will do whatever it takes to put your sister behind bars.'

There was a moment of silence between them. Kate didn't dare break it. In those moments she felt a connection with Alexandra. Two young women with more pain in their lives than they deserved. If Kate had any doubts about Alexandra's innocence, they vanished in those seconds of silent exchange.

Alexandra rubbed her face, then said, with a sigh, 'What am I going to do?'

'Hire me as your lawyer. I just quit Levy, Bernard and Groff. You pay me half of what you were going to pay them. I'll make sure you get justice, for you and your father.'

Kate wrote out a form of authority on a piece of paper, authorizing the transfer of files from Levy, Bernard and Groff to Kate Brooks, Attorney at Law. The authorization appointed Kate as Alexandra's sole attorney. She flipped the page around and handed it to Alexandra along with her pen. Kate knew that if Alexandra signed, this would be the beginning of her career, and the beginning of an almighty war with her old firm.

'When did you quit the firm?'

'When you opened your front door and let me in. I'm walking away from a dream job in one of the best firms in this city. I'm doing this for you, and for me. If I let Levy lose this case, or worse, if he strong-arms you into a deal with the prosecutor, I don't think I could handle it. Trust me. We can do this together. You will be my only client until this case is over. I promise I will work day and night for you. For your dad. I will not let you down.'

Alexandra took her time to read over the authorization. She put the page down, and stared at Kate. Then she picked up the pen, signed it, and extended a hand to Kate across the table.

'You remind me of, well, *me*, five years ago,' said Alexandra. 'We've both lost our moms. We're both dealing with that pain, and I know you'll use it to fight. That's what I did. I think you're smart and passionate. That's who I need representing me. Let's do this together.'

They shook hands, and both women smiled with some relief and excitement. Kate buzzed for the next ten minutes – expanding on her strategy, giving Alexandra the next steps. Her client drank it in, and by the look on her face Kate knew Alexandra was impressed.

'I do a lot of charity work with the homeless and some animal sanctuaries. Should I get references or maybe I could get someone to testify as a character witness? My dad knew a lot of good people – former mayors, people in congress, his old campaign manager, Hal Cohen?'

'Send me all those details. Character witnesses are self-serving so they would need to be someone of good standing who can hold up in cross-examination,' said Kate.

'I think I might have someone,' said Alexandra.

They talked some more, and Kate found herself enjoying Alexandra's company. She was warm, determined and positive. If Kate were in Alexandra's shoes she wondered if she would be able to maintain that kind of attitude. When she was done, Kate took a long drink of tea, finished toweling her hair while

Alexandra told her all about her father and how great a dad he was growing up.

'My sister, she's like a plague on our family. She broke Dad's heart a long time ago. She's crazy. I saw it when we were kids. She wasn't like anyone else I knew. She was cold, and weird.'

'You two don't talk anymore, is that right?'

Alexandra stared past Kate, out the window at the steel and glass towers of Manhattan – and Kate knew Alexandra wasn't taking in the view. She was miles away. Lost in decades' old thoughts and feelings.

'We haven't spoken since Mom died. It was a terrible accident, on the stairs . . .'

'I read about it,' said Kate. 'How old were you?'

'Eleven, twelve? I'm not sure. Part of me shut down that day. I can't really think of Mom's face. I can't picture it. Not clearly. She's with Dad now. They're back together as they should always have been.'

'Were you close to your mom?'

'Yes and no. My mother wasn't warm and affectionate. Not really. She showed her love in different ways. If I won a chess match, she would buy me a present, or take me for a treat. She didn't show love unless it suited her purposes. The love was there, but she rarely let it out.'

'I can understand that,' said Kate.

For the past few days Kate had lost count of how many times she had seen pictures of Alexandra online. The vibrant, nascent Manhattan socialite. She had money, beauty and relative celebrity. And yet looking at her now, Kate didn't see that. She saw a young woman in pain, struggling with her messed-up family, grief and anger too. Alexandra was not someone to be envied, and perhaps she never was. A sadness underlined her features – it was there just beneath her eyes.

At first, Kate's motivations for stealing Levy's biggest client were largely to do with her own revenge. Kate wanted the case to launch her career, and stick two fingers up at Levy. But while sitting in Alexandra's apartment, listening to her – those motivations had changed.

Alexandra was innocent. And Kate knew then she didn't just want to win the case for herself – for her career – she wanted to help Alexandra. She needed to save her. And send a murderer to jail for the rest of their life.

'Sofia ruined my life. She was just wrong. I hated her growing up. I hate her even more now. I'm sorry, I don't like talking about her. I want you to nail her for my father's murder. She should've been put away a long time ago.'

Kate rose to her feet to leave, and said, 'I promise I'll get justice for your father. And for you. Thanks for everything. The tea was delicious. Oh, should I put this towel back in the bathroom?'

Alexandra took the towel gently but firmly from Kate and said, 'Better not go in there. I just got out of the shower when you arrived. It's still a little messy.'

FIFTEEN

EDDIE

Harry took Harper's arm as we stood on the sidewalk outside the hotel bar, waiting on a cab. Harry's place was just a few blocks away, but he wouldn't leave until he saw us both into a cab. Harper's place was on my way home.

I stepped onto the street, looking straight down 2nd Avenue. While Harry and Harper talked, a dog made its way towards them. A small, mixed-breed mutt with sandy fur darkened in patches by mud and the grime of Manhattan traffic. The dog sat at Harry's feet, facing the street. Harry glanced down, patted the dog and stroked its head.

There were no cabs in sight.

Five minutes later a yellow cab pulled up at the curb. By this time, Harry and the stray were firm friends. Harper kissed Harry goodnight, said her goodbyes to Harry's new canine friend, and got into the eab. I got in the back beside her and as we pulled away we both watched Harry set off for home, the little dog beside him.

'He loves strays,' said Harper, looking right at me.

I suppose she was right. I had been a stray, probably in worse shape than that dog, when Harry took me out for lunch and changed my life from conman to lawyer.

We rode the rest of the way in silence, sitting close to one another, our shoulders touching. When the cab pulled up at Harper's place I looked out the window at the house. Her parents had left her money in their will some years ago, and now that her business was flourishing she had made the jump from an apartment to a townhouse. It was small, by comparison to some brownstones, but it was neat and well kept.

She leaned over and I lost myself in her eyes. My senses were filled with her.

'I had a great night,' she said.

'I did too. We should . . .' But I couldn't say anything more. I didn't trust what would come out of my mouth.

We were friends. I cared for her more than I'd cared for any woman since Christine. My marriage had failed both because of me and the job. My daughter was growing up in a house with her mom and another man. I was happy for Christine because I couldn't make her happy – but God, I missed my daughter. Amy was growing up fast. A teenager with a part-time father.

The crux of the matter was fear. I was scared to get into a relationship with Harper – I couldn't mess up someone else's life again and I loved our friendship. I didn't want to ruin that. It wasn't right. We were working together. If I made her uncomfortable or jeopardized our friendship in any way, I wouldn't be able to forgive myself. Her perfect, oval face was close to mine. She looked into my eyes. The tip of her tongue touched her upper lip. For a moment, I thought she was thinking the same thing as me. I didn't want this to go wrong. It meant too much. Harper had had half a dozen glasses of Scotch – she wasn't drunk but she wasn't sober, either. I couldn't make the first move. Not then. It just wasn't the right moment.

She kissed me on the cheek, said goodnight and got out of the cab. I shuffled over to her side so I could watch her make it to the front door. I wanted to make sure she got inside safely. She did, looking back and waving before closing the door behind her.

The cab didn't move. I looked at the driver and he was still gazing at the spot where Harper had last stood. He must've sensed me staring at him.

'Buddy, that lady has the hots for you. Poor bastard, you've got a lot to learn about women,' said the cab driver.

I couldn't argue with him.

A half-hour later, and after several pieces of advice on picking-up female signals, the cab driver dropped me at West 46th Street. I gave him a bigger tip than usual and thanked him for his advice.

I walked the short distance to the steps leading up to my building when I stopped dead.

There was someone sitting on the steps. Dressed all in black.

Street lights weren't good, and it was around one a.m. I couldn't see who it was. It sure didn't look like a homeless person looking for a place to bed down for the night. The shape was darker, smaller.

As I reached the base of the steps I saw a face, framed beneath a black ballcap.

Sofia.

She was dressed in a black Lycra jogging suit, and a black hoodie.

'Hi, Mr. Flynn. I tried calling. I looked you up in the phonebook and this is your only listed address. I didn't know it was your office. I thought it was your house. I was just sitting here trying to figure out how to reach you as I couldn't wait 'til tomorrow to speak to you.'

'What's wrong, did something happen?'

'It's just all getting too much for me,' she said, and pulled up the sleeve of her top. Below it I saw a dark slash on her forearm – she'd cut herself.

'Let's get you inside.'

We went up to my office, and I showed Sofia into the bathroom in the back. She took off her hoodie, and I saw her bare arms again, but this time her lip trembled, and she hung her head. She was embarrassed. The first time she'd shown me her arms was for a reason – to prove that she wasn't suicidal. Now I was looking at her arms because her compulsion had gotten out of control – and that was where the shame lay.

'It's okay, Sofia,' I said.

There was a new cut on her arm, laced over the multiple white and pink scars, which was still bleeding. It wasn't anything serious – she hadn't nicked an artery – but it looked deeper than most of the others.

I got some gauze and Band-Aids from the bathroom cupboard and cleaned and patched the cut. It bled through the Band-Aid. Her other wrist was still bandaged from the bite she'd taken out of it in the precinct. At that moment, I didn't really know what I should say. I decided she didn't need a lecture.

'Here's a towel. Keep pressure on it,' I said, ripping off the Band-Aid – it was too soon to apply one.

She thanked me and we moved back into my office. She took a seat on the couch and I fixed her a glass of bourbon.

'I don't have coffee. Ran out today. Just sip this, and when you're ready we can talk.'

She nodded and took off her ballcap, letting her dark hair loose. She took half the glass in one mouthful, and I refilled it.

'Take it slower. Just sips,' I said, pouring myself one.

I sat in my client chair, swiveled it around so I was facing her. We sat together, sipping our bourbon in silence.

'So do you live around here?' she said.

'I live here. There's a cot in the back, some books. A bathroom. That's all I need. But I need to get a proper place so my daughter can come and stay weekends.'

'Do you see much of your daughter?' she asked, and as she spoke her eyes took on a faraway glint. It was as if the question wasn't really about me at all.

'We spend time together every weekend. Saturdays in the mall, or Sundays in the park. She's fourteen now. She likes the mall more than the park now, I'm noticing.'

'You buy her things?' she asked, again with a thousand-mile stare.

'I do. Well, I give her an allowance and she spends it. I wouldn't know about make-up, or what magazines she's into these days. I do give her books though. She's a reader. Right now she's working her way through Ross MacDonald and Patricia Highsmith.'

'Smart kid. I couldn't concentrate on books. Being still, quiet . . . I could just never quite manage it. I was always bouncing off the goddamn walls, you know?'

I nodded.

'My dad put money in an account for me when I was that age. After Mom died I was sent to boarding school. He couldn't get the time to visit. Birthdays, holidays, he sent me money. There was a period when I was growing up when I saw him maybe two or three times a year at most.'

'What about your sister? Did you see her more often?'

'Less. That suited me just fine.'

'What about letters or phone calls?'

'Dad never wrote. Never called,' she said, adopting that faraway stare again. 'Before Mom died, Alexandra and I used to pass each other secret notes – so we could play a match together without Mom noticing. Each note was a chess move. It took months.'

'Who won?' I asked.

Sofia gave her attention back to me, looked into my eyes and said, 'Neither of us. Mom died before we finished the game. Her neck caught in the stair rails . . .'

'I know. A horrible accident.'

'Was it an accident? Sometimes I wonder if Alexandra pushed her . . .'

'Really?'

'I remember her standing there, frightened. She was clutching her blue rabbit, crying. But maybe she wasn't crying for Mom? Maybe she was crying because of what she'd done?'

'Did you ever talk about it with the police?'

'No, I didn't see the fall. I couldn't. I'm sorry about this, I shouldn't be burdening you with my family problems—'

'What? Look, I'm your lawyer, Sofia. This is all part of my job. I'm glad you're telling me this. And I'm sorry you couldn't reach me earlier. My cell was turned off. Harper's too, I guess. Did you call us before or after you . . .'

'I cut myself? After. It wouldn't stop bleeding. I thought I might need a doctor and Harper said not to call anyone. If something happened I should call her or you. She said there didn't need to be any more entries on my medical records. I know those look bad. I just got to thinking about my dad, about the case, and then it all builds up, you see. Like pressure. Sometimes running helps. When I nick my skin it kind of lets it *all* out. I didn't want to go to the emergency room, I don't want to make things worse.'

I didn't want to confirm that right now. It wasn't the time. But she was right. Her mental health history was a weapon for Dreyer to beat her with.

'It's very early days in your case, Sofia. When we have all of the prosecution evidence we'll know more. Right now, they have some forensics to tie you and your sister to your father's body and the murder weapon – a kitchen knife.'

'But I used that knife to slice chicken and vegetables. We both cooked for him. Well, actually, Alexandra cooked for Dad. I cooked for myself – he was never too keen on eating what I prepared for him. He was a fussy eater. Towards the end he didn't mind though. He was kind of . . . fuzzy in his last few months. I thought he was getting dementia, to tell you the truth.'

'Why did you think that at the time?'

'He was forgetful. Some days he was fine, some days he got my name wrong. Some days he called out for Jane.'

'Your mother?' She looked at the floor, took another sip, muttered, *yeah*, under her breath. Sometimes Sofia was like a kid. If I brought up something painful, she almost reverted to a child-like state – dealing with all that grief through a child's perspective. Even now, a glass of hard liquor in her hand, her fingers slid into the decorative grooves near the base of glass, and she caressed each cut and indentation, feeling the pattern. She brought the glass to her lips, took a long sniff, then a drink, and touched her lips – as if she had to confirm the alcohol would feel sticky and wet to the touch. She caught me looking at her, shook her head and put the drink down.

'Harper told me she talked to you. Said you talked about your dad, how he tried everything to help you. And your mom was a tough lady. I wanted to ask about your sister.'

'What do you want to know?'

'What was it like, growing up with your sister?'

'Hell. Total hell. She made my life a misery. We didn't talk, we didn't play together. It was kind of a war. After Mom died, Dad sent us away to different boarding schools. I couldn't have cut it in Alexandra's school, and he couldn't deal with two young girls *and* run the city. We were left alone. In our worlds, you know?'

I didn't know. I couldn't really imagine that.

'That must've made for a tense time growing up,' I said.

'Have you ever lived with your enemy? I have. I hate her. I wish she was dead. Getting out of that house was a blessing. Apart from that secret chess match, we didn't communicate. Even our notes were just moves, no narrative. I never got to beat her at the game, and I regret that, but I was glad when we parted. I could tell you stories that would make you want to vomit. No, my sister and I were not close. We were as far apart as two people could be. She told me Mom was dead because of me. That Dad withdrew from us because of me. I knew it wasn't true, of course. I never forgave her for saying that, making me feel that way. Mom was a real piece of work, but she was still my mom. I loved her. I don't know if she loved me back, but that didn't matter. Not really. I think about her a lot. I miss her.'

We talked a little more about the trial. I explained that the DA had forensics linking Sofia and her sister to the crime scene.

'I checked if he was breathing. I held him. Of course I had blood on me. His blood, but I didn't hurt him. I couldn't.'

'I believe you. There's something you should know. I was going to talk to you about it tomorrow, but we may as well talk now. The DA is offering a deal. He's going to try and have a joint trial, with you and your sister both up for murder in front of the same jury. I'm going to try and stop that and have separate trials. I don't know if I can split the trials up, but I'm going to try. I have a former judge helping me with that. The DA is offering a polygraph test to both of you. If you don't take it, he'll try to use that against you. It could go hard against you if your sister takes the test and passes. If you take it and fail, you're in trouble. On top of that, he's offering a plea deal. Plead guilty to the murder, and tell the court you did it with your sister, and you could be out of jail while you're still young. I can't let you plead to a crime you didn't commit, but I have to let you know about the deal.'

'I didn't kill my father. If I'd known that Alexandra was going to kill him, I would've killed her first.'

She spoke confidently and clearly for the first time. She made eye contact, no hesitation in her speech. No wavering up or down in her line of vision. No stumbling on the sentence. Her hands still and easy on her lap. No tells. This was the truth.

'In that case, we just have to think about the polygraph. It's your call. A polygraph is not an exact science. If you decline I can probably minimize some of that damage. If you take it and fail, you could be in trouble. My advice – tell the prosecutor to go to hell. I don't think it's worth the risk,' I said.

'No, tell him I'll do it. I didn't kill my father. I'm telling the truth. He'll see that and they will drop the charges,' said Sofia.

'He won't drop the charges, you should know this. He'll only make a deal for a guilty plea and testimony against your sister in exchange for a reduced sentence.'

'I'll take the test. I have nothing to be afraid of. I didn't do it.'

If she performed like that in the polygraph then she could probably pass. Suddenly, I felt a lot better about this case. Sofia had a well of strength, deep inside. I just had to mine it, keep it there for the trial.

I offered to get her a cab home, but she declined. Said she felt better. Her arm had stopped bleeding and she wanted to jog back to her apartment.

Said the run would help clear her head.

The talk with Sofia had cleared my head, for sure. She was innocent. I could feel it. I knew it. And what's more, I now realized what was wrong with the autopsy report on Frank Avellino.

It was Frank Avellino himself.

Frank was in great condition at the time of his murder. Apart from some signs of stress on the respiratory system, which could have been caused by the attack, he was in perfect shape. His heart, lungs, liver, brain, stomach, intestines – all pristine for a man of his age.

After Sofia left, I found the report at the bottom of the papers on my desk. I'd already made a few copies for Harper and Harry, but I wanted Harry to see it right away. I fed it into the fax machine and dialed Harry's number. After ten minutes, and another shot of bourbon, my phone rang.

'What am I looking for?' said Harry.

'Anything strike you as weird in that report?' I asked.

'Apart from the brutality, the bite, and the surgical skill, nothing.'

'What if I told you Frank Avellino was displaying dementia symptoms for a few months before he died?' I said.

I heard Harry flicking through pages. He paused. A small, weak bark sounded on the line.

'You took that dog home, didn't you?'

'What dog?'

'The dog that took you for a sucker on the street tonight.'

'He's my pal. He likes beef jerky and milk. I think we might be friends,' said Harry.

I gave him some time to read.

Harry said, 'His brain, aside from the injuries that occurred from the blade being rammed into the ocular cavity, was normal.'

'Frank didn't have dementia,' I said.

'Agreed,' said Harry.

Between the two of us, we'd read more than our fair share of autopsy reports. Anyone with dementia, or some other type of degenerative disease of the brain, will have signs of that disease visible to the naked eye during autopsy. The brain would look different. The ME said Frank's brain was entirely normal. That was what was bothering me. A dementia sufferer's brain doesn't appear normal – the disease ravages the brain. It's obvious. Frank's brain was not damaged by disease. Which meant he didn't have dementia.

'His lawyer, Mike Modine, told police Frank had called him to schedule an appointment to discuss changes to his will,' I said.

'What changes?' said Harry.

'We don't know. Mike Modine has gone AWOL.'

Harry sighed, heavily, and I could hear the squeaking of the old chair in his study. Then I heard Harry whispering to the dog, calling him a good boy. I had visions of the dog curled at Harry's feet, and I was glad. He needed a companion. And the mutt looked like it needed Harry.

'You know I just retired, right? Two hours ago, for Christ's sake.'

'Come on, Harry. Did you notice there's evidence of stress damage to the respiratory system? That's a strong indicator. You're thinking the same thing as me, right?'

'There are a few possible suspects. We need the toxicology report.'

'Okay, get some sleep, and say goodnight to the dog for me.'
He hung up.

Harry and I were on the same page. As far as I knew, the prosecutor hadn't noticed this. If Dreyer had noticed, there would be more tests and an amendment to the cause of death conclusion on the death certificate. Alexandra's lawyers might not have noticed it either. They had shown no signs of it anyway.

I knew now that Frank Avellino wasn't just stabbed to death.

For some months prior to his murder, he was being systematically drugged. Something to dull his brain, keep him confused and compliant. The damage to his respiratory system meant the drugging probably had an endpoint. Eventually, Frank would be poisoned to death.

But who was poisoning him?

The answer to the first question had a narrow field of possible answers. To poison a man like Frank over a period of time you would need very close, regular access.

There were two suspects.

Sofia and Alexandra.

I had a feeling whoever had been poisoning him had decided to accelerate the process of Frank's death with a twelve-inch kitchen knife, before he changed his will.

SIXTEEN

SHE

It was coming up on two a.m., the pavement a blur beneath her feet, the wind in her face, and her legs were burning with the effort.

Night running was one of her pleasures.

Tonight was not for pleasure. This was all business. The talk with her lawyer, earlier, had been a useful one. The lawyer was good and convinced that she was innocent. If the jury was as easily convinced as her lawyer, she would be just fine.

She reached East 33rd Street on 3rd Avenue and turned right at the corner. She increased her pace, feeling her heart rate jump, and now she had to concentrate on controlling her breathing. Her backpack was strapped tight so it wouldn't bump at her back. She swung her arms, finding the rhythm with her breath. In and out. Pumping her legs. Focused.

The sign for the parking lot loomed ahead of her. She slowed her pace, stopped and bent over to catch her breath. Sweat dripped from her forehead. Looking around, no one on the street, she went inside and took the stairs to the fifth floor. At the back of the lot on this floor the lighting was out. It was dark in that corner, which suited her just fine. She walked past a row of cars on both sides. There were some empty spaces, but not many. She found her motorcycle in the dark corner. The overhead light was still busted above this parking space. She had stood on the bike and swiped her helmet through the bulb two weeks ago when she last parked. God bless cheap parking-lot owners.

She slung her backpack to the ground, unzipped it and unfolded a Kevlar fabric motorcycle suit. It had been much more expensive to buy than leathers, but she needed something that would fold easily into her pack. She slipped off her running shoes, put her legs through the suit and then hauled it on over her Lycra. Zipped it up to the neck then closed the Velcro straps on the collar. From her backpack she drew out slip-on riding boots. They had a hard sole, but were foldable Kevlar. She put them on, and the gloves. While the Kevlar suit was practical, it did not have the same aesthetic quality as real leather. It lacked that delicious odor. The smell and feel of real leather was as intoxicating to her as a good red wine.

Packing away her running shoes in the backpack, she closed it and slung it over her shoulders, pulling the straps tight. She released the helmet from the lock on the seat, then put it on. It was a tinted visor, which cut down her visibility in the dark corner of the lot, making everything almost pitch black. She swung her leg over the Honda, turned on the engine and the lights, then eased it out of the space, along the lot and down the ramps to the street.

Ten minutes later she was on the Ed Koch Queensboro Bridge. She took Queens Boulevard, Van Dam Street and Review Avenue before she started making random turns. She made lefts and rights, trying to keep to a general south-westerly direction. Eventually she came to Haberman.

This was an industrial quarter that housed massive warehouses and distribution centers for UPS, Fed-Ex, and more. The industrial quarter sat below the shoulder of a massive turnpike, which linked the Long Island Expressway, the Queens Midtown Expressway, and the I-278. It was no accident that shipping and distribution centers chose to build here – it had perfect access points for Manhattan, New Jersey and anywhere else they needed to go.

These businesses needed workers. Workers needed somewhere to eat, rest and shop for essentials. There were a couple of sandwich shops, a McDonald's, a Burger King, Costco and a pharmacy.

She chose that particular pharmacy because it never closed, and it had quick getaway points. Same reason as the distribution companies. Within a half-hour of leaving the pharmacy you could be anywhere in a one-hundred-and-fifty-mile radius. Perfect.

The pharmacy sat in a strip mall along a road that was in constant repair due to the heavy goods vehicles that ripped up the blacktop twenty-four hours a day. The strip mall had a garment repair shop, a noodle bar and a dry cleaners, all of which were closed. The only thing open was the pharmacy.

She eased the bike to a stop, killed the light and the engine and kicked down the side stand. The pharmacy was part of a well-known chain. It had a long front window that spilled light to the lot, but not as far as her bike. From her vantage point she could see the cashier behind the counter to the left, just past the entrance. Her nametag read 'Penny'. She was in her twenties, blonde, staring at her phone and blowing bubbles of gum from her fat, pink lips.

In the back, she could just make out the pharmacist, Afzal Jatt. He was staring at a computer screen and nibbling at a Twinkie.

All was as expected. She had only ever dealt with these members of staff. When she picked up her supply, Penny would pop a bubble as she walked past. Then she would approach Afzal, collect her order, pay Penny and leave.

Once a month. Regular as clockwork. Thursday nights. Afzal and Penny always covered the nights, Monday through Thursday. On the one occasion she had visited and Penny was not on the counter, she waited until the following night. No point in more than one staff member seeing her, and potentially remembering her.

This night was always going to happen. She had known that from the start. Measures would need to be taken once her father was dead, and these were both necessary and messy.

She got off the bike, opened the storage compartment beneath the seat. It had been difficult to choose what to store in the seat compartment. It was larger and deeper than most seat compartments, which on average could hold about half a gallon of storage space. This bike had two gallons of space.

She reached inside, lifted clear the brown paper bag and closed the seat lid.

She stood facing the pharmacy. Helmet visor down. Bag in hand.

Once she got within a few feet of the store, the sliding doors opened. Penny, ten feet away at the counter, glanced up from her phone, then went back to the screen.

The store played a selection of nineties hits through its PA system. As the doors closed behind her she heard the opening bars of a Britney Spears song, 'Oops . . . I Did It Again'.

She went quickly to the door control panel, on the wall next to an umbrella stand, and hit the button marked with an icon of a padlock. Neither Penny nor Afzal had seen her do this, the display of umbrellas masking the move. The sliding doors closed behind her, and would not open unless Penny hit the unlock button. She walked past Penny, her eyes on the diet drinks and bars on the shelves, until she got to the end of the aisle, and then walked straight up to Afzal. He took the last bite from the Twinkie, rubbed his hands together to get rid of the sticky residue and placed both hands on the counter.

'Can I help you, ma'am?' he asked, still perched on his stool behind the counter. One eye on the customer, but also reluctant to stop watching what was on his computer screen. She figured he was watching a show, whiling away the late night hours.

The counter was below her waist, so Afzal, in a seated position, was the width of the counter away, but below her full height.

Perfect.

Her right hand dove into the bag and came out fast as she raised it overhead and brought the small hand-axe down with all the force and speed she could muster. There was a sound when the axe blade lodged an inch deep into the top of Afzal's skull. It was an unusual sound, like an opening being broken into a hollow trunk. A jet of blood splashed across the left side of her visor. She didn't want to wipe it away, it could smear the glass and then she wouldn't be able to see anything.

The axe came away easily, and one more blow into the skull broke it open. This was a wet cracking noise, and she quickly turned and ran toward Penny.

Penny had heard the noise and moved around the counter. Penny called out, 'Afzal, you okay?' but then Penny saw her, with the hand axe, dripping blood. Penny turned and ran full speed toward the doors. Penny screamed, but the sound died when the doors failed to open and her head smacked off the glass, sending a ribbon of cracks across its surface. Penny staggered, fell onto her back, dazed, her hand reaching up to her forehead.

She stood over Penny, who rolled onto her hands and knees and tried to get up.

She took the axe two-handed and swung it up high as she joined in the end of the chorus with Britney.

'. . . *I'm not that innocent.*'

The blade whistled as it cut through the air and cleaved into the back of Penny's neck. Penny's body instantly went limp, folding flat on the floor. The axe hadn't lodged, it had come free with the blow, but it had left a huge gash in the flesh through which she could see white bone. She struck again, this time at the side of the neck.

The axe bit deep, and stayed buried. She had to resist the urge to wrench it free and take it with her. The smell of the oiled blade, the feel of the hickory axe handle. Even as an adult, she felt the need to touch and smell certain objects.

She stepped over Penny's twitching corpse, hit the release button on the door control and walked through the doors as they swished open. She got on the bike, hit the ignition and pulled away fast from the strip mall, headed for the turnpike. With only light traffic on the interstate, she opened the pipes on the bike, let it roar underneath her for ten miles. She turned off, and meandered her way back to Manhattan.

Back to the parking lot.

She wiped the helmet clean with the suit. Put the suit, boots, gloves in her backpack and changed back into her ballcap and running shoes. The backpack would find its way into the river as she ran along the outskirts of the island, toward her apartment, and a long shower.

A good night's work. If the prosecution managed to work out that Frank was being poisoned they might be able to trace it to this pharmacy, and Afzal Jatt. That made them one step closer to her, and she couldn't allow that.

But there was more to be done. There was another possible link. A man. One who wasn't easy to get to. He was protected. He was smart.

He would be expecting her.

SEVENTEEN

KATE

Kate hit refresh on her phone, watched the screen change and then she saw it.

Fifty thousand dollars. In her account. A down-payment on legal fees. There would be more payments totaling two hundred and fifty thousand dollars. Her first fees as a lawyer. As a sole practitioner.

The waiter brought her coffee. She hadn't touched the cucumber and lettuce juice. The carrot and almond muffin in front of her was still as pristine as when the waiter had brought it fifteen minutes ago. She was too excited to eat.

Checked her watch.

Bloch was running late. Just a few minutes. Then, she walked in.

Her friend wore the same leather jacket, blue jeans and boots. Her tee had changed to navy blue, and now she wore a black and white scarf. She took a seat opposite Kate and picked up the glass of bright green juice.

'What is this?' said Bloch.

'Cucumber and lettuce juice. Want to try?' said Kate.

'You mean drink it?'

'Yes.'

Bloch made a disgusted face, shook her head.

She gave Bloch an update. Told her what happened yesterday in the office – that Scott had stolen her idea and used it to bag himself second chair in the Avellino case. And then, she told her what she had done in retaliation.

'Well done,' said Bloch. 'Have you told Levy yet?'

'I thought we might go see him together.'

Bloch nodded.

'I don't want you there just as a friend,' said Kate. 'I'm on my own. I need an investigator. You used to be a cop. You train cops how to investigate cases. I need help and I want you. What do you say?'

Bloch nodded.

'Is that yes? You'll do it.'

'Yeah. Cover expenses and—'

'Oh, I'll pay your going rate, or we can split my fees? I'm excited. And a little scared. I need you with me.'

Bloch nodded, said, 'Let's go ruin Levy's year.'

The red-haired security guard insisted that Kate sign Bloch in as a guest on the firm's premises. Bloch had to show ID, and once she was issued with a visitor's pass they rode the elevator together to the fourteenth floor. The office was alive when they stepped into the corridor. Paralegals, secretaries, associates were all milling around Levy and Scott who were in their shirt sleeves, in a glass-walled conference room issuing orders and stacking piles of paper. Motion production was in full swing.

Kate led Bloch into the conference room. Kate was in her business suit jacket, but she wore jeans and boots.

Levy noticed her come in and slapped down a bunch of loose pages on the desk, spilling them.

'Katie, where the hell have you been? And why aren't you properly dressed? What do you think this is? A rodeo?'

'I quit,' said Kate, and handed Levy a photostat copy of the form of authority signed by Alexandra Avellino.

'What the hell is this?' said Levy.

'It's payback. You can keep these motions, I just want the indictment, prosecution disclosure and then I'm on my way.'

Scott took the paper from Levy and his face turned pale as he read it. Which was a nice contrast to Levy, whose head looked like it was about to explode.

'You can't do this! Your contract forbids soliciting clients from this firm. I'll sue you for every cent you've got. I'll report you to the Bar Association too. You've just signed your death warrant,' said Levy.

'That was a threat,' said Bloch, stepping forward.

Two secretaries, both in their late twenties wearing the firm's standard grey and blue staff uniform, came into the conference room, folded their arms and listened.

'Who are you?' said Levy, then he noticed the secretaries and waved a hand at them to get out. They didn't move.

'I'm with Kate Brooks. Get the documents and we'll be out of your hair.'

'You're not taking a single page from this office. Scott, call security.'

Scott leaned over, grabbed the phone on the conference room desk and pressed an intercom button.

'If you fail to honor that form of authority then I can report *you* to the Bar Association. The documents, now,' said Kate.

Levy blew out his cheeks, huffed and puffed. He clenched and unclenched his fists, then came around the table with his finger raised. He started pointing it in Kate's face, spittle flew from his lips as he shouted and screamed at her.

'You're finished! I will RUIN you . . .' His finger poked Kate in the chest.

Block stepped in, took hold of Levy's finger in her fist and bent it, just a little. There was a tiny crack, but the finger didn't break. It was enough to shut Levy up, but not enough to cause serious damage.

Kate heard one of the secretaries behind her let out a *whoop*.

Scott talked frantically to security on the phone, told them to get here right away.

'Are you going to give us these documents so we can leave you alone?' said Bloch.

Levy's eyes were wide with embarrassment and fear.

'Let go of me, this is assault.'

She bent the finger a little more.

'Get them the documents,' said Levy.

The secretaries covered their mouths to hide their laughter, but between them they took two sets of papers from the other end of the conference room and handed them to Kate.

'You ever need a secretary, you call me,' whispered one of them, careful to make sure Levy didn't hear her. Her name was Jane, and Kate made a mental note. Kate couldn't afford an office, never mind a secretary, but some day she might.

Kate heard hurried footfalls in the corridor outside the office. Five security men ran in, almost knocking over Jane.

One of the security guards, a broad, tall man north of fifty-five with a buzz cut said, 'Bloch? Is that you?'

Bloch turned around, saw who it was and said, 'Hey Reggie.' She still had hold of Levy's finger, and when he tried to pull it away, Bloch added more pressure, buckling Levy's knees.

The other security guards all looked to the man Kate now knew as Reggie. He must've been their supervisor. They looked foolish and incompetent, just standing there while Bloch had hold of Levy.

'Get her off me, right this second!' said Levy.

'You on the job?' asked Reggie.

'I'm private now, like you.'

'Bloch, that's my boss. I need you to let him go,' said Reggie.

'He needs to apologize, first,' said Bloch.

The red-haired guard who'd been an asshole in the lobby made a move toward Bloch, and Reggie's huge arm snaked out, grabbing him by the shirt and hauling him back.

'Don't move. Let me deal with this. You can't cover shifts if you're in the hospital,' said Reggie.

Scott, who seemed to have found some nerve, started moving toward his boss. Levy's predicament merely gave Scott another chance to suck up to him if he made the effort to rescue him from his plight. He was trying to sneak up behind Bloch, his arms wide, ready to make a grab for her.

Bloch must've sensed this. She shot Scott a look and said, 'I've got *two* hands, hero.'

Scott stopped dead, backed up.

'Mr. Levy, I think you should apologize, sir,' said Reggie.

'What?! What am I paying you for? Get her off me,' said Levy.

'Sir, a month before my retirement, Bloch took my squad on an advanced driving refresher and a control and restraint course.

She's six feet away and there are only five of us. I think you should apologize, sir.'

'She's hurting me,' said Levy, forcing the sentence through the pain.

The security guards looked at Reggie, who was holding in his laughter, his mouth and lips trembling with the effort.

'Sir . . . I'd do as she says.'

'I'm sorry, alright, I'm *sorry*,' said Levy.

'Miss Brooks, do you have the papers you need?' said Bloch.

'Got them right here,' said Kate.

Bloch released Levy's finger, and he backed away, cradling his hand. Reggie stepped aside, leaving a space for Kate and Bloch to leave.

'This isn't over, Katie,' said Levy.

'It's Miss Brooks, to you,' said Kate.

Frank Avellino
Journal Entry, Wednesday September 5, 2018.
7:30 a.m.

Someone is following me.

It happened yesterday. A woman on a black motorcycle. It might be the same person I saw, all in black, last week.

I am not losing my mind.

I came out of Jimmy's restaurant after breakfast and she was on the other side of the street. This is the second time I've seen her in as many days. She gunned the bike and rode away just as Hal came out the front door of the restaurant. He said he didn't notice her.

Maybe Hal's losing his goddamn marbles.

I called Mike Modine, right then. I told him to hire the PI Hal had recommended.

10:30 p.m.

Sofia came over with some chicken noodle soup and we watched Jeopardy. After the show she made grilled cheese and gave it to me on a tray with some milk. It wasn't as good as Alexandra's cooking, but I didn't dare say that to her.

Alexandra made me pasta last night and it was great. Strange aftertaste. I had one of those smoothies so I couldn't tell if it was the pasta or the smoothie. It didn't matter, the meal was so good I slept for an hour afterwards.

I worry about Sofia. She's not like her sister. Alexandra is strong, organized and making her own way in the world. Sofia doesn't even have a job. No boyfriend either, although these days that's not such a bad thing.

Some of the guys she's dated were just junkies. I knew it soon as I looked at them. She tells me she's clean. I believe her.

As she cleared the empty tray away, I saw her arms. There was a bloodstain on her sleeve. On the forearm.

She's not using but she's still cutting herself. This is how it starts. In six months I'll have to book her into another clinic to dry out.

She tells me she's taking her meds. I tell her that her sister never missed her anxiety meds, and look how good she's doing. Sofia won't talk about Alexandra. These two will never make up. It just won't happen. I thought about telling her to watch out for a woman on a motorcycle, but then thought better of it. Sofia is paranoid enough.

When she was here she did something. A gesture, or a movement, or something I just can't remember and it reminded me of her mother. I wanted to tell her that but right then I couldn't remember her mother's name. I couldn't remember my own dead wife's name.

Maybe I really am losing it.

PART THREE

LIARS AND LAWYERS

EIGHTEEN

EDDIE

Nobody ran to Wesley Dreyer to make a deal. No plea agreements. This was a straight fight and today was the first major battle.

I arrived in court with Harry in tow. He'd prepared most of the motion briefs, which I'd filed last week. Today was arguments and judgments. No need to bring the client to court, for which I was thankful. After Sofia showed up at my office, she'd calmed down a little and between Harper and I we checked in on her almost every day. Yesterday she invited us over for coffee. Harper and I sat on her couch while she fussed over warming some cookies before she served them.

'She really is like a little kid, sometimes,' I said. 'Who serves cookies to their lawyers?'

'Look,' said Harper, pointing to the hallway. 'Go on, just a peek. It should be on her bed.'

I got up quietly, moved into the hall and there, on Sofia's bed, was an old, soft toy. Its fake fur had matted and was bald in other parts. It was a blue bunny rabbit. I sat back down before Sofia could notice I'd been snooping.

Harper whispered, 'She's had that since she was a kid. She said her mom bought one for her and her sister before she passed. She still sleeps with it.'

I nodded. I'd heard her mention her sister carrying a rabbit when she found her mother dead on the stairs.

'Did she mention the toy to you?'

'Yeah. She sleeps with it. Said she and her sister went everywhere with those rabbits when they were kids. I know it has sentimental value, but she's in her late twenties. She needs someone to look after her.'

Sofia was not cut out for the stresses of life even in ordinary circumstances.

I had no doubt that if she was convicted she wouldn't survive twenty-five to life in Bedford Hills Correctional. As prisons go, it's not bad. There are much worse. But it's still a maximum-security facility. The only max-security prison for women in the state. From the outside you can see the razor-wire-topped fences and what looks like an old Victorian house beyond. It's a large facility once you get inside, with buildings in a circular shape surrounding the exercise yards and training areas. Sofia would be placed on suicide watch – but not forever. I knew, first chance she got she would check out. Either deliberately, or she'd cut too deep and that would be it.

Sofia brought a tray of cookies from the kitchen. We ate and drank while I gave her an update on what was going to happen in court the next day. It looked like she understood – but maybe didn't fully appreciate – the turn the case could take if the hearing went badly.

Harper and I thanked her for the cookies, and we left her clutching her blue rabbit for comfort.

That was yesterday. Today was the beginning of the fight to keep her out of jail. The opening skirmish. And it had to go in our favor.

Her life was on the line. The only way to save it was to make sure we got a 'Not Guilty' from the jury. The pieces used to make that verdict a reality would be set in play this morning, in this courtroom.

I had copies of the motions under my arm, and I dumped them on the defense table. Harry had his copies, which he placed beside mine, and took a seat next to me. He looked around the room.

'It's weird being on this side of the judge's bench,' said Harry.

'You've had four weeks of retirement, don't tell me you're starting to regret it now,' I said.

'I didn't say that, I just said it's weird,' said Harry, who then used his feet to rock back on his chair, and locked his fingers together over his stomach. He had put some weight back on, and I was glad of it. It made him look more solid, curved out some of the lines on his face. We'd had a lot of late nights working on these motions, and those nights usually ended in Scotch and pizza at three in the morning in my office, with Harry's dog snatching the pizza crusts we tossed him. That dog would eat anything.

There was no one else in the courtroom. I liked to get there early. Get my seat. Get a feel for the room. Plus, I liked watching my opponents show up and find me already there – established and ready. It was a psychological thing. A subtle form of manipulation. I wanted my opponent to feel like they were stepping into my house.

'How do you think things will go today?' said Harry.

'Depends on the judge,' I said.

'I tried my old clerk three times, and she wouldn't tell me which judge was taking the case. Said she couldn't. She was sworn to secrecy. Loyalty ain't what it used to be.'

The doors at the back of the court opened, and I heard footsteps approaching. One pair of heels, and one pair of boots. I turned and saw Kate Brooks marching down the aisle, with a tall lady in a leather jacket behind her. Hardly the entourage I'd expected from Levy, Bernard and Groff.

Kate took a seat at the next defense table, furthest from the central aisle. Across the aisle was the table reserved for the prosecution. In front of us was a raised plinth, a mahogany bench and behind that a high-backed leather armchair flanked by the American flag.

Kate said, 'Hi,' as she passed my table.

Harry stood up and introduced himself, 'I'm Harry Ford. Consultant with Eddie Flynn. And you are?'

'Kate Brooks, from Brooks Law. That's my investigator behind you, Bloch.'

Harry turned around, and the tall lady with short black hair and the biker jacket shook hands with Harry. 'Ex-law enforcement, I presume?' said Harry.

Bloch nodded.

'Sorry, I didn't get your first name, Miss Bloch,' said Harry.

Bloch merely nodded in agreement. Harry sat his ass down.

I got up and went around to Kate's table. She stood behind it, arranging her papers. From her bag, she took out five different colored pads of Post-It notes and five different colors of highlighters and began arranging them. I didn't want to disturb her, but I wanted to make sure I'd heard her correctly.

'You said Brooks Law, right?'

'Right. I left Levy, Bernard and Groff about a month ago.'

'Shit, and you're representing Alexandra?'

'I am,' she said.

I stood back and took a second to look at Kate properly. She seemed to stand taller. She wore a nervous and excited smile, but now she looked like a lawyer rather than a beat-down paralegal who jumped and clapped for the boss every ten minutes.

'Congratulations, I'm really pleased for you. I do have one thing to ask though. I didn't get any of your motions to the court. I take it you're moving to split the trial?'

Kate took her own damn time to look at me now. She was gauging me, trying to figure out if I was a threat or if I was making some kind of play.

'We're not objecting to the DA's joint trial,' she said.

I heard Harry sucking air through his teeth, and the legs of his chair slapping down on the tiled floor. This was a major play from Kate. She'd realized that she had the better chance in a joint trial – that a jury would be more likely to believe Alexandra than Sofia. A brilliant strategy, but for one thing.

'I understand your thinking. But it's high risk, there's lots of ways that strategy might backfire,' I said.

'It can't backfire on me, only on your client,' she said.

'It can backfire if you destroy my client's credibility, and if I, in turn, destroy your client's. Then the jury won't believe either defendant and both get convicted. It's called a cut-throat defense – the DA just has to hand out the razor blades and sit back while we cut each other's throats.'

'I've considered it. I don't think you can lay a glove on my client.'

'Don't be so sure. I don't think this is wise. We should be fighting the prosecutor, not each other.'

'It's a risk my client is aware of, but we're confident. Tell me, is Sofia going to take the polygraph?'

'Is Alexandra going to take the polygraph?' I asked.

Kate folded her arms, shifted her weight. Her tongue grazed the inside of her cheek. She wasn't going to give that away so easily.

'Look, the way I see it, the prosecution is getting an easy ride with a joint trial. It will make us fight each other instead of fighting Dreyer.'

She pulled out a chair and sat down at the defense table, placing her three identical Muji pens in a neat row before her. The conversation was over. This was shaping up to be a war on two fronts for Sofia. It made it even more important that I got the trial split.

'Kate, I'm real pleased for you going out on your own. That's brave and no more than you deserve. I thought Levy was a creep. This is great for you, but I'm worried about making life easy for this prosecutor. At least don't object to my motion to split the trial? Don't muddy the waters.'

'I've got to do what I think is right for my client,' she said.

'Okay, let's see what happens,' I said. I didn't want to start a fight with Kate. I liked her. She was smart, and I was glad she'd ditched Levy and managed to wrestle his biggest case away from him.

I returned to my table, Harry giving me a worried look.

'If we don't split this trial—' he said, under his breath.

'I know, I know.'

Wesley Dreyer was the last player to show up and he looked like he'd been shopping for a new outfit for today. A pale yellow tie in a Windsor knot lay over a crisp white shirt. The combination was set off by a smart blue suit. Cut especially for him, of course. He looked like he was about to go for a photo shoot with a magazine, and in some ways that was exactly what would happen after the hearing. I'd no doubt Dreyer had called a press conference from the DA's office straight afterwards. He had one assistant with him, a young man in a suit that looked almost as smart as Dreyer's.

I did notice one other thing about Dreyer's outfit, though.

'I see you're not wearing your pin,' I said.

'I don't need to wear the pin today,' said Dreyer, a smug grin on his pink face.

The court clerk came through the chambers door and said, 'All rise.'

I stood with Harry. Dreyer was already on his feet. Judge Stone came through the door with our motions under his arm.

I heard Harry mutter, 'Shit. We're toast,' under his breath.

Son of a . . .

'Mr. Dreyer, you appear for the People. Mr. Flynn for Sofia Avellino and Miss . . .'

'Brooks,' said Kate. 'For Alexandra Avellino.'

'Very good,' said Stone. 'Mr. Flynn, I've read your legal briefs. I'm granting all three of your discovery motions. The prosecution is obliged to provide you with the evidence and documents listed in your affidavit by close of business today. I'm also granting the motion for inspection of the crime scene. That's for both defendants. The inspection will be done alone, without police presence save for an officer of the court who will video-record the inspection to ensure the scene is not tampered with. There will be unilateral disclosures of these videos. Edited to remove sound, so you can discuss the case freely at the locus.'

Dreyer's assistant lifted a box from the prosecution table, put it on my desk. He then picked up another box and put it on Kate's table.

'All documents and evidential reports have now been served. We have an officer with a video camera at the ready for the inspection of the Franklin Street property,' said Dreyer. He was expecting this. I'd no doubt he'd spoken privately with Stone about it before today. That would be a huge breach of ethics, but it happened and there was no way to prove it.

'Likewise, Miss Brooks, I'm granting your motions. Mr. Flynn had actually asked for more documents than you did, but you've got it all now and more.'

Kate stood, thanked the judge.

'Now, we come to the last order of business. Mr. Flynn, your motion to split the indictment and have separate trials for each defendant – I've read your motion and the brief. It was put together . . . *judicially*, you might say,' said Stone, giving Harry a sickening smile.

Harry mouthed something back to Stone. I'm no lip reader, but it looked like Harry said something that started with *mother*, and ended with *trucker*. Or something close to that.

'Your legal arguments are sound. The potential prejudices to your client are real. However, as you have alluded to in your motion, even the criminal code itself states that I have discretion in this matter, and that I can deal with it as I see fit as long as I have addressed the potential prejudices to both defendants. Even if both defendants are blaming one another, if both are willing to testify then it cancels out any constitutional argument that your client can't get a fair trial. And I can warn the jury about any fears of prejudice you may have. Those controls and warnings should stave off any substantial unfairness or prejudice. Miss Brooks, I take it your client is going to testify?'

'She is, Your Honor.'

'Well, Mr. Flynn, doesn't that mean that your client should be refuting that testimony with her own?'

'Your Honor, with respect, that means my client theoretically couldn't exercise her fifth amendment right against self-incrimination,' I said.

'It's up to you how you conduct your case, Mr. Flynn. Your client can take the fifth amendment all she wants, and I know you'll explain the consequences to her in advance. I have to be satisfied that there would be a substantial prejudice to your client before I split this trial. The word "substantial" is the key one, here. Any joint trial has some element of potential prejudice, but in my view it is not substantial. Also, I have to weigh up the cost to the taxpayer of two separate trials. On that basis, I'm denying your motion. The joint trial will begin in two weeks. We'll swear a jury this Monday. Court adjourned.'

'Your Honor . . .' I said, but he'd already gotten halfway to the door. He ignored me, and left.

'Shit,' I said, under my breath. 'Can we lodge an appeal today?'

Harry folded his arms. His eyes were closed and his brows knitted together. 'No can do. The trial hasn't happened yet, so we can't allege any actual prejudice. On appeal we have to show the judge wrongly exercised his discretion. When a trial judge has an inherent discretion built into their decision-making, it's hell to get an appellate court to overrule him. It won't work in this case. He's acknowledging our arguments, but he says that doesn't automatically mean a split trial if he can deal with any substantial prejudice to the defendants by warning the jury about certain aspects of the evidence. The Zafiro case kind of backs him up on that theory. Man . . .'

'But the criminal code says if the defenses are diametrically opposed—'

'I know what the codes say. So do you. So does he. And he still has the privilege of discretion. We can't appeal him unless his decision is perverse,' said Harry.

'What about arguing bias? Between Stone and Dreyer both defendants are going down.'

'Where's your evidence of bias? Especially given that he granted all your other motions. That kind of proves he's not biased. I'm sure that was in the back of his mind when he gave us everything we'd asked for in disclosure. If there's clear and substantial prejudice that emerges during trial, then our client has a good appeal. That's it.'

'But that prejudice would result in her conviction. We can't let that happen. Sofia wouldn't last inside. You know how long an appeal would take, and if we won we'd only get a retrial. She'd have to go through all of this again,' I said.

Harry shook his head, muttered, 'He's a son-of-a-bitch.'

'What was that you said, Mr. Ford? Did you say something about the Honorable trial judge?' said Dreyer with a serious tone. He wanted to embarrass Harry, mark his cards. It was a threat. You speak ill of Dreyer's white nationalist buddy, who just happens to be a judge, and he'll make sure that judge knows about it.

Harry said nothing, he just stared at Dreyer, his teeth clenched.

'I thought I caught you saying he's a *son-of-a-bitch*? Did you say that?' asked Dreyer. He was pushing it now, making his power play.

'I didn't call him a son-of-a-bitch,' said Harry.

'Good. That's a good boy,' said Dreyer.

Harry stood up, the word *boy* had set him off.

'I *said*, "he's a neo-Nazi *asshole* and you're his *bitch*." That's what I said, Wesley. Make sure you tell him I said that. You can both put on your white robes and have a good laugh about it.'

Dreyer wrinkled his nose, stood back. Harry was no longer a lawyer, nor a judge. He couldn't be reported to any professional bodies for that comment, because he didn't belong to any of them. Not anymore.

'In case you haven't worked it out yet, a joint trial gives me a guaranteed win. One of those women killed Avellino. The jury will convict one of them – at least. I don't care if it's your client, or Kate's. I'll try and have them both convicted, but even if one is acquitted I still get one conviction. I can't lose. Between you and Miss Brooks – one or both of you will lose. I'll see you gentlemen in court,' said Dreyer, and with that he left.

'Harry, that wasn't smart. We don't need the judge any more biased against us than he already is,' I said.

'Not possible,' said Harry.

Kate packed her files away, and as she was leaving she passed by my table and whispered, 'My client is taking the polygraph,' and then walked away.

Shit.

Now there was an even bigger problem.

NINETEEN

KATE

Kate watched Dreyer get into the old judge's face. She'd heard all about Harry Ford. Most young lawyers knew the stories. He was a legend. Smart, fair and fearless. What every judge should be.

She heard Dreyer call Harry *boy*.

At that moment, she wanted Harry to punch Dreyer in the face. Kate sniggered when Harry rose to the bait, called out Judge Stone, who was the exact opposite of Harry. She knew then that if her strategy paid off, Eddie's client was going to jail, and she was helping Dreyer to do that. A knot formed in her stomach. Bloch grabbed the box of prosecution discovery, Kate packed away her files and as she passed Eddie, she gave something away.

It was a little thing. Just to let him know Alexandra had decided to take the lie-detector test. This made Eddie's decision with his client a little less speculative. If both sisters had declined the test, the prosecution would have a better chance of convicting both of them. If Alexandra passed, Kate knew it would be a big point in her client's favor. Especially if Sofia failed the test, or didn't take it.

Sofia passing the lie-detector test didn't enter Kate's mind. Alexandra was convincing – even Bloch had been impressed. Kate had absolute faith in her client's innocence, which automatically made Sofia the murderer. And it was right that murderers were convicted and sent to jail. That's what she told herself. Yet something in the back of her mind hesitated at the thought of pointing her finger at another person and calling them a murderer. That was the prosecutor's job. She was a defense attorney at heart. Prosecutors were a different breed.

With Bloch beside her silently lugging the box of prosecution disclosure, she hung onto that thought as the pair of them walked silently out of the courtroom and along the corridor, and into the elevator to the ground floor. When she stepped outside into the cold sunshine on Center Street, that niggling thought had grown into a major concern.

What if her client was lying? What if Alexandra murdered Frank Avellino? Kate's strategy could send an innocent woman to prison for life.

Kate stopped, shook her head. It was as if she wanted to shake that thought loose and make it fall out of her ear onto the sidewalk.

'Kate Brooks,' said a voice. She looked up. A man in a tan coat and black wool cap approached. He had a kind face, and questioning eyes. He was just suddenly there, in front of her.

'Kate Brooks?' he said again.

This must be a reporter, thought Kate. Someone looking for an early story on the case. Reporters didn't tend to show up at the hearings until they were likely to catch a quote along with a snap of the defendant looking pained and paralyzed with fear.

'Yeah, I'm Kate,' she said.

The man opened his tanned coat, drew out a letter-sized envelope and thrust it at Kate. Confused and somewhat startled, the moment she took it from him he said, 'You've been served,' and then walked away. Kate ripped open the envelope.

Kate's cheeks flushed. She swallowed. She was now being sued. For two million dollars.

Bloch took the papers from her and glanced through them.

'It was bound to happen sooner or later,' said Bloch.

Since Kate took the case away from her firm she'd been through various skirmishes with Levy, Bernard and Groff. First there were the polite calls to Alexandra who proved as good as her word, refusing every one of Levy's calls and pleas to attend meetings. After a while, the phone calls to Alexandra stopped as the firm switched tactics. The first letter arrived in a brown envelope with all kinds of red stamps upon it bearing grave warnings to the recipient that if they didn't open the damn thing immediately it was likely to burn their house down.

The letter said that Kate was in violation of the non-compete, non-solicitation clause in her contract as she had poached the firm's biggest client. Second, she was also in breach of her confidentiality clause as she had used information held by the firm in order to solicit the client. In other words, she had checked the client database and found Alexandra's address in order to visit her. The last paragraph said that if she resigned as counsel for Alexandra, all would be forgiven. She had seven days to decide.

Seven days later another letter arrived. This one repeated the allegations in the first letter but this time it said that the firm was going to sue her for breach of contract, loss of revenue and damages.

Kate knew the game. She sent a simple reply stating that considering she had been forced to leave her job because of constant sexual harassment and discrimination, she didn't feel bound by any of her contractual terms. If the firm was going to ignore its anti-harassment policy, she was going to ignore the covenants that restricted her practice since it was the firm's fault she had to leave.

That stopped the letters. No more came after that.

She imagined the rest of the equity partners conducted a thorough in-house investigation and decided it wasn't worth it.

'I thought they were going to let it go,' said Kate.

'Nah,' said Bloch, 'not without a fight.'

It was going to turn into a fight, that was for sure. Kate knew then she would have to countersue, citing Levy's lecherous approaches, and while everything she would put in that suit would be true – there was no way of proving it.

Bloch put the box of discovery down on the sidewalk, took out her keys and blipped open her truck. Kate sat down on top of the box, cupped her face in her hands and tried to steady herself.

'Come on,' said Bloch. 'We can deal with that later. Right now we've got a murder case to win. I've got a feeling all the answers are under your ass.'

Kate smiled, stood.

Together they lifted the box into the trunk, closed the lid. Kate got into the passenger seat, Bloch the driver's seat. Kate buckled her seat belt, then noticed her hands were shaking. She gripped her knees and told herself everything was going to be alright. She didn't believe a word of it.

The engine roared into life as Bloch pulled into traffic. Fifty yards ahead a stop light turned from green to yellow. Kate heard a motorcycle beside her. She turned and saw the rider wearing a black helmet, with a tinted visor. The rider stared straight at Kate. She could tell by the tight biker suit it was a woman. Suddenly, the motorcycle roared and took off, accelerating rapidly, the engine like a turbine in her ear. The motorcyclist, all in black, tore through the intersection on the yellow light, making the other side just before the red and then weaving through the traffic.

Bloch brought the truck to a stop for the light and said, 'Nice bike.'

The rest of that day, and into the night, Kate and Bloch worked through the discovery in Kate's apartment. They ordered in food, Kate kept the coffee coming and at two a.m., Bloch put down the last sheaf of paper and rubbed at her temples.

'You finished?' asked Kate.

'I think both girls are finished,' said Bloch.

The prosecution case rested on forensic evidence.

DNA from both defendants on the victim's body.

Fingerprint and DNA evidence from both defendants on the murder weapon.

Hair fiber from Sofia Avellino on the victim's body.

Bite marks from Alexandra on the victim's body.

Both defendants had motive. Both had opportunity.

Both had a lot of the defendant's blood on their clothes.

'It's hard to split the responsibility. It'll come down to who the jury believe,' said Kate.

Pointing at the stack of forensic reports, Bloch said, 'That kind of evidence will put both of them away.'

The two-seater couch had a bow in the middle, where the central beam had broken. The rest of it wasn't too comfortable either, but Kate sat down in the middle of the couch because she knew from experience she'd slide to the middle anyway, no matter where she chose to sit on it. She put her elbows on her knees and curled her hair around her finger – staring into space.

'Let's see what she says in the morning,' said Kate. She saw Bloch to the door, then slept in her clothes until five a.m., when the cold got too much for her. Getting up, she brought her blankets to the radiator, and slept again, curled up on the floor.

By eleven that morning, Kate was showered and dressed in a new suit to meet Alexandra at her apartment. Her client let her in and offered her a seat at the small dining table.

'I love your suit. Is it new?' asked Alexandra.

'It is. Thank you.'

They sat together at the table, sipping hot herbal tea and making small talk before Kate got down to business. She explained the forensic evidence to Alexandra. How damning it looked. The only upside, maybe, was that it was damning to both sisters.

'There might be a way to minimize it,' said Kate. 'I want to stipulate we don't challenge the DNA, blood and fingerprint evidence. You told the police you went to your father and grabbed hold of him. You also used the knife before, when you were cooking. None of that evidence means you killed your father, just that it *could* have been you. I think if the jury has to sit and hear all this evidence from the experts, the sheer weight of it will make them think you had to have killed him along with your sister. This is about minimizing the case against you. Best way to deal with it is to say that it fits with your story.'

'So what happens, practically, if we don't challenge it?'

'We'll tell the jury this evidence exists, but we'll imply it's not important – that it doesn't prove anything. The bite-mark evidence is different, we'll fight that the whole way.'

Alexandra turned her head away, tears forming in her eyes.

'Whatever you think is best. I'm just so worried about the trial. I-I-I can't look at her. I don't want to be in the same room as her. She killed my dad, she wants to ruin my life. I don't want to see her. Is there a screen or something that could be put up, so I don't have to see her every day of the trial?'

'Not that I know of . . . I'll look into it. I know it will be hard . . .' Kate broke off when she saw Alexandra's fingers trembling. It occurred to Kate that her client's main concern wasn't whether she would be convicted – it was the loss of her father, and the deep, perpetual wound caused by his murder.

'Leave it with me. I'll see if something can be done. If it can't, then I will need you to be strong. You don't have to look at her. Look at the jury. Let them see what I'm seeing now.'

Alexandra met Kate's gaze, her chin wobbled, and she licked a tear from the corner of her mouth.

'I'll do my best,' said Alexandra, taking in a long breath and holding it. While she exhaled, her fingers pressed on the table, then slid around in patterns, as if she was feeling for every imperfection in the wood and exploring it.

She let out the air in her chest, drew a handkerchief from the sleeve of her blouse and wiped delicately at her wet cheeks. Kate detected the smell of lavender and spice in the air, probably from the handkerchief. Alexandra took a sniff at the scented handkerchief, rubbed the cotton between her forefinger and thumb, then unfolded it and held it up for Kate to see.

The corner of the material bore the initials 'FA', which had been monogrammed onto the material in black thread.

'Dad's smell is still on these handkerchiefs,' said Alexandra, fresh tears forming in her corners of her eyes. 'It's all I have left of him.'

Kate took hold of Alexandra's hand, and they exchanged bitter-sweet smiles.

'It's the polygraph tomorrow. Remember this feeling. This will get you through it,' said Kate.

TWENTY

EDDIE

'My landlord doesn't allow dogs in the building,' I said.

'No shit. You told me that yesterday. And the day before. In fact, you've said the same thing for weeks. Ever since I started bringing Clarence to the office. I'm beginning to get the impression you don't like him,' said Harry.

He was reading the final pages of the prosecution discovery. The bundles of documents were spread out on my couch and at Harry's feet was the dog he'd met the night of his retirement party. Harry had named him Clarence. They seemed to be at one with each other. The dog lay on its side and each time Harry reached down to grab the next set of pages, his tail would beat on the floorboards. Every hour, Harry would reach into his pocket and draw out a frankfurter from a baggie that he hand-fed to Clarence. He must've been on the streets a long time. When Harry first took the dog in, it was skinny and had lost a lot of fur. Now the bald patches were beginning to disappear, and you could no longer see the poor animal's ribcage.

Harry put down the last set of papers, patted his pal and gave him a frankfurter. I got up from behind my desk, retrieved the papers scattered around the couch and the floor and piled them on my desk. We had split the discovery. I read half. Harry read half. Now we swapped.

Two hours and two and half frankfurters later, all three of us looked like we could use a drink. I filled a cereal bowl with water from the faucet in the bathroom, and left it on the floor. Clarence lapped up the water greedily.

'He doesn't look like a Clarence,' I said.

'He's a dog. I didn't name him after Darrow because of what he looks like. Clarence Darrow was the best defence attorney who ever lived. And a survivor, just like this little one.'

'And does Clarence Darrow here have any bright ideas on how to defend our client?'

Harry wasn't even looking at me. We'd both finished reading the prosecution discovery – which amounted to the entire case against our client. Harry seemed to be more focused on Clarence. He rubbed the dog's belly, while Clarence kicked his little back legs in delight.

'Clarence says he's thinking about it. This one isn't easy. A drink might help?'

I poured Harry and I some coffee from the pot. I gave him his mug and he stared at it with open displeasure. Like I'd given him a mug filled with the leftover water from what was now Clarence's bowl.

'I thought we were going to have a drink?'

'That is a drink.'

'That stuff will kill you. Give me a large Scotch.'

He put the coffee as far away from him as he could, while remaining seated, and continued to massage Clarence while I poured him a real drink. He took the Scotch, sipped it, and Clarence let out a low, contented growl.

We fell quiet for a time, and I stretched my back and felt the dull ache leave the base of my spine.

'Talk to me,' said Harry. 'What are the main prosecution pillars?'

This was defense prep 101. It was up to the prosecutor to build their columns of evidence. They want to put a guilty verdict on the roof. The weaker we can make the supporting structure, the less likely it is that the roof will hold.

Simple.

'The crime scene investigator takes a single hair from one of the wounds on Avellino. This is hair that he says was partially trapped in the wound. It was a long hair, measuring nine inches. He says the only way that hair gets down into the wound is if it was trapped there when the knife made the incision. That has some logic to it.'

'On its own that's not too damning,' said Harry. 'Professor Shandler is the one who tested the hair. He's the one who really gives us the problem.'

The prosecutor's hair fiber expert – Professor Shandler – examined the hair and determined that it matched hair samples taken from Sofia.

'Hair-fiber analysis is not an exact science. There might be a way of attacking his findings. That's the only line of attack on this one.'

'Agreed,' said Harry. 'Let's ask Harper to research the good professor. With the amount of convictions overturned on unreliable hair-fiber analysis, somebody is bound to have questioned Shandler's methods before now.'

'I'll ask her to dig into the professor's personal history too. Maybe he has a few skeletons in the closet.'

'Good. So where does that leave us? The bite-mark expert says the wound on the victim's chest is consistent with Alexandra's teeth having made that mark. Good for him. Maybe we can use that to our advantage. If the bite-mark expert is good then it helps Sofia,' said Harry.

'Yeah, and if the hair-fiber guy is good then it cuts both ways. We could try and bolster the prosecution case on that point, throw their expert a few softballs in cross-examination and do real damage to Alexandra, but you know that just doesn't feel right to me.'

'What doesn't?' said Harry.

'We're defense lawyers. Anything that I might do to help a prosecutor just makes me sick to my stomach.'

'But it helps your client.'

'Maybe, but it doesn't feel right. From now on, let's focus on the case against Sofia. We have to forget about Alexandra.'

'I thought you wanted the guilty to be punished. Wasn't that always your way?'

It was part of the system – and it was part of my DNA. The innocent go free, the guilty pay for their crimes. If Sofia was innocent, then Alexandra had to be the killer. I should have been baying for Alexandra's blood.

But this case was different. It felt different. I believed Sofia didn't kill her father. When I'd seen Alexandra that night at the station, I couldn't say she looked like a killer, either.

'Do you believe Sofia is innocent?' I asked.

'It doesn't matter what I believe. She's our client. I know it matters to you a lot. It just so happens that I do believe Sofia. I can't see her doing that to her father.'

'That means it must've been Alexandra,' I said, but without much conviction. I believed Sofia was innocent. Trouble was I didn't yet believe Alexandra was the killer. There was evidence pointing to her, but I didn't yet feel it, in my gut.

Harry leaned forward, said, 'What about you? Having doubts?'

I shook my head, unsure whether I was trying to convince Harry or myself that there were no doubts in my mind. Clarence got up off the floor, nuzzled in beside Harry and used his snout to flick his hand off his lap and then leapt into the space. Clarence wanted some Harry time.

Harry stroked the dog, gently, and sipped his whiskey.

'Both sets of prints lifted from the knife match Sofia and Alexandra. Easy enough to explain. They both cooked for their father. Makes sense they both handled the knife. I'm not worried about that too much. Both Alexandra and Sofia were in the house that night, so opportunity is shared but . . .'

'But we're the only defendant with a documented history of mental health issues, drug addiction and violence. Alexandra is a poster child for stability and success. The murder looks like it was carried out by a raving lunatic. That's another big problem,' said Harry.

'Should I get a psychiatrist to minimize the damage?'

'You'd be wasting your time. I say we don't make a big deal out of her mental health. It doesn't prove anything, I suppose. The more we draw attention to it, the more it looks like there really *is* a problem.'

Harry had a good point.

Harper opened the office door and came inside. She ignored Harry and me and bent down to Clarence who leapt from Harry's lap and began rubbing his sides against Harper's legs. He whimpered and wagged his tail in excitement as Harper cooed and talked to him, telling him he was a good boy.

'Hey, defense attorneys are people *too*, you know?' I said.

'You're kidding. Not even you believe that,' said Harper.

'Is Sofia ready for tomorrow?' I asked.

She stood and said, 'She's gonna take the polygraph. She's calm, I've taught her stress management techniques I learned in the Bureau.'

'You think she'll hold up?' I asked.

'Polygraphs are all about managing stress so as not to give false positives. Some people who are naturally jittery can skew results – the data can't really determine between someone who is a nervous wreck and a liar. We'll see. She's as ready as she'll ever be. Big day tomorrow. I just got a call from the precinct. They're going to allow us into the Avellino house tomorrow night to look over the scene.'

'Great,' said Harry.

'It's a joint inspection. Lawyers and staff only. No discussing the case at the house – the DA is video-recording the whole thing.'

'He's being very careful,' I said.

'Wouldn't you be? This is a monster case. Last thing he needs is one of the defendants interfering with the scene, or worse – planting something to implicate the other. The co-defendant's counsel gets to see our inspection video, and vice versa. At least we can see what they're focusing on. Might give us a heads up.'

'Kate Brooks is probably thinking the same thing,' I said.

'Ah, I've already thought of that,' said Harper. She had a backpack slung over one shoulder. She removed it and handed Harry a large camera with a lens attached.

'If there's something we need to look at without the DA noticing, then we split up. Harry can use the camera, we use our phones. The cameraman can't follow three of us,' she said.

'I love you, Harper,' I said, and instantly regretted it.

It was meant as something flippant. A way to tell her I thought she was the smartest of all of us in this room. It came out wrong. It came out like it meant something else.

'I meant, I-I . . .'

'Who is the hair-fiber expert?' said Harper, ignoring my embarrassment.

'Professor Shandler,' said Harry.

Shaking her head, Harper said, 'Shit. He's legit. No adverse findings that I know of, but I'll check again.'

Hair-fiber analysis has been the subject of some criticism in appellate courts and there were several hair-fiber analysts who had been responsible for wrongful convictions. As their reputations went down the toilet, all of the cases they worked on went under scrutiny. We had been hoping the DA's expert would be one of those tarnished few. Harper had done her homework – she knew every hair-fiber expert on the East Coast who had a bad reputation. Shandler wasn't one of them.

Harper took her laptop from her bag, sat on the couch beside Harry.

'He's got a website,' she said. 'Lot of articles on his work. He's got a great rep. One of the top-ranked forensic fiber experts in the country. He's helped design a forensic lab for spectrometer analysis in Quantico. He built the Bureau's lab, basically. We're not going to get any dirt on this guy – he's the real deal.'

I finished my coffee, but instead of reaching for the pot for a refill, I picked up the bottle of Scotch. Unscrewed the cap. Began to angle the bottle to pour some into my cup. The liquid came to the neck of the bottle and I stopped. Alcohol rehab seemed a long time ago. I could drink in moderation now, but there was always the possibility that I might start to pour a glass of Scotch and never stop. I got up. Refilled Harry's glass with a smile on my face and then put the bottle back on my desk.

'The basis of any good con is a single principle – everyone wants to make a free buck. Greed and green. If Shandler is clean, looks like we'll have to dirty him up a little.'

'How?' said Harry.

'We'll get him to do what he does best.'

She looked up at me, momentarily confused.

'I'm not going to be involved in something illegal, if that's what you have in mind.'

'Don't worry.'

She looked concerned, her head went down, and her hair fell over her eyes. I didn't want anything to trouble her. Without thinking, my hand reached out and my fingers gently smoothed her hair away from her face.

Whatever thoughts or feelings she was having, they seemed to float away as she caught herself staring back at me. Her eyes darted around the floor, she took a step back and laughed nervously.

Now we were both embarrassed.

I could see a vein pulsing in her throat. She always wore a gold crucifix that hung around her neck on a thin gold chain. The chain looked cheap and the crucifix old and slightly tarnished at the base. I always thought it had been a gift from someone special. She wore it every day. I didn't know who had given it to her, or why. I wanted to know. I wanted to know every little personal thing about her. Every detail.

Fear held me back. I knew there was a line that I shouldn't cross. No matter how much I wanted to do it, and no matter how strongly I suspected she wanted me to step right over that line.

'Clarence, let's go for a walk,' said Harry.

Clarence got up immediately and followed Harry to the door. Before Harry left he said, 'You should try going on a date.'

I laughed, feeling like a sixteen-year-old kid again. The embarrassment, the sickening nerves.

'He has to ask me out, first,' said Harper, shouting though the door at Harry.

I could hear Harry's laughter in the hallway, and Clarence's paws on the wooden floor getting fainter as they got closer to the stairs.

'Hypothetically, if I *were* to ask you out, would that be a good thing?' I asked, trying to smile through the nerves turning my stomach to jelly.

'It depends,' said Harper. 'You'd have to make an effort. My dad bought flowers once in his life – when he asked my mom out on their first date. He wasn't the romantic type, so he must have really been in love. My mom talked about that bunch of flowers a lot. It didn't matter that they were cheap roses from the gas station. It was the thought that counted.'

'I'll see what I can do,' I said.

TWENTY-ONE

KATE

The morning of the polygraph test, Kate sat outside the examiner's office on a steel chair and wished with all her heart she could disappear into a hole where no one could find her. Her left hand wouldn't stop shaking, so she tucked it behind her knee.

'You're more nervous than I am,' said Alexandra.

Her client sat beside her, sipping from a half-gallon bottle of water. Kate had noticed that whenever she was with Alexandra, the woman nearly always had a big bottle of water close at hand, which she poured down her throat every five minutes. She was the most hydrated person Kate had ever met. As Alexandra drank from the bottle, Kate noticed the slight tremor in her client's arm. The heel of Alexandra's boot clicked on the floor tile in triple time.

Bloch leaned against the opposite wall. Cool, nonchalant, and switched on. Nothing escaped Bloch's notice. She was like a machine. Everything around her was data to be absorbed and perhaps noted. Never forgotten. Bloch kept looking between Kate and Alexandra.

'Just keep cool. Tell the truth,' said Bloch.

Alexandra nodded. Took another drink.

Kate nodded and bit the nails on her right hand.

Bloch was stone.

The door to Kate's left opened and a man in a suit came out. He greeted them, introduced himself as a licensed polygraph expert by the name of Carter Johnson, and invited them inside.

The room had no windows. One corner desk was lit with a lamp, and apart from an area no bigger than ten feet either side of the lamp, the room was in darkness. Beside the lamp sat a laptop and a desktop computer with two screens above it. Next to the desk was a chair facing into the room, its back to the wall.

Johnson beckoned Alexandra to the chair and began to attach monitors to her thumb, arms, forehead, and neck.

'I'm just here to observe,' said a voice in the dark.

Kate located the source of the voice and saw one half of Wesley Dreyer's face illuminated by the glare from his cell phone screen.

'I didn't agree to you being here,' said Kate.

'You never said I wasn't permitted to attend, either. I'm here now. I won't get in the way. I'll be in the corner. Quiet as a mouse,' said Dreyer.

As Kate became more accustomed to the gloom, she saw a bank of chairs in the opposite corner of the room. Kate and Bloch sat together, watching Alexandra settle herself. Taking deep breaths through her nose, and exhaling through her mouth. Long and slow. Then short and fast. She stretched her neck, closed her eyes.

Alexandra was ready.

The examiner, Johnson, explained he was going to ask her some questions to get a baseline response.

'Are you Alexandra Avellino?' he asked.

'Yes.'

'Do you have blonde hair?'

'Yes.'

'Do you live in New York?'

'Yes.'

As she answered the questions, she stared straight ahead, and kept as still as she could. The only movement came from her fingers as they stroked a leather and black pearl bracelet with a few metal charms. Alexandra didn't spin the bracelet on her wrist, as if she was fidgeting. Instead she rubbed the leather, turned the pearls, and felt the charms between her fingers as if she were exploring their feel for the first time.

'Is Hillary Clinton President of the United States?'

'No.'

While these questions went on, there were lines flitting across the twin screens, and Johnson was making notes and clicking on a mouse. This was new technology. Kate thought they were a long way from reams of paper feeding from a machine with a needle jumping across it in wavy lines.

'Is today Wednesday?'

'No.'

'Was it snowing when you came into the building?'

'No.'

'Did you murder Frank Avellino?'

'No.'

'Did your sister kill Frank Avellino?'

'Yes.'

'Have you lied in any of your answers so far?'

'No.'

Johnson glanced over his shoulder, nodded toward Dreyer who let out a sigh and then gave Johnson the thumbs up. Johnson reached down with his left hand, then came up with something in a clear plastic bag.

'Did you murder Frank Avellino with this knife?'

Pause. Alexandra stared at the thing in front of her as Kate got up and unleashed a tirade at Dreyer – her voice and indignation rising in her throat with every word.

'This is an ambush. This test is over. I agreed to let your examiner ask questions, not show my client the knife that was used to murder her father – that's completely outrageous. Have you no shame?'

Dreyer had his hands up in placation. Bloch strode over to Alexandra. She still hadn't answered the question. She had turned away from the knife, hiding her eyes from it. Her chest heaving. Bloch tore the pads and sensors from her skin.

'This is inadmissible. We've had enough and we're leaving. My client is a victim. How dare you show her the weapon used to kill her father? What kind of a sick animal does that?' said Kate.

'She's not a victim until twelve people on a jury say she's not guilty, Miss Brooks. You know that. The facts of what happened here can be referred to in cross-examination. Tell your client I'm not falling for her fake tears.'

Bloch walked Alexandra to the door, Kate followed them out. In the corridor Kate bumped into the back of Bloch. She was standing still, staring straight ahead. If Kate hadn't been standing behind them, she would've missed Bloch reach up and firmly take hold of Alexandra's right arm.

Stepping to one side, Kate looked ahead.

At the other end of the corridor was the reason Bloch stopped. Eddie Flynn, Harry Ford and Harper were coming toward them with their client, Sofia.

Kate swung around and saw Dreyer coming out of the examination room. He moved ahead of them and stopped. They would have to walk past him, and the other defense team, to get out of the building.

Kate didn't want Alexandra to have to face this moment so soon.

One of Alexandra's fears was having to sit in the same room as her sister. Facing your father's killer was one thing – but the fact it was your sister added only more pain.

'Alexandra, keep your eyes on the floor and walk with me. Don't look at her. Don't speak to her,' said Bloch.

They started walking.

'You set this up,' hissed Kate to Dreyer as they moved past him.

He said nothing. Alexandra's bail conditions were the same as Sofia's. Neither of them were to have contact, direct or indirect, with any of the witnesses in the case or each other.

'If you say one word to her, Dreyer will have you arrested and ask the court to revoke your bail. Don't speak to her, don't look at her, keep your head down,' said Kate.

Eddie Flynn looked like he was having the same conversation with his client. He found a door and stepped into it, Harper dragging Sofia in after her.

They were only ten feet away, Sofia was holding onto the doorway, Eddie shielding her from a view of the hallway. Sofia was telling them, 'No, no, no . . .' As they passed by, Kate caught Sofia peeking around Eddie's body. The look on her face was one Kate would never forget.

Sofia's eyes looked like fire. The skin around them was red, they were blazing with tears, hatred and sadness. Sofia didn't say anything more as they passed by. Harry Ford pressed himself to the wall, and Kate nodded in greeting. He nodded back, then looked at Kate's client.

Alexandra shielded her eyes, as if her sister were an eclipse and the mere act of looking upon her would render Alexandra blind.

Neither sister spoke. Kate put her hand on Alexandra's back, gently urging her to increase her pace. Kate felt a surge of tension – as if there was a toxic cloud emanating from that doorway.

They passed without incident, rounded the corner and made their way to the exit.

Bloch held open the door for them and then led the way to Alexandra's Land Rover, parked in the lot. Fumbling in her purse, Alexandra dropped the keys. Kate picked them up, opened the car and got Alexandra into the driver's seat. With the door still open, Kate waited while Alexandra cried.

'I don't know how I'm going to get through this,' said Alexandra.

'We'll be right by your side, every step of the way. You're stronger than you know,' said Kate.

Alexandra let out a peal of nervous laughter, said, 'I'm a mess. I can't sit in the same room as Sofia – knowing what she did. I just can't.'

'You can. And you will,' said Bloch.

No one spoke for a time. Alexandra nodded, blew her nose on a napkin and thanked Bloch and Kate. Kate said she would email the videos from the crime scene inspections later – see if Alexandra could spot anything useful. Kate closed the car door and watched Alexandra drive away.

'Dreyer wanted to see how she would react, to the knife and the presence of her sister. Smart,' said Bloch.

'He's not sure which one killed Frank Avellino. He's gauging them. I get the impression he's deliberately messing with their heads. He wants the sisters to tear each other apart, so he can mop up the blood and convict both of them. Let's hope Sofia's polygraph is a lot worse than Alexandra's,' said Kate.

*

Later that same night, Kate and Bloch made sure they arrived at Franklin Street to view the crime scene at the allotted time, and Alexandra was not present. They didn't want any more contact between Alexandra and Sofia.

A cameraman for the DA's office met them at the front door and an NYPD boy in blue let them both inside.

Kate had been hoping that seeing the inside of the property for real would trigger some additional line of defense – that she would see something which would help prove Alexandra's innocence, or rather, prove Sofia's guilt.

They took photos, and their own video.

When they left the property an hour later, both were disappointed not to have discovered a killer point to win the case. They did both have a better understanding of the geography and sheer size of the place, though, so it wasn't a complete waste of time.

By the time Kate got home, the DA's cameraman had sent both videos. Kate clicked on the email and forwarded it to Alexandra.

Maybe she could see something Kate couldn't?

TWENTY-TWO

EDDIE

Once I was sure Kate and her client had safely passed by the storage room, I let go of Sofia. She was already anxious about the thought of taking the polygraph and this only made things worse. When I'd seen them coming towards us, I knew I had to get her away. The room we were in had boxes piled up in the corner, and assorted stationery filling the rest of the wall space which had been taken up by shelves. At first she resisted. I could see the anger rise in Sofia. Hurt too. She resisted at first, telling me, 'No,' and repeating it as she held onto the doorway. She wanted to get to her sister. Alexandra had taken everything from Sofia. Then, the emotions overwhelmed her.

Sofia grabbed me, hugged me and buried her head in my chest. She moaned and held tight. I had put my arms on her shoulders, whispering to her that it would be alright. Now, having let go of her, I told her Alexandra had gone.

She took her arms from around me, stood back and adjusted her hair. She had been crying, and there was a wet patch on my shirt pocket.

'Sorry,' she said.

'It's fine. There have been a lot of tears on this shirt over the years. Mostly mine. Don't worry, she's out of here. You're safe.'

'Coast is clear,' said Harry from the corridor. We joined him and made our way down the corridor to the exam room. Inside, I saw Dreyer and the examiner in a lab coat typing on a computer with a bank of screens above it. Beside that was the chair for test subjects. I told Sofia to relax and go take a seat. Harry went with her to make sure she was settled and check out the exam process.

'I hope that was worth it,' I said to Dreyer. He ignored me. He was already making notes.

'We'll see, won't we?' he replied.

While the examiner in the white lab coat hooked her up to his machines, Harry spoke softly to Sofia and reminded her to tell the truth and, above all, to relax.

The examiner began the lie detector test with simple questions. After a few minutes, Sofia got into the swing of things. She was answering more confidently and sticking to her story.

'Did you murder your father?' said the examiner.

Sofia looked right at him, then at Dreyer, her face impassive. She had control. Dreyer, on the other hand, looked like a man who realized he might have gotten on the wrong bus. He bit down on the nail of his index finger, then adjusted his tie, and returned the already bitten-down nail to his teeth. Whatever charade he had arranged for today wasn't working out as he had hoped.

I returned my attention to Sofia, realizing she hadn't answered the question. Her lip trembled, and she said, 'No.'

The examiner had something in his hand now. It was in a plastic evidence bag. He dropped it beside Sofia and said, 'Did you put this knife though your father's eyes?'

Tears formed and quickly ran down Sofia's cheeks as she said, in a whisper, 'No.'

'Goddamn it,' I said, 'That's low. Stop this test right now.'

Before Dreyer could interject, Sofia said, 'No, it's okay. I'm okay. Just keep going.'

I shook my head.

'This is an ambush, Sofia. The results for this test are skewed. Your reaction to the murder weapon is natural and it's going to be recorded as a blip in the data by Doctor Dickface here, who will say you lied in that answer,' I said, gesturing at the examiner.

He turned around and said, 'Just doing my job.'

'If your job is to intimidate and frighten my client then you're doing it just fine. Come on, this is a freak show.'

'No, it's okay. I'm telling them the truth,' said Sofia.

Save for going over there and removing the pads and sensors from her skin, there was not much else I could do. I thought about it for a second. It was the right thing. I looked at the middle of the three screens in front of the examiner. Displayed was a wave of crazy lines and then more rhythmic, smooth curls after the wild scrawls. Those scrawls were the sensors going ape shit from Sofia's reaction to the murder weapon.

This was not going well.

'Ask her the last question again,' I said.

'Fair enough,' said the examiner. 'Did you put that knife in your father's skull?'

'No,' said Sofia.

I looked at the screen. Smooth lines.

The truth.

A bucketful of relief hit me. It was like a warm wave, washing me clean. I had called this one correctly. Sofia was innocent. But the comfort of that knowledge didn't last. As fast as that feeling had arrived, it quickly dissipated under an anvil of responsibility.

If I failed, this innocent, messed-up young woman would go to jail. And she'd tie a rope blanket around her neck first chance she got.

A murder trial with an innocent client is like saving someone who's fallen over a cliff edge. You've got their hand. You've got to hang on. You've got to haul them to safety. Their life is in your grasp. Your strength is all that separates them from a chasm.

Just a few more weeks. Then the trial.

While I was sure, Dreyer was the opposite. I'd bet he was expecting to put a little daylight between the defendants with his lie detector test. That had backfired for him. He chewed his nails, ignoring me. Watching the examiner's screen. He sighed, got up and said, 'Be ready for trial. I'm pulling no punches, Eddie.'

'Bring it on,' I said.

The inspection of the murder scene that night had been pointless. I got nothing other than a better understanding of the layout of the mansion. In the car, on the way back to my office, Harper and Harry confirmed they'd also got very little from the inspection. Nothing the cops overlooked. We'd taken photos, but there didn't seem to be much point. The DA would use their official photographer with the body in situ to show the jury. Our photos didn't have any evidential value.

Still, I might go over them again. See if it shook something loose, but I doubted it.

Two hours after I got back to the office, Harper and Harry having already left, I got the email with the DA's videos of our inspection. I checked Kate's video, and didn't seem to think they had had any eureka revelations from their inspection either – or if they did, they'd hidden their reactions well.

I forwarded the videos to Sofia to check over, drained my coffee and hit the sack.

TWENTY-THREE

SHE

The echo of her guttural, animalistic roar dissipated from the walls of her apartment. A large stain on the opposite wall dripped red wine to the floor. Below the stain, the shards of a wine glass that had shattered when she'd thrown it.

She swiped up on her phone screen, displaying the video controls. Selecting rewind, she moved the video back thirty seconds and watched again.

She'd seen both videos. Both defense teams looking around the house and the bedroom most especially. Taking photos. Making notes. She wasn't looking for anything that could help her defense, like she was supposed to. Instead, she was watching to make sure neither defense team discovered something in that bedroom that could tie her to her father's murder. Because there was something there. Something that she had overlooked. To the careful observer, the room was stained with all kinds of footprints on the rug and a large orange stain on the bare mattress. Nothing to separate her from her co-accused in the blood patterns. That's not the game she had been playing.

No, it was only when she'd watched this video that she had seen the single flaw in her plan so far.

It was plain and simple. And it looked like one of the defense teams might have exposed her mistake with a single photograph. The flash of their camera went off right at the very spot. If they didn't see it right then, which she was pretty sure they had not, they would surely see it when they got those photos printed. From their reactions in the video, it didn't look like the photographer had realized the significance of that photo. But they would, given time.

There were real risks here. Only one defense team had taken that picture. That picture could not see the light of day. If someone studied it, they would know she was the real killer. They would see. She had to stop it. There could be no one on the face of this earth who could know she killed her father. She simply could not allow it. All that she had worked for would unravel because of one stupid mistake and one lucky shot with a camera.

She needed to act. Tonight. Now.

Get the photos.

Kill the photographer.

PART FOUR

THE DARK RED NIGHT

TWENTY-FOUR

SHE

She carried a new backpack as she made her way along the dark row of houses, avoiding the pockets of bright amber thrown on the sidewalk by the streetlights. The pack held a Maglite, some rope, a leaf-bladed lock knife, a lighter, a small acetylene torch, a Taser and a pair of bolt cutters. This would be a quick kill. No body disposal required. She would make the crime scene look like a robbery gone wrong.

With any luck she wouldn't have to use the door-breaking kit. If they answered the door with the security chain in place, she would need to use the Taser. Then, when they were down, light the torch and apply it to the chain. Ten seconds on the brass chain and the bolt cutters would go through it like it was spaghetti. She guessed twenty seconds to gain entry if the chain was on. That's a long time to stand on a victim's doorstep. No other way around it. To go in from the back would be much riskier. She had never been inside and didn't know what kind of alarm system might be triggered. Plus, there were security lights at the rear. Probably on a motion sensor.

Entering from the rear of the property was not an option.

She circled the house.

A dog barked. It was inside. Too difficult to tell if it was coming from inside the target's property or one of the other houses close by. She stood at the rear of the house, in the alley. A light flickered into life on the second floor. A lamp. The light wasn't harsh enough to be a ceiling light. This was a muted, warm glow.

Maybe the dog had woken the target.

She moved from the alley, pulled her hood down tightly over her ballcap – the brim keeping the hood from affecting her field of vision. She liked the dark. She had never been afraid of the night. Not like her sister, who would whimper and complain each night when they were growing up. Sister always needed a light on to sleep. A lamp, or just the wedge of light coming into the room from a hallway.

She loved the dark. It was like putting on a cool, comforting cloak. She knew there was nothing in the dark that could harm her, even from a young age. She had never been a good sleeper. While her family slumbered, she would roam the silent house. Taking in the shapes made in the shadows – enjoying the familiar and yet strange angles of the rooms and furniture as they were transformed by the darkness and made anew. Moonlight seemed beautiful to her. It was the devil's neon.

Thunder cracked.

The rain came like someone turning on a shower. A heavy, thick downpour. Momentarily, she raised her face to the heavens, letting the rain fall on her cheeks – reinvigorating her with its cold caress.

She removed the backpack, held it in front of her as she opened the zip and drew out the knife. Flicking open the blade, she locked it in place and carefully put it in her jacket pocket.

It was time.

The dog barked again as she put her foot on the first step at the front entrance. Then another step, applauded by a volley of barks. She counted five stone steps to the front door. A porch light activated, illuminating her. She glanced around.

No one on the street.

The dog's barking abated, leaving only calm and the whisper of the wind in the branches of the trees that lined the other side of the street.

She checked the street again. It was empty. She knocked on the door, put down her bag. The bag was half open. Ready if she needed to dive in for the Taser.

She heard nothing more, didn't notice any lights coming on in the hallway. She would have seen them in the narrow window above the door.

She knocked again. Waited.

Stepping closer, she turned her head. Rested it against the door. She could hear the faint, rhythmic creak of feet on the stairs. Not a quick descent. Steady. Cautious because of the time of night.

Her heart began beating faster as she sensed a presence moving toward her, now only a few feet away, on the other side of the door. She stood straight. Forced down the excitement. She knew, in a matter of seconds, she would be inside, and hot blood would roll over her wrist as she turned the blade in soft flesh.

HARRY

He knew he was in the same damn dream, again.

In that strange, twilight state between dreaming and waking he told himself he was safe. It was just a dream. He wasn't really kneeling in that foxhole in a jungle twenty miles from Hanoi. The sweat that glued his combat fatigues to his skin wasn't real. His M-16 wasn't really sliding from his dripping wet hands. Hands bathed in the blood of his lieutenant, who'd stepped on a mine and lost both legs in a deafening, visceral flash.

He was dreaming.

He woke, like he did most nights, puffing and panting. Sitting straight up in bed and heaving great gulps of air into his lungs. Tonight he resisted the urge to check his hands, to make sure it wasn't real. Harry heard a whimper from Clarence, and the dog unfolded itself from the bottom of the bed and gently came toward him. Clarence's wet nose brushed Harry's cheek, and then he felt that rough, cold tongue on his own nose.

'It's okay, there's a good boy,' said Harry, patting the dog.

After a few minutes, Harry's breathing had returned to normal. It was then he noticed he really was soaking in sweat. His white vest was awash. He took it off, threw it in the corner. He would pick it up in the morning and add it to the laundry. The most recent, former Mrs. Ford would have yelled at him for such a thing. She was in Hawaii now, presumably with her tennis coach.

'It was just a dream, boy,' said Harry, stroking Clarence.

But it had been real once. Many years ago. And it would never leave him. No matter how long he lived, there was always a part of Harry Ford that never left that foxhole.

Clarence's head turned around, sharply, toward the bedroom door. A low growl came from him and then he leapt from the bed and barked at the door. Harry turned on the lamp on the nightstand, found his glasses next to it and put them on.

'What is it, Clarence?'

The dog turned to Harry, barked once, then returned his watchful gaze to the door.

Throwing back the bed covers, Harry felt the chill air on his legs. He swung his feet out of the bed and stood up.

'Well, it ain't the Viet Cong, that's for damn sure,' he muttered, under his breath.

Thunder cracked.

Almost immediately Harry heard a deluge of rain hitting the roof. Clarence didn't flinch, his gaze unwavering from the door.

He felt the need for the bathroom. Old age. He used the en suite, and listened while Clarence continued to growl and bark at the door. Harry told him to be quiet, but now he was sure the dog had heard or sensed something other than the thunder, and that he should check it out. He flushed the toilet, then washed his hands and splashed water on his face for good measure. Already the images from the dream had faded from his mind, for another night at least.

Harry came out of the bathroom and saw Clarence scratching at the door with his paws. Something was wrong. For a second he thought about his old army service weapon, safely secured in a lock box in his closet. The key was in a pot on the bureau, buried beneath a layer of coins.

He shook his head, opened the bedroom door. Clarence twisted and jammed his nose into the open door space and wriggled through it as fast as he could then ran down the stairs.

Harry was about to follow when he heard something. He stopped. Listened again.

There it was. A faint knocking sound.

As Harry descended the stairs he couldn't tell if the groaning sound was coming from the old staircase or his knees. It didn't matter. Neither was about to get fixed anytime soon. He got to the bottom of the steps, expecting to see Clarence standing guard at the front door.

Only Clarence wasn't there.

He looked around and saw him, cowering in the corner of the hallway. His little head was down, his tail between his legs. His body was quivering. He didn't growl, or pant. He was silent. Frozen in what Harry thought was fear at whatever lay on the other side of the door. Clarence was a street dog, and God only knows what he'd been through, or who might have harmed him in the past, but Harry now saw fear in his little dog's face for the first time. It was clear he was afraid of whatever was outside, because as terrified as the animal was, he never took his eyes from the front door.

Harry moved forward, toward the door. His mouth felt dry. The hallway felt cold, and the gold chain around his neck seemed to amplify the chill, hanging around his body like an icy noose.

He turned the deadlock bolt, took hold of the door handle and began to turn it.

BLOCH

Sleep never came easily to Bloch. Even when she was little, she would lie awake in bed for hours on end, staring at the light fitting on the ceiling and the shadows it threw across the room from the glint of streetlights outside.

Now she lay in what had been her parents' bedroom. She had moved in months ago, but she'd yet to unpack or properly furnish the place. A futon, some bedroom furniture and a couch made up the sole items of furnishing for the entire house. She'd driven past three home and garden stores, but the thought of putting new furniture in her childhood home was still a little weird. Somehow, her mom and dad wouldn't approve. She knew this didn't make sense, but it was enough for now to keep the place sparse. What if she bought something and it didn't quite fit with her sense of the place? That worried her. She wanted everything to be perfect.

The mattress was unforgiving, but comfortable in a strange way. She had an old desk lamp that lay on the floor, the cable too short for it to sit on her new nightstand. It would take some time to get the house into shape, so she would have to put up with some imperfections until then. She bent over, clicked on the lamp and cracked open an Elmore Leonard novel she had read years ago but could not now remember.

Her jaw began to ache, and she reminded herself to stop grinding her teeth.

It was the lamp lying on the floor, not on the nightstand, that was making her grind her teeth until it hurt. She always had a lamp on the nightstand.

Bloch liked everything to be just so. Something out of place in a room would feel like a stone in the bottom of her shoe. She thought about where she could get a socket extension lead at this time of night. Bloch told herself she was letting this get way out of control. She got out of bed and went to the bathroom. A dental night guard lay in a glass by the wash basin. She was supposed to wear it every night to stop her grinding her teeth, but it hurt her gums and made it even more difficult to get to sleep. She rinsed the guard, and was about to put it in her mouth, when she heard a dog barking.

It wasn't coming from Kate's father's house, next door. Louis didn't have a dog. Must've been the other neighbor, the young couple from San Diego who drove the Taurus and kept parking it too close to Bloch's driveway.

Thunder cracked.

The dog let off another volley of barks. It wasn't too loud. Bloch could tell the dog was inside, somewhere. If it had been in the back yard the barking would've been much louder. These houses were not built to keep out noise. Rain hit the house like a hose. Bloch put in the bit, switched off the bathroom light and was on her way back to the bedroom when she heard something other than the rain.

It sounded like tapping.

It was coming from downstairs.

She leaned over the rail and cast an eye into the gloom below.

Listening, she could hear nothing.

She straightened, raised the bit to her lips, opened her mouth, and then she heard it again.

It wasn't tapping.

Someone was knocking on her door.

It was late. So late it was actually early.

She walked briskly to the bathroom, dropped the night guard in the glass and then slowly walked down the stairs. There were two pictures hanging on the staircase wall. A picture of her on her graduation day from the police training facility, and another one of her mother and father together on a beach somewhere. They looked happy. Her mother held an ice cream cone to her lips while her dad planted a kiss on her cheek. The kiss had caused her mother to half close her eyes. Bloch could tell by the wrinkles at the corner of her mother's eyes that she welcomed the kiss – that it was as sweet as the ice cream.

Bloch continued down the steps, but as she passed the picture of her mother and father, she bent low and took up the claw hammer she had left on the stairs earlier that evening after hanging the pictures.

The hammer felt good in her hand. Ideally, Bloch should have gone back upstairs and picked up her gun before even approaching the front door. Whoever it was at this time of night – they sure as hell wouldn't have anything good to say.

Bloch padded, barefoot, dressed in her cotton pajamas to the front door. She stood there for a time, listening. She tightened her grip on the hammer, let it fall to her side and then turned the latch, which disengaged the deadbolt. It clicked when the bolt retracted back into its housing within the door.

She put her hand on the latch, unlocked that too, and turned the handle, wary of what she might find on the other side of that door.

SHE

She locked her fingers around the hilt of the knife, drew it out, and held it behind her thigh. Angling her body to the left, she made sure it would not look obvious that she was holding a weapon out of sight.

Her senses heightened. She felt at one with the world. With nature. A natural predator at the top of the food chain. Her ears picked up the mechanical click of the door unlocking, the almost imperceptible scrape of metal on metal as the door latch drew back, drawn into retreat by the turning handle, and then the door opened just a fraction. Dark hallway revealing itself in slow motion, the drawing in of breath, and she readied herself to move suddenly, violently. Her shoulder muscles bunched, she stood on her toes, like a tigress primed to leap from the tall grass for its prey, maw open, claws bared.

The door opened further . . .

HARRY

Harry pulled open the door slowly, his left hand on the handle, his right bunched into a fist. As the street slowly revealed itself, he saw a figure standing there. The figure wore the night like a shroud.

Clarence began to whimper and howl.

SHE

There was no security chain to bar her entry. She moved fast, hitting the door with her right shoulder, surprising her prey. Inside, the hallway was dark, but her eyes were already accustomed to the gloom.

A dog howled.

While the target rocked backwards, she took three careful, quick steps and rammed the knife into flesh.

The blade bit below the ribcage. The angle perfect. It slid beneath the ribs, with a trajectory just off the vertical, the tip of the knife searching for the heart.

Her fist drew tightly around the hilt and she twisted the blade. The twist brought with it a flood of arterial blood through the channel in the center of the blade, and it flowed over her hand and wrist. She let go of the weapon and the body fell to the floor. Her victim was dead before the back of their head hit the carpet.

She kneeled, searched the body. Nothing. She ran upstairs to the bedroom, retrieved the cell phone with the pictures, rifled the drawers and spilled their contents to the floor. She found a small stash of ready cash, which she put in her pocket. She smashed the phone to pieces, and then ran down the stairs.

She bent low, grabbed the lifeless body and dragged it further into the hallway.

She saw something glint on the floor.

A fine gold chain hung limply around the neck. When she had picked up the corpse the chain must have caught on her. A link must've broken, and the chain had snapped and half lay on the floor. It looked cheap. She decided no intruder would think it worth taking. She left the house, closed the front door behind her and ran from the scene, her pack bouncing on the small of her back.

BLOCH

The night air sent a chill through Bloch as she opened the door. When she saw what was on the other side, she drew her hand across her mouth and closed her eyes in horror.

A large fat raven stood on top of a small green bird. One of the Quaker parrots. The raven pecked so hard at its prey that its beak broke through the body and hit the boards below. The large black bird was so ravenous that the parrot's flesh covered its head, and blood had spilled across Bloch's porch.

Bloch shouted at the raven, and it drew back. Fluttering to the porch rail. Bloch took one of the few empty packing boxes, split it open, and used the bottom to scoop the parrot's remains into the box. She closed the bottom, then the top of the box and brought it inside.

As she closed the door she saw the raven staring at her before it let out a cry of protest at being robbed of its feast.

The bird was dead. Bloch couldn't abide watching its body being torn apart on her front door. She would bury the bird, box and all, in the back yard come the morning.

HARRY

The figure that stood outside his front door looked odd. Twisted, slouched as if carrying some great weight.

Clarence whimpered again.

The figure stepped forward quickly, into the light.

Eddie looked as though he was half drowned in the rain. His suit and shirt clung to his frame. He raised his head and Harry saw his face was wet with more than rain. Eddie's face was contorted in pain and suffering. He couldn't speak, although his lips moved.

Instinctively Harry's fingers reached for the gold chain around his neck, from which hung the dog tags of his two best friends who never made it out of their foxholes one dark red night in a hot jungle east of Hanoi. Eddie raised one hand. There, entwined between his fingers was a chain. Dangling from the chain was an old tarnished cross. Even in the rain, Harry could see blood on the chain, on the cross.

It was Harper's necklace.

Only then did Harry notice what was in Eddie's other hand. A drenched bunch of flowers with wrapping from the Circle K.

Cheap, gas station flowers.

'She's gone. I went over there to give her these and I saw the cop cars outside,' said Eddie, his voice giving sound to the wound that threatened to tear him apart. 'Harper's been murdered.'

PART FIVE

THE TRIAL
Three Months Later

TWENTY-FIVE

SHE

It was just after midnight. The trial would begin in nine hours. Her feet were a blur on the sidewalk. She'd found a steady rhythm in her stride and there were miles ahead of her. The run let her mind wander to the recent days' events.

She had not looked at her sister those first two days in court as the lawyers chose the jurors. She could feel her eyes on her, but she didn't look. Couldn't look. She focused on the judge, her lawyer and the jury. That was it. She knew if she turned to look at her sister she would not be able to resist a smile and she couldn't let anyone see that. She could not let her mask slip during the trial. All of her work had come down to this.

The chess game in her apartment was an exact match of the old game she had played with her sister. All the pieces in their positions from when the last move had been made. Before Mother broke her neck.

Since that day, she had been playing the match against Sister in her head. Setting up her pawns. Moving a knight and a rook into a perfect position for attack. Her queen in reserve. Soon the queen would come out to play. The most powerful piece in her arsenal.

Taking her father's fortune wouldn't be half as sweet if her sister wasn't also punished.

The final moves in this lifelong game would happen in the courtroom, in nine hours' time.

She would need all of her strength to see it through. During the day, she was the innocent sister, falsely accused of her father's murder. During the night, she would have work to do.

Her pace slowed as she approached the restaurant. She jogged by, glancing through the window. Hal Cohen took the hand of the young woman across the table. Cohen dressed in a smart black suit, Armani or Lagerfeld. The woman wore a red dress so tight it cut off her circulation, but, conversely, was sure to get Cohen's blood pumping. She guessed the woman was half Cohen's age, and at least twenty years' younger than Cohen's wife.

She stopped outside the large side window of the restaurant. Her cell phone sat in an armband with a clear plastic cover on it. She wore wireless ear buds. Tapping the button on her ear bud, she triggered the camera on her phone. Her arm at the perfect angle to capture the clandestine couple.

She took the phone from the band, selected the photo and texted it to Hal as she walked around the corner toward the alley. Before she turned into the alley, she took a photo, pressed send on that one too. Hal would come through the kitchen and meet her out back.

There was little light penetrating the alleyway. She moved further along, past the dumpsters, to the steel doors at the rear of the restaurant. One of the doors opened, Hal stepped out and shut it behind him. If what he'd told her was accurate, there was business to be done. The kind best completed in darkness.

'I got your message. Is it true?' she asked.

'See for yourself,' said Hal, removing a single piece of paper from his inside jacket pocket and handing it to her.

Using the torch on her phone, she scanned the page, her heart quickening.

'That's a Xerox, of course, but you can see I'm telling the truth,' said Hal.

She nodded, said, 'You wrote in the text that we should talk about a deal. Aren't you forgetting we already had a deal?'

'That was before,' said Hal.

'Before what?'

'Before I found that,' he said, pointing to the page.

'And this changes things how?'

'Well, I'm thinking your sister might pay more?' said Hal, a mischievous grin appearing on his darkened features. It looked more menacing in the half-light, like a dog baring its teeth before it bites.

'Where's the original?' she asked.

'The DA's office have it. I sent it in a few days ago.'

'What?'

'It has no value without me. Don't you see? It's practically worthless without my testimony.'

'What have you told the DA about it?'

'Very little, but they're anxious to talk.'

'How much is your testimony worth?' she asked.

'Ten, to you. Upfront.'

'I don't have that kind of cash,' she said.

'That's your problem. You've got till nine o'clock tomorrow morning, then I'm talking to your sister. I can swing my testimony either way, depending on who is willing to pay more.'

He flung open the back door to the kitchen, returned to his mistress in the restaurant and let the door close behind him.

She put her hands on her hips. She didn't have ten million dollars right now. When her inheritance came in, she could realize that kind of cash without much difficulty, but right now – impossible.

Breaking into a run, she pounded down the alley, and by the time she reached the streetlights she had a plan.

TWENTY-SIX

EDDIE

'I don't know how long it's been since that night,' I said. 'When I think of it, I can't quite piece it all together. The memory is not all there. Just fragments. Maybe that's a good thing. A shrink would tell me that's a symptom of trauma.'

I ran my fingers along the lettering on the tombstone.

MARY ELIZABETH HARPER

I couldn't bring myself to read the rest. Even though Harper, and her partner in the PI firm, Joe Washington, had been out of the FBI for almost two years, the Bureau gave her a full honors funeral. Joe wouldn't talk to me. Her former colleagues were more accommodating. They let me stand with the rest of the mourners at the graveside, probably because I'd come with Harry. When the service was over, one agent approached me. Paige Delaney. Together with Harper, we'd worked a case not so long ago. Paige and Harper saved my life. She was an analyst at the FBI Behavioral Analysis Unit. And one of the smartest people I knew. She'd been in New York for months, tracking the Coney Island killer.

'Joe will come around,' she said. 'He's hurting because he wasn't there to save her.'

I nodded my thanks, but I knew things would never heal. Joe was blaming himself, and me, for not being there when she needed us. I didn't blame him. I should have been the one there. I should have told her sooner how much she meant to me. Maybe if I had just gone to the house earlier she would still be alive. The night of the killing, I'd stood in front of the mirror, trying to psych myself up to go over there and tell her. If I'd been a braver man none of this would've happened.

Paige put a hand on my shoulder, said, 'I asked NYPD if I could take a look at the file. I'm working a profile of Harper's killer. If I hear anything . . . I mean . . . if they catch somebody, you'll be the first to know.'

'Thanks, I appreciate it.'

With that, she turned and left, joining her fellow agents. Paige was in her fifties, single and married to the job. Her silver hair blew around her black suit jacket, and I felt another thump in my chest. Harper would never get to that stage of life. My marriage had ended partly because I pushed my family away for their own safety. My line of work brings me into contact with bad people, but that's not it. Somehow, my life has brought nothing but pain and loss to those around me. To those who I loved most dearly.

Not only had Harper lost her life, I felt like a part of mine had been taken. A chance to be happy with someone that I loved.

Harper's death turned something over in me. Something dark that had always been there. I had suppressed it, fought it down with friends, with Amy, with Harper. Now I could control it no longer.

I peered over the headstone. Sun was almost up on the first day of the Avellino trial.

My lips touched the marble, and I got to my feet.

'I'll find whoever did this,' I said. 'I'm so sorry.'

The base of the headstone was still covered in flowers. Tributes from friends. Cards, washed into pulp with snow and rain. One card looked fresher than the others. It was sitting behind plastic that wrapped a dozen roses together. It was from Sofia.

It read – 'I'm sorry.'

Tears masked my way back to the car. I drove into Manhattan with my knuckles white stars on the steering wheel, my teeth clenched.

I parked outside my office and went upstairs. Harry and Clarence were already inside. Harry sat behind my desk. Clarence lay in his bed; he spent enough time here that I at least wanted him to feel comfortable. Clarence and Harry came as a pair now. Harry was looking over the defense exhibits, which we'd shared with the prosecution and Kate Brooks only last week.

'Don't you think it's been long enough?' said Harry. 'You can't keep doing this.'

'Can't keep doing what?'

'Going to her grave every day. The funeral was almost three months ago now. It's time to start thinking about letting go. A wound won't heal if you keep picking the scab.'

'I don't want to heal. I want to get Sofia acquitted and then find out who did this to Harper.'

My office phone rang. I picked up.

'Eddie Fly, I'm downstairs. Come on outside. We need to talk.'

The voice was New York Italian. Jimmy the Hat Fellini. No one else called me Eddie Fly these days. It was a name that once echoed off the walls of bars, bookies and pool halls. I'd grown up with Jimmy, learned how to box in the same gym. Once you make a friend of Jimmy the Hat you need to have a surgical procedure to get him removed. He was always there when you needed him. Most of the players in New York, in every sphere, had a friend in Jimmy. The head of the New York crime family was a good man to have in your corner.

'Hi, Jimmy. I'll be right down,' I said.

'Eddie—' said Harry, but I cut him off.

'I won't be long,' I told him.

Harry frowned on this side of my personality. Before I was a lawyer, I had a life on the other side of the law. Sometimes I had to step back over that line.

I went downstairs and out onto the street.

A limo sat in the middle of West 46th, its motor running. A garbage truck pulled up behind the limo and the driver stood on the horn. The garbage truck couldn't get past. The limo didn't move. I opened the rear door of the limo. The crew from the garbage truck got out of the cab, and some came around from the rear and began shouting at the limo to move. They were big men. Five of them. With a job to do. And they didn't appreciate being delayed by a limo.

'Move your ass, pretty boy!' they cried.

Jimmy got out of the car, turned to the men and asked, 'Do we have a problem here?'

Everyone knew Jimmy the Hat. If not in person, they knew him by reputation.

The men threw up their arms, instantly, and backed away, apologizing profusely.

'I'm real sorry, sir. We'll reverse back up the street, don't worry about it. We didn't mean no offense.'

Jimmy was a hand grenade. I got into the limo and sat opposite him. He wore black pants, polished handmade Italian shoes, a white button-down shirt open at the neck, and his grandfather's cap, of course. I hadn't seen him without that cap since he took over the Fellini crime family. Nowadays, Jimmy's business was ninety-nine percent legit. He owned a lot of property, had a big slice of legitimate and profitable private businesses, and he had a direct line to the New York planning office. Any developer in Manhattan who wanted a permit could spend two years buried up to their ass in paperwork, or they could call Jimmy. For a fee, they could start building within the month.

He reached over and we embraced. He slapped my back as he released me, in the way of hard men who express their affection with slaps and kisses on both cheeks that kind of hurt but meant well. I didn't know a kiss could cause me physical pain until I befriended Jimmy.

'You look terrible. Are you eating?' he asked.

'I don't have much of an appetite these days.'

'I'm sorry to hear about your girlfriend. I've asked the mayor's office to keep me informed.'

'She wasn't my . . . we were close.'

Silence filled the leather interior of the limo. Jimmy nodded, wet his lips.

'Like I said, the mayor's office will let me know if the cops find a suspect,' he said. Jimmy was practical – if someone hurt a friend, or God forbid a member of his family, Jimmy would ensure that justice was served. He had been a longtime associate of Frank Avellino, and Jimmy still had friends in the mayor's office it seemed. If Jimmy wanted information on any murder case in the city, he could get it in a heartbeat.

'Was she working any dangerous cases? Anyone have a grudge against her?'

I shook my head.

'Far as I know the only case she was working was mine – the Avellino trial. She put some bad people away when she was a fed. I think the cops did a full check on her previous cases – making sure no one with a reason to kill Harper had recently been released from federal prison. They got zip.'

'It looked like a professional job,' said Jimmy. 'You don't take somebody out like that in their own house and disappear. At least it was quick, Eddie.'

'She died instantly. That's what the cops told me. I don't know. Did you get what I asked for?'

Jimmy glanced to his left and the brown envelope that sat beside him.

'Cops say you were there that night,' said Jimmy.

'Yeah, but I don't remember much about it. She'd already been taken away by the time I got there. I pushed my way into the hall, found her necklace lying on the floor and I just knew she was dead. I took the necklace. I just couldn't leave it lying there.'

At that moment, I felt the need to touch my neck. I wore a Saint Christopher's medal on a chain, for good luck. I'd kept Harper's necklace, got the links mended, and wore it alongside my own. It felt good to let something of ours be together, even if it was only cheap gold.

'I need what's in that envelope, Jimmy. I wasn't thinking straight that night. There might have been something I missed,' I said.

'What's in here ain't good for you to see. I got it, but I don't think you should look.'

'I have to,' I said. 'I can't trust the cops on this one. It's too important. She was too important.'

Jimmy nodded, handed over the envelope.

'You get anything on Frank?' I asked.

'Sure, I've been busy is all. One of my guys from the restaurant, Little Tony P, he's in the goddamn hospital with a brain injury. He got run over crossing the street, for Christ's sake. I'm gonna go see him when we're done here. I got a lot on my mind. Sorry it took so long, but I also had to wait until all my little birds came back to tell me their tales. Frank had a lot of friends and a lot more enemies. I had to be sure his murder wasn't a hit. All the little birds have come home with the same story. There was no motive, no opportunity, no old scores that needed to be settled, no money floating around in the wind, and no contracts on our dearly departed Frank either.'

I had thought as much, but I had to be sure. Jimmy confirmed my fears – this was not a hit on Frank. It was patricide. No question.

'How close were you to Frank?' I said.

'Depends who wants to know. If you're asking me, yeah, we were close. If the DA is asking, then I hardly knew the guy.'

'Did you know Sofia or Alexandra?'

'Frank kept family separate for the most part. Like a lot of my business partners, it's better if the IRS, the FBI and any other three-letter government organization are none the wiser about our relationship. We didn't socialize together when he was in office, but have no doubt, I put his ass in the mayor's chair. He wouldn't have gotten past the primary without the unions. His girls? Birthdays, family celebrations – not that there were many of those – Frank came to the restaurant with them.'

'Either of the girls strike you as peculiar?'

'Peculiar like they could chop up their old man for no reason? No. They didn't like each other, I knew that. Frank was always bitching about it. I know they had a lot of money in that house, but green isn't everything. Family is the most important thing you got. Frank was a widower twice over. You know? That's gotta leave a mark. That wasn't no happy home for those kids. Frank told me . . .'

Jimmy hesitated.

He liked to talk. We had grown up together. Jimmy didn't see me as a lawyer, and I knew enough details to put him in jail for the rest of his life. Not that I would. Ever. We had a mutual trust. The fact that he had hesitated meant he didn't want to betray a confidence that had been given to him by someone else – Frank. Jimmy was old-school that way.

'You can trust me,' I said.

Jimmy looked out the window, gazing up at my building.

'Why don't you got somewhere nice to live, Eddie? This place ain't fit for a man like you.'

'I do fine. Come on . . .'

'Look, what I've got to tell you may not help. It may not help at all. It's probably nothing but . . .'

'Jimmy . . .'

'Frank's first wife. She fell down the stairs, got her neck caught in the bannister. Both girls were in the house. They saw the body. It was fuckin' tragic, you know? Frank came to see me the next day. I got a guy in the city morgue on my payroll. Don't ask me why . . .'

If I was sure of one thing, it was I didn't want to know why Jimmy had a man in the morgue. I could guess though. It didn't take a genius to figure out that some body bags might go into the furnace with an extra corpse inside.

'He asked me for a favor. My guy spoke to the medical examiner. I took care of it.'

'What did you take care of?'

'The autopsy report.'

Harper had obtained this as part of our background. I'd read it. Accidental death. Cause of death was massive trauma to the spinal cord from the tumble on the stairs, resulting in instantaneous death.

I didn't press Jimmy. I simply stayed quiet and let him come out with it.

'There was something missing from the report. It wasn't related to the cause of death. Jane Avellino had a mark on her calf. A bite mark. Small. About the same size as a child's.'

An image flashed into my head, causing me to squeeze my eyes shut. The image felt like a sharp blow, painful, but not physically so. I saw Sofia in the interview room at the First Precinct – blood on her lips and cheeks, a bite mark on her wrist. I shook the thought away, shivered and told myself that was something totally different – it wasn't the same as biting someone else – and she only did that to herself because she didn't have a razor. The scars on her arms spoke to that. Then there was the bite expert, who said the mark on Frank Avellino's chest matched Alexandra's dental impression.

I began to wonder whether Jane Avellino's death was accidental.

'Jesus, you think Sofia or Alexandra bit their mother, she fell down the stairs and broke her neck?'

A darkness drew upon Jimmy's face.

'No, whether she fell or she was pushed is impossible to say. The medical examiner said the bite mark came after.'

'After she was dead?'

'None of this helps you because Frank never found out what really happened. He put both girls into boarding school the month after the funeral. Who could blame him? He made sure the girls saw shrinks while they were away and they kept Frank informed of progress. One of them shrinks told him the bite could've been a reaction to the trauma of finding their mother dead, and maybe they were trying to wake her up. Some shit like that,' said Jimmy, rolling his eyes.

'You don't think so?'

'Frank told me Jane was a hard woman. Tough on the kids, you know? Frank was a tough guy, but he loved his girls. Jane though, I only met the once. I didn't take to her. She was cold. Frank told me she hit the girls. Bit them, too. My old man was good with his fists, but I loved him and I never raised a hand to him. He was my poppy. One of those girls was as tough and cold as their mother.'

'Abuse can scar people. It ruins lives.'

'There's more to it than that. It's a sickness, too. In the soul. All I'll say is this. I don't know no little girl who would find their mother dead on the stairs and then take a bite clean out of her corpse. You still go to church?'

I shook my head.

'I go every Sunday. I spoke to Father Loney about it. He said Frank had a demon living in his house. One of those girls was evil.'

'I don't put much stock in what priests think,' I said.

Jimmy leaned forward, and when he next spoke his voice never rose above a whisper. It was as if he was fearful of someone, or something overhearing him.

'I done things in the past that would make you puke. What happened in Frank's house was something else. One o' them girls took a bite out their dead mother. That's not some little girl that's sick in the head – that's *evil*.'

TWENTY-SEVEN

KATE

The consultation room in the Center Street courthouse was both cold and uncomfortable. Alexandra dressed in a smart black pantsuit with a white silk blouse beneath the jacket. She shivered, and Kate couldn't tell if it was due to the temperature or the thought of the trial due to begin in the next hour.

Bloch wore a navy blazer, blue shirt and tan chinos. This was Bloch dressing up for the jury. She looked professional, and yet casual enough not to be uncomfortable. Kate had suggested Bloch wear a suit for court appearances. She had said nothing in return, and Kate accepted the outfit as a fair compromise.

Pulling down the hem of her skirt over her knees, Kate read the notes for her opening speech to the jury. She had been preparing it for almost a week – practicing in front of the mirror. She had cut it down from an hour and ten, to just ten minutes. The speech touched on all the main points of evidence, highlighted the presumption of innocence, and laid the groundwork for the case against Sofia.

An old, scratched-up table sat between Alexandra and Kate. Alexandra's fingers drummed on the tabletop. In the past weeks, Alexandra had become increasingly nervous, her anxiety building with each passing day. It seemed natural. As long as Kate could keep her own worries and anxieties from the client, things wouldn't get too much for Alexandra.

Sliding her notes to one side, Kate turned her attention to her client.

'You're really scared, and that's completely natural. It's okay to be scared. I'd be worried if you were calm. You just have to get through the next few days. That's all. Remember what I told you?'

Alexandra nodded, said, 'Okay, I'll try it.'

Her fingers quieted and became still. She took in a long breath, and instantly an air of something approaching calm settled over her.

Kate had told Alexandra to wiggle her toes if she was nervous. No one would see her do it. It was an anti-anxiety trick Kate learned in law school. Witnesses, defendants, even lawyers, can't help getting nervous. There was no way to stop it, but there were ways of dealing with it. Consciously wiggling your toes gives anxiety an outlet. No one can see you do it, so you have a calm and confident exterior.

'I'll take two of my meds – that'll help ease it,' said Alexandra. She popped two pills into her hand from a blister pack and swallowed them with water. They were low-level anti-anxiety meds. Alexandra took one every day. Doubling the dose on the first day of a murder trial didn't seem like a bad idea to Kate.

There was a knock on the door behind Kate. Moving off the wall, Bloch unfolded her arms. Opening the door an inch or two, she peered out. Somehow, between Kate and Bloch they had managed to avoid the journalists and hacks that surrounded cases of this type like scavenger birds feasting on a corpse.

'It's Dreyer,' said Bloch.

Kate stood and followed her into the corridor.

'God, what is it? Is it bad?' asked Alexandra. Any pretense of calm evaporated. Her shoulders tensed, her hands came up as if she were about to fend off a blow.

'I'm sure it's fine. Wait here. I'll be back,' said Kate.

In the corridor Dreyer stood with three assistant DAs behind him. All were thin, youthful men who looked at least five years younger than the prosecutor. Little Dreyers in waiting, thought Kate.

In his hands he held a bound document with a laminated cover marked, 'Further Disclosure.'

'What's this?' said Kate. 'Don't tell me this is something I should have been given months ago or I will file notice with the judge – you're giving me great points on appeal before we've even begun.'

'Can we talk alone?' said Dreyer.

Kate eyed the young men behind Dreyer and said, 'Bloch stays.'

'As you wish,' said Dreyer. He stepped forward and the entourage scattered. He held out the document like it was toxic. Having been served with a lawsuit not long ago, she was wary of accepting papers without first knowing what they contained.

'What is it?' said Kate.

'We had a request from Flynn for a toxicology screening on Frank Avellino. Blood and organs were tested. These are the results. I'm not obliged to share them with you, but I figure you and Flynn should at least have a fair fight.'

Kate took the document, flicked through to the conclusion.

'What is Haloperidol?' she asked. Traces had been found in Frank Avellino's liver, brain and blood.

'You have to figure that out for yourself. We're tearing apart the property now, looking for any trace of it. What you should really be pondering is how Flynn knew to test for it when we didn't, and why it was present in Avellino's system at all. My guess is the answers can't be good for your client, Miss Brooks.'

Kate handed the report to Bloch as Dreyer walked away.

Bloch flicked through the pages, read the conclusion and handed the document back to Kate in under a minute. In that time, Kate had accessed her phone's Google search facility and was looking for an academic article on Haloperidol – something, anything more reliable than Wikipedia.

'You don't need to search it,' said Bloch. 'It's a pacifier. An old girlfriend of mine used to work in a geriatric care home in Bay City. Said most of her job was cleaning up shit. In Bay City they liked to keep the patients docile. Liquid Haloperidol in their oatmeal did the trick.'

'It's an antipsychotic. Jesus, they give that to old people?'

'They used to in Bay City,' she said.

'And they don't anymore?'

'Not after I heard about it. I paid a visit to the care manager. Seems like most of their stock of Haloperidol was accidentally poured down a drain in the middle of the night. Same night that the manager had a nasty fall on a torn piece of carpet and broke both of her arms.'

Kate reminded herself how glad she was to count Bloch as a friend. She would never want her as an enemy.

'Why was Frank Avellino taking it? There's no mention of it in his medical records?' said Kate. There was something in that statement that made her think more. Like she was on the precipice of something key to the whole case. Bloch got there before her.

'Maybe Frank didn't know he was taking it,' said Bloch.

Alexandra's head shot up from the desk as soon as Kate returned.

'What did he want?' asked Alexandra.

Kate brandished the document, let it fall on the desk dramatically.

'It's a toxicology report. It says your father had large amounts of a drug in his system when he was murdered – Haloperidol. You ever heard of it?'

Alexandra's shoulders relaxed, her expression changed. Where she had been tense and worried before Kate returned, she now had a very different aspect. Her lips set in something like determination – a fire lit behind her eyes – she said, 'Yes, I've heard of it. I've known about it for years. My sister used to take it when she was young.'

TWENTY-EIGHT

EDDIE

I found a bathroom in the Center Street Courthouse that didn't smell like Marlon Brando's pants in *Apocalypse Now*. The faucet ran cold after a few seconds, and I splashed water on my face and looked in the cracked mirror above the basin.

It was time to flip the switch.

When you're a trial attorney, you have people who rely on you. Lots of people. In a trial, there's one person who has placed their whole life in your hands. You can't let your own shit get in the way. You have to find a way of turning it off so you can do your job. Your kid is sick – *flip the switch*. The bank just took away your house – *flip the switch*. You're sick, depressed and an alcoholic with a dark grief that's eating through your bones – *flip the goddamn switch*.

You have to be able to shut all of that shit out. Get rid of it. Put your head in the game. If you don't, you'll never forgive yourself and your client sure as hell won't forgive you.

I blew out my cheeks, dried my face with a paper towel and flipped the switch.

It was the first day of trial. My priority was to stop it – kick the judge off the case and put the hearing back a few months. I needed some time to get my head straight. It was a risky play, but I had to get rid of this judge.

I came into court late.

The courtroom had been set up for a joint trial. Prosecution table on the left, filled with Dreyer and his cronies. On the right were two defense tables, six feet apart, side by side. Harry sat at the first table with Sofia. There were two empty chairs at our table. One for me, one for Harper. I asked for this seat to be kept empty, and Harry had agreed. Kate Brooks, her investigator, Bloch, and Alexandra sat at the other defense table.

All the tables faced the judge's bench, with the jury seated to the right of the defense tables. To the left of the room, beside the witness stand, a large projector screen had been erected. It sat white and idle. I took my seat beside my client. She held out a hand, I took it and gripped it lightly. It was as reassuring a gesture as I could manage.

'You don't look well,' said Sofia.

'I'm fine. Don't worry. I've been working hard on your case, is all.'

A false smile spread over her lips, which quickly pursed. It was Sofia who then squeezed my hand to reassure me. I didn't look over at Kate or Dreyer. It was game time, and I didn't need any distractions. My head felt like it was filled with cement and if I didn't hold it up straight then it would fall to the desk and crack open.

'ALL RISE,' said the clerk, and Judge Stone swept into court, his black robes billowing behind him like the wings of some black, carnivorous bird. His face was pinched, his nose and lips pointed in a scowl at me and Harry.

The gallery was filled with members of the public, journos and TV reporters. Every man and woman in the courtroom stood to attention, answering the clerk's call to be upstanding for the honorable Judge Stone.

Sofia stood. The prosecution team. Alexandra Avellino, Kate and Bloch. They remained standing until the judge got to his seat, flapped his robes around his midriff and bowed. Standing as the judge enters and exits the courtroom is a mark of respect.

Harry and I didn't move our asses from our seats.

Not one goddamn inch.

Stone noticed this. He gave me a look like I was the worst scum of the earth. Beneath his contempt.

He sat down, his gaze boring into mine. There was a rustle of clothing, creaks from the public benches behind us, and squeaks from the defense and prosecution team as their chairs grated over the parquet floor as they took their seats.

'Something wrong with your legs, Mr. Flynn?' said Stone.

I stood slowly, stretching up to my full height, and said, 'Absolutely nothing, Your Honor.'

'What about you, Mr. Ford?'

'Both legs are in top physical condition, Your Honor,' said Harry.

'I see. Well, then, I think I should probably take this matter up with the Bar disciplinary committee.'

'As a former Justice, I'm one of the disciplinary committee chairs,' said Harry. 'Do you want to hand me the complaint now or email it later? Not that it matters.'

'I think he should write it out now if he has a crayon to hand,' I said.

Slowly, and with all the grace he could muster, Judge Stone rose to his feet. As he stood, his face changed from grey to pink, then a shade close to red.

'I have never been so . . .' He was too angry to speak. White bubbles of spit formed at the corner of his trembling mouth.

I glanced at Harry, he returned the look.

It was working.

'Your Honor!' cried Dreyer. 'These are matters for another time, perhaps? There are more pressing issues than Mr. Flynn's disregard for this court. We wouldn't want to give him ammunition to make an unfounded claim of bias against you.'

Shit.

Harry sighed.

It had almost worked.

We had planned to make Stone explode. He had a weak pressure valve. All racists and bigots do. One word against Harry or me and we were going to make an immediate motion for Stone to recuse himself from the trial on the grounds of bias. He would've denied the motion, we would have had a chance for an immediate appeal, which would have been successful. No appellate judge would take the risk of sending a defendant for trial before a potentially biased judge, because if they were convicted they would be straight back to a higher appellate court, complaining not only about the initial judge but the appellate judge who let the trial go ahead. If the motion for a new trial judge had been granted, any other judge but Stone would split the trials, giving Sofia a fair chance.

Dreyer had spotted our play and took out the quarterback before he could release the ball. Goddamn, but Dreyer was quick-witted. I made sure I would not underestimate him again.

Judge's Stone's eyes narrowed in realization. He worked out that Dreyer was warning him. It took a while, but Stone got there. He sat down, said, 'If there are any further outbursts or episodes of insubordination I shall refer this to the superior judge and he can deal with you two after the trial. Is that clear?'

Harry and I both nodded.

I whispered to Sofia that our attempt at removing this judge and splitting the trial hadn't worked out. It had always been a long shot, and she appreciated this. We would just do our best. She knew the risks and we figured it was worth it, considering the major risk to Sofia was in a joint trial.

At least now Stone was aware of the danger of a bias claim; he would be seen to be fair to the defense in order to distance himself from any such allegation. We wouldn't get an easy ride, but Stone would be careful not to prejudice our client in any of his statements and perhaps give me some extra leeway with my cross-examination. Nothing had been lost with the play. Stone was never an ally. If Judge Stone was in your corner, then you probably needed to take a long hard look at yourself.

'Jury keeper, let's have the jury in court. It's time to get this trial started,' said the judge.

A door opened to our right, and the jury was led in. I was reasonably happy with the jury when we finished selection last week. They looked to be a fair split of people who were as impartial as I could have wanted. Men and women. Some were religious, some weren't. They had a broad spread of backgrounds, careers, and ethnicities. I didn't care about anyone's background. They were all Americans. They were ordinary people who were now under a tremendous burden. They alone would decide this case. I just had to make sure they made the right decision.

Dreyer stood and introduced himself. He had dressed more demurely than usual. He looked formal and plain. Gray suit, white shirt and dark tie. An instrument of the state.

'Members of the jury,' he began. 'I thank you for your service to this court. At the end of this case I will ask the judge to excuse all of you from ever having to serve on a jury for the rest of your lives. Have no doubt, this case will change you. You will see images in this courtroom that will haunt your dreams. You will never be the same. Because for the next few days you will be in the presence of evil. Before you are two women. Sisters. Take a look at them, please.'

Out of the corner of my eye, I caught sight of Harry leaning forward to watch the jurors. I tried to focus on their faces too. I wanted to know if any eyes lingered on either of the defendants. So far, most of their attention tended to focus on Sofia. Her sister, dressed in a black business suit that complimented her tan, and with her blonde hair tied back, appeared the confident, professional woman. Before this day had come, I had meant to ask Harper to take Sofia shopping for a trial outfit – I knew she wouldn't really bother otherwise. She was not confident about her appearance and I could tell she was conscious of the network of scars on her forearms. With Harper gone, I'd forgotten to speak to Sofia about her outfit for court. That's what happens when you don't flip the switch. Sofia wore black pants, and a long-sleeved black sweater. Her dark hair contrasted her pale skin. Alexandra looked as though she'd just come off a private jet after a fruitful Paris business meeting. Sofia looked like she'd just come from an AA meeting.

'The prosecution will show you evidence that ties both women to the brutal murder of their own father – a great patron and public servant of this city – former mayor of New York City, Frank Avellino. Now, take a real good look at these women. They murdered Frank Avellino, their own father, in cold blood.'

Dreyer let that hang there, and the jury took their time to make their evaluations of the defendants. Judging by the looks on the jurors' faces, they didn't seem too impressed – least of all with Sofia.

'These sisters are blaming each other for their father's murder. They will seek to cast doubt on the prosecution evidence, but the evidence in this case can't lie. Both women are tied, by our forensic officers and crime scene specialists, to the murder. We will show you that evidence. It's up to you to evaluate it, make up your own mind and come to a verdict.'

The jurors were still new to the case. They hadn't heard any evidence, hadn't been bored or confused by experts, hadn't had the worry of when the case would be finished so they could get back to their jobs and their lives. Every juror gave Dreyer their undivided attention. And he used every second to the full.

'Last October fourth, a knife was taken from the block in the kitchen. A twelve-inch long kitchen knife made of good steel. One used to prepare family meals. The type of knife any of us could have in their home. This bloodied knife was found in the bedroom. The fingerprints of both defendants were found on this knife. The prosecution accepts that it's possible the prints may have gotten on the knife in a manner not connected with the murder, but they may not. That is up to you to decide. What is clear, is that knife was taken up to Frank Avellino's bedroom, and one or both of the defendants did *this* to him.'

He walked away, back to the prosecution table, and an image flashed up on the projector screen.

Juries aren't supposed to talk. They stay silent. This jury looked at the screen, and they were silent no longer. One juror, a middle-aged woman who worked in home design, let out a wail as she covered her mouth, and then her eyes. Expletives, gasps, even a muted scream erupted from one of the jurors but I couldn't tell which one.

On the screen was a picture of hell.

Frank Avellino lay on his back in his bloodied deathbed. His shirt had been ripped open, and it hung in tatters as if a wild bear had ripped into him with both claws. He no longer had a face, just a mass of tissue and exposed bone and teeth. His eyes were gone, only what looked like dark red pool balls in his sockets.

'Both defendants had the victim's blood on their clothing. Again, this could be because one of them touched him, or tried to revive him in that dark bedroom without realizing he was dead. It's up to you to decide if you accept that explanation. One or both of the defendants murdered this man. This case should result in at least one conviction for one of the defendants. It can end in convictions for both. The evidence against Sofia and Alexandra Avellino is clear.'

He paused, pointed at the picture and concluded his speech with a flourish.

'I know some of you are not religious and that doesn't matter in this courtroom,' said Dreyer. 'But I defy any of you to look at Frank Avellino and say you don't believe in evil. Ladies and gentlemen, that evil is in this room. With you. Right now. Don't let it go unpunished.'

TWENTY-NINE

KATE

Kate made a note on her yellow legal pad in blue ink.

Dreyer is a shock jock. He'll use the violence in this crime to his advantage. He's playing on the jury's emotions. Use it.

She got to her feet and watched Judge Stone introduce her to the jury as counsel for Alexandra Avellino. The speech she had rehearsed had to go out the window. She'd cut it down while listening to Dreyer – there were other plays to be made, and she wanted to turn the tables on the prosecution.

Kate moved out from behind the desk, and walked in silence to the well of the court. This was the center of the courtroom. The equivalent of the pitcher's mound at Yankee Stadium. She laced her fingers together and let her arms fall. She faced the jury. And waited.

Then she turned to the judge and said, 'Your Honor, respectfully, I think the jury have seen enough of that image for now.'

Stone flicked his index finger to Dreyer, and one of his assistant prosecutors killed the projector, returning the screen to a blank canvas. The relief on some of the jurors' faces was welcome. Kate wanted to get up into position to address the jury quickly, and make sure it was her who gave them that relief from the nightmare on screen.

Dreyer wanted that image burned into each juror's retina, but he'd left it up there too long and Kate had swung it to her advantage. That was her play. Take everything Dreyer threw at her and either bat it out of the park or hit it straight at Eddie's client.

'Members of the jury, my name is Kate Brooks. I have the honor of representing Alexandra Avellino.'

Kate paused, and looked at Alexandra. The image had reduced her client to tears. Alexandra sat with her head up and tears lining her face. She dabbed at them with a handkerchief. Kate said nothing for a time. She wanted the jury to see her client's grief. Drink it in, just as much as they had bathed in the prosecution's hellish photograph.

'You will hear a lot of evidence in this case which is circumstantial. My client was at home when her father was murdered. She called the police in a panic when she discovered the body, and hid in the bathroom fearful that her sister would kill her too. All of these circumstances I don't have to prove. They're in black and white in the 911 phone call she made to the police. Before she made the call, she tried to save her father, having discovered him bloodied and torn apart, lying on his bed. Alexandra is not evil. She is a victim here.'

She paused, looked around the jury and saw some of them nodding. This was going better than she had expected. She had to finish it now, get out on a high.

'Alexandra has had an upbringing stained by the loss of loved ones. Losing her mother, and then her stepmother in tragic circumstances. Now that her father is gone, my client believes she no longer has family left. Her sister is no longer family. Her sister took everything from Alexandra. There is one killer in this room, ladies and gentlemen. And it's the person with a history of complex psychiatric conditions, with a documented history of using knives, of self-harm, of addiction and criminality. The killer is on trial. The killer is Sofia Avellino, and you have a duty to my client as a victim to acquit her, and send her sister somewhere she can never harm anyone else again.'

Kate paused again, and noted the smiles and the nods and the attention the jury had given her. It was all about rapport, and she was off to a great start.

She glanced at Bloch and saw her friend sitting with bold admiration on her face. Kate made her way back to her seat.

Bloch leaned over and said, 'You're amazing.'

Alexandra whispered, 'Thank you,' and gave Kate a tearful hug.

The jury watched every moment, and then turned toward Sofia, and Eddie Flynn, with something like contempt in their eyes.

THIRTY

EDDIE

I'd never stood up to give my opening speech to a jury so hostile.

They weren't looking at me, they were focused on Sofia. She looked like a rabbit in the middle of the road, with headlamps coming toward it. Frozen and shivering, waiting to be run over flat.

I told her it was okay, and Harry patted her hands. She had both hands spread out on the table, one on top of the other. Her fingers were shaking. Harry steadied them, but really he was using his palm to cover them. Sofia's anxiety could translate as fear. The fear of someone who has done something terrible and has just been found out.

I didn't stand in the well of the court. Kate had done such a number on us, and the jury had clearly liked her, that I didn't want any comparisons in the jury's mind. Instead I walked right up to the jury and stopped only a few feet from the first row. I put my hands in my pockets and I thought about what I was going to say.

I had a speech prepared, but now it sounded flat in my head. I couldn't use it. I had to come up with something new. Kate was riding on Dreyer's coat-tails. Every point Dreyer made in the case, Kate was going to deflect it onto Sofia. There were no easy plays. The jury was being told a story in this case. And right now they liked the one they were hearing.

My story had to be different. It had to be better.

Whoever tells the best story wins.

I cleared my throat, and took my time to make eye contact with some jurors. The jurors that I had selected in the last few days. Seven women. Five men. One male alternate, one female. Most of the women on the jury were at least ten years' older than Sofia. All of them held jobs. A cleaner. A van driver. A chef. A hotel maid.

A coffee shop manager. A retired teacher. The female juror who was about a year or so younger than Sofia was a student at NYU. She at least held my gaze without defiance. This juror hadn't made up her mind yet.

The men were a mix of laborer, telemarketer, web designer and two wannabe actors who both waited tables in chain restaurants while they waited for Mr. Spielberg's call.

I was tempted to ape Kate's chosen line of defense. Whatever she and Dreyer hit me with I could throw it back at them. Kate, despite her inexperience, was a natural. Perhaps an even better opponent than Dreyer.

I looked at Alexandra now. And the jury followed my gaze. To save Sofia I should destroy Alexandra. That's what the job demanded. If the jury believed Alexandra then Sofia was in trouble. To top it all, I believed in my client, which made Alexandra the murderer. I should be going all out to destroy her.

The innocent should be set free. The guilty punished. All of that goes out the window in a joint trial. The only real opponent is the prosecutor – they have the burden of proving guilt beyond a reasonable doubt. If you lose sight of that, and start a war with your co-defendant, they'll fight back and you destroy each other in front of the jury, who will inevitably think both are lying. All the while, the prosecutor gets to put his feet up, and occasionally toss in a ball for the defendants to fight over and hurl at each other.

The best way to lose this case was to fight with Kate Brooks. I believed Sofia was innocent, and the only thing I cared about right then was getting her an acquittal. To do that, I had to focus on Dreyer as much as possible and ignore Alexandra.

Alexandra wiped her red, raw eyes. She looked like any other successful, attractive Manhattan socialite in her business suit, manicured nails and five-hundred-dollar haircuts. She didn't look like a killer. She looked nervous. One hand reached out and I saw her touch the defense table, running her index finger over the wood grain in small, concentric circles. Nerves, I guessed. I glanced back at Sofia, and saw again a young woman in so much pain, just trying to hold it together.

I couldn't do the job of prosecutor and defense attorney. It just wasn't in me.

'Ladies and gentlemen of the jury. I represent Sofia Avellino in this case. Like Alexandra, she has lost her father too. I won't say to you that the killer is in this room. That's far too presumptive of me. The only people who get to decide this case are you. Each one of you will listen to the evidence in this trial and then you will decide upon a verdict. I don't have to prove to you that Alexandra is the killer, nor do I have to prove my client's innocence and anyone who says differently in this case, be it Miss Brooks or Mr. Dreyer, well, they're wrong.

'It falls on the prosecution to prove their case, but guess what? The prosecutor isn't going to tell you who killed Frank Avellino. Mr. Dreyer will present evidence that it could have been either one of the defendants. And he'll leave it up to you. I say that's not good enough, members of the jury. You cannot fill in blanks for the prosecutor. He might say both women carried out the murder, but why then did they blame each other and call the cops on each other?'

I paused and took a step forward, so I was closer to the jury. It was working. I asked them a question and beyond all my hopes, some of them were actually thinking about it. I needed them to think, to question everything, not to be blindly fed the facts by the other lawyers.

'It doesn't make sense, does it?'

Two jurors shook their heads.

'Maybe one of the women in this room did kill Frank Avellino, but the prosecutor isn't going to tell you which one. He wants both of the defendants convicted if possible. But I think you know that's not possible. And if the prosecution does not prove, beyond all reasonable doubt, who killed Frank Avellino then there is one thing you must do, ladies and gentlemen – you must acquit.

'And I will only ask you do to two things in this case. Listen to the evidence. And if by the end of this trial you are not sure who killed Frank Avellino, then you must acquit both defendants, because the prosecution has failed to make its case. Thank you. I know I can rely on you all.'

I sat down, in better shape than when I first stood up. Some of the jury would think and evaluate the case properly and that's all I could ask.

Sofia leaned over, fresh tears in her eyes and determination on her face, and she said, 'Alexandra killed my father. I want you to make sure she pays for it. Don't do it this way.'

'Sofia, I'm trying to save your life. Let me do my job.'

She blinked, and tears fell on the papers laid out on the table. 'He was my dad. And she killed him. She has to pay for it.'

THIRTY-ONE

KATE

Eddie's opening speech had surprised Kate. She felt sure he was going to lay some bombshell in the middle of the court, and watch it blow her defense wide open.

He didn't.

He wasn't coming after Alexandra. It was a high-risk strategy, but smart. It relied on the jury taking their oath seriously, and deciding that if they couldn't choose between Alexandra and Sofia as to who was the real killer, then they had to acquit. Technically, the argument was sound.

Bloch whispered, 'He's good, but that's never going to work.'

'Why not?' said Kate.

'This jury saw that photograph of Frank. If they believe one of the sisters did it, they're not leaving this courtroom unless someone is made to pay for it.'

Kate nodded, then saw Dreyer stand and call his first witness.

'Detective Brett Soames,' said Dreyer.

Kate flicked through her legal pad, looking for the notes she'd marked with pink tabs. While she found the pages, she heard Soames come forward. She recognized him from the night of the murder, when she first met Alexandra in the cells. He had worn a truly awful yellow shirt. The shirt had been terrible enough to stick in mind. It was that bad.

Soames was tall, mid-fifties, with tight greying hair. The yellow shirt had been given the day off, but the replacement didn't look much better. He wore a navy suit and green shirt with a blue and white striped tie. It looked like an odd ensemble. Kate wondered if he was color-blind. As Soames held up the Bible, Kate noticed the notch on Soames' left ring finger. He had been used to wearing a wedding ring, until recently. Made sense – no spouse would let their man walk out of the house wearing a suit and tie combo like that.

Once Soames had been sworn in, Judge Stone told him to take a seat and then took a moment to make sure the detective had water and whatever else he needed to make himself comfortable in the witness stand.

To settle the witness, Dreyer asked some easy questions about the detective's length of service on the force, and his experience. He was a career cop. He'd been in homicide for the best part of fifteen years. This was not his first rodeo.

'Detective, how were the police first alerted to this crime?' asked Dreyer.

'The defendants both made 911 calls from their cell phones,' said Soames. As he spoke, he made a point of turning toward the jury and delivering his answer to them. He didn't smile, didn't even appear friendly to the jury. He struck Kate as an honorable cop who was simply here to do his job and tell it like it was. A prosecutor's dream witness.

'Your Honor, I think it would be prudent at this time to play the 911 calls for the jury.'

'I agree, that okay with you, detective?' asked the judge.

Kate had never seen a judge be so pro-police before. You can score all the high marks you want in the bar exam, you can know every piece of case law and precedent and ace your way through every mock trial that's thrown at you, but nothing prepares you for this. Even if you're completely factually and legally accurate in your argument – you can still lose in front of a biased judge. This was the real world now.

Dreyer signaled to one of his assistants, and Kate put down her pen and listened while the PA system kicked into life and the first tape was played.

It was Alexandra.

Bloch opened a file and read along with the transcript. Alexandra swallowed and closed her eyes as she heard her own voice, and the fear that was rifled through each word like a fat seam of gold running through bedrock.

The jury listened too, and Kate paid close attention. They were drinking it in.

The tape finished dramatically, with the dispatcher losing Alexandra on the line, not knowing her fate.

'And the second call, please,' said Dreyer.

This was Sofia's call, which had come into the 911 emergency response center almost a minute after Alexandra's. The tremors in Sofia's voice sounded real enough to Kate. If she had to make an assessment of both calls, she would say Sofia was the most scared on the phone.

Closing the file with the call transcript, Bloch folded her arms and leaned back. She must've made the same assessment.

Sofia sounded more real.

Kate had no doubt her client's fear had been very real at the time; this just meant that Sofia was better at faking it.

'Detective Soames, you were tasked to the scene by the NYPD response unit?'

'Yes,' said Soames. 'The response unit had secured the property, and the scene. Given that both occupants of the property had blood on them, and were both reporting that the other had carried out the murder, the response officers had placed them both in custody. When I arrived at the scene both defendants had been arrested, and read their rights. I then spoke to both women.'

Kate's pen, which had been moving across the page, making notes of every word of evidence given by Detective Soames, suddenly halted.

Soames had not previously disclosed any conversation with the defendants at the scene. It wasn't in his deposition. This was all new. She shot a look at Eddie and saw his jaw tighten, the muscles creasing above the jawline. He hadn't seen this coming either.

Both were in uncharted territory.

'Who did you speak to first?' asked Dreyer.

'I spoke to Alexandra Avellino.'

'And what did she say?'

Before Soames turned his head away from Dreyer, and delivered his answer to the jury, he gave Kate a passing look. Kate knew, right then, this was bad.

'Can I refer to my notes?' asked Soames.

The judge and Dreyer nodded. Soames reached into his jacket pocket and produced a notebook. Copies had not been served on Kate, and she doubted Eddie had seen them either.

'Alexandra said – *Arrest that bitch. She killed my father. She'll kill me.* I noted this and then I spoke to Sofia Avellino.'

'What did Sofia Avellino say?'

'She said – *You have to arrest Alexandra, she did this. She's evil. She's ruined my life.*'

Dreyer nodded.

This wasn't as bad as Kate had first thought. The accusations kind of cancelled each other out – but only so far.

'Before we go on to talk about the crime scene, I noticed that when you spoke to the defendants at the scene, neither Sofia Avellino nor Alexandra Avellino asked about their father's condition. Did you tell either of them he was dead?'

'I did not.'

'And at any point, either at the scene or in the precinct during questioning, to your knowledge, did Sofia Avellino or Alexandra Avellino ask about their father's current medical condition?'

'No, sir. They did not. I guess they already knew because—'

'Objection,' said Kate. 'The officer's guesses are not evidence. He is not giving expert testimony.'

Kate's knees had already bent, and she was in the process of sitting down, her objection clear, precise and one hundred percent correct when she heard Judge Stone say, 'Overruled.'

Kate got back up, 'Your Honor, the witness is speculating on—'

'Miss Brooks,' said Stone, 'I realize you are not overly familiar with courtroom proceedings, but your objection has been ruled upon. This is a highly experienced homicide detective who has no doubt attended at hundreds of serious crime scenes and spoken to thousands of people at those scenes over the long course of his distinguished career. If he wants to give his opinion on this matter, the court would welcome it.'

Kate felt like she was five years old. Knowing the rules, and expecting the judge to abide by the rules in the real world, appeared to be two different things. She had to learn fast.

'Sorry, could you repeat your answer, detective?' said Dreyer.

'Yes, whenever we speak to relatives of the victim, it's my experience they just want to know if that person is still alive. Doesn't matter how badly they appear to be injured, it's always the first thing they ask. They're hoping, beyond hope, that their loved one is still going to make it. In this case, it was unusual that neither of them asked if Frank was still alive. Highly unusual. I think that's because they both knew he was already dead.'

'In both 911 calls they say their father was attacked. They don't say he is dead, is that correct?'

'Correct. They would also know that all 911 calls are recorded.'

'And did they ask for a paramedic in the 911 calls?'

'Yes, both of them asked for an ambulance.'

'And yet they didn't ask about their father's condition when police and ambulance arrived? Why is that?'

'They knew he was dead already,' said Soames.

'Why do you think they knew he was dead?'

'One way is putting a twelve-inch knife through both of his eyes. That'll do it.'

Kate objected, the judge nodded.

'Let's move on, shall we? I'd like to have photograph E.3.8 on screen, please,' said Dreyer. And sure enough the screen was soon made up of a picture from a horror movie. A wider shot of the decimated corpse of Frank Avellino lying on his back, in bed.

'Can you describe the scene for us, detective?'

'This is the master bedroom on the second floor of the deceased's property in Franklin Street. The photo was taken at the door to the room. There were no lights on in this room when the patrol officers arrived, they turned them on when they saw the dark staining on the carpet around the bed. You can see multiple footprints. One is patrolman Jacobs – wearing standard NYPD issue boots. The tread is distinctive so we can pick it up easily at this type of crime scene. He had felt for a pulse on the victim, found none. The other sets of bloodied footprints surrounding the bed belong to Sofia Avellino and Alexandra Avellino.'

The jury focused their attention on Soames, and only a few occasionally flicked a glance at the photograph.

'Can you describe the condition of Frank Avellino's body when you arrived?'

Clearing his throat, Soames took a sip of water before he spoke. As if he was steadying himself for what was to come.

'My partner, Detective Isiah Tyler, we've been together now for five years. We've seen some things in our time. Nothing like this. Tyler saw the body, and had to leave the room. There was a very strong smell from the blood, and the body. We were used to that, but we weren't used to seeing wounding this extensive on a victim. At first I thought the victim had been shot point-blank, center mass, with a shotgun. Then, when I got closer, I saw it wasn't a gun wound. These were individual strikes with a long-bladed knife. Most were stab wounds, and I think I lost count when I hit forty. There were slashes with the knife too. As you can see, part of the victim's nose has been cut away, there are horizontal slashes across the throat and . . .'

Soames stopped talking, looked down, then looked up and continued.

'. . . and the sternum. There were stab wounds to both eye cavities, and the eyes had eight-ball hemorrhages due to massive trauma. It looked to me like any number of those wounds could have proved to be fatal. Yet the killer continued to mutilate the body. There were two wounds which were significant in the investigation.'

'Which were?'

'A stab wound to the chest, which I saw had a long brown hair protruding from it. And a bite mark on the victim's chest.'

'Tell us about the stab wound first,' said Dreyer.

'I used a set of pincers, and carefully removed the hair, while the crime scene forensics officer looked on and photographed it. The hair had been stuck, deep in the wound, as you can tell from the blood staining on the last two inches of the hair. The hair was sealed in an evidence bag and submitted for further testing.'

'And the bite mark?'

'It was photographed and was the subject of specialist analysis.'

Dreyer turned the pages of notes on his desk.

'In your experience as an NYPD homicide detective, would you say these wounds were inflicted by one person?'

'That's impossible to say. It could have been a single assailant, or two or three. From the looks of it, they used the same knife. The knife we found on the floor, by the bed.'

'Is this the knife?' said Dreyer, holding aloft a kitchen knife wrapped in plastic.

'That is the knife.'

'One last question. Were there any defensive wounds on the victim? Any signs that he had struggled with his attacker, or tried to defend himself?'

Soames turned to the jury and said, 'No. In knife attacks we sometimes see wounds on the hands or forearm. There were none on this victim. He was taken unawares and probably fatally stabbed before he could take defensive action.'

'Thank you, Detective Soames.'

Kate got up out of her seat fast. There was a lot of evidence she didn't need to challenge right now. Some she could not let pass, and it had to be dealt with immediately.

'Detective, you wrote down in your notebook the statements made by Sofia Avellino and Alexandra Avellino at the scene. Yet you neglected to mention these in your deposition. Why?'

'My deposition charted my investigation. The statements were entered into the record when both defendants were booked into custody. I didn't need to mention them in my deposition as they had already been accurately recorded in central booking.'

Kate's breath caught in her chest. She had messed up the question. Made it much too loose. She had asked for an explanation, and she'd gotten one. The jury was nonplussed. She could have handled that better. She thought carefully about the next question, framed it in her mind before she opened her mouth.

'Looking at that picture of Frank Avellino, isn't it obvious, even to a loved one, that Frank is dead?' she said.

'I couldn't say,' said Soames.

'He looks dead, detective, doesn't he?'

'He appears to be badly wounded. No one could say those wounds are fatal just by looking at him. Both defendants asked for a paramedic in the 911 calls,' said Soames, formally.

'Both my client and Sofia Avellino approached him, and touched him. Might they have realized that he was dead then?'

'They might. But then why ask for a paramedic when they dialed 911? That doesn't make sense.'

'If they held him and thought he had died from those terrible wounds, that would explain why Alexandra did not ask you if her father was dead, wouldn't it?'

'It might.'

'It does, doesn't it?' said Kate, pressing for a better answer.

'It's one explanation, but I don't buy it,' said Soames and she thought that was the best she could get out of him. 'The other explanation is that your client knew Frank was dead because she'd spent time ripping him to pieces,' said Soames.

Kate nodded, and on her way back to her seat at the defense table, she saw two or three jurors look at Alexandra curiously. It was look of wonder, and disgust. She'd lost some jurors on Soames. This was going to be harder than she'd thought.

THIRTY-TWO

EDDIE

I was tempted not to ask Soames anything at all. His testimony had been damaging, but not too bad. Kate had done her best to minimize it, but her opening question wasn't tight enough. Not her fault. Some witnesses need a tighter leash than others and you can't know that until you ask your first question. Years of experience can give you an advantage, but Kate was doing better than I did on my first murder trial.

I stood, decided I had to shake the tree some more. See what fell out.

'Detective Soames, when the defendants made these statements to you at the scene, I suppose both defendants had been arrested, and read their Miranda rights before they spoke to you?'

'Of course,' said Soames.

Even if that weren't true, that was the answer you got from every cop in the city when you asked that question. No cop is going to admit a suspect said anything significant without first being given their right to remain silent. If they didn't have their rights read to them, the statement was largely inadmissible. Soames would never admit to talking to a suspect without them being Mirandized.

'Are you sure both defendants had been arrested and Mirandized before you spoke to them at the scene?'

'I am one hundred percent certain,' he said, with a degree of satisfaction. He had delivered this affirmative answer with a smug smile to the jury. Little did he know, he'd just handed me his heart on a plate. I wouldn't rip it from him yet. I had to wait until the right time.

'Detective Soames, you consider the statements made by the defendants at the scene to be significant, yes?'

'Correct.'

'I thought so. You seem to be implying that because Alexandra and Sofia did not ask you if their father was still alive, that means they killed him?'

'It's a logical conclusion.'

'Let us remind ourselves here that the prosecution maintain there is evidence against both of these defendants. If one defendant makes a significant statement to you, at the crime scene, well, isn't that vital evidence for the prosecution case?'

'Yes.'

'You knew this was important evidence when you wrote it down in your notebook at the scene, didn't you?'

'I guess I did.'

'And given that it's so vital, you didn't think to include it in your deposition or give copies of your notebook to the prosecutor so they could be disclosed to the defense teams?'

'I gave all relevant information to the DA's office.'

'But not a copy of the relevant pages from your notebook?'

He paused.

If he lied and said yes he could jeopardize the credibility of the prosecutor; if he told the truth then he had no way of knowing what kind of blind alley I was leading him down.

'I must've overlooked my notes. I don't think I gave a copy to the District Attorney's office.'

'You don't think you did? The former mayor of New York City is lying dead, torn to pieces in his bedroom, you have two suspects in custody, according to you both of them made significant statements, and you don't think you handed over a note of those statements? Either you did, or you did not. Which is it?'

Soames cleared his throat, tried to regain some composure, then looked to the jury and said, 'I did not.'

It was my turn to hit the pause button. Let that sink in for the jury. It was a minor point, but I wanted to let it chew up the furniture for a while.

'Are you incapable of conducting a basic investigation, Detective Soames?'

He didn't bother to look at the jury for his answer, he shot it straight back at me with a little heat on the return.

'My record speaks for itself. My department has one of the highest homicide clearance rates in this city, or any other city for that matter.'

'Then as an experienced and talented investigator you wouldn't make such a basic error of not handing over vital information to the DA's office?'

'I guess . . .'

'Detective, the statements made by the defendants at the scene are not significant at all, are they?'

'They are. Alexandra and Sofia didn't ask if their father was alive because they both knew he was already dead, because they had made *damn sure* he *was* dead.'

'There's another reason neither of the defendants asked if their father was alive, isn't there?'

'Not one that I can see. In all my years as a homicide detective, it has never occurred before.'

'Earlier, you confirmed that before the defendants were questioned at the scene, they had been read their rights, remember?'

'I remember. I'm certain. They had been read their rights.'

'Suspects are only read their rights after they are arrested, yes?'

'Correct,' said Soames, who was tiring of this.

I took a page from the prosecution disclosure and handed it to the clerk.

'Look at this document, please. This is the arrest record. Arresting officer was patrolman Jacobs?'

'Correct,' said Soames.

'And both defendants were arrested on a single charge?'

'Yes,' said Soames, wary now of where this might lead.

Time to take him out.

'According to the record, patrolman Jacobs arrested both defendants for murder. Might that be where they got the idea that their father was dead?'

Soames swallowed, his Adam's apple bobbing up and down in his throat.

'You can't be arrested for murder unless there's a dead body, right?'
He didn't answer. He didn't need to.

'Detective, there is precious little evidence against these defendants. You and the prosecutor are clutching at thin straws trying to make a case, isn't that what's really happening here?'

Soames cleared his throat, took a sip of water, leaned toward the mic and said, 'No, sir.'

Soames had taken the hair from deep in the wound on Frank Avellino's chest. The hair-fiber expert and Detective Tyler would have more to say about it, but I just needed to cover my bases with Soames.

'You testified that you removed a strand of hair from a wound in the victim's chest, detective. You are not a hair-fiber analysis expert, are you?'

'No sir, we have Professor Shandler for that.'

'Good. Nothing further.'

Dreyer didn't try and repair any of the damage, not that there was much he could have done. It did look to me like the DA was scrabbling for any scrap of evidence that tended to show guilt – anything that could be spun in the prosecution's favor was going to be thrown at us along with the kitchen sink.

'The People call Detective Isiah Tyler,' said Dreyer.

Soames left the witness stand and exchanged nothing more than a look with Tyler. It was a warning. Be careful. Tyler was much younger than Soames, and more hot-headed. More easily led into an ambush by a clever lawyer.

Tyler dressed all in black, as befitted the occasion. Shirt, tie, suit, shoes. He took the oath and got comfortable in the witness stand.

'Detective Tyler, you carried out investigations in relation to the victim and his family?' asked Dreyer.

'I did,' said Tyler. 'My partner and I shared the workload on this case. It so happened that I took a call from a lawyer named Mike Modine, the night of the murder. A Saturday. He told me that he had an appointment to see the victim on Monday to discuss a change to the victim's will.'

'Did you obtain a copy of the victim's will?'

'I did. The executor of the will is Hal Cohen. Mr. Cohen was the campaign manager and friend of the victim. He provided a copy of the last will to me. It's marked Exhibit 6 in the bundle.'

There was downtime while the jury, who now had cause to open the papers in front of them, flicked to the correct exhibit and began reading.

'This will is five years old now, is that right?' asked Dreyer. He was leading the witness, but I didn't object. It wasn't prejudicial and he was moving things along.

'That's right. The will was made in 2014 at Mr. Modine's offices.'

'What is the effect of this will, detective?'

'The will leaves some charitable donations totaling a million dollars, and then the remainder of the deceased's estate is divided equally between his daughters, Alexandra and Sofia Avellino.'

'Were you able to ascertain the value of Frank Avellino's estate?'

'Yes, Mr. Cohen had been given a valuation for tax purposes. The total estate is forty-nine million dollars. After taxes are paid, and the charitable donations performed, the residue of the estate totals forty-four million dollars.'

There was a wolf whistle from someone in the crowd behind us. The judge mustn't have heard it because he didn't remonstrate with the people in the gallery. There were more than a few whispers, murmurs and intakes of breath at that figure. Even some from the jury. That was a shitload of money by anyone's standards.

'Now, we know from Mr. Modine's call that the deceased wished to make changes to his will. And had arranged to meet Mr. Modine on Monday morning for those purposes. Do you know what changes were to be made?'

'I can't say for certain. However, we have reason to believe that the deceased was subject to undue influence at the time of his death.'

'What do you mean, undue influence?'

'Frank Avellino was being drugged, without his knowledge. We believe, from the type of drug used, the purpose was to exert some measure of control over Mr. Avellino and his money.'

The jury leaned forward. I couldn't help looking at Sofia at this point. Her hand was drawn across her open mouth, and she turned and gazed with hurt and pain at her sister. We'd told her about the theory, and the toxicology report. Hearing it from your lawyer was one thing, but listening to it going on the record in a public court was another.

Alexandra had her head down, her shoulders heaving as she wept.

Taking his time, Dreyer took Tyler through the results of the toxicology report, and explained it to the jury. Haloperidol was an antipsychotic drug that, administered in the right doses, rendered people docile, suggestible and easily controlled.

'Detective, you said the victim was drugged with this substance, but why do you say that? Could Frank Avellino have been taking this drug himself?'

'I don't believe so. His medical records show that this was not a drug which had been prescribed to him. Also, he had seen his family physician in the months leading up to his death as he had been experiencing symptoms that could have been early-onset dementia. This could also have been because the drugs in Mr. Avellino's system were producing the symptoms of dementia. The physician recommended an MRI scan for December. Mr. Avellino never made it that far.'

'If someone is administered Haloperidol without their knowledge, what does that suggest to you?' asked Dreyer.

'That someone wanted Frank Avellino under their control. They could have persuaded him to sign a power of attorney, say.'

A chill flooded through me. Dreyer was going somewhere with this that I hadn't foreseen. I turned to an exhibit page in the prosecution bundle and looked at the document again. Dreyer had been working his way up to this, and Tyler opened the door a little wider to let him in. Dreyer directed the jury and the witness to the same page.

'Detective, what is this document at Exhibit 228?'

'This is a power of attorney, executed on September fifteenth. It grants his appointed representatives power over all Mr. Avellino's property and affairs.'

'And who are the named representatives for Mr. Avellino?'

Tyler spoke slowly and carefully as he said, 'They are Mr. Hal Cohen, and Miss Alexandra Avellino.'

Frank Avellino
Journal Entry, September 15, 2018

I don't know what to believe anymore. Either I'm going crazy or someone is trying to kill me.

In a way, I kind of hope someone has taken out a contract on my life. That's preferable to me losing my mind. I can deal with a contract. Jimmy can take care of it.

I spoke to Jimmy this morning and he said I was paranoid. No one would dare put out a hit on me. And no one would think of robbing me, not when I'm one of Jimmy's old friends. That shit just doesn't happen.

An old man slipping into my goddamn dotage. I was convinced he was wrong. I'd hired a private investigator who was keeping an eye out for anyone following me. Hal thought it was a waste of time and money, but it made me feel better. The PI was a big guy named Bedford and he told me I wouldn't even see him. True enough, since he started two weeks ago, I hadn't seen him so far. That didn't help. I felt that maybe he wasn't watching me at all – maybe he was at home in bed watching TV, thinking I was just another paranoid schmuck. But I knew it, I'd seen the biker watching me.

Then when I left the restaurant, I stood on the sidewalk and noticed my shoe was untied. I knelt down, and goddamn it, I must've been down there ten minutes and I couldn't remember how to tie my shoe. I just knelt there on one knee, the laces in my hands, staring at my brown shoe until tears fell on the leather toecap.

I tucked the laces into the sides of the shoe and took a cab home.

10 p.m.

I wasn't hungry tonight. Just made myself a sandwich.

The soup Sofia made yesterday was still in the fridge. The stew Alexandra sent over from the deli sat beside it. I made myself a peanut butter and jelly sandwich with a glass of milk and watched the news. Feeling better tonight. My head is clearer, for the first time in days.

Call from the PI service. I told them Bedford hadn't been in touch with me by phone or text. No, I didn't know where he was – he'd told me that I wouldn't see him, for Christ sake. They are assigning a new operative in the morning.

Bedford is missing. There's a police appeal for information on the news.

I'm in bed now. Can't sleep. Headache that won't quit.

And a bad feeling in my stomach. I called Alexandra, left a message. Called Sofia and she picked up, said she would come and see me tomorrow.

THIRTY-THREE

SHE

For all her preparations, both physical and psychological, nothing had prepared her for the feeling she experienced seeing Father's bloodied corpse blown up on a large screen. She had kept no trophies from her kills. Nothing as a reminder of those moments of exquisite pleasure. Seeing the photographs gave her a warm feeling, low in her stomach, and sent her heart fluttering.

She could almost taste his flesh.

This was overwhelming. She tried to think of the song in her head; the rhythms of that song would dissipate the rush that was coursing through her system. She noticed then that her right hand was touching the table, her index finger working into the notches on the desk made by a thousand heavy, metal-edged folders. Abruptly, she took her hand away, placed it in her lap.

The day was going fine. As she had expected. Detective Tyler had exaggerated the effects of Haloperidol in his testimony. It was not a drug that caused people to become completely compliant; in some ways it had made Father more difficult – but he had signed that power of attorney. A few months of poison in his food and poison in his ears would have turned him against her sister. Then, she would have persuaded him to change his will, then let him slide away in a gentle overdose. The drug itself doesn't kill, but enough will shut down the respiratory system, or cause heart failure in the process. No medical examiner or pathologist would look beyond respiratory failure or a cardiac arrest in a man of her father's age.

The problem was, she had underestimated Father.

If she had paid more attention to him then she would not have had to bring forward her plans. Somehow, deep down, she thought

Father had always known about her. He had seen the bite mark on Mother's leg, and he had covered it up. Or perhaps, on some level, he could not face the sure knowledge of who she really was. Her nature would horrify any parent. And yet he never confronted her, but he could not live with either of them in the wake of their mother's death.

He had sent them away. She felt that in the years immediately after her mother's death, Frank blamed them both. He knew one of them bit Jane, but he never spoke of it. The shame, perhaps. When she graduated high school, Frank seemed to have forgotten, or at least put his doubts to one side.

Four years ago, when she had fed three bottles of OxyContin into Frank's second wife, Heather, he should have known that things had not changed. That his daughter had not changed. Heather had her own problems, addiction the most prevalent. He could accept an accidental overdose easily – so had the authorities.

Heather had not accepted it. Not at first.

She had called at the family home knowing Frank was out of town, and that Heather would be alone and drinking. Popping pills was part of the fun. When Heather got too drunk to hold onto her glass, she still hadn't had enough Oxy powder in her vodka and soda. She had to hold her down at one point and force a rubber funnel into Heather's throat so she could pour a bottle of Oxy-laced Chablis into her stomach.

She had stayed with Heather while she died, quietly, and then removed any trace of her presence in the house that night before leaving Heather for Father to find on his return the following week. The house had retained that smell for some time. Heather died in high summer. After the funeral, Frank had to hire an expensive bio-remediation crew to get rid of the smell of her rotting flesh.

Heather's funeral was the last time she had seen Sister. They stood at opposite sides of the open grave. Father in between them at the head of the grave. His head bowed, tears falling onto Heather's casket. Sister didn't look at her. Sister blamed her for everything. She suspected that secretly Sister was jealous.

She had power. Her willingness to do whatever it took gave her that power. Sister was weak. Always had been. Even when they were little, Sister could always be manipulated. A promise of candy, or a book. And then Sister would do what she was told. Even bad things. The difference was when Sister was caught by Mother, she would cry and cry.

Sister cried that day when Mother died on the stairs, and as far as she could tell, Sister hadn't stopped crying since. For some acts, there was no forgiveness. They stained the soul. She knew it that day as her teeth sunk into her mother's skin. Mother didn't cry out, didn't flinch, nor pull away. Some part of her thought that maybe Mother might still be alive. Some part of her brain that hadn't fully shut down from the break in the spinal cord. A part of Mother's brain that made her conscious, and able to feel the pain of the little teeth piercing the skin. She knew this was unlikely, but the frisson of wondering if Mother could feel it made the act all the more important, all the more defining.

She listened to the lawyers battling first with Detective Soames, and then Detective Tyler.

None of it mattered.

Her sister would be convicted. And she would walk free.

There was no doubt.

Her thoughts dissipated, bringing her back into the courtroom. She looked down, her fingers stroking the table again. She tucked both hands between her thighs, then glanced up.

She didn't know if anyone had seen her. It didn't matter.

Sister's fate was sealed.

Soon, there would be nothing standing between her and her father's fortune.

All of it. And yet, it wasn't about the money. It was about keeping it out of Sister's hands. Money is also power. Sister was the only one who knew about her true nature. It had to be this way, both of them on trial. Murdering her sister and then Father would have raised too many questions, even if she made their deaths look like accidents. And where would be the fun in that? Hearing that Father and Sister dear died in a car wreck would give a certain sense of comfort – but absolutely no pleasure.

Father murdered, and Sister convicted of that murder and disinherited was perfect. She would take the money – the power. Frank would finally pay for the years he neglected her, kept her away from him in cold boarding schools, the way he had let Mother beat her and bite her – Frank Avellino deserved that death.

And Sister deserved to pay for it.

THIRTY-FOUR

KATE

The full effect of Tyler's testimony hit Kate like a dump truck.

Detective Tyler alleged Frank Avellino was being drugged against his will, so someone could take control of his affairs and his money. Then he confirmed a recent power of attorney had been executed in favor of Alexandra and Hal Cohen.

It looked awful. It looked like Alexandra had manipulated her way into a position of trust by drugging her father. Another step closer to his fortune.

Dreyer didn't ask anything else. He sat down.

He let the implication of Tyler's testimony float around the courtroom like a bad smell – a gaseous vapor that would descend on the jury as a fine mist, and stink up their clothes, and their opinions.

Kate could sense the tide had turned against Alexandra. She needed to blow this cloud of suspicion away, right now, before it poisoned the jury against her client. She had to do something, and whatever it was she needed to do it right now.

The legs of her chair barked against the parquet floor as she shot her seat back. Her heels came together and braced beneath her. She placed her hands on the armrest of her wooden chair, ready to spring up, but her mind was blank.

She'd prepared for this trial like nothing else she'd ever done. She knew every word of every deposition, every document down to the page number in the trial bundle. But the toxicology report coming in today had been an unexpected curve ball. Suddenly that trial bundle, her strategy, her prepared cross-examination questions, everything felt alien now instead of familiar and practiced.

The power of attorney document was already in the bundle. It hadn't meant much before now. It wasn't that important. But with evidence that Frank Avellino was being drugged into submission around the same time the power of attorney had been executed – well, that threw everything into a new light. A mundane legal document that had been signed by her client now looked sinister. The whole trial bundle was now new territory. Each document could be a time bomb, waiting to blow up in her face.

She was about to stand up. All eyes on her.

When she stood she would need to ask a question. A good question. Something to quell the brush fire of imagination that now swept through the jury. There was only one problem. She didn't have a question. Her mind was blank.

Sweat bled through her skin like she was a peach being crushed by the heavy silence. Even if she did think of a question, she now couldn't be certain the panic wouldn't strangle her before she could ask it aloud.

A strong hand took hold of her wrist. She turned. Bloch was holding her, drawing her closer into a whisper.

'Buy some time. Get a short continuance. I've got new information,' said Bloch, and she angled the large screen of her cell phone toward Kate. The screen display read, 'Two New Files Shared to Dropbox.'

Before she forgot what she was going to say, Kate rose.

'Your Honor, we request a short continuance.'

Stone looked lazily at the jury, and then the clock on the wall behind them.

'Looks like we've had a long day. Ten o'clock tomorrow morning, ladies and gentlemen,' he said, and stood up. The courtroom gathered itself to stand as the judge made his exit. Eddie and Harry remained seated the whole time. Kate could almost feel the shade being thrown at those two by the judge as he made his way to his chambers.

'What have you got?' asked Kate.

'I've no idea. Not yet,' said Bloch. 'It might be nothing. Or it might be a new lead on Frank Avellino's killer.'

*

It took five minutes to deposit Alexandra in an Uber. Kate and Bloch couldn't wait until they got back to Kate's apartment so they found a quiet corner in the Corte Café on Lafayette and sat down with coffee. Bloch ordered a meatball sandwich. Kate, a chicken salad. With fries.

Since they were handed the toxicology report that morning, Bloch had been busy. She'd maintained a close relationship with several law enforcement agencies and various precincts in the New York area. The feelers went out ten minutes after she'd read the toxicology results. Word got around that Bloch needed help and all New York's finest and available hands went to work. It didn't matter that Bloch was now a private detective, working for a defense lawyer. She was a name, and her father had been too. NYPD look after their own. She asked them to look for any pharmacy or pharmaceutical wholesaler robberies in the last year.

The first Dropbox file revealed the results of the search.

There had been thirty-seven robberies of interest. Most of them on pharmacy premises, but two were wholesalers and there had been one hit on a transportation truck.

In none of them had Haloperidol featured or been part of the haul.

'Zip on the robberies,' said Bloch.

'What about drug dealers?' asked Kate.

'Nah, Haloperidol is not a recreational drug. There's no high. No buzz, either. It's not exactly a downer. More of a knock-out punch. It messes you up. Turns people into a pile of paranoid jello.'

'But I thought every kind of drug was on the black market, surely.'

'Not when it's so readily available with the right pharmacist. You hand over a fake prescription and five hundred bucks and you're lit.'

Swiping the document away from her phone screen, Bloch then accessed the second file. Inside was an email and video.

'There's a ViCAP hit,' said Bloch. 'Looks like NYPD are investigating this as a hate crime. An Indian pharmacist and a cashier were taken out last month. There's video.'

Mercifully, the video had no sound. This was a public coffee shop, and there were customers all around. It looked like security camera footage from a large chain store of pharmacies. Kate recognized the branding on the counter. Someone dressed in black leathers and a crash helmet entered the store, moved away out of shot then walked casually up to the pharmacist at the counter and took an axe to his head. Flinching, Kate looked away and mouthed the word, 'Jesus.'

When she opened her eyes, she found an old lady at the next table looking at her strangely.

'Look at that,' said Bloch, pointing to the screen.

Rewinding the video with a turn of her finger on the screen, Bloch played it again. The cashier saw what had happened to the pharmacist and made a wild run for the front doors. Only they didn't open, not one inch, and the cashier slammed her head into the glass, cracking it. She bounced back off the doors and fell to the ground. The figure in black was upon her in seconds. Two blows to the back of the neck with the axe. Then the figure moved out of shot to the right-hand wall, the doors opened, and they left.

It was one thing seeing the aftermath of violence. It was quite another to see it happening, even if it was just on a large phone screen.

'I don't think this helps,' said Kate, shaking her head. 'It's probably nothing to do with our case. I can't see how it relates.'

Bloch went back to the email, read over the notes that accompanied the video.

'This is important. I think this could be Frank's killer,' said Bloch.

'How?' Kate shook her head again, this time in disbelief. 'Why do you think that?'

'I need to do some more digging. But there's something here. I can feel it. Did you see how she moved?' asked Bloch.

'She?'

'She. That's a woman. You can tell by the hips. A confident woman. This was no racially motivated crime. For a start there's no graffiti, no message left. Dumb racists who are violent and stupid enough to kill always have a message from some group or cult.'

'Plus, she killed the cashier. The cashier was white.'

'Nation First, the KKK, or whatever white supremacist group you care to mention, have no qualms about killing white people if they have to. But in this case, they didn't have to. She planned to kill the cashier. Look . . .'

The video played, and Kate watched the figure more closely this time. It was clear to her now that it was a woman. The figure moved out of camera shot as soon as she came into the store.

'There. She came in, and the first thing she did was lock the sliding doors. So when the cashier saw what she did to the pharmacist, the cashier would run headlong into the doors, only they wouldn't open as she expected. She could've left the cashier alive. She didn't. Nothing was taken from the pharmacy. No cash. No drugs. The killer used a blade. The axe is perfect for this. Heavy enough to cause massive damage, but light enough to wield and conceal.'

'Why not use a gun?'

'Guns leave rounds behind. Rounds can be traced. Plus, it's noisy and it draws a lot of attention. Professional killers. Real pros. They get up close and personal with hits after a while. This woman . . .' said Bloch, pointing to a frozen image of the figure in black on the screen. 'This woman has killed before. She didn't even run from the pharmacy desk to the cashier. She walked. Took her time. No panic. If . . .'

'If what?'

Bloch studied the screen for a long time then said, 'I'd say she enjoyed those kills.'

The waitress brought over a meatball sub, filled with marinara sauce. Kate's salad and fries came next and Kate pushed the food away. Her appetite had left the building. Bloch picked up the hoagie and bit into it. Marinara sauce dribbled over the side of her mouth and she wiped it away with a napkin.

'I thought you were hungry?' said Bloch.

Kate flipped her the bird. Bloch smiled.

'I still don't see how it's related to the Avellino case,' said Kate.

'Well, it might not be. I need to check the sales records and stock reports for Haloperidol and take a look at the pharmacist. He was the main target. Have to be sure this wasn't a revenge hit for him prescribing the wrong meds or something. I doubt it. All the same, I'd like to rule it out. There's something else though, relevant to this case.'

Kate waited patiently.

Bloch took another bite of the sandwich. Swallowed it down, wiped her mouth and said, 'You remember a few weeks ago – motion day? We saw a biker. All in black. A woman. She cut us up and then burned a light right around the corner from here.'

'Come on. That's nothing. Coincidence.'

Bloch used her tongue to dislodge a crumb of hoagie that had become stuck in her teeth. She took a long drink of coffee, leaned back and said, 'I've seen her a few times since that day. Black leathers. Black helmet with a tinted screen. I saw her last night.'

'Where?'

'Across the street from your apartment.'

Kate froze, her mouth open, then she broke into easy laughter.

'You almost had me, there. Come on, Bloch. You're reading too much into this. Why would anyone be watching us?'

Bloch didn't look like she was joking. She put down her sandwich and put Kate straight.

'If I was on trial for a murder I committed, I'd be watching the lawyers too. Both sides. Making sure no one figures it all out, and if they get too close – bam.'

Kate thought for a moment, said, 'You don't think this case has anything to do with what happened to Eddie Flynn's investigator?'

'I can't say for sure, but I wouldn't be surprised.'

The conversation trailed off as Bloch ate her hoagie, and Kate picked at the fries. They finished and together made their way back to Center Street. It was dark now, with no wind, but the temperature was already below freezing and falling fast. Bloch had parked in Leonard Street, and it was time to head back to Kate's apartment together and do some serious preparation for tomorrow.

As they passed Hogan Place, Kate saw Dreyer standing outside with his assistants. They were huddled into their overcoats, their breath misting in the cold, drinking coffee and smoking cigarettes. Their conversation petered out as they saw Kate and Bloch approach. Kate didn't acknowledge Dreyer – she kept her head down and moved past them. No sooner had they moved out of earshot, Kate heard Dreyer mumble something and it was greeted with a chorus of derisory laughter. She didn't doubt the laughter was aimed at them.

It didn't seem to bother Bloch at all.

They stopped at the cross walk for Leonard Street, and Bloch hit the button. This part of Center Street was one-way – all the traffic coming from their left. A truck blew by, and then some cars. On the other side of the crosswalk Kate saw a woman, heavily pregnant, with a big red coat bulging over her stomach. The woman laid a hand on her stomach, protectively, in the manner some pregnant women find comforting. The gesture made Kate smile. That kid was already loved and it wasn't even born yet. A man with gray hair and a cashmere coat came and stood beside the pregnant woman. The man hit the crossing button again, angrily, as if the traffic light system would only work for him.

A car stopped in front of Kate, at the stop line. Beyond the car, a bus came to a stop. The light changed. Kate and Bloch began to cross the street.

So did the pregnant woman, and the gray-haired man.

Kate and Bloch passed the car. Before they reached the bus, a sound began to roar off the buildings, vibrate through the blacktop before finally landing in Kate's chest. The noise increased – the volume rocketing – and suddenly Kate knew what it was.

It was a high, mechanical whine accompanied by a base roar of throttle.

A strong arm thrust out in front of Kate, across her chest, holding her back. Bloch had stopped dead, just before the front of the bus. Kate looked to Bloch, then she heard the explosion of sound from a blast right in front of her.

Something dark shot past the bus, the pregnant woman screamed and fell back onto her behind, clutching her stomach, her legs splayed out. The gray-haired man fell forward, first onto his knees, then flat on his face. He didn't put his arms out to arrest his fall, and there was a wet crunch when his nose hit the blacktop. Kate's mouth opened but no sound came out. She could still hear that roar and looking to her right, she saw a motorcycle, with a rider all in black, mount the sidewalk and drive straight into Collect Pond Park.

The arm that restrained her disappeared as Bloch ran after the motorcycle. Kate looked back at the scene in front of her. The doors of the bus opened and the driver got out. He went straight toward the pregnant woman who was still screaming. Kate moved forward toward the man lying face down.

'Oh my God, are you alright? What happened?' she said, kneeling, her hands shaking, her heart pumping. She touched the man's shoulders, and then recoiled as a pool of dark blood spread from beneath him.

Footsteps behind her, coming up fast. Suddenly Kate was surrounded. She fell onto her side, pushed out the way by a man in a suit. She looked up, saw it was Dreyer and his assistants. One of them turned the gray-haired man over, and that's when they began to shout in panic.

The hilt of a knife jutted from his throat. His eyes were open and lifeless, his face a bloody mess. His nose sat at an odd angle, flattened to the right against his cheek by the fall. Kate's stomach heaved, and she covered her mouth and got up.

Bloch came charging back and knelt down beside Kate.

'The rider got away,' said Bloch.

One of the assistant DAs got up to help the pregnant woman, trying to calm her, for the baby's sake at least. Someone, Kate couldn't tell who, was on the phone to a paramedic.

Dreyer turned toward Kate and said, 'This was my witness. We were waiting for him to come in and be deposed.'

'Who is he?' asked Kate.

'His name was Hal Cohen.'

THIRTY-FIVE

SHE

She had timed it just right.

It took a lot of work, but it was worth it. She knew that Hal Cohen couldn't see Dreyer before five o'clock, because Dreyer was in court along with her. Dreyer would want to depose Hal personally. He would have been a key prosecution witness.

She had other uses for Hal. He had fulfilled his purpose, and she didn't even have to pay him a dime.

What Hal had discovered and turned over to Dreyer would be interesting. Even without Hal, Dreyer could spin that particular piece of evidence any way he wanted. It had less impact without Hal, was much less important, but still usable.

Killing Hal had taken split-second timing. She had a window of four seconds, and it had proven more than enough time. She had left the courthouse, taken a cab to her garage and suited up in her leathers. From there, she waited outside Hal's office for him to leave, having first made an anonymous call to make sure he was still in there. Once he left, on foot, she tracked him the four blocks to Hogan Place, and the DA's office. Taking him out in Center Street was the perfect spot.

She idled the bike to the traffic light, waited and then when she saw Hal begin to cross, she spun the back wheel, let it go, drew the knife and pointed it at Hal as she shot past. The speed of the bike did the work. There was a shockwave that travelled up her arm when the knife hit bone.

This time, she didn't miss.

No need to stick around to make sure Hal was dead – she knew it was a fatal stab wound. She struck a glancing blow to the pregnant woman, but thankfully it was slight enough not to send the bike over. There had been a wobble, but she corrected it quickly and burned the tires as she shot across the street, through Collect Pond Park and onto White Street.

Within minutes she was several blocks away, and, managing to use some of the few alleyways in this part of town, she avoided the last five traffic cameras before she entered a ten-story parking lot. In the lot, she parked the bike in the back of a brown panel van, then drove the van out of the lot. The cameras were looking for a black bike with false plates, not a busted-up van.

The risk had been worth it. Hal was dead.

And her sister had no idea the storm that was about to land in court.

THIRTY-SIX

EDDIE

Harry rested his elbows on his knees and studied Clarence. The little dog sat there transfixed by his master, his tail wagging.

'If someone was drugging Frank, taking control of his empire, making him submissive, and getting away with it, why was it necessary for him to die?' asked Harry.

Clarence licked his chops, moved forward onto all fours and stuck his nose under Harry's arm, prodding it away. Obliging his friend, Harry stroked his fur in something approaching contemplation.

Clarence didn't have an answer for Harry's question. Neither did I.

'We can't assume anything here,' I said. 'Frank was being slowly poisoned and controlled, but we can't know for sure that it was the same daughter that ended up killing him.'

'True, but it makes the most sense. My guess is Frank found out who was drugging him, called up Mike Modine to cut the culprit out of his will. That forced the hand of the poisoner – they had no choice but to kill Frank before he could make that change.'

'That explains why they had to take drastic action before he met his attorney on Monday. Kinda strange the cops haven't found Mike Modine, don't you think?'

'I'd say it's darn right suspicious. One thing I know is lawyers like Modine never run off to join the circus unless they're scared about going to jail.'

'I checked in with his firm. Everything's in order with Mike's files. He wasn't about to get sued, he was already divorced, and as far as anyone in the firm knew he wasn't seeing someone new. He just disappeared. It stinks, Harry.'

'Seems to be a lot of people involved with the Avellino sisters end up dead. Their mother, their stepmother, now Frank. Maybe Alexandra killed Modine too?'

'You still think Sofia is innocent?' I said.

Harry stood, attached Clarence's lead to his collar and made a few grumbling sounds as he straightened up. Harry wasn't getting any younger.

'I had my doubts in the beginning, but I trust your judgment. The more time I spend with her, the more I think she's just a mixed-up kid from a bad family. She needs help. She needed her father. I can't visualize Sofia hurting anyone. Alexandra – I can picture it more easily,' said Harry.

'Why?'

'Whoever did this must've known they'd get caught. You don't kill your father with another witness in the house. No one does that. Even if you're in a blind rage – it would be stupid as hell unless you killed the witness too. I don't get why both women are still alive. One of them is a liar and a killer. Sofia is volatile, but Alexandra gives me the impression of someone who can be calculated in their actions. There's a lot about this case doesn't make sense, unless there's a whole other side to it that we can't see. Anyway, I'm not going to see much more tonight. Adios. Me and my amigo are hitting the sack.'

Harry and Clarence left the office just after eleven. I looked over the trial bundle again, then when I raised my head and checked my watch I saw it was coming up on midnight. I should sleep.

The thought of lying down in that cot in the back – I couldn't face it. Not tonight. Every time I closed my eyes I saw Harper's face. It was beyond grief now. It had become something else. I had cried for her, for weeks. It felt like bleeding. That some part of me had been hurt, and it was only making me sicker and sicker and I didn't know how to fix it. The pain of losing her had given way to guilt. No way to know when that happened, but I felt it all the same. I'd already lost or pushed away one family for fear of them getting hurt. Three years ago Amy had been taken by the Russian mob. If it hadn't been for Jimmy the Hat I would never have gotten her back. That changed things in my marriage. The biggest threat to Christine and Amy was my work, and the bad people who came along with it. Part of me had cut off my family, for their own safety. Now I was paying the price. I was a weekend dad, with all of the troubles and worry that came with it.

Did Harper's death have something to do with me, too? Would she still be alive if she hadn't met me?

That was a question I wanted to ask myself, but I was afraid of the answer.

I played the video again, for the fifth time that day.

It was us. Harry, Harper and me in Frank Avellino's house. Taking pictures. Whispering theories so the sound guy wouldn't pick it up on the recording. This was one of the last things Harper ever did. These were the last images of her.

I cracked open the Scotch, poured a glass way too big and settled back in my seat to watch, my laptop perched on the desk in front of me. I studied every movement she made. I'd never noticed how graceful she was. I knew she was beautiful, but this was something else. She moved like she wasn't human, and yet was more human than any of us. Her heart was right there in her smile.

Cops thought Harper's murder was a robbery gone bad. There had been a spate of home invasions, but then again, there were always home invasions. It was part of the turf. Maybe it was my guilt, maybe it was grief, but I couldn't shake the feeling this was down to me. Every time I felt this I tried to rationalize. Tell myself what I wanted to hear. That it couldn't really be connected to the Avellino case. There was no reason to target her. If someone had killed Harper because of this case, I couldn't figure out why. Why target Harper? Why not me?

It should've been me.

Slam.

It should've been me.

Slam.

It. *Slam.* Should've. *Slam.* Been. *Slam.*

I stopped when I heard the crack. Didn't know if it was the desk or my hand. I looked down and the wood at the corner of the desk had split along with my knuckles. In the bathroom I put on a Band-Aid and returned to my chair. The image of Harper, frozen on screen.

My head went gently to the desk, resting on the back of my hands. I wanted to sleep, but I knew it wouldn't happen.

The killer took some cash from a bureau in her bedroom. Five hundred in twenties. Maybe they'd thought about taking her necklace, and then thought again. And they smashed her phone.

The images from the night of her murder would never leave me. I saw blood on her hallway floor. The broken necklace in the blood, the little gold cross in the middle of the chain. There was something else I needed to remember. Something important. I squeezed my eyes shut.

There. I saw it. Playing out in my mind like a nightmare.

Beyond Harper's hallway was a set of French doors leading to a kitchen. Her laptop lay open on the kitchen table. I'd seen it when I came in. Although I hadn't registered it at first. I was too busy looking at the blood on the floor.

They took the money. Left her necklace. Smashed her phone but left the laptop.

My head shot up to the video. I played it again from the beginning. Harper's death had not been part of a robbery. She had no defensive wounds. She'd been stabbed as soon as the killer had stepped into the house. If it had been a robbery, the phone would've been fenced for a hundred dollars, and the laptop five hundred, easy.

This was no robbery. It was just supposed to look like one.

Sofia had gotten a copy of this video. So had Alexandra.

What if Harper had seen something? Something none of the rest of us had seen. Something implicating the killer.

What if the killer had known this?

I clicked the track pad and started the video again.

When I was done, I scanned most of the Avellino case, started composing an email and then attached the file and the video, and hit send.

There was one person in the world who I trusted to look at this. Maybe she could see something I couldn't.

THIRTY-SEVEN

KATE

The house in Edgewater, New Jersey, felt both familiar and new. Kate remembered the house when Bloch's father had filled every corner with Christmas lights and refused to take them down until Easter. Every time Kate saw him he had a smile on his face, a ready joke and candy in his pocket. Every single time. Until he got busted out of the NYPD and then all of that changed.

Now, instead of lamps scattered around the rooms, Bloch had put up strings of fairy lights. Said it reminded her of her father, and besides, there weren't enough plug sockets for adequate lighting and the overhead bulb was too harsh. Bloch liked the fairy lights. Kate said she liked them too.

What remained of an extra-large pizza had grown cold as it lay in the takeout box in the center of Bloch's dining table. Beside it was the Avellino trial bundle. Kate popped another Diet Coke, Bloch pulled the cap on a Michelob. They saluted each other with fresh drinks, didn't say cheers, but each swallowed a mouthful and eased back in their seats at the table.

'You okay?' asked Bloch.

It took some time for Kate to find the right words. 'I've never seen anyone die. I can't get that sound out of my head. When his face hit the road . . .'

'I'll look into the pharmacy murders some more. A biker, female, all in black. Tinted visor. It could've been the same person.'

'You think it was Sofia?' asked Kate.

Bloch shook her head, 'I don't know, to be honest. This is a whole new ball game. I don't think Alexandra is a killer, and I would be surprised if I was wrong, but I can't say for certain. She said she went straight home after court when I called her. I can't verify that, and we have no way of knowing where Sofia was at the time Cohen was murdered.'

That last statement drew a heavy silence into the room. The temperature seemed to drop. If Hal Cohen, a witness in the case, was targeted, then it meant he must've had information that could nail the killer. Neither Bloch nor Kate knew what that might be. The events of that day had rocked Kate. She was going to stay at Bloch's house tonight – work on the case – try to sleep. She felt safe here.

'I don't sleep much,' said Bloch. 'If you want to turn in, the spare room is ready.'

'It's okay. I don't think I'll sleep much either.'

Since the murder of Hal Cohen, and Bloch's revelation that the figure in black leathers had been outside her apartment building, Kate decided there would be safety in numbers. As long as the other number was Bloch. No point in denying it, she felt safe around her. Two nails above the front door held a twelve-gage pump-action shotgun. Bloch would need to stretch for it, but it was within reach. On the kitchen counter, beside a bottle of tomato ketchup, lay one of Bloch's personal firearms. A Magnum 500. Earlier that evening, before the pizza arrived, Kate had felt the weight of the gun, and wondered how the hell Bloch carried it around all day. The Magnum held five rounds in its cylinder. Each round looked the same size as a cigarette lighter and cost two and a half bucks.

No matter what kind of problem you had, as long as you were carrying that gun, two dollars fifty was probably all you needed to spend in order to solve it.

'What's it for? A gun that size?' Kate had asked.

'Wildlife rangers carry them. It's one of the few handguns that can stop a bear.'

'We don't get many bears in Central Park.'

'It works real good on people, too.'

Kate picked it up, in a two-handed grip, careful not to let her finger stray to the trigger.

'Don't worry. You have to *really* pull that sucker to fire it.'

'How'd you even get a carry permit for this? In New York?'

Bloch took the gun from Kate, set it back down on the counter. 'Who said I had a permit?'

Kate glanced over at the weapon now, her stomach full of pizza, and an uneasy feeling spread. It would be good for Bloch to have it if they were attacked. And at the same time, Kate knew she never wanted Bloch to use it.

'Seriously, why the heavy artillery?' asked Kate.

It took a while for a response. Bloch liked to chew on things for a while. Like there was only a certain amount of words she could use before they all dried up. Bloch didn't talk about her feelings, or her fears. They were spending more and more time together, and Bloch was slowly opening up.

'I took a couple rounds in the vest a while back. It scared me. I bought the Magnum when I quit the force. Had to put on eight pounds of muscle before I could shoot it straight, but it was worth it. Sometimes you only get one shot. With that thing, one shot to the center mass is all I need.'

Kate wanted to probe further, ask how such a terrifying experience affected her friend, make sure she was okay, ask her if she wanted to talk about it. But she knew from the look on Bloch's face that this tiny piece of information was all she was going to get. Bloch was staring at the bookcase. There was only one book placed face out. A novel – *Twisted*, by J. T. LeBeau.

Glancing at the trial papers on the table, Kate said, 'I think I've got a shot at destroying the prosecution case tomorrow.'

'You got some questions for Tyler?'

'A couple. I need to speak to Alexandra in the morning.'

'Do you really think she's the innocent one?'

Draining the last of the diet soda, Kate crushed the can, tossed it into the lid of the pizza box.

'I do. I think her sister could be setting her up.'

'Strange way to frame somebody – putting yourself on trial for murder,' said Bloch.

'I have a feeling we haven't seen everything this trial will throw at us. Alexandra is innocent. I can feel it.'

THIRTY-EIGHT

EDDIE

The ping of incoming mail jolted me awake.

I'd fallen asleep at the desk, again. I looked at the screen. Just after five a.m. The alert message read, 'New Message from Kate Brooks.'

The email said Hal Cohen had been murdered last evening. What looked like a female in black biker leathers rode past him at a crosswalk, put a knife in his neck. It said no more than that. Attached to the email was a zip file. I clicked on the zip file to open it. The compressed file contained a video. Nothing more.

The video filled the screen. Security camera footage from a pharmacy. A figure, clad in black and wearing a motorcycle helmet, entered the store. I watched as a gruesome double murder played out on the screen. I stopped the playback as the figure in black left the store, then I ran in the back and dry-heaved. My stomach settled, my anger did not. I showered, put on a fresh shirt and tie and then dialed her cell phone, finding her number at the bottom of the email.

She picked up almost immediately.

'We need to meet. Our clients can't know we've talked. This is between us.'

'Come to my office,' she said.

A half-hour later I parked my Mustang outside an apartment building called Lexington Village, but could easily have been called Demolition by Fitzpatrick & Sons. The front door was wide open, like the large crack in the wall beside it. A smell of stale vegetables filled the hallway and I was surprised that one elevator was working. I rode it to Kate's floor. The hallway on this floor didn't smell any better. The carpets were dirty, and more large cracks ripped apart the walls. This place should be condemned. Kate opened the door to her apartment already dressed for court, but her hair was still wet at the edges.

'Come in. Sorry about the mess, I stayed at a friend's last night. Haven't had time to clean up,' she said.

She wore a pair of Adidas Superstars to go with the business suit. Inside, the apartment reminded me of my first place in Manhattan. It was smaller than most tombs. Somehow, the kitchen, bedroom and living area had been fitted into a single space, and with little forethought. Compact and uncomfortable. The two of us made the place look crowded.

'I'm sorry I asked you to my office. I work from home,' said Kate, sheepishly.

'That's fine, I live in my office, so we're kind of even.'

Kate had an easy laugh, and she appeared to relax just for a moment – no longer embarrassed. She ushered me towards the single stool at what she said was the breakfast bar. It was a sheet of Formica sitting on a plank. I sat down, facing the small kitchen area. Kate busied herself making coffee. She set out two mugs, not asking if I wanted any. She wanted coffee and she wasn't going to drink it alone.

The coffee machine began to gurgle, and she poured it out. She took a sip from a mug that said 'Ravenclaw' across it, and gave me a mug with a picture of Harry Potter on the side.

It was good coffee, and I thanked her, then took a look at the mug. The picture of the kid wizard had faded, like it had been through the dishwasher way too many times.

'I like *Harry Potter*. Sue me,' she said.

'No, that's fine. My daughter loves the books.'

'Smart kid. How old is she?'

'Fourteen.'

'That's a tricky age,' said Kate.

'Being a teenager sucks for most people. She'll get through it. How about you? How are you coping with your first trial?'

Kate nodded as she drank, then set down her mug and said, 'It's exhausting. That's one thing I didn't expect. Soon as I got out of the courtroom I realized how tired I felt. It's really draining.'

'You get used to it. Adrenaline will ca
dozen trials. That, and fear. Eventually you
to the effort required to get through a trial.

I paused, let her take in the complime
happened yesterday with Cohen?'

'I didn't know who he was until Dreyer sho
outside Hogan Place, waiting for Cohen. We were cro
and this bike shot past. The rider put a knife in Coh
couldn't believe it. I spoke to the cops afterwards, gave a .   .ment.
So did Bloch. They think it might have been an attempted robbery.
I told him it was too fast for that. The motorcycle rider didn't even
say anything. Just stabbed him.'

'You think someone was taking out a potential witness in our case?'

'No, I think Sofia was taking out a witness.'

'Wait, the cops haven't come near Sofia. If she was a suspect,
she'd be arrested. What about Alexandra? Has she been arrested
or interviewed?'

'No. Either it's NYPD incompetence or it's Dreyer. This is his
big case, with a guaranteed win one way or the other. Maybe he
doesn't want to jeopardize the trial by hauling the defendants into
custody on an unrelated matter.'

It made sense. Dreyer was probably thinking that at least one
of the defendants would be convicted, and then they wouldn't be
going anywhere anytime soon. Plenty of opportunity to question
them on Cohen's death when they're locked up.

'It was a woman on the motorcycle, in black leathers, tinted
visor. Did you watch the video?' asked Kate.

'I did. I checked the time and date stamp on the footage and
found a report in the *New York Post*. A pharmacist and cashier
murdered in their store in Haberman. Nothing taken. The reports
worked on the basis this was a racially targeted murder, and the
white cashier was a just a witness that needed to be taken out.'

'That pharmacy was one of the top five suppliers of Haloperidol
within a fifty-mile radius of Manhattan. Their sales of the drug had
spiked in the months leading up to Frank Avellino's death. They
re-ordered every month, which makes me think someone came in

their stock. There's an opioid crisis in this country,
of friendly pharmacists for the right price. Before this
period, they ordered Haloperidol from the suppliers once every
nine to eighteen months.'

'Where'd you get your information?'

'My investigator – Bloch.'

I swallowed down a tightness in my throat. Every now and again
I'd bump into a reminder of Harper, and it felt like being hit with
a baseball bat. I coughed, and took a real effort to control my voice,
fighting to keep the emotion from it.

'She sounds really good.'

'She is. Maybe not as good as your friend was. Sorry . . .'

'It's okay. I need to keep my head in the trial. It's the only thing
keeping me going.'

We both fell silent for a time, while I flipped the switch. Head
back in the game.

'You really think the figure in black is one of the Avellino sisters?
Killing the pharmacist and Cohen to cover their tracks?' I asked.

'I think it has to be,' said Kate.

I paused, let that sink in while I drained the coffee and Kate
gave me a refill.

'What do you know about Mike Modine?' I asked.

'Not much. He was a Wills and Probate attorney – specializing
in estate wealth management. He helped the dead pass their money
to the living with as few deductions for tax as he could manage. He
says he doesn't know what changes Frank wanted to make to his
will, and he's taken off. Probably having a mid-life crisis in Malibu
with a twenty-one-year-old volleyball player,' said Kate.

'Mike Modine made two-and-a-half-million dollars last year
before taxes. Due to some creative accounting on his part, he's
got five mil in a bank account in Zurich which he thinks the IRS
don't know about, and at the time he went missing he had a dozen
credit cards in his wallet. He's been a partner at this firm for eight
years. Before that, he was an associate for fifteen, working his way
up to the big bucks.'

'How do you know so much about Modine?'

'I did my homework. If he was making cash on the side he had to put it somewhere. There's no indication he was skimming clients, as all of the bank records on his files are audited. I just don't buy him up and leaving a job he worked his ass off to get.'

Kate lowered her head. Something seemed to flash before her eyes. Maybe the moment she'd upped and left Levy, Bernard and Groff. I got the sense she was rethinking that decision. Whatever it was, it passed quickly.

'You think Modine got fired and went into hiding?' asked Kate.

'No.'

'What then? You don't think he ran, you don't think he got fired and . . .'

The realization spread over Kate's face.

'You think he's dead, don't you?'

'I'm pretty sure of it. I think Modine had an idea why Frank wanted to change his will. That, or maybe the killer didn't know what Modine had been told by Frank, and had to take him out anyway – just to be sure.'

I laid out my theory for Kate. Told her about the deaths of Heather and Jane Avellino, the suspicions, the bite mark on Jane's thigh post-mortem.

'I've felt like I'm being watched. That someone has been taking note of my every move. I think that someone is the killer. Whichever one of our clients murdered Frank, it wasn't their first time. I think they murdered their mother, stepmother, the pharmacist and cashier, Hal Cohen, Frank and Mike Modine. And I think they might have killed Harper too, but I'm really not sure on that one. Maybe there are others we don't even know about. This is all connected. One of us is representing a very dangerous woman. I think it might be you,' I said.

'Wait a minute, *my* client? You're the one representing the sister with severe psychiatric problems. And all of these killings . . . I think that might be taking things too far,' said Kate. 'We don't have evidence to—'

'Of course we don't. They aren't on trial for those murders because there *is* no evidence. That doesn't mean I'm wrong. And just because Sofia has had mental health problems in the past doesn't make her a killer. There's a degree of skill, planning, and timing in these murders which I think Sofia simply isn't capable of.'

'Well, Alexandra is no killer. I watched a man die in front of me yesterday. Do you think that if I, for one moment, thought it could be Alexandra, I would still be in this case?'

'I think you're not sure about your client.'

'Well, I am, pretty sure. You? You can't be one hundred percent certain your client is innocent?'

She had me there. I believed Sofia. Whether that was because I *wanted* to believe her, I couldn't say. My heart, and my head, told me Sofia wasn't the killer.

'There's always a small doubt in the back my mind. That's all.'

'Same here, I can't be certain, but I'm as sure as I can be that Alexandra is innocent. I've put my career on the line for her.'

'We have to remember that one of us *is* representing an innocent person. I think we just let it play out for now. I think the killer is on trial because they think they have to be on trial.'

'What?'

'There's something close to fifty million dollars on the line. What did Dreyer tell us? Forty-four million after taxes? That kind of money, I don't think it can be anything other than motive. Forty-four million isn't just money – it's power. I think the killer knows she will be acquitted. That you or I will get them off somehow.'

'That's ridiculous, you couldn't slice this decision any thinner. It's fifty-fifty down the line.'

'Right now it is. And we have to keep it that way.'

'What?'

I paused. Thought. 'I think there's something we haven't seen yet. A witness or a piece of evidence that is coming down the pipe which tips the scales. There's a get-out-of-jail-free card coming our way. When we see that, we'll know who the killer is.'

Kate shivered and said, 'You think one of them planned this from the beginning?'

'I think they planned to dope Frank into submission, and when that didn't work, or Frank found out about their plans and wanted to change his will, then they had to take alternative action. What's the best way of making sure you inherit forty-four mil, and your sister doesn't?'

'You make sure your sister is convicted of killing the legatee,' said Kate. 'The Slayer laws prevent murderers inheriting their victim's estates. And if you're acquitted you can't be tried again, that would be double jeopardy. So one of us is part of this plan?'

'Maybe not part of it. I don't think it's about us. It's evidence or testimony. Something we haven't seen yet. If that smoking gun comes up we'll need to talk again. Look, I've never asked this question of another attorney and for most it doesn't even matter, but I *have* to ask this. Do you really think Alexandra is innocent? Honestly, no bullshit.'

'I do. What about you? Do you think Sofia is innocent?'

I nodded, said, 'I wouldn't have taken the case otherwise.'

'Shit,' said Kate.

'We can't speak a word of this to Dreyer. Nor anyone else. We have to trust each other,' I said. 'There's something coming – a witness or a piece of evidence that proves the case against one of the sisters, or exonerates one of them. I just know it. When we see that get-out-of-jail card coming – we know it's false and the other sister planted it. I think one of them killed Frank, and is dead set not only on convicting her sister, but making sure she herself is acquitted.'

Kate held out a hand.

'But what do we do with this *card* if we see it?'

'We lay down our arms. If I see Sofia playing that card, I'll sink her case.'

'Do you mean you'll walk away?'

'No, I mean I'll make sure she's convicted. I won't fight her case anymore, and I'll do my best to destroy her defense without getting disbarred.'

Kate looked to the ceiling, ran her hands down her throat before she spoke.

'My mom sacrificed everything so I could be a good lawyer, in a top firm. Now I'm being sued by that firm. I've put my life on the line for this case. Helping a murderer go free, or getting disbarred wasn't part of my plan,' she said.

'I didn't know you were being sued. You should have told me. Do you have a lawyer?' I asked.

'No, can't afford one.'

'Let's get this trial out of the way. If you want, I might be able to help.' I reached into my wallet, there was something there that I'd put away for a rainy day. I took it out and handed it to Kate.

'What's this?'

'It's a card I found in Levy's wallet,' I said. 'I don't know what it is, it's not for any kind of service or company I've ever heard of. It's kinda mysterious. It might be something, it might be nothing. Tell you the truth, since you took over the case I haven't even looked into it. Thought I might need leverage on Levy someday and this seemed like it could be something.'

As Kate took the card, I said, 'I sent an email last night to a friend. She's an analyst in the FBI. I want her take on this. I'm going to call her later. If I get anything from her I'll share it with you. This is beyond attorney-client privilege now. One of us is a pawn in a killer's game.'

Kate nodded, turned the card over in her hands – examining it.

'It's weird. I've never seen a card like this before,' she said.

'I know. Guys like Levy have secrets. Maybe this is one. Maybe not. Just promise me one thing,' I said.

'What's that?'

'If it turns out to be a bullet for Levy, make sure you shoot it.'

THIRTY-NINE

KATE

Detective Tyler took his seat in the witness stand, and this time Kate was prepared. She stood, with a legal pad on the desk in front of her. Scanning her notes one last time, Kate looked up and made eye contact with Tyler. He had the same cocky look on his face that he'd worn yesterday. It was Kate's job to change that look.

'Detective Tyler, the victim's home was searched following the murder?'

'I believe so.'

'And to your knowledge, no Haloperidol was found on the property?'

'Correct.'

'NYPD also searched my client's apartment and no Haloperidol was found there either, correct?'

'That's correct.'

'So there is no evidence linking my client to that drug?'

Tyler sniffed, blinked, and said, 'We believe—'

Kate cut him off, 'You're not sitting as an expert witness here, detective. Your belief doesn't matter. Please answer the question – there is no physical evidence linking my client to the drug found in the victim's body, is there?'

'There's no physical evidence. However, your client had the opportunity to place that substance in the victim's food.'

'And did you find food laced with Haloperidol in the victim's home?' asked Kate, struggling to keep control of her voice. She didn't know the answer to this question for sure, but she guessed that if the DA had found poisoned food, it would have appeared in a report before now and been served on her.

'Not to my knowledge.'

'So, again, there is no evidence linking my client to this drug?'

'There's no physical evidence, other than the symptoms Frank's medical records discuss, and the drugs found in his system at the time of death,' said Tyler.

'And no forensic link between the drugs and my client?'

'No,' he said, reluctantly.

Kate nodded. She'd done her best. Kept Tyler on a short leash. She was tempted to keep going. One more question. She decided against it. One loose question now and she could undo all her hard work. Instead, Kate thanked the witness and sat down.

Alexandra whispered, 'Thank you.' Kate nodded. She didn't know how to feel about Alexandra anymore. Was she thanking her because she was innocent? Or because Kate was doing a good job of helping her to get away with murder?

Kate shivered, and picked up her pen. She didn't think Eddie would ask any questions, and indeed he didn't. It was time to move on to the next witness.

Dreyer stood up and said, 'The People call Professor Barry Shandler.'

Kate could breathe easily. Shandler was the hair-fiber expert, and he didn't link anything to Alexandra. She'd read Shandler's report, and was curious to see how Eddie would handle it. The doubts creeping into Kate's mind seemed to fade away as she recalled the details of Shandler's report. If Shandler was right, then Sofia was most likely guilty. And she couldn't see how on earth anyone could challenge Shandler's testimony, but this evidence was already out in the open. This wasn't the get-out-of-jail-free card she'd discussed with Eddie that morning.

A hand brushed against her arm. Alexandra, staring at Shandler as he made his way to the witness stand. Kate smiled at her client, patted her hand.

She felt better about this case. She felt, for sure, she was on the right side.

Alexandra was innocent. She had to be.

FORTY

EDDIE

Professor Shandler was one of those guys who didn't much look like a professor. At least no kind of professor that I'd ever seen. For a start, he wasn't old. No wispy white hair. No bushy white eyebrows that looked like clouds. No cardigans, no corduroy, no wide leather shoes that a grandpa would wear.

He couldn't have been older than fifty. Jet black wavy hair that looked as though he'd put some product in it. No beard or moustache. He had pale skin that looked like it would burn if he went south of the Mason–Dixon line, and a blue pin-striped suit in a modern cut over an expensive silk shirt – blue, and silk tie – purple. The expensive suit went well with his narrow chin, high cheekbones and walnut-brown eyes. He looked more like a model in a high-end fashion magazine.

Several of the female jurors sat up a little straighter when they saw Professor Shandler. He'd worked in the NYPD forensic science lab, and had since gone out on his own into private consultancy work, where the best money lay.

He took the oath, sat with the judge's permission and Dreyer took him through his long history of qualifications and experience. At every question, Shandler gave a nod and a simple 'yes.' He had an air of authority about him. A deep voice tinged with a slight rasp that made every word sound like the gospel. Once Dreyer had impressed the jury with Shandler's credentials, he cut right to it.

'Professor, you were sent a number of hair fibers for analysis in this case, perhaps you would take us through the samples first of all, and then we'll talk about your testing?'

'Of course,' said Shandler, angling his seat to get a better look at the jury. 'I received three items for testing from the District Attorney's office. One was a hair, with at least part of it buried in a wound on the victim. The second was a sample of hair from Alexandra Avellino, and the third a sample of hair from Sofia Avellino. I refer to the latter two samples as control samples, whose origins are known to me.'

'And the first sample? Sample one?'

'This was the hair which I was to analyze and compare with the control samples.'

'Before we begin, can you tell us a little bit about human hair?'

'I can. Most of us have thousands of hairs on our body. An individual scalp hair is grown in a follicle of skin, which also contains a root. None of the samples I examined contained a root. Unfortunately the hair shaft, which is what I work with, is not a living part of the body that contains DNA. However, hair strands do contain certain characteristics which I can examine.'

'What are those characteristics, Professor?'

Without taking his eyes away from the jury, he set out his schtick. It was practiced, and smooth.

'Ladies and gentlemen, imagine a round target,' said Shandler. As he said the word, 'round,' he traced a wide circle with his finger, to help illustrate his point.

'The only thing in this target is a bull's eye, in the center. That is what the inside of a hair looks like. On the outer shell, we have the cuticle. This cuticle will have a pattern. Then, in the space between the outside of the hair, and the bull's eye, you have the cortex and depending on the level of melanin in the cortex, this determines the color of the hair. And then the bull's eye – this is called the medulla and it too can have a pattern and distinct structure. I look at all of these characteristics, on a microscopic level, when I examine a hair for comparison purposes.'

'What were the results of your tests?'

'Sample one, the comparison sample, shares distinct characteristics with the hair sample provided from the defendant, Sofia Avellino.'

Dreyer paused, again, to let the jury absorb this.

'Can you be more specific on how you came to this conclusion?'

'I can. The morphological characteristics were identical. The samples shared an imbricate cuticle pattern. They were also of the same pigmentation. The medulla of both samples was of similar diameter, identical continuous pattern and identical vacuolated structure. The only conclusion, based on my forensic examination, is that the hair found on the body of the victim probably came from Sofia Avellino.'

'May I remind the jury, this hair was actually embedded in one of the many stab wounds found on the victim's body. What does that tell you, Professor?'

'I am a scientist, ladies and gentlemen of the jury. I follow logic and established scientific principle. The Locard Exchange Principle states that when two people are in contact with each other, there will be some transference of material between the two. It is probable that the transference of this hair took place at or close to the time of the murder, given the hair from Sofia Avellino had been pushed into the wound, presumably by the blade.'

'Thank you, Professor.'

I glanced to my left, saw Sofia with her lips set firm, shaking her head. It's hard to listen to someone who is telling lies about you. In front of you. Her forehead wrinkled, and she wiped at her eyes before the tears came, shunning them and willing them not to come.

Harry patted her arm, leaned behind her and caught my attention.

'I'm going to pick up our friend. Text me when you're ready,' said Harry.

I gave him the thumbs up, and Harry left the courtroom.

I looked around, and noticed then that Dreyer had sat his ass back down. A tapping noise distracted me and I saw Judge Stone, prodding the face of his watch with his finger and looking directly at me.

'Apologies, Your Honor,' I said, getting to my feet.

Beneath my file of papers I had five brown envelopes. I picked them up and made my way around the defense table. I handed one to Dreyer, one to Kate, and gave the other three to the judge's clerk.

'Your Honor, Professor Shandler is one of many witnesses on the prosecution's list. I didn't know if Professor Shandler would actually be called to testify until now, and that is the reason why I have not served this report on my colleagues or the court. It is relevant evidence that I may have to use in my cross-examination of this witness.'

Stone refused to take an envelope from the clerk, and whispered, too loudly, 'Get that out of my face.'

He realized he'd been overheard, and coughed. Then said, 'Whatever it is should have been served weeks ago. I have no inclination to admit this evidence.'

'Your Honor, failing to admit the evidence at the appropriate moment would be grounds for a challenge for bias.'

I could see his ears pin back, the creases disappear from his forehead. Last thing Stone wanted was this case to be halted and his decisions thus far to be put under scrutiny from another judge.

'Very well. If you have an argument as to why I should allow this witness, your co-defendant and the District Attorney's office to be ambushed by your material, then I'll allow it.'

'I can deal with some general matters first,' I said.

Stone waved his hand at me to get on with it.

'Professor Shandler, good morning.'

'Good morning, Mr. Flynn.'

He was courteous, professional. Calm. He'd testified in almost twenty high-profile cases in his career, and never once had his findings or testimony been successfully challenged in an appellate court. The corner of his mouth turned into a half-smile.

I glanced at my phone on the defense table. I had a text ready to go to Harry. All I had to do was hit send, and he would come in with the cavalry. The empty seat beside Harry sent a black cloud into my head. She should be here. Harper should be alive.

I closed my eyes, just long enough to flip the switch.

When I opened them, Shandler's expression had changed. He looked almost sorry for me. He must've thought I was a rank amateur, struggling to come up with a decent question.

'Professor, before we go any further, I will give you one opportunity to recant your testimony to this jury. I want you to explain to the jury that you have exaggerated your findings, and your report and analysis is fundamentally flawed. I'll give you ten seconds.'

FORTY-ONE

EDDIE

I counted down from ten, silently.

My gaze never broke from Shandler. And his eyes never left mine.

He'd already made a big mistake. He'd been suckered into a fight with me. Now the jury didn't matter to Shandler. There would be no more eye contact with the jury, no more careful explanations, nods and gestures. He was locked in on me. Where I wanted him to be. Easier to get him riled up and get his mouth moving faster than his brain.

'There have been a huge number of convictions overturned due to unreliable expert testimony from hair-fiber analysts, isn't that true, Professor?'

'I wouldn't know. None of my cases have been challenged, Counselor.'

'Until the current administration shut down the investigation, the FBI were reviewing three thousand convictions in which their hair-fiber analysts testified. In almost two thousand of the cases they managed to review before they were shut down, they found flaws in the hair-fiber analysis and testimony in ninety percent of those cases. Would you agree that hair-fiber analysis as a whole is fundamentally flawed?'

'No. Like I said, I have never had one my cases successfully appealed.'

'It was the FBI's hair-fiber analysts that provided your initial training, isn't that correct?'

Shandler shuffled around in his seat, leaned forward and said, 'Yes, my initial training. And I say again, I stand behind every single test and analysis I have provided. Not one has been challenged successfully.'

'Just so we're clear, you're saying you stand by every hair analysis opinion you've ever given?'

This time he turned to the jury, said, 'Yes. I stand by every single one.'

'You are aware of the concept of confirmation bias?'

'I am familiar with the concept. I am never biased in my approach.'

'Just so the jury understands, confirmation bias occurs when an expert is given a low number of samples to compare – say two to three. You are looking for similarities in those samples, aren't you?'

'And differences.'

'There's no hair-fiber database, is there?'

'No.'

'So when you're asked if a hair fiber matches a suspect, you're only comparing two samples, you're not looking at hair samples from the general population.'

'Correct. But if they don't match, I say so. When they do match characteristics, then I am happy to confirm this.'

I took a moment. Let Shandler get a little more comfortable. I wanted him to think he was making a comeback.

'In hair-fiber analysis, it's possible that two hairs, from the same person's scalp, won't share the same morphological characteristics, isn't it?'

'It's possible. It's not likely.'

'But it is possible. In that scenario, by looking at the hairs through a microscope you might think they came from two different people? So you can't with certainty match two hairs that belong to the same person?'

'Like I said, that's rare but possible.'

I turned to the judge, 'Your Honor, I'd like to admit the defense hair analysis report in those envelopes. If one could be handed to the witness, please?'

Dreyer was quick to object. He spat out his case to the judge while his assistant opened the envelope I'd given them.

'Your Honor, if the defense has obtained its own expert witness report, then we should have been on notice so that our expert witness had some time to consider it. This is an ambush.'

'Mr. Flynn. I take this objection very seriously. Who is your hair-fiber expert?'

'His name is Professor Barry Shandler,' I said.

The court fell silent apart from the tearing of envelopes. I interrupted to state my case before Dreyer could recover.

'I'm not ambushing this witness, because the report in the envelope was prepared and written by this witness. He can't be ambushed with his own report. The findings in this report do not relate to his analysis for the prosecution – this is a separate matter that goes to credibility.'

Judge Stone flicked through the report, as did the DA and Shandler.

'I'll allow this to proceed. I can't rule out a report from the District Attorney's own witness, however much I think it is irrelevant,' said Stone.

'I'll allow the witness, and the jury to read the report. It's short. Only two pages.'

One of the envelopes held the jury copies. They were quickly distributed and the jury began to read. Once everyone had finished reading, I saw the confusion on their faces.

'Professor Shandler, in this report, commissioned by Harper Investigations, you examined two hair-fiber samples. A sample labeled F1, and CD, correct?'

It took a moment for Shandler to answer. He was looking around nervously, as if he was liable to be swallowed up in a trap at any moment.

'I carried out the analysis.'

'And your findings were that the samples were a probable match?'

'Yes.'

'And your testimony today is that the hair fiber from the victim's wound is a probable match for my client?'

'Yes.'

'And you've already confirmed to the jury, earlier, that you stand by the accuracy of all of your reports?'

'Yes.'

I hit send on the text.

'The report that you prepared for Harper Investigations, just six weeks ago, confirms the probable match of samples F1 and CD. I can tell you that the hair sample F1 came from me. It's my hair. Does that change your opinion?'

'No, not at all. The sample CD must've come from you too,' he said.

'Actually, no. This is CD.'

I stood back, pointed to the rear doors of the court and Harry walked in. Shandler put his hands on the armrests of the chair, and levered himself up so he could see over the heads of the crowd in the public seating area. When he saw Harry, he sat back down, with a smug grin on his face.

'That cannot be possible. With respect, microscopic analysis would show a clear differentiation between Caucasian hair and African American hair in many respects. The sample CD did not come from this gentleman,' he said, pointing at Harry.

Harry reached the end of the aisle, and stood in the well of the court in open view of the witness stand, the judge and jury. He'd heard what Shandler had just said, and couldn't keep the smile off his face.

'You're correct, Professor Shandler. Sample CD did not come from Mr. Ford. Sample CD came from him.'

Shandler's mouth opened as I pointed to Clarence Darrow, who sat beside his master, and licked his chops with a long tongue before eyeing Shandler and letting out a sharp bark.

'You stand by your analysis in every case, Professor. Yet you can't tell the difference between my hair and the hair from this dog's belly. Would you like to change your testimony now?'

'This is outrageous!' yelled Shandler, getting to his feet, shaking a finger at me. He was shouting, swearing. I felt sure if I was closer he would've hit me.

The crowd burst into laughter, the jury looked at Shandler like he'd just grown another head, and Judge Stone started to bang his fist on his notebook.

'Get that animal out of here,' shouted Stone.

Harry took the final word – 'Which one, Your Honor? Clarence or Professor Shandler?'

FORTY-TWO

KATE

Kate had never seen anything like it.

Judge Stone called a break for lunch, and had the court cleared. Eddie hadn't torn the DA's expert to pieces, he'd simply allowed the expert to tear himself to pieces. Kate would never have brought the dog into court, no way she would've had the nerve. The jury liked it, and by the time Eddie and Harry were leaving the court, Kate knew this was as close as it could possibly be. She'd hoped Professor Shandler's testimony would put a target on Sofia Avellino's back.

Now, this was anyone's case. All that could change with the next witness.

On the floor above, they found a quiet room and put Alexandra there, away from the press, with a salad and a bottle of water. Kate and Bloch took the stairs two floors down so they could talk as they walked the corridors. Neither of them felt hungry, and Kate didn't want anyone overhearing, especially her client.

'This thing is wide open now,' said Kate. 'You still feel confident we're on the right side of this?'

'You're a defense attorney,' said Bloch.

'What do you mean?'

'There isn't supposed to be a right side. You just do your job.'

'That's bullshit, and you know it. You know me. And you wouldn't be here if you didn't believe Alexandra.'

'I guess you're right,' said Bloch.

Sometimes Kate found her friend a little frustrating. In those moments, Kate just wanted to listen to a long explanation about why she was still doing the right thing, why Alexandra was innocent, and how they were going to win this case. She wanted the words to drown her. Consume her doubts. Wash them away.

They walked and talked strategy for the bite-mark expert. His name was Peter Baumann. No state or federal law enforcement agency could analyze bite marks. They had to go to a recognized expert. Baumann was the bite guy. He had been working with law enforcement for years and was a seasoned expert witness, even if his methods weren't exactly state of the art. Kate knew that prosecutors chose their experts based on two criteria – their seniority and expertise in the field, and possibly more importantly, their ability to withstand cross-examination. There was no point in the DA engaging the best bite-mark analyst in the country only to find that when they got on the witness stand they folded like a hot Hershey bar.

The lunch hour passed quickly, and neither Bloch nor Kate ate. A cup of coffee from a vending machine, or at least something *supposed* to be coffee, was all Kate could manage. All too soon she was back in court. There was no re-examination of Professor Shandler by the prosecution – Dreyer knew that witness was a lost cause. It's bad when one of your witnesses gets pummeled with hard questions – it's ten times worse when the witness is reduced to a laughing stock. Kate actually thought that Eddie could have achieved the same result without bringing Harry's dog into court – but the dog made the jury laugh at Shandler, and once they did that it was game over.

Peter Baumann didn't look like Kate had imagined him. She thought he would look a lot more like Professor Shandler. Tall, wealthy and good-looking. Baumann was short. Five foot nothing. He was clean-shaven and completely bald. His eyebrows were so lightly colored that Kate hardly noticed they were there at all. When he walked past the lawyer's tables at the front of the court to get to the witness stand, Kate caught an unusual odor emanating from Baumann. It wasn't unpleasant – the smell of dental putty, bleach and cinnamon. He smelled kind of like a dentist's treatment room, which Kate found both strange and comforting. She wondered if she smelled of ink and paper.

Baumann refused to take a religious oath, and instead affirmed that he would tell the truth, and nothing but the truth. Prosecutors liked it when their experts took their oath on the Bible. And for Christian expert witnesses, this was no problem. The atheist experts weren't happy. Prosecutors thought it played better with the jury, and might offend some Christian jurors if their experts were seen to shun the Bible. Some scientists pushed back against this, said they already felt like frauds swearing on the Bible when they weren't in the least religious.

This jury didn't seem to have a problem with Baumann refusing the Bible. He wore a pastel blue suit, white shirt and bright green silk tie. Kate found the tie distracting. You could land a plane with that thing.

'Mr. Baumann, would you explain to the jury your area of expertise?' said Dreyer.

Surprisingly, Baumann didn't make eye contact with the jury. He didn't even turn his head to look at them. His gaze fixed on a point on the back wall, behind Kate. A vague, faraway look in his eyes as he answered the question.

'I am a forensic odontologist, a fellow at the University of Texas, San Antonio, and a member of the American Society for Forensic Dentistry and Bite Comparison Odontology. I have been examining bite marks for over thirty-five years, and providing expert testimony in more than fifteen states across the US,' said Baumann, with a strong Texan lick to every syllable. Odontology came out Baumann's mouth as *O—don—tology*, as if the word were too long to be said in that accent, and required considerable effort to spit it out.

'Did you carry out an examination of the bite marks on the victim?' asked Dreyer.

'I did. The medical examiner found what looked to her to be a single bite mark on the victim's left breast area. There are seven different types of bite mark. The particular type I identified is known as an incision bite. This is a skin puncture, made with the teeth. This was not an avulsion bite as no skin was removed. Nor was it an artifact bite, where flesh is removed. This was a simple puncture wound. I was able to identify eight punctures, in an oval pattern, which correspond with anterior teeth marks.'

At this point, Baumann pointed at the screen opposite, and Dreyer's assistant pressed a button on a remote, bringing up a full-color image for the benefit of the jury.

'I took this photograph during my examination of the victim. As you can see, this is a life-sized close-up of the bite. It's oval in shape, and the puncture wounds are clearly defined. There is some hemorrhaging beneath the skin, caused when the teeth closed around the flesh, pinching it in the bite.'

'How did you carry out your analysis of this bite?'

'I took measurements from the bite marks, and then, from the life-sized photograph, I compared those measurements to make sure they matched. Then I was provided with dental impressions of the two defendants in this case. From those impressions I made two master casts, and carried out my analysis on those casts in comparison to the bite marks.'

'How can you be sure the casts are an accurate representation?'

'The casts are perfect. The mold is the same used in all orthodontic practice. It's very accurate.'

'Once you had the casts, what did you do then?' asked Dreyer.

'I carried out measurements, and bite simulations using both casts. I measured canine to canine distance, incisor width, and rotational angles of the incisors. Comparing the measurements on acetate to the life-sized photograph provided a match from one master cast. The simulated bite from that same master cast also produced a simulated bite which precisely matched the bite pattern on the victim.'

'Which master cast was this?'

'Master cast two. This was the cast taken from Alexandra Avellino.'

'From your tests and analysis, what is your conclusion, if any, regarding your investigation and comparison of the bites and the teeth of the defendants?'

Baumann cleared his throat, leaned forward, and said, 'The defendant Alexandra Avellino bit her father on the chest with enough force to break his skin. That's my conclusion.'

The jury, who had sat silently listening to Baumann's soft, southern gentleman tones, now looked to Alexandra. Some of them with disgust, a few with disappointment.

'Nothing further. Miss Brooks may have some questions, so please remain seated, Mr. Baumann.'

FORTY-THREE

KATE

Abandoning her notes, Kate stood and moved around the defense table so she could be closer to Baumann. His eyebrows knitted together, but he retained a genteel smile. It was a condescending look.

'Mr. Baumann, you said that you are a member of the American Society for Forensic Dentistry and Bite Comparison Odontology?'

'I did indeed, ma'am.'

'There are at least three other organizations in the United States whose members practice forensic odontology. The Bureau of Legal Dentistry, The American Board of Forensic Odontology, and the International Organization for Forensic Odonto-Stomatology. You are not a member of these organizations?'

'No, ma'am.'

'Why not?'

Baumann exhaled, loudly, as if this was all a waste of his goddamn time.

'Well, the organization I belong to has its head office in Houston. It's only a few hours away. It's convenience, more than anything else.'

'The other three organizations I mentioned have, over the past few years, attempted to set down forensic guidelines for the standardized examination and comparison of bite marks. Your organization has not, correct?'

'Those organizations are based in New York and California, and we don't hold much regard for their practices. We do things our way.'

Kate paused, raised an eyebrow at the jury. New Yorkers don't much like any perceived slight at their town, or their people. Kate paused long enough to let the jury feel aggrieved at Baumann, then continued.

'So you don't, for example, carry out three-dimensional computer imaging of the suspect's teeth?'

'We do not.'

'You don't have a standardized scoring system so that the levels of similarity can be graded?'

'No, ma'am.'

'You only compared the suspects' dentition to the bite marks. You didn't, for example, set up a number of master cast bite simulations, with, say, ten or eleven casts, like a police line-up, as recommended by the Bureau of Legal Dentistry?'

'I did not.'

'You were called in to carry out your analysis of the bite mark when?'

'I got the call on a Saturday. I flew out Sunday and examined the body that evening.'

'Where did you examine the body?'

'In the morgue.'

'So you made no account for the distortion of the wounds?'

'I assumed a level of distortion, but it did not effect my findings or measurements.'

'Let's be clear what I mean when I talk about distortion. Human skin has a high degree of elasticity. It can expand, contract, swell, and shrink?'

'It can.'

'And when a body is moved, there has to be some element of force applied to the skin. The body is lifted from the crime scene into a body bag, taken on a trolley to the city morgue, and once in the morgue the body must be lifted again from the bag to the examining table.'

'I guess.'

'And when the body is lifted, it is common for hands to be placed beneath the body's arms, in the armpits? Persons at each side of the body and one person who will lift the legs?'

'I assume you are correct.'

'When skin is pulled, if any part of it is already torn, this can cause further tearing of the skin, isn't that correct?'

Baumann chewed on this for a moment, then said, 'It's possible.'

'It's likely, isn't it?'

'Could be.'

'Given that your measurements were taken to fractions of a millimeter, it's entirely possible that the cuts you measured were widened during the process of the body being moved.'

'It's possible. Anything is possible.'

'When you examined the victim, rigor mortis would be present, which tightens the skin and would widen any puncture wounds, correct?'

'I suppose.'

'One of those odontology organizations I mentioned states that no accurate bite-mark comparison can be made when a body has undergone rigor mortis, or it has been moved, isn't that correct?'

'I feel like I'm repeating myself, ma'am. I already told you I don't ascribe to those methods.'

'Isn't that half the problem with bite-mark comparison, Mr. Baumann? There is no accepted standard of comparison?'

'I don't believe so. The accuracy of the comparison is down to my expertise.'

Kate took a moment to stop and think. She was at the point where things could all go very wrong from here on in. She could stop, use what answers she had already gained, or throw everything at Baumann. Glancing over her shoulder, she saw Bloch. Her hands cradled below her chin. Bloch closed her eyes, and nodded.

Go for it.

'Mr. Baumann, there is no bite-mark database in the United States, is there?'

'Not to my knowledge.'

'So you cannot compare the bite marks on the victim to any other set of teeth other than the two master casts in this case?'

'Why would I want to compare the bite marks to every person in New York? I can see and measure the similarities. I don't need to compare it to the general population.'

'We all have the same type of anterior teeth, bar losing or damaging a tooth, correct?'

'That's true. There are central and lateral incisors, and canines. A set of two of each, on the maxillary and mandibular arches. That's twelve individual teeth. I examined each one and compared them to the bite mark. The odds of someone having the same distance measurements between each individual tooth . . . well I couldn't even calculate those odds, they're so high.'

'The purpose of general dentistry is to keep teeth and gums healthy, and ensure uniformity, correct?'

Baumann's face began to redden. This quickly spread to his scalp, making him look like an angry tomato. Still no answer came.

'Uniformity is not always the goal.'

'It is when someone has had braces applied to their teeth, isn't it?'

He growled, 'That's right.'

'Your statement that the odds of a member of the general population making the same bite mark as Alexandra Avellino is based on the probability that the position of each individual tooth is unique in relation to the other teeth?'

'It has to be.'

'Not if, like Alexandra Avellino, you wore a brace for twelve months to alter the position of your teeth. To make them more uniform in appearance.'

'I was not aware she had worn a brace.'

'Does that alter your findings?'

Baumann shook his head, 'I wouldn't think so. Not by much.'

'I see. And the fact that no other forensic odontologist would even have tried to compare the bite mark in this case, because of rigor mortis, because of the movement of the body, that doesn't give you cause for doubt in relation to your findings?'

'No, ma'am.'

'In relation to your bite-mark simulation of the master casts, what did you use to simulate the bite?' asked Kate, already knowing the answer. She just wanted the jury to hear it.

'Pig skin. It's the closest material we can ethically use.'

'And you think pig skin is equivalent to a human body, in rigor mortis?'

'It's the best we got.'

'In summary, your analysis failed to account for various changes in the bite-mark appearance since the wound was inflicted, and you cannot conclude that my client's bite mark is unique?'

'I guess so, ma'am.'

Kate turned away from the witness, and watched the jury as she walked back to her seat. Some were shaking their heads at Baumann, others were either not convinced by Kate, or not convinced by Baumann – they seemed almost indifferent. Hard to tell how well this cross-examination had gone, but at least she had a few converts on the jury. Her cross was damage limitation – and no more. On that basis, she counted it successful.

Reluctant to let two expert witnesses be annihilated, Dreyer spent ten minutes trying to patch up Baumann's testimony, but enough damage had been done. That same handful of jurors seemed to look at him with suspicion.

That was enough.

As Baumann left the witness stand, he mouthed the word, 'Bitch,' in Kate's direction. At first she was shocked, then she focused on Baumann's face. He'd mouthed something else as he passed her table.

He wasn't looking at Kate when he said this. Nor Bloch.

No, this was directed at Alexandra. She couldn't look at Baumann and avoided his gaze. Alexandra missed him mouthing, 'Murdering bitch.'

Kate thought about complaining, highlighting this to the judge and asking him to discipline Baumann. But then, she didn't want the jury to hear what Baumann had called Alexandra.

Maybe Baumann had bought his own bullshit science, thought Kate.

Then she had another thought.

What if Baumann was right?

FORTY-FOUR

EDDIE

Judge Stone allowed Dreyer to call one last witness this afternoon, with Kate having demolished the bite-mark expert in double-quick time. I thought Kate had enough to throw shade on the bald Texan – more shade than a ten-gallon hat.

While Dreyer consulted with his team, I took my time observing the jury. Some of them were still reeling from Baumann's evidence. I'd say that seven looked downright confused. The remaining five unconvinced by Dreyer's bite guy. Probably Dreyer had asked half a dozen bite-mark experts to look at the marks on the victim, and most of the more reputable ones had probably said *no* when they found out the body had been moved.

There's always one expert who will sign his name to any kind of opinion-based report as long as they're getting paid. Forensic science in the US legal system was driven by money, and the desire for convictions more than science. Money talks.

'I have one final witness for the day,' said Dreyer. 'We had intended to call Hal Cohen, a longtime friend and colleague of the victim. Sadly, Mr. Cohen was fatally stabbed yesterday on his way to my office. The police manhunt continues for the perpetrator. The police believe that this may have been an attempted robbery that went wrong, or there may have been other motives in play.'

'Have the defendants been questioned by police?' asked the judge.

'No,' said Dreyer. 'This trial is too important for any potential interruption. I'm sure the NYPD will question the defendants to establish their whereabouts when this trial is completed.'

During a trial, your senses are all on high alert. You're attuned to reading body language, both from the witness and the jury.

Listening to, and evaluating, every word spoken. It's like being on a high wire for seven hours, and one moment's loss of concentration sends your client plummeting to the bottom of a ravine. When Dreyer answered that question, I sensed a change in the room. Something happened.

Sofia.

Her hands were clasped together under the table. She had drawn her fingers together, her hands pressed so tightly that her arms shook with the effort. Her face had a faraway expression, tears in her eyes and she rocked back and forth ever so slightly. It was like she was waiting for an executioner.

I glanced over and saw Alexandra was jittering up and down in her seat, her left leg bouncing with nerves.

Both of them had known Hal Cohen. I'd told Sofia about Cohen's death that morning. She had looked sad and confused. Shocked, maybe. I wondered how Alexandra had taken the news. Right now, at the mention of his name, one of them should have been saddened, and one of them trying to hide the fact that they killed him.

'Your Honor,' said Dreyer, 'as I was hoping to call Mr. Cohen, I will have to call another witness earlier than anticipated. I need some time.'

'How long do you need?' asked Judge Stone.

'An hour at the most.'

'Recess for one hour,' said Judge Stone. The court clerk called, 'All rise,' Harry skooched down in his seat, and I leaned back in the chair and folded my arms. Harry and I had already made our point. Now it was a matter of principle.

Glancing over, I saw Kate looking worriedly at me.

I'd rarely had a trial like this. I had no idea what witness Dreyer had in his pocket.

And no clue what would happen next.

Stone would let Dreyer get away with anything. Any kind of ambush. It didn't matter. Stone wanted a conviction, just as much as Dreyer.

We took Sofia to a quiet room, got her settled down. The trial, although it was proceeding quickly, was taking its toll. The faint lines around Sofia's eyes had deepened and stretched, and now dark circles grew beneath them. Her fingers trembled, and her voice was both breathy and erratic in pitch. Like something inside her was shaking her every now and then.

'I think we're about even with Alexandra at the moment. I don't know what the prosecutor has in the pipeline, but whatever it is we'll deal with it. You're doing great. You're holding up. I just need to you to keep things straight for another day or two. Then it'll all be over,' I said.

She nodded, and said, 'I don't know how much more I can take. Being in the same room as her. Jesus, it brings back a lot of bad memories. Things I haven't thought about in a long time. And what she did to Dad . . .'

Harry put a hand on her shoulder, squeezed. She put her palm on top of Harry's hand, and then rested her cheek against it. Her eyes closed on a reservoir of tears, and set them running. They dripped, one by one, onto Harry's fingers.

'It's gonna be okay,' said Harry.

We sat in silence as she gathered herself. In those quiet moments, the river of pain I was holding back threatened to burst the dam. I could flip the switch, but the grief and the guilt were always there. A pressure, at the bottom of my skull. I knew when the court day finished, the dam would open sometime tonight. Another night not sleeping. Another night punching the walls. I took a breath, forced the dam closed. I would deal with it later.

'Who killed Hal Cohen? Could it have been Alexandra?' she asked.

'We don't know,' I said.

We stayed in the room until one of Dreyer's assistant DAs found us and knocked on the door.

'Mr. Dreyer would like to see you,' said the assistant.

Sofia insisted she was okay, and it took some persuading for Harry to leave her, but eventually he relented and both of us made our way down the corridor to where Dreyer waited on a bench set against the painted yellow wall. The paint peeled away from a seam in the wall and flecks had settled on one shoulder of Dreyer's immaculate suit, but he hadn't noticed yet.

I sat down beside him. Harry stood, folded his arms.

'If you asked the judge to strip naked and dance the light fantastic with you in the middle of the courtroom, he'd do it,' I said.

A dry, mirthless smile spread over Dreyer's face, revealing small white teeth.

'The judge and I are getting along famously. I've got something here for you. You'll be angry when I hand it over, but I assure you, on my professional word, that this is the first time I've been in a position to serve this.'

Sitting on the other side of Dreyer was a small pile of pages. Maybe a hundred, at most. They'd been placed on the bench face down, so that no casual passer-by could see the title of the document.

'Hal Cohen brought this in. I saw it three days ago. This is a Xerox. The cover sheet is a report from a Sylvia Sagrada. It's legit. I'm introducing it as evidence and I'm calling Sagrada to testify.'

I took it from him, and without looking at it I gave it to Harry.

'How long have you been holding onto this, really?' I asked.

'I only saw it three days ago. I didn't serve it on you until I knew it was genuine. Ms. Sagrada says it's the real thing. Hal Cohen, for what it's worth, would've given testimony as to how he'd come by it. But he's not here, is he?'

'Eddie—'

'Wait a second, Harry,' I said, 'Dreyer, you expect me to believe this crock of shit? This is an ambush. You don't do this in a murder trial.'

'Like you don't introduce your own hair-fiber report until you begin to cross-examine the state's witness?' said Dreyer.

He got to his feet. 'I'm telling you the truth. Cohen gave this to my office a few days ago. I had to be sure it was real before I served it. If it was a hoax, I wouldn't use it and we wouldn't be having this conversation. Be ready. I'm calling Sylvia Sagrada to the witness box in ten minutes.'

We both stood, facing one another. I was a little taller, but Dreyer stood straight and tried to stretch to my height. His eyes locked on mine. He shot his cuffs, puffed out his chest and the corner of his mouth curled into something approaching a snarl. If I didn't know better I would've sworn he was about to start a fight.

I looked down at his feet. He was on his toes.

'If you want to intimidate me you might think about a bigger heel on those Hush Puppies, pal.'

'I don't like you, Mr. Flynn.'

'I'm not crazy about you either. You've deliberately gotten close to a right-wing, racist judge just to advance your career and get an easier ride in court. You make me sick.'

A mocking laugh rang out of Dreyer.

'I don't need Stone for this to go my way. Between you and me, I'm glad I didn't use the polygraph tests. Your client's result was inconclusive. I guess the case law excluding lie-detector experts is still good. This evidence buries your client. She's the killer. I think her sister had something to do with it too. I think they both killed him. Maybe I can't prove that, but at least I can put your client behind bars where she belongs.'

He looked over my shoulder at Harry and said, 'Happy reading.'

FORTY-FIVE

KATE

Kate and Bloch read the report from Sylvia Sagrada in five minutes, then flicked through the attached Xeroxed pages. Bloch said nothing. When Kate was about to ask her a question, Bloch simply shook her head. She was processing. Too early for questions. But Kate saw the look in Bloch's eyes. This was the piece of evidence they'd been expecting. She'd told Bloch all about the conversation with Flynn. There was a killer moving amongst them, killing witnesses, manipulating the case, with a surefire piece of evidence planted to get them an acquittal, and their sister a conviction.

Kate explained the report to Alexandra, and watched the light come on in Alexandra's eyes.

'I knew it. I knew this would happen. Oh, thank you, God,' said Alexandra, her fingers laced together, her head tilted back and eyes to the ceiling. This new evidence would put Sofia away for murder. Alexandra knew it.

'This is your get-out-of-jail-free card,' said Kate.

'It's the truth,' said Alexandra. 'Finally, the court will hear the truth.'

Bloch shook her head.

They went back into the courtroom, Alexandra almost bouncing along in her heels, a new hope alive in her face. Kate felt like she wanted to be sick. There was a tightness in her stomach that spread to her throat. She'd called it all wrong. She was representing the killer. Kate swallowed down the bile building in her throat. She told herself she should have known it was her who was representing the killer. Eddie Flynn was too experienced to let himself get played by a client. They took their places at the defense table and waited.

The judge returned, and Dreyer said he was calling a new witness. Sylvia Sagrada. Eddie got up and objected, but Stone waved it away, dismissively. He would allow the new witness and assess the evidence for admissibility.

Kate felt like she was strapped into a fast-moving car. Her arms pinned, the steering spinning left and right, out of control, her foot flat on the gas pedal as the car veered toward a solid brick wall. She opened her eyes, took a breath.

She'd talked to Flynn about what they would do. Kate couldn't be a part of framing an innocent woman and letting a murderer go free. When she'd made that deal with Flynn, she never thought it would be Alexandra who was the killer moving the pieces on the board. Kate couldn't be a part of that. She would no longer do anything to assist her client in getting off. If she tried to fire the client, then she would only make things more difficult. The judge probably wouldn't let her walk away from a live murder trial. Even if the judge did allow her to exit the trial, that didn't solve the problem. All she could do was make sure she didn't become part of the weapon used to beat an innocent Sofia Avellino into a murder conviction.

The courtroom was silent. She felt Bloch nudge her in the ribs. She looked up, and Bloch pointed at the judge.

'Miss Brooks,' said Judge Stone, 'I hope you're still with us. Tell me, have you taken your client's instructions on this matter? I take it you have no objection to this witness?'

She didn't even have to turn her head. In her peripheral vision, Kate could just see Alexandra shaking her head, whispering 'No, not at all,' under her breath.

'No, Your Honor. My client does not object at this time,' said Kate.

'Good, then proceed, Mr. Dreyer,' said Stone.

'Thank you, Your Honor. The People call Doctor Sylvia Sagrada.'

A petite woman in a gray pantsuit came forward. Her heels *thocked* on the floor, her long hair was so dark it shone under the ceiling lights. When she took the oath, Kate saw that she was younger than Kate had expected, and had an aura about her. There was something authoritative in her speech. Firm. When Doc Sagrada said something, you believed it.

'Doctor, that title, let's just clear this up for the jury – you're not a medical doctor, is that correct?'

'I have a doctorate in Forensic Document Examination and Comparison, from the University of Mexico. I'm currently based at NYU.'

'You were sent a brief by my office. Please tell the jury what that brief contained.'

'A memo, a toxicology report on Frank Avellino, several pieces of contemporary correspondence we know to have come from Frank Avellino, and this,' she said, holding something aloft.

Kate saw a small black book in Sagrada's hand.

'It's a journal, kept by Frank Avellino in the last months of his life,' said Sagrada.

A murmur rippled over the masses in court. This was new. This was very crucial new evidence.

'This journal came into the possession of the District Attorney's office a few days ago. It was provided by Hal Cohen, who found it during a search of the victim's personal papers. He did not get the opportunity to comment, for the record, or appear in this trial, to give his opinion on the authenticity or otherwise of this journal. But are you able to tell us if this is indeed Frank Avellino's journal?'

'In my opinion, yes, this is Frank Avellino's journal.'

People shifted in their seats, moving forward, eager to hear this testimony. It sounded like an army getting ready to march. It began behind Kate, from the gallery, and spread like a brush fire.

'Silence in court,' said Judge Stone.

'And with the materials provided, which you mentioned, what did you do to examine the journal, Doctor?'

'I carried out a forensic examination of the control samples, the known examples of Frank Avellino's handwriting, and I compared it with the handwriting in this journal.'

'And what were your findings?'

Before answering, Sagrada picked up the water jug in the witness box, poured some into a plastic cup and took a drink. She set the cup down and angled her gaze to the jury.

'The control samples were all good. Some letters, some signatures. This gave me a good base of comparison for the victim's handwriting. I then took into account known factors. From reading the toxicology report, I knew the victim had Haloperidol in his system, and this accorded with some of my observations of the handwriting in the journal. There were passages in the journal that very clearly correlated with the victim's handwriting, and some, which did not. These passages looked like the author was under the influence of drugs or alcohol, although the style was the same, the hand was clearly loose and difficult to control. But, in my view, the same.'

'Just to be clear, Doctor, what was your conclusion regarding the identity of the author of the journal?'

'In my professional opinion, Frank Avellino wrote this journal,' she said.

'How certain can you be?'

'In this case, because of the influence of drugs, I can only say that in my professional judgment, authorship lies with Frank Avellino. There is enough consistency in the formation, construction and pattern of letter formation, syntax and sentence construction to lead me to that belief.'

'Thank you. Would you read the last entry in the journal please? October second, I believe. Two days before the murder.'

Kate fixed her view on the jury. She'd already read the entry. She wanted to see how the jury would react.

'October second,' began Sagrada. 'I know what's been going on. She's been poisoning my food. I saw her tonight. She poured something into the soup from a white bottle. Then hid it in her purse. She thought I didn't see. I bet she's been putting it in my smoothies too. I'm going to change my will, then I'm going to call the cops. I'm not crazy. I'm not sick. It's her. I asked her what she put in my soup. She said I was imagining things. I need to act fast, so I didn't push the issue. My God, I never thought it would have been her who betrayed me . . .'

Sagrada looked up from the notebook; she didn't need to read along with the last sentence. She knew it by heart.

'It was Sofia.'

A wail erupted. Kate turned and saw Sofia on her feet, Eddie holding her back. She was screaming, her face red, hair stuck to her skin as she pointed at the witness, then shouted again and pointed at Alexandra.

'No, it's all lies. It's Alexandra. She's the murderer! I'm innocent!'

Alexandra sat passively beside Kate, ignoring Sofia. For the first time in the history of this trial, Kate saw her client sitting in a relaxed, almost calm state. Kate knew then, without question, that this journal was what Eddie had predicted. This was the get-out-of-jail-free card for Alexandra. A piece of evidence that frames an innocent woman. Kate would have no part in it. She couldn't directly challenge her own client in court. She had to trust Eddie to do something and the best Kate could do would be not to get in his way. Her first case as lead counsel. Her very first murder trial, and all Kate could think was that she hoped she would lose.

FORTY-SIX

EDDIE

'We know the journal is a fake. We just have to prove it,' I said.

The red blotches on Sofia's face looked raw and angry. Her eyelids were swollen, along with the skin around them. She hadn't stopped shaking all day. I'd called a friend, got Sofia something to level her out.

The Valium was taking her down a notch. Straightening her out of a hyper-tense state. At least she could speak now. She could breathe more easily. The panic had stopped choking her.

Sofia looked back into her apartment, and Harry was closing her blinds, checking the doors, making sure the place was secure. 'Eddie, tell me straight – am I going to jail?' she asked.

'No,' I said. Right then, it felt like a lie. 'You'll be fine. Put on one of those old black and white movies you like so much. Order in. Harry and I need to work tonight. We need to concentrate and we won't be able to do that if we're worrying about you.'

Sofia rushed forward, letting go of the door. She threw her arms around my waist, her head rested on my chest. I was surprised by this, and at first I didn't know what I should do. Then I put my arms around her, and patted her on the back, told her things would be okay.

She let go, thanked me, and Harry came out of the apartment into the hallway.

'Don't worry, sweetheart, this guy is the best trial lawyer I've ever seen. He's not as good as me, he's not perfect, but he's pretty damn good,' said Harry.

'How can I be in second place to you if I'm the best trial lawyer you've even seen?' I asked.

'Well, I've never seen myself. How could I?'

For a second. A split second. A smile appeared on Sofia's face as Harry and I argued good-naturedly.

'Thank you,' she said, and closed the door.

I followed Harry to the elevator. We got in, and before the doors closed I asked, 'Do you think you got everything?'

'I got the kitchen knife, and a pack of razors from the bathroom.'

He opened his jacket. Sofia's kitchen knife was secreted in his inside pocket.

'We've done everything we can. She'll be okay. We just have to figure out how we're going to win this,' said Harry.

The 2nd Avenue Deli is no longer on 2nd Avenue. Hasn't been since 2006 when the landlord and the owners couldn't come to an agreement. The restaurant moved to East 33rd and 3rd Avenue, and New York moved with them. Abe Lebewohl, an immigrant to New York, had worked his way up from busboy to counterman in a deli on East 10th Street, and finally opened his own place in 1954. Abe loved food, people and New York City. Everybody loved Abe. He was murdered on the street in 1996, on his way to the bank with the cash from the restaurant's takings. New York mourned him, and family took over the business.

I first came here with my mom and dad when I was a kid. When Abe put a pastrami sandwich in front of me that was bigger than my head, and took time to talk to my family and get to know us, I knew I would always come back.

I went upstairs to the second floor. Harry had reserved a booth in the back corner. When I arrived, Kate, Bloch and Harry were all seated. There was an empty chair at the corner of the booth for our fifth guest. She hadn't arrived yet. I sat down beside Harry, Kate and Bloch opposite.

'I'm sorry, Kate,' I said. 'We expected this, and it would've been a shock to me too, but we talked about it. Alexandra is trying to frame Sofia. That journal is dynamite to this jury.'

She was nibbling at a bowl of French fries, her head down. Bloch drank coffee and Harry had a beer. There was a heaviness in the air. A weight that sat on all of us.

'I just didn't think it was Alexandra,' said Kate. 'But it has to be. She's the only one that benefits from this. I watched the jury – they ate up Sylvia Sagrada. They believed every word. You should've seen how they looked at Sofia. With hatred. Jeez, I'm sorry too. Your client is innocent. I can't be a part of putting her away . . . I just . . .'

Elbows on the table, Kate's fingers massaged her temples. She was going through hell. She'd given up her career in a firm to go out and defend a woman she believed to be innocent. Now, every-thing had changed. Her first case turned out to be a nightmare. Representing a murderer. And no matter what the cost to her, I knew Kate wouldn't set a killer free. She was here, which meant she would help if she could. She hadn't yet been crucified by that numbing code of ethics that keeps lawyers sane and out of jail – you don't speculate over your client's innocence, you don't ask if they're guilty, you do your job and the jury decides. Lawyers get asked it all the time – how can you represent someone you know is guilty? Our job tells us never to ask about guilt, never to put ourselves into a position where we question our client's guilt or innocence – we just put forward their case. That's the job.

A crock of shit. A lie we tell ourselves so we can sleep at night. Kate hadn't been taught to park her conscience yet. The one thing that was saving her was inexperience. She hadn't been to the other side of that door. The door where you turn off your instincts, and you do your job no matter what, even if your client is guilty. I'd been through that door, and I'd spent the rest of my life trying to make up for it.

'I think you're both right,' said Harry. 'There's a whole degree of planning involved in this murder to make it look like something else, and too many people who could tell the truth about what really happened are dead or missing. It's not a coincidence. None of it. Alexandra wrote that journal. She killed those people.'

Kate leaned back, closed her eyes and shook her head.

'I can't let her get away. I have to nail her, Kate. The more I think about it, the more I wonder if Harper's death is linked to this case,' I said.

The chair at the edge of the table squeaked on the floor as it was pulled out. Paige Delaney sat down. I introduced her to Kate and Bloch.

'Paige is a fed, but don't hold that against her. She's seen the case files and videos. I asked her to help us with a profile,' I said.

'I haven't quite finished it yet,' said Paige. 'And I don't know how useful it will be. You should have it tomorrow at the latest, but I can talk through some of it now. First thing is that I believe we're dealing with a serial killer. And that's where the problems with a profile begin.'

'I thought the FBI had profiling down to a fine art,' said Harry.

'Not yet we don't, there's a kind of rift happening in the Bureau. We're working on definitions, categories and sub-categories of killer types that have existed now for forty years. I think we need to overhaul the entire process.'

'Why?' asked Harry.

'Because we're working from a baseline simplicity. Our work has always been focused on creating a profile that every law enforcement officer can understand. The reality is never that simple. In this case, it's even more difficult because of the lack of research into female serial killers. Even our sub-types and categories of serial killer are based on male-focused research. Female serial killers have been overlooked for decades. About fifteen to twenty percent of all serial killers are female, and they make up only about three percent of the research.

'Even our methods of tracking and identifying serial murder don't work as well as they should. In order for a cop on the beat to enter details of a murder on our ViCAP database, they have to fill out a form, which asks one hundred and fifty questions. It takes a couple of hours to do it right. You think a cop has a couple of hours to help us with research?'

Bloch leaned forward, but said nothing. Other than nodding her head in a greeting, she hadn't said a word, but I could tell she was taking it all in.

'Upshot is the FBI will tell you there are perhaps fifty serial killers at large in the United States. The real figure could be closer to two thousand. Statistically, that means there are between three and four hundred female serial killers operating right now. And we have no idea who they are, or the extent of their crimes.'

'Jesus,' said Harry. 'What about this case?'

The waiter brought a selection of sandwiches and sharing platters, and we fell silent until he was done.

'So, what do you think? Is it Alexandra or Sofia? I don't want to prejudice your view with my own opinion. I just need to hear from someone outside this trial,' I said.

'Which Avellino sister is the killer? That's a tough question. Neither fit a typical profile exactly. Both have experienced significant childhood trauma with the death of their mother. There's suspicion over that death, and what you told me about the bite mark is interesting. Both girls were sent away from their father after their mother's death, different schools, separate lives. Yet . . .'

'What?' I said. 'We need you to make a call, Delaney. We think the trial is being rigged here.'

Delaney took a bite from a sandwich, wiped her lips with a napkin and thought it over. I could see her wheels turning.

'Most serial killers are not mentally ill,' she said.

'You're kidding me,' said Harry.

'A lot of them are psychopaths, but that's not a mental illness. If it was, half the CEOs of Fortune 500 companies would be in psychiatric hospitals. Most serial killers function normally in life, they actually learn how to fit in. One of the first major works on serial killers was by Clerkley – it's called *The Mask of Sanity*. Back then, in 1941, they figured if you did insane things then you were insane. Not so today. Looking at your girls, Sofia's self-harming doesn't fit well with the profile. People self-harm for all kinds of reasons, but it's one of the factors that is steering me away from her.'

'Gun to your head – which one is the killer?' said Kate.

'Alexandra,' said Delaney.

Harry told her about the journal, and our line of thinking now that it had emerged as evidence in the trial.

'It's smart. That journal will have a big sway on the jury. If the journal implicates Sofia in the poisoning, and this killing and trial is part of some plan, which is what it looks like, then sure. Alexandra has faked the journal well enough to convict her sister and get herself an acquittal. She doesn't have to be a master forger either – Frank's handwriting was debilitated because of the drugs. Smart.'

'So what do we do now? We can't let her get away with this,' I said.

'If I put her on the witness stand you can cross-examine her?' said Kate.

'You'd be knowingly throwing your client under the bus. You can't elicit false testimony from her either – what if she convinces the jury she didn't do it? She's managed to convince both of you. If I call Sofia and Dreyer does a number on her then it could make things even worse,' I said.

We sat in silence for a few moments, lost in thought.

'Don't call the defendants,' said Bloch. 'The problem is the journal. We show the jury it's a fake. The DAs spent all their time proving it is *authentic*. I don't think they've had time to consider if it's *accurate*.'

With the exception of Kate, who was casually eating a French fry while her friend talked, Harry, Delaney and I were all open-mouthed. These were the first words Bloch had spoken since we'd sat down. I guess she didn't talk unless she had something damn important to say.

'Holy shit, that's exactly what we need to do,' I said.

Bloch said nothing.

'Damn, that's the whole nine yards right there,' said Harry. He stared straight at Kate and said, 'Does she do that a lot?'

Kate raised her soda to her lips, hesitated and said, 'Welcome to my world.'

FORTY-SEVEN

EDDIE

The sound of Sylvia Sagrada's heels on the floor. It was a clock ticking down to my cross-examination. Another night with no sleep. This time, I'd been working. I was ready to take down Sagrada this morning. I'd done the work. Made the calls.

And yet I wasn't ready. I didn't feel it.

Sagrada took her seat in the witness box and began to pour a glass of water.

'Eddie . . .' whispered Harry.

He began talking softly, but I couldn't hear him. I wasn't thinking about the journal, or Sagrada, or Sofia or Alexandra. Because my head had been filled with those thoughts all night, and the only thing on my mind this morning was Harper. I'd spent every night since her death thinking about her, and last night felt like a betrayal. She was on my mind. I'd tried to flip the switch, but it wasn't working.

'Remember, you're still under oath, Miss Sagrada,' said Judge Stone. 'Mr. Flynn, do you have any questions for this witness?'

I did. And I couldn't ask any of them. The pain felt like living inside one of those old deep-water diving suits. The ones with the copper helmet and bubble visor, the lead boots and weighted belt. I was protected from the world by this pain, and it weighed heavy on me. Dragging me down.

'Eddie, let's go. This is for Harper,' said Harry.

I stood, deciding not to hide this pain, but to use it.

'Dr. Sagrada, do you accept that some members of your profession could examine this journal, and come to a different conclusion about the identity of its author?'

'I accept that. We can only give our opinion. I understand others may have a different opinion.'

First step.

'You accept that your interpretation of who wrote the journal may be flawed?'

'It may be. I don't believe it is, but it may be.'

She was careful not to back herself into a corner. She needed a way out with her professional credibility intact if I happened to nuke her opinion in the next twenty minutes. Smart. Plus, it gave the jury some confidence in Sagrada's credibility – she was stating an honest belief, and her mind was open to other possibilities. This made her testimony even stronger. I had to be careful here.

'You based your opinion on letter formation – the style, if you will? And syntax and sentence construction, is that right?'

'Principally, yes.'

'But the handwriting in the journal did not exactly match Frank Avellino's known handwriting samples, correct?'

She looked away from me, gave her explanation straight to the jury.

'Handwriting can change over time and circumstance. It's all similar. Some of it more than other sections. The known variable here is that the victim was being drugged at the time he wrote this journal.'

'Someone who knew the victim's handwriting well, someone who knew how the victim spoke, they could produce a pretty good approximation of the deceased's handwriting, couldn't they?'

'Depending on their skill level. Yes, I suppose it's possible.'

'The first entry in the journal is dated August thirty-first last year. I'll just read some of the opening page – *I hate writing this shit. Never done it before. I'm not a man who wants to have his memoirs published. There's enough skeletons in my closet to fill a goddamn graveyard – twice. This is on doctor's orders. This is for me only. And Doc Goodman . . . If it's not my prostate it's my brain. Hal Cohen finally persuaded me to go see the doc about both. I'm on pills for the prostate, and I have to write this shit for my brain. Doc asked me some questions, which I answered, and he said I was fine. But to please him,*

he wanted me to write down my thoughts and any symptoms I notice.
He'll see me in a couple of months. I think it's fair to say that this
journal was written on advice from the victim's neurologist, Doctor
Goodman, who wanted to get an overview of symptoms?'

'I'd say that's accurate. The doctor probably wanted to know if
this was stress-related, or something else, before he performed brain
scans. I imagine the doctor was concerned it may be early-onset
dementia.'

'I think that's accurate. And you were given the victim's medical
records, correct?'

'Yes, I wanted to know if the victim was being treated for
any conditions that could affect his fine motor skills, ergo his
handwriting.'

I leant over the defense table, took a page from the pile in front
of me and approached the witness.

'This is an extract from Frank Avellino's medical records. This
is an attendance with Doctor Goodman, the victim's neurologist.
It records blood pressure and vitals, and the results of a physical
examination. The last handwritten entry reads – RV 3/12 DY, can
you see that at the bottom of the page?'

'Yes, I do.'

'I wasn't sure about the abbreviations and their meaning. I think
RV 3/12 is review in three months?'

'Yes, that's right. It accords with what the victim wrote in his
journal.'

'And DY, for a time it had me foxed, but do you concede it's
probably shorthand for diary?'

'I do more than concede, I agree. Dr. Goodman probably
recorded that he wanted to see the results of Frank's diary in three
months' time. And, of course, the letter formation and sentence
construction in that journal entry is consistent with that of the
victim.'

'Thank you. The next entry in the diary, or journal, is September
fifth of last year. Again, I'll just read a section – *I am not losing*
my mind. I came out of Jimmy's restaurant after breakfast and she
was on the other side of the street. This was the second time I'd seen

her in as many days. She gunned the bike and rode away just as Hal came out the front door of the restaurant. He said he didn't notice her. Maybe Hal's losing his goddamn marbles. I called my lawyer, Mike Modine, right then. I told him to hire the PI Hal had recommended. Was this section consistent with the victim's letter formation and constructions?'

Sagrada nodded. 'It is.'

'The next entry is September fifteenth, and again, I'll just read a short passage – *The soup Sofia made yesterday was still in the fridge. The stew Alexandra sent over from the deli sat beside it. I made myself a peanut butter and jelly sandwich with a glass of milk and watched the news. Feeling better tonight. My head is clearer, for the first time in days. Call from the PI service. I told them Bedford hadn't been in touch with me by phone or text. No, I didn't know where he was – he'd told me that I wouldn't see him, for Christ sake. They are assigning a new operative in the morning. Bedford is missing. There's a police appeal for information on the news.* Is this consistent with the victim's letter formation and sentence construction?'

'It is consistent,' said Sagrada.

I took a moment. I'd planted some explosives in those questions. Before I hit the detonator, I wanted to see who would be caught in the blast.

Alexandra's right hand closed over her left fist and she placed both elbows on the defense table, and then her chin on top of her knuckles. I could see the whites of her teeth, biting down tight on her lower lip. Eyebrows creased together, in concentration or concern. Both, maybe. People used to say that the eyes of a murder victim still retain the image of their killer. An old superstition. Yet when I looked into Alexandra's eyes, I could see a red tinge at the corner, as if her gaze remained tainted with blood.

Sofia's expression was soft. Her hands on the table in front of her, fingers outstretched, as if she were reaching for something – truth, maybe. Or mercy. I didn't see a killer in Sofia – only a victim. Someone who had suffered at the hands of others. I guessed that she had been so badly hurt in the past that the pain was almost nostalgic. A comfort, or a reminder that she was still alive. Still hurting. Still bleeding. There are victims who get drowned in their loss. It takes everything away from them – taste, smell, love, security, sanity. Grief is a great thief. It will steal everything unless it is checked. Sofia looked like she couldn't lose anymore. She knew the journal was a ticket to life imprisonment. I just had to tear it up.

I turned back to Sagrada.

'You've stated, quite fairly, that your view is largely opinion-based, and opinions on authorship may vary. If new information challenged the authenticity of this journal, would you be willing to change your opinion?'

Forensic document analysis isn't quite reading finger bones in a wooden bowl, but ain't a kick in the ass away from it either. Sagrada thought about her answer carefully, then said, 'It would depend on the nature of the new information.'

'What if the new information revealed this journal has been written purely for the purposes of this trial?'

'I'm not sure I follow,' said Sagrada.

'Let me put it another way – the journal is a forgery.'

Sometimes a line is spoken in court that feels like a blast of cold air. Everyone sits up a little straighter, eyebrows are raised, people exchange surprised looks, as if they're about to open the popcorn and enjoy a show. It's the rousing final chords of the overture, and the curtain is about to go up.

'I've already given my opinion on the handwriting,' said Sagrada.

'I'm not talking about the handwriting, I'm talking about the contents of the journal itself. The first entry in the journal is dated August thirty-first, and discusses the victim's recent visit to the doctor and the need to keep this journal for medical purposes. The medical record of that appointment is dated September first. The entry above this reads August thirty-first – DNA. DNA stands for Did Not Attend. Mr. Avellino missed the appointment, rescheduled for the next day – September first. The journal records this appointment on the wrong date, August thirty-first. Maybe someone who knew he had an appointment that day wrote the entry, but didn't realize Frank had missed the appointment and gone the day after?'

Sagrada looked at Dreyer, but said nothing.

'On September fifth the journal entry mentions the victim having breakfast at Jimmy's restaurant, just as the victim did every morning. However, on September fifth the restaurant was unexpectedly closed due to a gas leak in the neighborhood. There's no mention of the gas leak, nor is there any mention of having breakfast somewhere else. Only someone who wasn't there that day would leave out those details and assume Frank had breakfast at Jimmy's. On September fifteenth the journal mentions the disappearance of the PI, Bedford, mentioned on the news – yet the first media broadcast of this story happened on September eighteenth. Doctor Sagrada, this journal was written by someone who had knowledge of Frank Avellino's general movements, but it was not written by Frank Avellino.'

'I didn't have this information when I compiled my report. I was not fact-checking the journal.'

'No, you were not. If you had this information when you were compiling your report, I take it this would've better informed your opinion?'

She hesitated. I'd handed her a way out, without affecting her professional judgment. If she was smart, she'd take it.

'The job of verifying the accuracy of the information in the journal belongs to law enforcement. Not me. With this new information I cannot stand over the veracity of my earlier opinion. With the benefit of this new information, I have to doubt the authorship of this journal.'

Some intakes of breath, low grumbling from the jury. They had a clear shot at one of the defendants in this case, and now it had been taken away. The guilt or innocence of the defendants was now as muddy as it ever was. Until my next question.

'The District Attorney's office came into possession of this journal via Hal Cohen. Mr. Cohen is now deceased. We have undertaken some investigations into Mr. Cohen's financial dealings. Would you be surprised to learn Mr. Cohen recently had one million dollars paid into his account?'

'I was not aware of this.'

'It was transferred from an account in the name of Alexandra Avellino. This begs the question: who would benefit from writing a fake journal, pointing at Sofia Avellino as the one who poisoned the victim?'

'Objection,' cried Dreyer, 'relevance and calls for speculation.'

'Your Honor, this is an expert witness who is permitted to give her opinion.'

'I'll allow the question, but be careful how you answer,' said Stone.

Sagrada was careful alright. This cross could be professionally damaging to her. She hadn't been given the time to look at the journal properly, and the NYPD had not investigated it for accuracy. Her only way out of this without a single blemish on her record was to take a dump on the DA and the police department.

'I'll ask again, who would benefit from forging this journal?'

'Well, clearly Alexandra Avellino. She has to be a strong candidate for authorship of this journal. The journal implicates her sister, and I believe the journal may well be false, and it's possible she paid Mr. Cohen that money so he would bring the journal to the police.'

All twelve heads on the jury swiveled an accusatory look at Alexandra Avellino. I sat down. And left them staring at the woman who had killed her own father.

FORTY-EIGHT

KATE

Kate could not sit silently in front of her client and not try to limit the damage from Sagrada's testimony. Bloch had told her about the million dollars, but they had not mentioned it to Alexandra. It looked like she was bribing Hal Cohen, and it's possible Cohen was murdered because either he asked for more money, or he was going to spill his guts to the NYPD. Either way, Alexandra had potential motive to kill him.

It was Alexandra's defense that was dying now. Kate doubted she could do anything to staunch that wound, but it would look suspicious to Alexandra if she didn't try. She had to do something – Alexandra was muttering 'no, no, no,' under her breath. The tremors were back in her arms and legs. She took a pill from her purse and swallowed it dry. It didn't seem to do any good. Kate had to at least put on a show.

'Doctor Sagrada, you may not have heard all of the testimony from the previous witnesses, and I just want to remind you that Detective Tyler confirmed that after a forensic examination of the victim's home, and my client's apartment – no traces of Haloperidol were found. None. Do you accept that?'

'I do.'

'And is it fair to say that you now don't know, with any certainty, who really wrote that journal?'

'I think that's fair. Part of the journal could've been written by the victim, or all of it, or none of it.'

Kate had gotten all she could. She sat down. No re-direct from Dreyer. The prosecution closed their case. Flynn stood and told the court the defense calls no witnesses.

Last thing a defendant wants to do is put themselves through the ordeal of cross-examination. Not if they're smart enough to avoid it. If the defendants didn't testify, it meant they didn't get to tell the jury that they didn't do it, but at the same time they didn't have that assertion torn to pieces by the prosecutor either.

'I want to testify,' said Alexandra.

Kate had moved her seat away from Alexandra, by a few more inches, at the start of the day. She felt the need for distance. Alexandra was a multiple killer. A psycho who had manipulated, killed her father and framed her sister for it. And had taken many more lives to ensure she was never convicted. Kate wanted the trial over – fast. More than that, she wanted her client to be convicted and locked away for a very long time.

'I don't think it's wise. You could face more charges for attempting to bribe a witness. What was that about? You never told us about Cohen.'

Alexandra began to cry. Kate thought she might be able to turn on the waterworks and hysterics like a switch.

'I wanted him to tell the truth. He said he would go to Sofia for money, and whoever paid him he would be on their side – either saying the journal is real, or a fake. I-I-I'm so, so, sorry. He told me not to tell my lawyer.'

'It's up to the prosecution to prove their case. If Dreyer destroys you in cross-examination, you've just done his work for him. And if you tell that to the court, you'll definitely face more charges. Let's leave it to the jury.'

'Are you sure?' asked Alexandra.

'I'm sure. I think you testifying has more downsides than you can imagine. It won't be pretty. And it will give Dreyer an advantage – you'll be the only defendant he gets to accuse in person, and the only one he gets to tear apart.'

Kate watched her client's wheels turning. Calculations running alongside fear. Five seconds. Ten. Biting her wet lip, Alexandra looked toward the jury. A couple of jurors stared right back. Kate tried hard to discern those looks. Were they looking at someone they thought was innocent – or were they waiting for their chance to punish a killer? Kate's best guess was they were looking at Alexandra the way a ten-year-old kid looks at a tiger in their enclosure: an element of fascination, but the knowledge boiling behind it that this thing could kill.

'Alright, if you think it's for the best then I'll take your advice. I trust you. I won't testify.'

Kate confirmed to the court she would be calling no witnesses.

'Well that just leaves closing arguments. Mr. Dreyer . . .'

The prosecutor stood and approached the jury. He took his time. Confident of the win. Kate knew he could smell the blood in the room and he wanted to strike now.

'We've all learned something during the course of this trial,' began Dreyer. 'We've learned that Sofia and Alexandra Avellino are rich enough to buy themselves good defense lawyers, that's for sure.'

Dreyer's face pulled his lips apart into something that would resemble a smile on a human face, but Kate had never seen Dreyer smile. On the prosecutor, the smile was as fake as watching a jaw move on a ventriloquist's dummy. Dreyer had chops as a prosecutor. Tactically sound, smart, ruthless and determined. But in that moment Kate saw what he lacked – humanity. There was no rapport with the jury. No relationship there at all. She guessed that Dreyer recognized this deficiency, or that it had been pointed out to him before, and he was desperately trying to work on it.

He'd tried to crack a joke, and almost cracked his own face.

Dreyer just looked creepy.

'But those expensive defense attorneys cannot get in the way of the truth. There is one truth, one fact, one absolute that no one in this courtroom has challenged, and it's the key thing for your consideration – when Frank Avellino died, his daughters were in his mansion. His body was still warm by the time the paramedics got to him. One of the defendants killed him. Or both of them did. But it had to be at least one of the defendants who sit before you today,' he said, pointing first at Alexandra, and then Sofia.

'Sofia Avellino has chosen not to testify in this case. Same with Alexandra. That is their right. Their silence means you don't get to hear them say they didn't kill their father. Each of them deny it, through their counsel. But if you are denied the opportunity to hear from the defendants, then you must use your judgment and assess the evidence and testimony against them. And there's plenty . . .'

He went though the testimony from the police and experts, in detail, and said the challenges to that evidence from the defense attorneys may be valid, but the jury may decide it was just court-room tricks.

'Members of the jury, I ask you to return the verdict of guilty for both of the defendants. If you think one deserves the benefit of the doubt, then give it to them. But at least one of these women is a killer. Maybe it's Alexandra, who tried to buy a witness, and falsify her father's journal? Maybe it's Sofia, whose hair was found in a knife wound to her father's chest? We, the People, invite you to consider that they both had motive and opportunity to murder their father, and that forensic evidence links both sisters to this horrific crime. Thank you.'

Eddie stood. He had half a dozen pages in his hand. A speech, written and ready to be delivered. Kate thought it would be some-thing bold, something stirring about the presumption of innocence, and the foundation of our justice system and constitution. She thought Eddie would have begun working on this speech days ago, adding and editing it as the evidence mounted. And once complete, he would have practiced it in front of a mirror like she had. Honed it. Polished every word so that the delivery was perfect and the message was loud and clear.

The jury waited in silence. Eddie threw the pages on the defense table, scattering them.

'I don't need to read my speech. I don't even need to talk to you about the evidence in this case. You've been paying attention carefully. I know this. So, I won't waste your time. Do the right thing. Acquit Sofia Avellino.'

And with that he sat down.

If he had a mic, he would've dropped it.

'Miss Brooks,' said Judge Stone. 'Do you have anything to say to this jury?'

Kate swallowed, looked at the speech she'd written, and turned the pages over, laid them face down on the desk. She rose to her feet, adjusted her blouse, and came around the defense table to stand in front of the jury.

'My client . . .' she said, and then froze.

My client killed her father, his friend Hal Cohen, a pharmacist, a cashier, probably Mike Modine, maybe her mother and stepmother too, along with Jesus knows how many more.

How do you represent someone you know is guilty? How do you stand there and tell a jury that they're innocent? Why did this have to happen in her very first trial? These questions rolled around her mind like bingo balls in a tombola.

'Members of the jury, I had written my closing speech before this trial began. That's the way I was taught to do it. Before the trial started I had prepared my client's defense. I knew the points I had to make, and I knew what the issues in the case would be. I wrote my speech with those points in mind. I wanted to remind you of those points. The unreliability of forensic evidence, the holes in the prosecutor's case, the co-defendant's motives for murder . . .'

She took another pause. Let the silence into the room. Two jurors sat up a little straighter, they were listening. They didn't know where this was going.

Neither did Kate.

'But I'm not going to do that. I think you already know your own minds. I think you already have a good grasp of the evidence. I would ask you to be fair, and impartial, and to return the verdict which my client deserves.'

Kate didn't tell the jury which verdict her client deserved. She had gotten through her speech, and she hadn't lied to her first jury.

She stood straight and true and returned to the defense table with her head up, and her conscience intact.

Until the verdict.

FORTY-NINE

EDDIE

For a trial lawyer, there are two words in the English language that terrify us more than any other. These two words stared back at me from my phone. They'd come through by text message seconds ago.

THEY'RE BACK.

The jury had been out for all of forty-eight minutes.

There's a lot you can do in forty-eight minutes.

But one thing you can't do in forty-eight minutes is come to a fair and balanced verdict in the most complex murder trial in the history of New York City. That's not possible. The jury probably has a question to ask, I thought. This isn't the verdict.

It can't be.

But it was. Deep down, somewhere, I knew it. I dumped my coffee, turned back toward the courthouse.

Walked beneath the flapping, torn, faded stars and stripes that hung from the flagpole outside the court building. The raven protested my arrival.

So many had died. And perhaps more would die before the end. When I was a kid, growing up in a small, cold house in Brooklyn, my mom told me there was no such thing as monsters. The stories I'd read as a kid about monsters and witches and taking children away from their parents, into the forest, well, she said they were just fairy tales. There are no monsters, she said.

She was wrong.

The Criminal Court building elevators were old and painfully slow. They took me to my floor, I got out and walked the corridor to the court room, following everyone else inside. I took my seat at the defense table next to my client.

A hush fell as the jury filed in.

They had already given the paperwork to the clerk. Paperwork they'd completed in the jury room. My client tried to say something, but I didn't hear her clearly. I couldn't. Blood roared in my ears.

I was a pretty good judge of which way a jury would fall. I could call it. And I was right, every single damn time.

This was the first verdict that I couldn't call. I was too close to it. In my mind, it was an even split. The verdict may as well come down to a coin toss. A fifty-fifty. I knew what I wanted to happen. I now knew who the killer was. I just didn't know if the jury would see it. I was jury blind.

The clerk stood and addressed the jury foreman. A tall man, with a plaid shirt and rough hands.

'In these matters, have you reached verdicts upon which you are all agreed?' asked the clerk.

'We have,' said the jury foreman.

The clerk said, 'In the matter of the People versus Sofia Avellino, do you find the defendant guilty or not guilty?'

The foreman looked straight ahead. Not a good sign. Usually if the jury is going to acquit they look at the defendant – they're waiting to watch that tsunami of relief wash over the innocent defendant. It's what makes justice great. It's power.

I hung my head. I couldn't look. Harry grabbed my shoulder, I could feel his tension in his grip.

Not a single noise could be heard. Not even a breath. The courtroom was a tomb. And I had a creeping dread that Sofia would be buried in it.

The foreman cleared his throat, and when he spoke, he sounded like he was shouting from the rooftops, far above my head.

'Not guilty.'

A rumble of noise, building. Sofia grasped my arm and cried out. It sounded both human and animalistic. A grunt of pain and relief, like a thorn being pulled from flesh.

'In the matter of the People versus Alexandra Avellino, do you find the defendant guilty or not guilty?'

No pause this time. No hesitation of any kind.

'Guilty.'

There was no quelling the noise now. The guttural sound that came from Alexandra's throat was the opposite of Sofia's. There was no relief, just pain and anger. Her hands flew from her sides and Kate tried to calm her.

There was no way to quiet this courtroom. The gallery erupted in chatter, and it was all Judge Stone could do to tell Kate that her client would be sentenced at a later date, before he discharged the jury, revoked Alexandra's bail and adjourned the court.

Dreyer was still pumping his fist, a grin of angry satisfaction on his face as the court security guards approached Alexandra with a set of cuffs. She recoiled, yelling, *'No, no, no, they got it wrong, it was my sister!'*

They held her down, cuffed her and took her away, Kate following behind them. Before they disappeared through the side door, Kate turned, saw me, gave me a thumbs-up. It was bittersweet for Kate. She'd backed the wrong sister, and she knew it. And yet, she had done the right thing.

A large hand slapped me on the back.

'We did it, Eddie. We got her,' said Harry.

'I didn't know what that jury was going to do. I had no clue.'

'From the moment you exposed that journal, it was always going this way,' he said.

'Really? I didn't think so. I just couldn't call it one way or the other. I got lost in this one, somewhere along the way.'

'You haven't slept in a long time. I'm surprised you can still stand. It's okay, you can't call the verdicts all of the time. Get some rest,' he said.

He sniffed, and followed Sofia as she was swallowed by the crowd. The reporters were barking questions at her, a melee of noise and camera flashes. Dreyer was besieged by reporters too. He put on that hellish, triumphant look and thanked his team.

I pushed through the edge of the crowd, kept my head down and made for the door. It was over. The killer was in custody. Sofia was free. Justice, if there was such a thing, rarely saw its reflection in a verdict. Justice is not about right and wrong. People make mistakes.

Criminals and jurors alike. Verdicts are often flawed because people are flawed. This verdict was right, and as I left the courthouse I stared up at the stars and stripes, and felt that maybe they weren't in such bad shape after all. I needed to get back to my office.

I wanted to sleep until next year.

FIFTY

EDDIE

Within an hour of the verdict I was in the back room of my office, lying down on my cot, eyes closed, two-fingers of whiskey rolling around in my empty stomach and my eyes shut tight.

My body wanted sleep. My brain, too. I'd never felt so tired. Months of sleepless nights and long days were finally taking their toll.

But no sleep came.

All I could think of was Harper. Her killer was still out there. It was possible that Alexandra had killed Harper, and that thought was hard to resist but there was nothing linking her to the murder apart from Harper working on Sofia's case. If Harper saw something during that visit to the Franklin house, and had to be taken out by Alexandra, I couldn't see what it was. I only had theories – nothing approaching a solid.

Thoughts were banging around in my head so much I could almost hear them.

I sat up.

I really did hear banging.

On the front door to my office.

I threw on a tee, a pair of jeans and made my way into the office. The outer door was frosted glass, and I could see someone on the other side. I opened my desk drawer, took out a pair of brass knuckles and slipped one of them onto my right hand. Unless the person on the other side of the door was Harry, or Kate, I would punch their lights out and ask questions later. Harper died opening her front door.

More banging on the door. This was not just knocking. Whoever was on the other side didn't seem friendly.

I took a breath, stepped forward, shot my right arm into a firing position and flung open the door.

It wasn't Harry. And it wasn't Kate.

And I didn't punch them out.

The person on the other side of the door wore tight grey jeans, black boots, and a blue blazer over a dark patterned shirt. Bloch didn't say hello. She didn't say anything. She stared into the floor, as if she was looking through it to the concrete and metal below. Lost in thought, and something else. She looked like she'd had bad news – a relative in a car accident maybe. Whatever it was, she had trouble spitting it out. I wanted to say something but I got the impression that if I did she might put one of those Doctor Marten boots through my face. But then I remembered Bloch didn't talk much, and reasoned that I should at least risk the boot to get things started.

'Bloch, you okay?' I said.

She didn't move. Didn't flinch. Didn't look at me. She just said, 'I don't think so.'

'What's wrong? Is it Kate? Is she okay?'

'She doesn't know I'm here. Not yet. Can I come in?'

'Sure,' I said, stepping back. I slipped the brass off my fist and let it fall on the desk.

Bloch didn't sit down, even after I offered her a seat. She shook her head at the suggestion of a drink.

'Okay, you gotta help me out here. Something's wrong, I get that. Talk to me.'

'In the end, it was just too easy,' said Bloch.

Sometimes it takes a simple statement to change the way you look at something. I felt like part of this case was a closed door, and Bloch had just cracked it open an inch.

I should've known the jury was going to convict Alexandra, and acquit Sofia. Harry had been sure of it – the only one who didn't see that verdict coming was me. And now I knew why. I could see it on Bloch's face. Not only was I tired, I was unsure. Unsure about everything, and that doubt had unmoored me. I was adrift on water, surrounded by the fog of grief. And I wasn't paying attention. The forensic evidence in the case couldn't be relied upon – the hair-fiber expert and the bite guy were both as unreliable as each other. I wouldn't have been surprised if Dreyer had influenced their reports somehow, so he could point the accusing finger at both suspects. In the end, it didn't matter because the jury didn't take to either expert.

'Two things bother me,' said Bloch.

She paused. Talking wasn't easy for her. She had to build up to it. The last rays of sun blared through a grime-colored window opposite. She gazed at the dust motes floating in the beam of sunlight.

'I think part of the journal is true. Frank found out who was trying to poison him, and he was going to change his will – that's why he was murdered. The Haloperidol. It's in liquid form. Big white bottle. How come the cops didn't find any trace of it and how come Frank didn't notice her putting it in his food?'

'Well, maybe she was careful?' I said.

'She gives it to him for months, he doesn't see it and she doesn't spill a drop? But somehow he figures it out anyway?'

'She was *very* careful?' I said.

'That's the second thing that bothers me. This was almost the perfect crime. She's been really careful. Killing witnesses, taking her time to plan this and yet she was sloppy enough to put *three* factual mistakes into the fake journal,' said Bloch.

That door in my mind flung open. We both looked at each other. Proving the journal was fake had been all too easy. That thought locking our eyes and minds like a pair of cuffs.

Those simple words from Bloch were enough to tilt my world on its axis. Sometimes you just can't see something because you're looking at it from completely the wrong angle.

'Are you thinking what I'm thinking?' I said.

She didn't answer, just flicked her eyes at me, then back to the floor.

'We still don't know why Harper was killed. I've watched those videos of the Franklin Street inspection over and over. I thought maybe she'd seen something in the Franklin Street house that implicated one of the sisters, and taken a picture of it. Maybe she didn't even see it at the time, but she had a picture. Maybe I'm wrong, and I don't have her phone pictures to check, but it's the only thing that could have made her a target for Frank's killer. Harper was smarter than me. Better than me. I owe it to her to find out.'

'It'll be dark soon. I want to look inside the house on Franklin Street again,' she said. 'You want to come along?'

I did. I wanted to look for myself, but before I did anything I had to be sure of the course of action. I needed confirmation. I had an idea about the Haloperidol, and I had to run it down.

'Take Harry with you. If the cops find you it helps if you've got a former senior judge along for the ride. There's not a cop in this city that wouldn't know Harry Ford. Are you going to tell Kate about this?'

'Not yet,' said Bloch.

'Don't tell her anything until you leave Franklin Street. She'll want to come with you. If she's caught breaking and entering her legal career is over before it's even started.'

Bloch nodded, asked, 'Are you coming with us?'

'I can't come, I've got other things that are more important.'

'Like what?'

'I've got to make a call to an old friend. Then I need to buy a newspaper and go to the hospital.'

'You feeling alright?' asked Bloch.

'No, I'm pretty far from alright.'

FIFTY-ONE

HARRY

The ride only took an hour from Bloch's house in Edgewater to Franklin Street, but Harry was already regretting his decision to drive. A twenty-year-old convertible with a soft roof is not the ideal car for a long drive on a cold night. A light snow began to fall and a steady drip of water started to flow onto Harry's left thigh from a leak in the roof. At his age, Harry felt the cold more assuredly than most. His scarf and long overcoat were pulled tight around him, collar up, gloves on, and still he shivered.

The conversation wasn't much warmer. Bloch had wanted Harry to drive. She had to concentrate, think things over. Harry didn't object, but he wished he had now.

Harry had barely gotten a dozen words out of Bloch. Her address. 'Wait here,' when they arrived at her house, and then, 'Let's go,' when she got back into the car. That's it. They were now only a few minutes from Franklin Street.

'Don't park outside the house. Drive by. Park in the next street,' said Bloch.

They drove past the house where Frank Avellino had been so brutally slain. It was in darkness. Cold as the night. Harry did as she asked, and parked a block away.

'I swear to God it's warmer outside,' said Harry as he stepped onto the sidewalk. Bloch unfolded herself from the little green sports car. She stretched her back, and looked down at the car with disapproval.

'It's a classic,' said Harry.

'It's a shitbox,' said Bloch, retrieving a bag from the front seat.

They made their way in the light snowfall to the house. There were few people on the street, and no one in Franklin Street save for the occasional passing car. Harry took a beanie hat from his coat pocket and put it on his head, pulling it down over his ears as far as it would go. Bloch didn't seem to mind the cold, and if she did, it didn't show.

She put on a pair of green leather gloves and opened her bag as she approached the front door of the house. She took something from the bag and climbed the three steps leading to the door. She stood there, making it look as though she was fumbling for the keys to the lock with cold hands. Harry stood behind, blocking the view of any passing cars as best he could while he listened to the whirr and buzz from what sounded like a small drill.

They were at the door for thirty seconds, no more, when he heard the lock engage and the door swung inward.

No words passed between them as they stepped inside and Bloch closed the door behind Harry.

She gave him a small flashlight, no bigger than a pen, and said, 'Keep the light away from the window.'

'Don't you think Dreyer would've let you and Kate come back here to inspect the place after you filed your appeal?' asked Harry.

'And how long would that take?' she asked.

It wasn't a question so much as an end to the matter. Technically, this was breaking and entering. Not the first time he's been on the wrong side of the law. It was surprisingly difficult being friends with Eddie Flynn and staying on the straight and narrow. Sooner or later Eddie led everyone astray – for the right reasons, of course.

At least the house was warm. The heating was on a timer, to keep the pipes from bursting in the cold. He followed Bloch into the kitchen. It was different to the last time he'd been here but at first Harry couldn't quite figure out why. Bloch opened the fridge, slowly, just an inch or two. She didn't want to flood the place with light. She dipped her head toward the open fridge door, and Harry came over to take a look. Inside it was empty. They'd even taken the shelves. It was then that he realized what had changed. The last time he was here some of the cupboards had glass panes, displaying crystal wine glasses, high-balls, and whiskey glasses. Now, there was nothing behind those decorative panes. Harry opened a drawer. No cutlery.

A quick sweep of the kitchen revealed every mug, cup, glass, bowl, plate, pan, knife and fork had been removed for testing. Everything that could've been used to eat, drink, or cook was gone. They had even ripped the dishwasher out and taken that with them, too.

'And not a trace of Haloperidol on any of it,' muttered Harry.

Bloch said nothing. Instead she moved upstairs. She was taking the same path that Harper had taken in the video. Looking at the same things, trying to see what she had seen.

Sighing, Harry followed her to the top floor. To Frank Avellino's bedroom.

The double doors leading to the bedroom lay open. Bloch stood on the threshold, her flashlight angled into the room. Her eyes followed the beam as it slowly swept, first the floor, and then every corner. She took a step forward, and then another, all the while the torch moved slowly, her focus absolute.

'See anything?' said Harry.

Bloch didn't reply. He wasn't even sure she had heard him. Harry moved into the room, keeping a respectful distance behind Bloch, not wanting to fall beneath her flashlight beam. The floors were solid. Not a single creak no matter where you stepped. Harry kept his flashlight on the floor, and as Bloch came to the bed, and zeroed her attention on the bloodstained mattress, Harry moved toward the en suite bathroom. Most of the blood had soaked into the bed, there was little on the floor. It was rich, thick pale carpet. The stains stood out. Spatter only. No pools of blood. Both women had heavy bloodstains on their clothes, which they said came from holding their father to see if he was still alive. Hard to disprove that assertion. Harry had seen the photographs, and anyone who came into contact with Frank Avellino in that bedroom would've been a bloody mess.

There was a nightstand table with no books on it. Just a lamp and some tissues. A chest of drawers on the opposite side of the room looked untouched. A mirror rested on top of it, and the blood spatter had not reached this far. Harry pointed his flashlight at the ceiling. There was nothing there. No stains. And apart from some streaks on the wall above the bed, there was no staining on the walls either.

Bloch took her time, getting close to the bloodstains, the only real physical evidence that remained in the house. Harper had spent time doing the same. Harry watched, but after a while he could no longer tell exactly what Bloch was looking for. He turned off his flashlight, opened the door to the en suite and went inside. There were no windows in the bathroom, and Harry closed the door and flicked on the lights. There was no shower – just a toilet and small sink. It had probably once been a closet. There was a large and luxurious bathroom next to Frank's bedroom with a Jacuzzi tub and shower big enough to fit a basketball team.

A combination of the cold and time meant Harry needed to use the bathroom. He lifted the toilet seat, and bit the finger on one glove when he heard something. He stopped dead, a chill running over his skin.

'Harry!' came the shout, again.

It was Bloch.

'There's no windows in here. I needed to put the light on to use the john. Sorry, I'm an old man.'

'Harry!' came the shout again, more urgent this time.

'What is it?'

'Come out,' said Bloch.

Harry turned one hundred and eighty degrees and took two steps forward. He reached for the handle. Grabbed it, turned it slowly. The metal catch groaned as it was turned.

'Stop,' said Bloch.

'What?'

'Are you turning the handle?'

'Yes. Don't worry about that noise. The mechanism squeaks. It's just me.'

As much as Harry liked Kate, he wasn't warming to Bloch so much. She hardly spoke, and had as much personality as the john behind him. Still, he knew she was smart and spoke when she had something to say, irrespective of how she said it. If Harry was on a case, he'd want Bloch with him, but he knew that he wouldn't want to share a beer with her after hours. At his age he didn't think he could survive too many of Bloch's conversations.

He turned the handle, slowly. The handle stopped once it had fully turned, and Harry flicked off the light and opened the door. He came out to see Bloch staring at him, a strange look on her face.

'I know why Harper was killed,' she said.

Harry's lips moved, and a sound even came out, but it wasn't a word. He just mumbled until he'd recovered enough to get control of his tongue.

'Y-Y-You what?'

Bloch's lips parted, she breathed in, about to tell him what she'd discovered while Harry was in the john, but she never got started. Instead, her eyes flared wide. Both of them stood still.

There was a noise.

A door closing.

The front door. A metallic slam and jangle as keys were dumped on the marble kitchen top. Someone was downstairs.

Bloch put her index finger to her lips. Harry stood very still. He took shallow breaths, and held Bloch's gaze. If the cops were downstairs, they were in serious trouble. If it was Sofia, they had a lot of explaining to do.

'Under the bed. Now. Quietly,' whispered Bloch.

Harry got down on his hands and knees, then lay flat on the floor. The bed was tall enough for his purposes, and he shuffled his body beneath it. Bloch came in from the other side. They could see the open door to the bedroom. No lights on in the hallway. Not yet. They were trapped up there. Bloch took out her phone and began typing.

FIFTY-TWO

EDDIE

In a private room in Mount Sinai Hospital, a man I'd never met lay asleep in his bed. He looked peaceful. There were bandages still on his head and at the side of his face. His right leg in a cast, elevated on a hoist, didn't seem to bother him too much. It was hard to tell. His right arm was also in a cast, and draped over his large belly.

I opened the door to his private room and waited at the threshold until he saw me. He didn't seem to recognize me. I'd been staring at him for a few minutes, and I was sure I hadn't seen him before.

'Who are you?' he asked.

His skin looked deathly pale, to match his death-rattle voice. His lips were angry red, and cracked.

I didn't answer him. Instead I came into the room for a better look.

'Are you a doctor?' he asked.

Another man came into the room. Jimmy the Hat took up a seat at the side of the bed.

'How you feelin'?' asked Jimmy.

'Good. Better,' said the man.

'Tony, this is Eddie Flynn. He's a good friend of mine. Eddie, this is Little Tony P. This is the guy I told you about. He got run over crossing the street.'

'Good to meet you,' I said. 'I have a couple of questions about your accident.'

'You the lawyer? I-I-I don't want to sue nobody. I didn't get the license plate. I don't know who ran me over.'

Sweat broke out on his face. A light tremor in his good hand. He was nervous when he had no reason to be.

329

'As I understand it, you parked your car close to Jimmy's restaurant. It was early in the morning, before you started your shift there. And when you got out of the car a motorcycle rammed straight into you, crushing you between the bike and the car door. That's what you told Jimmy. That right?' I asked.

'Yeah, yeah. I probably didn't look in my mirror before I got out of the car. It's probably my own damn fault.'

Jimmy looked at me. I nodded.

'The way some witnesses described it, the motorcyclist almost took the door clean off, then walked the bike back, and slammed the front wheel down on your head? Doesn't sound like an accident to me?'

'I don't know what happened. I don't remember. Last thing I remember was getting out of the car,' said Tony.

'This was your new car?'

He swallowed, said, 'Yeah, yeah. Brand new. A bet came in for me. One hundred Gs. Just when I thought my luck had changed, this happens.'

He raised his good arm, as if to remind us that he was badly hurt.

'Broke my goddamn skull. I don't know. I guess I should've looked before I got out of the car.'

'I asked Jimmy to speak to his bookies, and anyone else who runs a book in Manhattan who paid out a hundred grand in the last six months. Guess what they said?' I asked.

'I don't know, I mean I . . .'

'The bookies who knew you said you were betting more, but you weren't winning. And they didn't pay out six figures to anybody in the last year.'

'Look—' he began.

'Tell him the truth,' said Jimmy. 'If you lie, I'll know it. And then I'll get angry.'

'I'm not lying,' said Tony.

No one in their right mind would lie to Jimmy the Hat. Especially if you worked for Jimmy – that was a one-way ticket to the bottom of the Hudson. I needed this guy to open up.

'Tony, you got one way out of this,' I said, 'and that's to tell me the truth. Here's what I think, and if I'm right, then you say so. If I get it wrong, you say so. Okay? Telling me the truth is the only thing that can save you right now.'

'I—'

'Shut up and listen. You're a short order cook. You've worked at Jimmy's restaurant for two years now. A friend of Jimmy's, Frank Avellino, used to come to the restaurant every morning for breakfast. He had a few meetings there over coffee and then went about his day. Am I right so far?'

He was shaking now. He blinked sweat out of his eyes and nodded.

'Good. Now, Frank Avellino was being poisoned – drugged. For months. Turns out the cops can't find any trace of the poison in his house. Not a single drop. I'm thinking maybe the poison was never in the house. I'm thinking maybe somebody paid you to put it in Frank's eggs every morning. I think they paid you a hundred grand. I think you did what you were told and then I think the person who paid you got scared. Scared that maybe a hundred grand wasn't enough to keep your mouth shut. So they tried to shut you up permanently. How am I doing so far?'

'It wasn't poison. I swear to God. She told me it was medicine. Medicine. Said he wouldn't take it at home and I should slip it into his eggs and sausage . . .'

Jimmy wiped his face, lowered his head and breathed out in a long, exasperated sigh.

'A hundred grand is a real generous tip for putting medicine in someone's food,' I said.

'I swear—'

'Shut up,' said Jimmy.

At my side I held a copy of the *New York Times*. I put it in front of Tony, the front page facing him.

'You met this woman. The same woman who paid you, gave you the Haloperidol, and then tried to kill you. Her picture is on the front page,' I said.

There were two pictures on the front page. The trial had captured the lurid imagination of readers, and below the fold were photographs of Alexandra and Sofia as they left court yesterday. Close ups. Showing their grim determination in the face of their personal nightmare.

'Which one?' I said.

He closed his eyes. Tony had gotten in way over his head and now he was having to pay the price.

'She tried to stab me in the face, but she missed and dropped the knife. It must've fallen under my car. Then she landed that bike on my head. She's crazy,' he said.

'Hey, Tony,' said Jimmy. 'I know you're probably scared of this lady. She nearly killed you, after all. But look, she ain't here. And you don't need to be scared of her no more. You need to be scared of me. Because I *will* kill you. Do you understand?'

Tony opened his eyes, nodded rapidly, and stuck a finger into the paper. I leaned over to see who he had pointed out.

'You sure?' I asked.

'I'm sure. It was her.'

Now I needed to save Tony P.

'Jimmy, Tony is going to testify that he sourced the Haloperidol for her, and he was paid handsomely. He's also going to say that after her father was murdered, she asked him where he'd gotten the Haloperidol, and he told her he got it from a pharmacy in Haberman. He's then going to say that she tried to kill him on the street. You are going to do all of that, aren't you, Tony?'

'I'll do whatever you say.'

'Because if you tell the truth to the cops, and testify that you poisoned somebody in Jimmy's restaurant, that would be bad for Jimmy's business. And if you don't testify at all that means there's no reason for Jimmy to keep you alive. So you'll do it?'

'I'll do it, I swear.'

I left the newspaper, thanked Jimmy and ran for the door.

'Don't kill him. I need him.'

'He'll still be breathing when the cops come to talk to him. Who knows how long he'll keep breathing after that?' said Jimmy.

FIFTY-THREE

EDDIE

The house on Franklin Street looked quiet. There was an old van parked outside. I glanced through the rear door windows of the van and saw boxes stacked inside, and something else, too. I stood for a second in the night air, listening. The city was quiet for once, just the distant traffic.

I approached the house. The front door was open. Even so, I knocked on the door and hollered a greeting as I came inside.

The hallway had a lamp burning on a side table. I called out again, and moved forward until I saw the kitchen and lounge.

Sofia stood in the lounge, in semi-darkness, the light from another lamp burning on the table caught in her eyes, making them look ablaze.

'Eddie, what are you doing here?' she said.

In front of her, on a coffee table, was a chessboard. The pieces laid out as if a game was in full flow.

'I came by to see how you were doing.'

'How did you know I was here?'

'There was no answer at your apartment. This house is yours now, I guess, and I thought you might be here. I saw a van outside, are you moving in?'

'I thought I'd move a few things into the house. I wanted to keep busy,' she said.

'Is that your chessboard? Did I interrupt a game? Is someone else here?' I asked.

'No one else is here. Yeah, this is my board. This is my sister's game. The game we played when we were kids, and didn't get to finish.'

She reached down, moved a knight.

'And now it's over,' she said. 'I've won.'

The light seemed to move deep into her eyes, making them luminous, like a predator caught stalking its prey in the moonlight. The frightened, meek Sofia was gone. Her sister was awaiting sentencing for Frank's murder, and Sofia was in the clear. She no longer had anything to fear. Her confidence all but glowed around her like a halo.

'You definitely won,' I said, nodding. 'You must really hate Alexandra.'

'I hated her long before she killed my father. She took everything from me when she pushed Mom down the stairs,' said Sofia. 'It was an accident. A stupid accident. She didn't mean to kill her. I wasn't angry at Alexandra for taking our mother away. It's that it happened too soon. I hated my mom. I wanted to beat Mom at chess one day. I wanted to grow up, and for my mom to know I was better than her. Better than Alexandra, too. I wanted to hurt Mom, and she took that away from me. I couldn't hurt her in death, even though I tried. Then Dad sent us away. I lost him, too. She deserves to rot for what she did.'

There was a seismic change in Sofia. She looked and held herself differently. I felt like I was really seeing her for the first time. Things were beginning to make more sense. The real reason for the hatred between her and Alexandra was clear now. When she said she'd tried to hurt her mother in death, I knew exactly what that meant. Alexandra pushed Jane at the top of the stairs, but it was Sofia who bit her after she was dead.

Sofia shook her head, as if coming out of a dream. 'Do you want some coffee?'

'Thank you, that would be great. There's been some developments and I wanted to fill you in.'

She led me to the kitchen, turned on the rest of the lights. There was a new coffee machine sitting on the counter, fresh out of the box that lay beside it. Frank never drank coffee, she told me. He preferred tea toward the end. She filled the bun flask with water, plugged in the machine, filled it with fresh grounds and set it to percolate.

'Killers always make mistakes,' I said.

'And you found one?' said Sofia, her tone even and inquisitive.

'I found two. She left a witness alive. Someone who could identify her.'

She opened a cupboard, looking for coffee mugs. There were none.

'They took all the mugs,' she said. She opened more cupboards,
found nothing.

'I guess coffee is off the menu,' I said.

'Looks like it. Sorry, what were you saying about a witness?' She
came around the small breakfast diner in the center of the kitchen,
and stood just a few feet from me. She still wore a long coat and
boots, even though the house felt warm.

'The guy she paid to put the drugs in Frank's food. He used to
work in Jimmy's restaurant.'

'Oh my god! And what did he tell you?'

'He's talking to the cops, right now. He told me he was paid
to do it.'

She looked down at the tiled floor while she processed this.

'I still can't believe she did it. She's my sister,' said Sofia.

'That wasn't her only mistake.'

'Really?'

'Yeah, but you don't need to worry about it. Honestly. It's over
now, Sofia. You're not in danger anymore. I just wanted to come
by, make sure you're okay and then I'll leave the rest to the police.'

'Are you sure you don't want to go and get something to eat?
Or we could stay here and have a bite?'

'I'm sure,' I said, approaching her. 'I'm glad it's over. I was so
worried that if you got convicted you wouldn't make it inside. You
can move on from this. I know it will take time, but you can do
it. You're a millionaire now. You have everything.'

She held out her arms as she approached me. I walked toward
her and embraced her. I'd left the front door open, and now I
took a moment to listen, hard. I could hear sirens in the distance.

'Thank you,' she said.

I patted her arm, and we released one another.

'I'd better get going,' I said, backing away.

The coffee machine started to gurgle a fanfare, to announce it was ready.

'What was the other mistake? You said you found two? Just out of curiosity?'

I heard a faint screech of brakes from a car pulling up outside. 'The 911 call,' I said.

'What about it?'

'Well, when somebody takes a life, there's a lot of emotions flying all over the place. Adrenaline spikes, blood coursing through your veins, that kind of thing. It's easy to make a mistake right in that moment. See, when she called 911, she said she could tell her sister was in the bathroom. Said she could see shadows of feet beneath the door. I got a text from a friend about twenty minutes ago. Turns out, from your father's bedroom, you can't see any shadows of feet or legs at the bottom of the closed bathroom door. Not even when someone is standing on the other side of the door, turning the handle. So how did she know her sister was in there?'

Sofia's face changed. What had been a warm, contented expression, morphed into something else. Her eyes narrowed, her lips drew tight across her teeth.

'It wasn't Alexandra who said that in the 911 call,' she said, stepping toward me.

'I know. You knew Alexandra was in the bathroom because you watched her go in there. Then you called 911. Harper took a photo of the bathroom with the door closed and light on inside. If we had examined that picture we would've seen there's no light cast beneath the door. That's why you killed Harper before she looked at those pictures more closely. And Little Tony P didn't pick out your sister, either. He identified *you*.'

I stepped back, said, 'You can take her now.'

Detective Tyler came around the corner into the kitchen, followed by Soames.

'Sofia Avellino, NYPD. Turn around right now and put your hands on the counter,' said Tyler.

I stepped back, waited.

Sofia shook her head, and said, calmly, 'This is bullshit. Utter bullshit. I've already been acquitted of my father's murder. You cannot put me on trial again – that's double jeopardy.'

'Ma'am, turn around and put your hands on the counter, right now,' said Tyler, reaching to his side arm.

Sofia put her hands in the air, slowly turned around, and placed them on the counter.

Tyler let go of his gun, approached Sofia and said, 'I have to search you – do you have any weapons on your person?'

'No, I don't.'

Tyler put his arms out and placed both on top of Sofia's shoulders. He began feeling through the fabric of her coat, then moving his hands down her back, searching for any hidden knives. While he searched, he read Sofia her rights.

'I'm arresting you on suspicion of the murder of Afzal Jatt, Penny Letterman, Hal Cohen, and Elizabeth Harper. You do not have to say anything—'

'That's a crock of shit. There's nothing to link me to any of these murders. Nothing. The word of some coked-up short order cook isn't enough. You've got nothing.'

'We've got this,' said Tyler as he pulled something shiny from Sofia's coat pocket.

A gold crucifix on a cheap gold chain. There were bloodstains still on the cross. Harper's blood. At least, they had still been there when I planted the chain in Sofia's pocket thirty seconds ago.

'No,' she said, when she saw the chain in Tyler's hand.

Soames kept his distance. He was happy for his younger partner to do most of the physical parts of the job. He turned to me and said, 'Thank you.'

'No need,' I said. 'Just do as you promised, and everything will be fine. Also, the van outside. There's some packing boxes in the back, but there's something else too. A black motorcycle.'

Tyler took a step back, and put his other hand into his coat pocket, searching for an evidence bag into which he would place the chain.

Soames turned to me to say something, his mouth opened, but before he could speak there was a terrible crack.

It didn't sound like any kind of gunshot, or even a gas tank going up. It sounded wet and hollow.

Tyler had turned toward us, his back now to Sofia. And his face had almost gone. Something splashed on my cheek. Something hot, that burned.

Sofia dropped the handle of the bun flask. It was all that remained of the coffee pot. The rest of the glass was in Tyler's face. While she dropped the handle, she fell to her knees, pulled at Tyler's jacket and then crawled, fast, around the other side of the dining table.

I turned to Soames who was wiping frantically at his face. He must've caught more of the splash of hot liquid than I did.

Another sound, and this time it *was* a gunshot.

Soames fell back. I ducked, put my head down. The first thing I saw was a gun hitting the floor, followed by Soames. He'd taken one in the stomach and he was bleeding badly. He'd tried to draw his gun but had dropped it. Too far away for me to reach.

Footsteps.

I looked up and saw Sofia holding Tyler's gun. It was pointed at me.

'Alexa, play my song,' she said.

A sibilant voice erupted from somewhere in the kitchen, electronic, and cold. 'Playing "She" by Elvis Costello.'

The music started up, and Sofia smiled.

FIFTY-FOUR

SHE

Sofia glanced toward Soames. He was bleeding out. Dark blood was already pooling beneath him, his stomach awash with it. Sofia could smell something bad too – maybe the bullet had ruptured part of his gut and bile was leaking into the wound. Soames wouldn't last long. No need to worry.

Still keeping the gun on Eddie, she looked at Tyler. A long shard of glass was in his cheek, another in his neck. He was spasming on the floor.

Eddie Flynn was on his back, on the floor, under the gaze of the .45 in her hand.

'You almost got clear, Sofia. If you hadn't killed Hal Cohen we wouldn't have connected you to the pharmacy murders. Why did he have to die?'

She cocked her head. Smiled. Flynn was far too smart for his own good. She needed a lawyer like him. He was one of the best in the city, and he only defended those he believed to be innocent. He had been perfect for her. She relied on him figuring out the journal had been forged. Sofia had been careful to copy Frank's handwriting, but not perfectly. Enough to throw some doubt on who wrote it. Including hidden inaccuracies in the journal was a risk, but one she needed to take. It was the only way to prove the journal was written by the real murderer. Only someone who was guilty would write a fake journal framing someone else for their crime. It had been the killer piece of evidence in the trial. One that she was still proud of.

'Hal Cohen was like my father, and a lot of other men in this city. They made money from the suffering of others. I needed Hal

339

to find the journal. I'd hidden it in Frank's personal papers after the cops had searched the house. I wanted to Hal to find it, because he would try to exploit it. He was predictably corrupt. He gave the journal to the DA, then tried to make a buck. Depending on who was paying him the most, he would testify for them either saying the journal was real or a fake. I was never going to pay him. I wanted him to give the journal over, and for Alexandra to pay him to testify that it was real. Then, when you burned the journal in court, it would look like Hal and Alexandra had been in on the fraud the whole time. Especially when she was paying him. I couldn't have Hal turn up in court and say I'd offered to bribe him. That wouldn't do. He'd given the journal to the DA, and taken Alexandra's money. After that he'd served his purpose.'

Flynn backed away, using his feet and elbows to move toward the hallway. Sofia followed, keeping the gun on him. Her knife was in her backpack in the living room. The smell of the blood, the feel of the weapon in her hand – it was intoxicating. She gestured with the gun that he should keep moving.

She wanted the knife for this.

She wanted to feel it in his flesh.

FIFTY-FIVE

EDDIE

She motioned with the gun that I should keep backing up, toward the lounge. This wasn't the first time I'd had a gun pointed at me, but I got the impression she didn't want to use it. She liked to work up close and personal. There was a look on her face that I couldn't place. She wasn't panicked, she wasn't even breathing hard.

She was enjoying this. Every second. She had fooled me, but I wasn't the only one. Sofia Avellino was a monster, and she'd worn a mask her whole life. Now, she had become who she had always wanted to be – a winner. She had all of her father's money, and Alexandra ruined. She had her revenge on those she thought had wronged her, and she was almost pulsing with the power it gave her.

'Keeping moving,' she said. I was almost halfway across the hallway between the kitchen and lounge.

'How does it feel? Knowing you're going to die?' she asked.

I said nothing, I kept moving.

'Harper died too quickly. I wanted to cut her up, like I did with Daddy. But that would've looked too suspicious. You'll die slow, Eddie.'

I should've been afraid. Fear could shut down a body just like a bullet. I wasn't afraid. I was furious. I wanted to get up, grab that gun and put it under her chin. Keep it there, let the thought of death linger for Sofia and then pull the trigger.

The song playing through the house was kicking into gear, and Sofia was getting more excited with every passing note. 'You want to kill me, don't you?' she said. 'For what I did to Harper? Well, that's not going to happen. You're not going to kill me, Eddie.'

'Had she still been alive, Harper would've caught you earlier,' I said. 'And you deserve to die for what you did to her, but you're right. I'm not going to kill you.' I stopped moving. 'She is.'

Sofia's eye's blazed open, and then she wasn't there anymore. A deafening boom filled the hallway. I cried out, but my voice was drowned by the sound. An explosion. One second Sofia was there, standing over me. The next, she was lying face down in the hallway, five feet away. She'd lost the gun, and there was a massive pool of blood coming from beneath her arm. I looked up and saw Bloch standing at the other end of the hallway, a huge silver revolver in her hand. Harry behind her.

I took out my phone and dialed 911.

FIFTY-SIX

EDDIE

One Month Later

'Don't I know you from someplace?' said the hotdog vendor.

'I'm a lawyer,' I said.

'Yeah, you represent that girl who killed Frankie Avellino.'

'Not anymore.'

'She fire you?'

'No, I fired her.'

'What do you want on your dog?'

'Chili, cheese, jalapenos – the works,' I said.

He handed me a huge hotdog on a plastic tray. I gave him a ten and told him to keep the change. He wasn't the first person who'd recognized me in the past few weeks. It still burned that I hadn't been able to spot Sofia. That she had managed to con me, Harry and . . . Harper. She'd made me feel sorry for her. And I hadn't seen the monster behind that mask. If I had, maybe Harper would still be here.

That night, while the paramedics loaded Soames, Tyler and Sofia into separate ambulances, I called Kate. I told her everything. She had cried on the phone. The relief she felt hit me even harder. Kate had been right about Alexandra all along.

'I should have listened to you. You called it right from the beginning.'

'You were conned, Eddie. Not just you. Sofia convinced everyone. It's not your fault.'

'Don't worry about me. Go get your client out of jail.'

Soames and Tyler survived the attack, and Alexandra Avellino became the first defendant in the state's history to have her conviction overturned before she'd even been sentenced.

Sofia was facing multiple murder charges. She would plead not guilty by reason of insanity. It wouldn't work. Her mental health problems were real, but none of them made her a killer, or explained the evil that came from within her. She'd survived the gunshot to the shoulder, but she'd lost the arm in the process. Maybe that was justice for Frank – because he would never have his killer put on trial – double jeopardy prevented it. Not that it mattered to Sofia – she would spend the rest of her life in pain, and in a cell. The pain would be made worse by the knowledge that Alexandra would inherit Frank's estate.

I crossed the street and went through the glass doors of the building that was home to Levy, Bernard and Groff, attorneys at law. A receptionist gave me directions to the correct floor and I took the elevator. There were two guys in suits who were there to escort me. I recognized one of them as Scott. Levy's blue-eyed boy. In the elevator, Scott wrinkled his nose and stared at my hotdog in disgust.

'Sorry, you can't have any,' I said.

The doors opened and I was led to a glass-walled conference room. In the center of the room was a long table. The three managing partners of the firm sat at one side. John Bernard was in his seventies, well-groomed and wearing a tailor-made pin-stripe suit. Matthew Groff was a little younger, and paler, if that was possible. Levy was the youngest, and he sat in the center of the group. They were flanked by a group of security guards and associates. I'd heard about Bloch's little incident with Levy. I liked Bloch.

Kate and Bloch sat facing the opposing army. Kate directly opposite Levy. Bloch on her left. I took the empty chair to the right of Kate. A view of the Manhattan skyline opened up behind Levy and his partners.

Kate had a laptop open in front of her. Bloch had a cardboard box at her feet. The associates that sat around the table all had iPads, legal pads or huge stacks of legal papers in front of them. Same with the partners.

I put my chili dog in front of me, and asked Bloch and Kate if they wanted a bite. Kate politely declined. Bloch just shook her head.

'This is a without prejudice negotiation, in relation to the matter of Levy, Bernard and Groff, a firm, versus Kate Brooks. Do we have any questions before we commence?' said Levy.

'Yeah,' I said. 'Could I get a fork? This hotdog is a lot messier than I thought.'

Levy looked at my lunch, then me, and said, 'We've been waiting for you for ten minutes. We couldn't start the negotiation without the defendant's attorney. I'd hoped you'd be bringing more than cheap junk food to the table.'

'Oh, I'm not the attorney for Kate,' I said.

'What?'

'Nah, she's doing just fine on her own. She doesn't need me,' I said and I took a bite from the hotdog. It was hot, and delicious.

'Then why are you here, Mr. Flynn?' asked Bernard. He had a voice that sounded like it was coming from the back of a deep, oak wardrobe.

'I'm just here to watch. I wouldn't miss this for the world,' I said.

'Alright, for the record we can ignore Mr. Flynn. Miss Brooks, I've spoken to my partners, and we have arrived at the figure of two-point-three million dollars. That's our bottom line. You stole our client. That means you stole our fees. We want that money, and your law license. Final offer.'

Kate produced the black plastic card I'd taken out of Levy's wallet, and placed it on the table.

'I have a counter offer,' she said.

Levy's face took on a strange look. It was like he'd seen a ghost pull down its pants and shit on his lawn.

Kate picked up the card and pressed one side of it. A small, metallic connection point flipped out of the side. It looked like a micro-USB.

'This card belongs to Mr. Levy,' she said as she slotted it into her laptop.

'No,' said Levy. It didn't sound like a denial. It was a plea. A cry for mercy.

'The card acts as a kind of digital portal to a site on the dark web,' she said.

As she turned the laptop screen around, I caught a glimpse of the site. I didn't read the name, but I saw the bank of pictures. One of them looked a little like Kate. And she was bending over. The photo was taken from behind, probably on a camera phone. There were other pictures, even worse. Some were photographs taken under tables, with the camera angled up a woman's skirt. There were more graphic photographs of Kate changing, or on the john. Levy must've had cameras hidden all over the office, beneath desks, in the female bathroom, and God knows where else. Suddenly I'd lost my appetite.

'These are photographs of me, which Mr. Levy took, surreptitiously, and uploaded onto this site – *Co-workers I'd Like To Rape.*'

'Jesus, Theo!' said Bernard.

Theo Levy put his head down as it started to turn bright red.

'For what I'm sure is a substantial annual fee, Mr. Levy can look at other pictures taken by powerful men of their female employees, some are even naked, and engaged in what looks like non-consensual sex. The users can even rate the women, and the pictures. I see that my home address was also put on the site. I will withdraw my counter-suit for sexual harassment, you will withdraw your suit for breach of contract and—'

'Kate,' said Bernard, interrupting her. 'You don't need to say any more. We'll withdraw our lawsuit. You do likewise and sign a non-disclosure agreement. We'll pay one million dollars in compensation and that will be an end to it. Okay? Can you turn that computer off now?'

'I'm sorry, Mr. Bernard, I hadn't finished. There will be no non-disclosure agreements. This is a one-time offer. We withdraw our respective lawsuits, Mr. Levy resigns from the firm and you put out a press statement to say that sexual harassment has been a problem at Levy, Bernard and Groff, but that you're calling in expert human resources teams to address the issue. That's it.'

'Look, Miss Brooks, you're clearly a talented lawyer, but you'd be a fool to turn down a million dollars—'

'No non-disclosure agreements. I think I said that already. This shit has gone on too long behind closed doors. It will continue to go on unless you deal with the problem,' said Kate.

'Two million,' said Groff.

Kate shook her head.

'One time offer,' said Kate again. 'If you don't take it, the offer is walking out of this room with me. And I'm going straight to the *New Yorker* with this card.'

'Goddamn it,' said Bernard. 'Just do it. Just give her whatever she wants.'

'You can't—' said Levy, but Bernard cut him off.

'You don't get a vote in this, Theo. I have a feeling your ass is going to be thrown out the door before the end of the day.'

'You have a deal. The case is settled,' said Groff.

'Wait,' said Levy, but they ignored him.

'Thank you,' said Kate.

Bernard and Groff both turned on Levy and began to berate him. Not for being a creepy pervert, but for getting caught. He was trying to speak but they weren't listening.

'Oh, one more thing,' said Kate.

Reaching down, Bloch grabbed the cardboard box at her feet, and put it on the table.

'What's this?' said Bernard.

Kate opened the box, and started bringing out bundles of legal documents.

'These are lawsuits on behalf of fourteen Levy, Bernard and Groff associates and secretaries. They're all female. They've all had their picture taken by Mr. Levy, and we have screenshots of them. When you calculate the salaries owed to these women, because they weren't getting paid anywhere near their male counterparts, and you figure in damages for sexual harassment, I'll recommend two million dollars to settle.'

'Two million? We can do that,' said Groff.

'Two million each,' said Kate.

Through gritted teeth, Bernard said, 'How many of them did you say?'

'Fourteen.'

'We need to check the paperwork and interrogate these claims. We'll get back to you before the end of the week on those,' said Bernard.

'No problem. If I don't hear from you by Friday, the price goes up

'Wait a second,' said Levy, no longer willing to be shouted down. His career was over, and he was desperate to try and save himself. 'I'm not going anywhere. We can win these suits. She stole that card from me. She can't use it in court!'

'Actually, I stole it, Theo,' I said. 'Do you want to report the theft of your pervert passport to the police?'

Levy's mouth opened and shut like a fish.

'I didn't think so.'

Within an hour the paperwork was done on Kate's case, and she was pretty sure she could collect at least twenty percent on each of the new claims from the associates. This was a nice payday for her.

Outside the building, Harry waited with Clarence on a leash. It was a gorgeous day. Bright, sunny and cold.

'Why do I have a feeling that once those cases are settled and the damages are paid that the card will somehow find its way to the NYPD?' I said.

'I have no idea,' said Kate. 'These things happen all the time. Bloch definitely wouldn't put it in an unmarked envelope and send it to the sex crimes unit.'

I bent low and patted Clarence on the head. I was beginning to like Clarence a lot more.

'You know there's a vacancy on the tenth floor of that building,' said Harry.

I turned and gazed up at the glass tower.

'Nah,' said Kate. 'Too many bad memories in that place. Does this mean you've considered my offer?'

'I have,' I said. 'People around me get hurt, Kate. Harper was killed. It's my fault. She was working my case and I didn't see Sofia Avellino coming. I believed her, and it cost Harper her life. I can't let you—'

'She knew the risks, Eddie. It's not your fault,' said Kate.

'Harper loved you,' said Harry.

'I should've known. I got conned by Sofia,' I said.

'You couldn't have known,' said Kate. 'Sofia manipulated everyone. The problem was we were on opposite sides. If we had been working together from the start this wouldn't have happened.'

'Kate's right. You've been on your own too long, Eddie. Time for a new start. A new firm,' said Harry.

'Come on, I have to go see Dreyer and convince him to drop the charges against Alexandra for paying Hal Cohen to be her witness. I want to tell him I've got a new job. That we're a team now.'

'You think he'll drop the charges?' I asked.

'I'm pretty sure. Soames and Tyler will be there, with their war wounds. They said they would do their best to persuade him. I think it'll work. Come on – are we partners? You've got the reputation and the clients, so a seventy-thirty split in your favor sound about right?'

'No,' I said. 'If we're going to be partners then it's got to be fifty-fifty.'

We shook hands. Right then, a new firm was born. Flynn and Brooks, attorneys at law. We had a consultant, an investigator, and even an office dog. Now we only needed an actual office, and a phone.

And some luck.

I left Harry, Kate and Bloch in a bar at around three o'clock in the afternoon. Alexandra would have one year of probation for attempting to pervert the course of justice, we were celebrating Kate's latest victory, and the new firm. Harry already liked Kate, and he was warming to Bloch. Both women loved Clarence. The sound of their laughter followed me into the street. I'd only drunk Pepsi and water. At the moment I had no stomach for booze. I thought I might finally kick it for good this time.

I got into my car and drove. There was no conscious plotting of direction. The wheels just kind of took me there. By the time I arrived at the cemetery the sun was setting. With my head down, my feet found my way to Harper's grave. I sat down on the wet grass beside it, leaned my head on the cold stone, and within seconds I felt myself drifting off to sleep.

LOOK OUT FOR STEVE CAVANAGH'S
EXPLOSIVE NEW THRILLER – COMING SUMMER 202

ACKNOWLEDGEMENTS

I've often said that there would be no books written by me if it wasn't for my wife, Tracy. This continues to be the case, and I'm ever grateful to her for everything she is, and everything she does. Without her I would be absolutely nothing.

My thanks also go to the work done by my editors Francesca and Christine. Thanks to Orion Books, especially Emad, Katie, Sarah, Harriet and Lynsey.

Research into neurological matters was greatly assisted by John Cane and Dean Burnett. Pharmaceutical advice was provided by A. A. Dhand, a rather gifted thriller writer in his own right. You should check out his books. Chess advice came from Alan Bradley, another excellent writer, and I'm very grateful for all of it.

This book was hard to write. I don't mean the story necessarily, I mean physically. At time I was writing this novel I was still a full-time lawyer, and I had been writing at night for eight years. This took its toll. In previous years I might get three or four hours of work per night, but in 2018/2019 I was often too tired to write. A good deal of this novel was written in the River Mill writer's retreat, in Downpatrick. And my thanks goes to Paul Maddern, celebrated poet, and generous host of the River Mill. And more thanks to Tracy, for sending me there at weekends to complete this book. I am now a full-time writer, and for that I have to thank Tracy, and you.

Yes, you. The reader, who has bought my books and read them. Thank you.

Thanks also to friends, family and colleagues for your support There's more Eddie Flynn on the way.

And thanks to Shane Salerno, the man with the plan.

Eddie Flynn used to be a con artist.
Then he became a lawyer.
Turned out the two weren't that different.
Win the trial.
Or lose his life.

'A deliriously fast and enjoyable ride from the
next big Irish crime fiction star. Highly recommended'
ADRIAN McKINTY

Your client is innocent.
Your wife is guilty.
Who would you fight for?

'Quite simply, *The Plea* is one of the most purely entertaining
books you'll read this year'
JOHN CONNOLLY

'Plotting that takes the breath away'
IAN RANKIN

THE LIAR

It takes one to CATCH one.

FROM THE AUTHOR OF
TH1RT3EN

Steve Cavanagh

Who is deadlier –
The man who knows the truth?
Or the one who believes a lie?

A missing girl, a desperate father and a case that threatens to destroy everyone involved – Eddie Flynn's got his work cut out.

'Plotting that takes the breath away'
IAN RANKIN

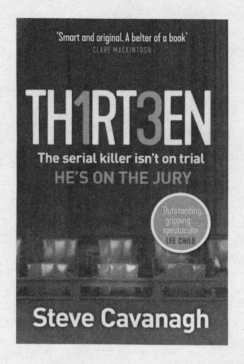

'Smart and original. A belter of a book'
CLARE MACKINTOSH

TH1RT3EN

The serial killer isn't on trial
HE'S ON THE JURY

'Outstanding,
gripping,
spectacular'
LEE CHILD

Steve Cavanagh

THE MURDER TRIAL OF THE CENTURY IS HERE.

A ruthless prosecutor.
A brilliant defence lawyer.
A defendant with a secret.
And a serial killer on the jury . . .

'Books this ingenious don't come along very often'
MICHAEL CONNELLY

'This guy is the real deal. Trust me.'
LEE CHILD

TWISTED

Never let MURDER get
in the way of a good story

FROM
THE AUTHOR OF
TH1RT3EN

Steve Cavanagh

**BEFORE YOU READ THIS BOOK
I WANT YOU TO KNOW THREE THINGS:**

1. The police are looking to charge me with murder.
2. No one knows who I am. Or how I did it.
3. If you think you've found me. I'm coming for you next.
After you've read this book, you'll know:
the truth is far more twisted . . .

'Punchy, ridiculously gripping, fast-paced, clever.
Beautifully plotted and incredibly fun to read.
He's done it again. SUPERB'
WILL DEAN